I0782457

Blade Upon the Vein

Book One of the
Dragonbone Blade Series

Asf DeWeese

Copyright © 2024 by ASF DeWeese

All rights reserved.

No portion of this book may be reproduced in any form without written permission from the publisher or author, except as permitted by U.S. copyright law.

Contents

This book is dedicated to my mom, my dad, and the Blizzard of
'77.

and

In Memory of Katrena.

I could almost feel you standing behind me as I wrote Porta and
Morti, urging me to make her sassier and him just a tad uglier.

From the Nightmare

Excerpt from The Rise of the Warlock Emperor - via the translations of Korvaeulous Sinclayre

OUT OF THE NIGHTMARE, a hero was born.

Jettisoned from the shadows and smoke of a dying dream, he would prove the salvation of a civilization upon the cusp of destruction. From ashes to accolades, he would bring light to the darkness encasing the night.

This is his tale. This is his triumph.

The light of the gods shone softly that first true morn, for they had spent all their Brightness on creating a being they deemed incorruptible. A savior true, with a heart both bold and strong, bearing the last solace of the beings of an era bygone. A song, sadly dying upon ancient lips, of a prophecy, the promise of Dusk and Dawn.

A light unfolds in the darkness, beginning what will have no end.

Son first born of a noble knight and a maid most chaste, Praxxys R'nevoran, was destined to be one of the fortunate among the people of Noxia. While fate placed him amongst riches and privilege, Praxxys, himself, was solely responsible for the depth of his own greatness. Cognizant of the power that the Brightness of the gods gave him, he was diligent in his quest to pull his people from the chaos in which the Nightmare had left them. To free them, to protect them, to bring the capital city of Vaeyn to prosperity and become a kingdom above all others.

...To make sure no one forgot his name.

He rose swiftly from warrior to honored knight, from trusted general to beloved king. From battle-hardened leader to loving husband and doting father. On the cusp of his third decade of life, Praxxys was legend, the powerful force of his goodness renowned throughout all lands.

But even gods must take chances on the fickle creation they call life, for Fate is a capricious monster with its own curious peccadillos.

We are born, we live, we die. This has ever been the terms of our sentence on this world. We are blessed, but doomed, to grow old, love hard, and leave behind a legacy to entertain, to guide, to enthrall the generations to come.

This way of things did not satisfy Praxxys. As one of the Bright, perhaps the only one so blessed by the gods, he did not visibly age past his thirtieth year.

But his friends did.

As did his most beloved bride. Their son grew frail, a prince without progeny himself, and passed while his father still very much resembled a man in his prime. Awash in a flood of grief for those he'd lost, Praxxys searched for the gods that had made him different, desperate for a cure for the immortality he did not want.

But the gods could not, would not, be found.

Decades passed for the Lonely King, as he then became known to his subjects, days filled with ever-changing faces and bodies. The sun rising and setting, seasons frozen then thawed, their passing empty of any true meaning for the grieving hero. Until a time the scurrilous gods were found, Praxxys vowed he could not, would not, allow his soul to connect with another. Better to remain a lonely man than one built of continuous grief and sorrows.

Determined to find some worth within his immortal existence, he filled his days bettering the lives of his people. Fighting wars on behalf of the downtrodden and weak. Expanding his empire past the tempestuous currents of his native shores and into lands previously only mentioned in the vaguest of myths.

Through both the rages of war and negotiations of peace, the Brightest Emperor emerged. A hero so brilliant and cunning, many speculated he was no longer a man at all, but a god sent to replace the missing entities to which his very existence was due. Though he fervently denied this claim, in time, Praxxys, himself, began to wonder.

Each year seamlessly poured into the next for Praxxys until the day he fell in lust with a maid of prestigious lineage amongst her people. The finest of ladies, to be sure, and seemingly beyond reproach. Tired of his lonesome existence and deciding he could seek companionship where love would never blossom, he asked for her hand in marriage. The people rejoiced to have a queen once again.

Solay Cartyn was, undeniably, a woman of great beauty and quick mind, but her heart was as untrue as each word that slipped from her lips. Hidden beneath her flawless skin, dark magics danced in her veins and blackened her soul. Although most were none-the-wiser in regard to her shadow-self and chose to be enthralled by her stunning facade, Praxxys began to get glimpses of the monster he had married.

As serendipitous fate would have it, the full knowledge of his wife's perversions coincided with the announcement of her pregnancy. Even as gut-wrenching fear seized his every waking moment and featured in all of his nightmares, Praxxys became a father once more.

To the Brightest Emperor was born a daughter as fair to look upon as her mother, and as noble in heart as her sire. Though determined not to become attached to the spawn of a woman he suspected he would someday have to kill, Fate decided to have a laugh once again.

On the third day of her life, the court gathered to acknowledge the tiny princess as heir apparent to the mighty throne of Noxia, and, for the first time, Everlain Moniq R'nevoran was placed in the arms of her father. Praxxys fought as well as he could to ignore the thrum of energy connecting the child he held to the heart within his chest, but the gods had finally granted him the weakness he craved...a love so precious only the hardest of souls could resist.

Finally, the hero was humbled, irrevocably and unquestionably conquered...by a little girl with the reddest of curls. No more did the prospect of war bring excitement. Nor did the worries of the world he ruled hold Praxxys' attention as they should. More and more, he passed his duties to trusted advisors, unconcerned that the consolidated powers of a century were slowly returning to the people. Filling his days with tea parties and pony rides, then dances and debuts, he eagerly spent his free moments indulging his daughter's every whim while the steady rein of the Brightest Emperor seemed to slip from his hands unremarked.

But from the depths of her dark library, amongst her grimoires and potions and diabolical dreams, the Wicked Empress did notice. No longer satisfied by her mean-spirited plotting and small-scale schemes, Queen Solay began in earnest her own quest to become the ultimate power in Noxia, however she must.

Turning further to the darkness that encased her shriveled soul, she ate, slept, and breathed the black magics that brought her a power most unsavory...but a great power, nonetheless. Years came and years went as Solay refined her hold on the empire. The whispers of discontent did not touch her as her once lovely appearance faded, and the truth of her evil grew.

When plague and disease and the undeniable signs that the creatures of the Deep Nothing had returned once again, Praxxys could no longer retreat to the idyllic existence he had deluded himself into thinking was his. The empire was suffering, and he could no longer hide from its wounded cries. It was beyond time for the Brightest Emperor to show his light once more.

As he gathered up the most trusted of his warriors, neither Praxxys nor Everlain held any doubt about what they must do to reclaim their realm, to restore honor and goodness once again to Noxia. The Queen must die for her unnatural crimes. With this intent, they crossed the eerie threshold of her personal chambers deep under the palace, uncertain what they would face from this monster that was once wife and mother.

To their astonishment, there on the cold stone floor of the largest chamber, lay the mangled body of the aged sorceress queen. Her corpse was shriveled and her opulent blood red dress in tatters, as if unseen claws had, with great pleasure, torn through fabric and flesh alike.

Surrounding her was a circle of sacrifices, remnants of creatures cruelly deprived of life and violently splayed between black candles, their flames still dancing with glee in the damp. Near her hands, the blood-flecked pages of a grimoire sat pale and triumphant, its leather binding scored by desperate nails at the moment of her grotesque death. Most horrifying to the onlookers who stood shocked, weapons in hand, was the pulsing gold and red glow of an open portal standing proud and sinister above the body of its last sacrifice.

And through this gate, she let in true evil. The evil that had, itself, given rise to the Nightmare.

With a heavy sigh, Praxxys turned to his sweet Everlain and kissed her upon the forehead. His heart was heavier than it had ever been before. The world required a hero once again.

What came next will be forever known throughout our history as the Second Night, a time of monsters and death and chaos. It was a world awash in blood and terror. Year bleeding into year until a decade had passed in battle. Once again, Praxxys R'nevoran raised his flag above the rotting detritus of a vanquished foe, conqueror supreme, beloved by all once again.

Only to return to find his precious daughter frail and wasted from the last plague to sweep the land. They say, on that day, that the heavens split from the force of his despair and tremors wracked the foundation of the palace. He turned every ounce of his indomitable will to finding a cure for her malady, to prolong her life and, when that failed, he began to wonder why death should claim her at all.

In the shadows of the forbidden caverns, he turned to the books and black magics that had once held his second wife enthralled. So soon did he forget the tragedy these ancient spells had brought upon his people. He ceased to sleep and rarely ate, all his attention focused on not losing his daughter. His days were spent by her side, selflessly nursing her fragile shell while encouraging her to hold strong. Endless nights were consumed by candlelight, chasing rumor and wild tales and dead ends, until he came to the very last book, a grimoire so old and tattered that every fiber of his being rebelled at the thought of touching it.

But open it he did, and inside, the answer he sought buried deep within the fear he suffered.

His eyes devoured each line of the spell, and even as his mind memorized, his soul balked at the horror his life had become. He was the Brightest and had never fallen before the foe in all his many ages. Surely, he could survive the effects of one dark casting? He wasn't a man prone to failure. But, his conscience battered him, what if he did? The gods, after all, had deserted him long ago. Seeking solace, he returned in the dark of night to Everlain's bedside. He sat quietly with his hand upon hers as a wheezing shudder weakened her body without remorse.

This was the night that all good broke inside the Brightest Emperor.

Naught but an hour passed before Praxxys determined to take Fate into his own hands, gathering the bartering chips he would need in this, his last true battle. Dawn found him with the ancient spell book in his hands, the words that would cement his destiny bitter on his tongue. With one last lament for his lost honor, he tossed the remaining offering on the sweltering stones where once his damned queen had given her life, and muttered the final word of the incantation, "Solay".

Thunder filled the cavern, and every last glimmer of light was smothered in a frightening red haze. From out of that miasma of grief and torture walked the ghostly figure of the woman he had once called wife.

"Praxxys." She stretched her transparent arms, ending in wisps of smoke where once she had graceful hands, "never would I have assumed you would say my name with such longing." A teasing smile lit her features, turning the emperor's stomach at the thought that he had once lusted for this woman.

"From the stony look on that handsome face, am I to guess you are not happy to see me?"

Praxxys' fingers left angry divots in the pages of the grimoire as a myriad of emotions flashed through his body, none of them pleasant.

"One cannot miss what was never truly real." He spat at the dripping clouds of gore that once served as her feet.

"The demise of my pathetic human flesh opened so many new doors for me. Vast is the power filling every last molecule of my existence, there for my every desire, should I just ask. That, I feel, is the ultimate reality." She pulled back from where she'd been caressing the flames dying in the pit, the emptiness where her eyes once gleamed now two sparkling craters of nothingness, ringed in flashes of red. "Although," her head tilted to consider him in a way she had never deigned to do when alive, "you have made my master suffer more than most. I hope you come to me bearing news that will increase his joy at my continued servitude. He does get quite moody from time to time."

Praxxys stood stalwart. Patience had never been Solay's strongest quality.

"Well," she glided slowly around his tautly held frame, sneaking glances at him for the sole purpose of increasing his discomfort, "why did you summon me?"

"I seek life for Everlain. An immortal life."

The tortured spirit that was once Solay crossed her arms dramatically and stared at the underside of the castle lurking dark and oppressive above them. A second passed, then two.

"Done." She smiled, her lips devious and empty, like a cat who had eaten the court pigeon.

"Why should I trust you, charlatan of curses that you are?" Surely, Praxxys felt, bargaining your very soul should be a much more involved process.

"You fear death for her but have no regard for your own. Here you call me from the depths of my eternal pain, begging for a reprieve from your tender feelings, yet giving no regard for my own? How easily you despise me, cruel husband, when I am but a different version of the creature you have become." Her ghostly image took on a sulky, sultry air as her vaporous body curved around his. "Do you not remember that she is my daughter too?"

"You had little feeling for her when you were alive. Why would you care now?"

"Hmmm." She made a mockery of smoothing her hair, gathering the wispy curls into gorgeous swooping twirls and pinning them to her head in jolly whirls. "I suppose one can find regret in the afterlife, such as it is. And," faintly pointed teeth punctured the bedamned smile she shot him, "my master has declared he has been waiting an eternity for this very moment."

He placed the worn grimoire down carefully on the altar. Despondence made his every move slow and heavy. Of his many adventures and countless achievements, only Everlain had ever brought him true joy. In his heart of hearts, he knew he had no choice.

"What is it you want me to do?"

A jester-worthy flourish of her hands produced a weapon made not of metal, but of bone, blood, and shadows. As her incorporeal form began to slip back into the source of the Deep Nothing, her voice whispered encouragingly in the stale air.

"Take the knife."

And so he became the immortal Warlock Emperor.

He stands upon a hundred thrones, ruler of a thousand years. Thus, was the world broken.

This is his tale. This is his travesty.

This is our torment.

Woe that the strength of the Nightmare should reign eternal.

Chapter One

DAMNED WAS THE DAWN that never came.

Long into the night the drums of an army rampant sent trills of terror echoing up and down the spine of ridges that encased the land at the Edge of the World. It was thought to be an untamable region, filled with sheer stone rises, arid tundra, and the most unforgiving flora and fauna in any of the known kingdoms. Its people, Edgers as they were derisively called, were whispered to have an obscure magic of their own and drew strength from a life lived in the light.

From the ashes surrounding the people he'd claimed for Noxia, Praxxys watched the golden rays of the sun caress the summit of the jagged mountains in its picturesque climb to the sky. If the light dared place its claim so boldly upon them, so too could he.

The Warlock Emperor wrenched his hungry blade from the heart of the nameless village elder who had the audacity to reject his rule. He released the dry husk of his corpse to crumple slowly to the scorched ground. The man, though feeble, had attempted to keep him from his rightful claim on the equally nameless village now being consumed in the purple flames of his rage. The man may have been no one, from a nowhere place that Praxxys would not remember past this evening, but his soul had been filled with valor. Solay's rumble of satisfaction echoed through his head.

Be still, bitch. You always were a noisy eater.

He could feel her pleasure pulse through the Dragonbone dagger as if his long dead wife, trapped forever in a prison of her own making, were laughing hysterically. If there had been one thing she loved more than a sacrifice to her greatness, it had been irritating him.

Determined to ignore the choices he couldn't unmake, he lifted the bloodied knife high and swept it in a sharp circle, the signal to his men to prepare to depart. He knew his officers would be diligently prodding the foot soldiers under them into action. Orders dispatching the wounded to healing tents would be brusquely given or, if they were beyond the help of the hedge healers that followed the camp, to see that they were dispatched in general and left for the vultures.

Once, a gentler emperor would have mourned the loss of his soldiers and insist they received a proper warrior's burial, but Praxxys had long since left that man behind. The shadows of the

Nightmare demanded their due and what need did a soul have of its lifeless body anyway?

Stepping imperiously over the dusty remains, Praxxys wasted no time assessing the spoils of such an unsatisfying battle. He could feel, his heart pulsing in time to the cries of the unwilling souls bound within the blade he shoved resolutely back into its golden sheath, that a greater challenge and reward awaited. A shrill whistle brought his mount to his side, the massive phantom-hearted beast stomping readily on anyone unfortunate enough to be standing between him and his master. The last shards of the old man's bones were ground into the earth beneath his soot-black hooves.

"Ah, Tramoxxys! Never was there a more worthy steed." He patted the gelding's broad shoulder affectionately, taking the time to brush at the flecks of blood marring his white coat. A few softly muttered words initiated the dark healing spell that had allowed his horse to survive many years longer than any of its brethren. A quick ripple of magic flickered through the people standing nearest him, stealing minute bits of their lifeforce and redirecting it to cure his mount's injuries.

One of Praxxys' lieutenants paused as he approached, a groan ripped from his throat as the spear slice trailing along his ribs suddenly split further. Years of service to the emperor should have prepared him for the effects of the spells the emperor cast but, as they all well knew, being a trusted soldier for the empire required great sacrifice.

"Your Eminence," he collected himself and bowed low despite the pain, "do you wish a contingent be left behind to battle the flames? Your new subjects are known for their prosperous farms and the remaining elders are vowing to see that they continue to flourish for the good of the empire..." He stuttered to a stop as the emperor's eyes landed on him in full force. While it was considered an honor to be seen by Praxxys, it was also unnerving and terrifying in equal measure. The soldier broke under that icy gray gaze, his head falling to his chest in an effort to become unseen. A cold chill suffused his body as he waited for the emperor's response. He began to tremble, now in fear, the pain in his side forgotten in the dread that swept over him.

"Let it burn." Praxxys' response was nonchalant. "A forest grows stronger for the flame. I'm sure the same applies to the field. Let us see how adversity lifts these peasants." He swung himself up in the saddle and nudged Tramoxxys past the nameless soldier, his brief good mood ruined slightly by the terror emanating from the man. That kind of response fed into Solay's pleasure but left him with a sour taste in his soul, even after all these years.

He turned his horse toward the mountains and urged him forward at a quicker pace, needing to put the noise and smell of the chaos he'd created behind him. There was no room in the life of the Warlock Emperor to mourn the loss of weaker emotions. Longing for true respect and loyalty was futile. There was only the drive to conquer. He lifted his eyes, cold at the best of times but now frigid in the aftermath of battle, to the ridges separating him from his next victory.

Held securely within the fortress-like embrace of those ageless rocks, he'd heard a special breed of Edgers lived, a supposedly unconquerable race of barbarian warriors. Praxxys didn't doubt they existed but, although the common peoples he'd encountered along the Edge whispered tales of their heroic deeds, he did not believe they had a chance to defeat his numbers.

Perhaps he could never again return to the days when he was Brightest, but at this he could excel. He could revel in the satisfaction that being Emperor of All would bring. Despite the hate and fear that he now brought to the masses, he would never apologize for uniting the entirety of the continent under Noxia's banner. He didn't have to. Tramoxxys reared suddenly, a jolt of ambitious energy filling his tired muscles with strength and impelling in his hooves the need to run, to tear divots in the already disturbed earth.

Praxxys' smile was grim but not displeased. There was no one to stop him.

While the slow thud, thud, thud of a thousand feet heralded the ominous beat of the coming battle, the Salvadonians resolutely prepared to meet an army that had never known defeat. Through nearly invisible trails and rock-hewn shafts carved from the mountains by blood and toil centuries ago, the indomitable warriors slipped past the dangers that stalked them daily. Courageously they ran through the night, never tiring, never stopping, so that they could ambush their attackers as dawn broke across their land.

Theirs was never an easy existence. They had banded together many centuries ago, a worn people fleeing from a world filled with violence and invaders without mercy. Struggling, the few lucky to be left after what they referred to as The Exodus, settled warily in the last place available to them. It was a place filled with monsters and hardship, but safe from the wars that would see an end to their people. They made it a home, but they never forgot the feeling of vulnerability that had plagued them. They raised their children and their children's children as warriors, whetting their blades and honing their survival reflexes on the dangerous creatures that ran rampant at the Edge of the World.

Some chose the murky swamps to call their own, building floating fortresses and laughing as the water dragons beat their heads in futility against their hulls. Others picked the mountain crevices and caves, spending their days soaking up the rays from their beloved sun, then retiring to their rock enclosures when night fell, bathing their precious crops in the light resonating from their sleeping bodies. The royal family chose to conquer the Foldtswood proper. Admittedly the most dangerous part of the Edge, they prospered nonetheless, growing strong and tall amidst the dark forest and harsh steppes.

As one people, the Salvadonians greeted the seemingly endless onslaught of invaders. Weapons held firm and hearts steady, they looked to the sun for one last blessing, only to be encased in unnatural shadow.

Valiantly they fought, led by their beloved prince, Roryn T'Yanil, a warrior like no other, his growing legend second only to that of the dark-souled emperor encroaching upon their peace. Against all odds, they not only held the passes that day, despite the false dark drawing endlessly at the strength they received from the sun, but they managed to advance, pushing back an army renowned for its inevitable momentum.

But even the lion cannot stand the sting of a thousand scorpions. For the first time in their history as a united people, Salvadon was defeated.

Bruises covered the entirety of Roryn's noble face, their pattern echoed by the splatters and seep of blood from the many cuts he'd been dealt from the unforgiving gauntlet-clad fists of no less than five enemy soldiers. It had taken that many of the emperor's highly trained lackeys to bring him down from the murderous fugue that the heat of battle had provoked. Even then, if it hadn't been for a disabling bolt of unnatural purple magic, he knew he'd be fighting still.

Around his neck a collar of rough gold burned unnaturally against his skin. A bare hundred warriors, the proud men and women of Salvadon who had survived the wicked lash of Praxxys' power in the last torturous minutes of the battle, lay bleeding beside him. The indignity of a forced march back through their own territory had broken more than the warrior's bodies.

As they came before their king and elders in defeat, shame stood heavy upon their souls. All but the most stalwart were unable to keep their feet under the pulses painfully flashing through their bodies from their own golden shackles. Sweat dripped from every inch of his body from the effort but, gallantly, Roryn stood tall.

It wasn't in his blood to surrender. The Foldtswood was a more dangerous place than most, and it bred survivors who had no concept of pain or dishonor. Centuries of fighters raising fighters in an unforgiving land left no room for the weak, but from the defeated look pulling his older brother's face into a shape he'd never witnessed before, he could surmise the old blood of T'Yanil was fading.

"You have been defeated this day, people of Salvadon." The Warlock Emperor raised a hand, halting the front lines of the large army spreading into the valley behind him. Acres of forest burned frantically along the tops of the mountains, surrounding the village itself in a halo of flame and smoke. "However," his voice echoed, horrifically sweet, in the ears of everyone gathered, easily heard above the wails of the dying and the cheers of the victorious, "now is not a time for despair. This day could bring your destruction, or," a smile curved the already chiseled planes of his face into a cold ravine of pleasure, "you can accept salvation and become a part of the Glorious Empire. Who now shall be the voice of Salvadon?"

With his dark hair shorn but for a long, thick tail braided proudly down his back and his broad shoulders bronzed under an intricate scrollwork of dark tattoos, Tarwyn T'Yanil was the epitome of Salvadon royalty. When he stepped forward to stand fearless before the Warlock Emperor, a grim smile erased the pain from Roryn's face. A gore wound had kept his older brother from this battle, but his ferocity in the face of danger was unquestioned.

"I speak for my people, though what words I have shall not change whatever Fate has decreed."

"Fate?" Praxxys spat and shook his head, as if disappointed. "I'm not a cruel Emperor, you'll see. I ask not for any more of your lives or even this desolate land you chose to flourish in. All I require is your obedience, an oath of your fealty...and the sacrifice of your truest soul."

"For your goodwill toward the people of Salvadon, I pledge our oath to uphold the empire and obey the dictates of its emperor." The words were pulled from a reluctant mouth. The citizens of Salvadon, those from the marshes and the mountains and from the royal city itself, hung their heads in defeat, shame in their inability to preserve their sovereignty written plainly upon their stoic faces.

"And the soul?" An elegant eyebrow arched toward Praxxys' hairline. "A benevolent emperor expects to be gifted with only your finest."

Tarwyn's face grew painfully blank as his eyes dipped to his younger brother, standing sure and cocky before an unde-featable foe as a true T'Yanil warrior should.

"Take the boy."

A strangled gasp issued from more than one mouth, but Roryn's gaze went instantly to his mother. Her brilliant blue eyes, near mirror images of his own, were filled with shock and her horrified tears barely held themselves at bay. Roryn turned his head quickly. His heart faltered to see her coming so close to losing the composure no queen of the T'Yanil blood would ever compromise.

Torn between the urge to challenge his brother or take a chance that he could break through the line of unnaturally enhanced warriors surrounding the Immortal Emperor and wipe the superior smile from his never-dead face, Roryn's resentful glare reluctantly turned to the man he had aspired to be his entire childhood.

"Has your blood turned cold, Tarwyn, and frozen your manhood? We fight, Brother!" His disgust was evident in the way he spat the words but, in the crowd, his mother bit her lip at the betrayal and hurt rolling off of him in waves. "Have you forgotten our creed, the essence at the very marrow of our ancestors?"

Salvadon Never Serves.

The words echoed through the soul of every Salvadonian. Already rigid spines straightened further, weapons shifting from guarded to aggressive. Even the smallest children held back their fear and flexed their tiny fingers around rocks and sticks. Fire seemed to light Tarwyn's eyes, burning fiercely as his muscles tightened at this primal call to battle.

Roryn met his brother's gaze, unspoken words dancing in challenge between them. An energy outside of the control of any warlock swelled in the bloody meadow and arced in the veins of every Edger. At his feet, warriors once frozen growled their defiance and began to rise against the sorcerous pain still pounding through their bindings. Without his volition, the spear within Tarwyn's hand began to rise.

A throaty laugh filled the air moments before the Warlock Emperor waved his hand and unleashed a crashing wave of destruction. An unholy wind swirled around the basin, seeming to cackle and scream with the cries of the tortured dead bound to his power.

Its fetid heat brought down the brave warriors surrounding Roryn, creating a silent circle of battered flesh. Even he fell to one knee, his locked elbows and fists burrowing into the arid grass the only things keeping him from full submission.

"T'Yanil doesn't disappoint." Praxxys dropped the reins of his destrier and slowly pulled the heavy gloves from his hands. He tossed them haphazardly to a slight serving waif trembling beside the massive horse's hindquarters. His hand caressed the handle of a bone white blade sheathed in a gold band across his chest.

"Your sacrifice will be a very satisfying one, to be sure." He slid gracefully down to the ground and pulled the blade slowly from its resting spot. "You honor your Emperor this day."

Fear, a feeling uncommon to him despite the dangers that stalked him unceasingly, filled Tarwyn for the first time. He helped the elders around him stand, whispering at them to spread word for the people to retreat to the high mountains. He felt the edges of the crowd begin to melt away as his command filtered through. He knew they would gather the children and flee. Even if most of them should perish here today, Salvadon itself would not die.

Roryn watched his death approach...no, a fate much worse than death. To be struck down by the evil that owned the Warlock Emperor was a horror no warrior could imagine. Anger swelled in his throat until it erupted in a mad, guttural scream directed at his brother. He lunged past the pain, past the magic, past all reason, gaining his feet as his end neared.

"Fight...fight for T'Yanil. Fight for what our ancestors died to build. Fight for the freedom of the young learning to take their first kill." His eyes were awash with emotion, not with tears but with rage. With desperation. "Fight...for me." Roryn's challenge was an unspoken plea.

Tarwyn's broad shoulders fell, his pride melting alongside his honor. His younger brother had always been keen of heart and stalwart in his resolve. It was one of the many things he had admired in what he saw as a younger, more carefree version of himself. Unlike Tarwyn, who had the duties of ruling thrust upon him at a young age, Roryn was equal parts admirable, stubborn and hotheaded. He wouldn't understand that this was a battle the people of Salvadon couldn't lose...and it was one they could never hope to win. All their weapons and determination could not triumph over so dark and limitless a magic as Noxia held.

This way, his people kept their lives, despite that they should lose their most beloved prince. Even though it would destroy the king himself to condemn the person in this world he loved most.

"For your people, Roryn," His voice didn't reflect the choking emotion that centered around his throat, nor the pain stabbing repeatedly in his heart at what he must do. "I order you to kneel."

This time, a soft wail shook the queen, more powerful for the fact that it was a sound never heard before within the Foldtswood. Roryn swallowed back an answering cry of frustrated grief at this betrayal. He didn't fear death, but they had all heard the rumors of the horror that befell the souls given to that unnatural blade. A torturous afterlife bound in the Nightmare, an endless eternity of being fodder for the dark shadow awaited him. A fact Tarwyn knew as well as any and was willing to accept for his only sibling.

Roryn turned his back on his brother and faced his destiny like he always had, bravely. As Roryn's bright blue eyes locked in a rebellious glare with the stormy ice that encased those of the emperor, he kneeled. He did not break, did not flinch. His thunderous expression made it obvious that he did not accept this as his end. A flash of white and gold preceded the blade in its deadly arch as it descended.

Only to score the unprotected flesh of Roryn's right forearm. Lightning ricocheted within the now churning black clouds overhead, mixing ominously with the booming thunder of the ancient spell Praxxys chanted. Anger seemed to pulse within the very atmosphere as the Nightmare was denied its victim. With force, the Warlock Emperor slammed the bone blade back within its sheath with finality.

A thousand unlucky dead I've fed you, Heartless Shrew. Begone now, this one is mine.

The screech of betrayal that roiled through the valley burst every eardrum it touched. An evil wind swept violent tornadoes of rage throughout the valley, its fury burning with its very presence and smothering the purple flames dancing on the mountaintops. Praxxys smiled.

"Come now, my son. The Glorious Empire awaits its prince." His extended hand was grasped readily, and he pulled Roryn to his feet. Praxxys smiled at the former king of Salvadon over his shoulder as he walked away, taking perverse pleasure in the tears rolling down the man's face.

Roryn never looked back.

Tarwyn stood tall among the remnants of his once great people, fully shattered. He watched with no emotion on his face, aside from the painful streaks of his sorrow, as his brother mounted the destrier he'd been given and willingly rode away beside the Warlock Emperor.

His people melted away, unsure whether to applaud his resolve or let him dissolve in his own shame. Tarwyn was as empty inside as if the cursed blade had stolen his own soul.

But he lived...and so, too, would Salvadon.

Chapter Two

S HADOWS FLICKERED THROUGH THE underbrush, shrouding, then revealing in bare glimpses, the nearly silent hunters in diligent pursuit of their prey. Softly shod feet crept forward, inch by careful inch, one after the other, delicately feeling the detritus of the forest before committing to completing a step. Once, this grace would have been displayed through glorious spins and heart-racing twirls on the marble floors of their childhood. Now, each motion was thoroughly considered and made with grim determination.

It was a dance that would bring death or cause their own.

The summer sun broke through the canopy above, its rays penetrating the gathered gloom and glinting off the brilliantly golden hair of a young woman crouched behind a curtain of wild grape vine, its grasping tendrils tenaciously hanging onto the corpse of a long-fallen tree. One of the bolder beams of light filtered through the bracken to outline the sharp edges of the arrow she slipped into place on her short bow. Her attention was focused on the deer that had just entered the small clearing, her movements flawlessly silent as she lifted her weapon, pulling the feathered shaft back on its string, the rough sides of her fingers trailing along her smooth cheek.

She let out her breath, a second away from releasing the arrow, when the wind shifted, casting her scent directly at her quarry and causing the animal to toss its head into the air, its body turning away from her, making her shot impossible. Cursing under her breath, she withdrew the tension on the bow, resigned to another day filled with the unhappy rumbling of her stomach. She could sense the deer's muscles begin to bunch as it turned to escape, its tail lifted in the white flag that would herald its flight.

Then it froze, its giant swiveling ears the only movement for a swift heartbeat. A breathy warble of song filled the air, silencing the birds and jerking the buck's attention away from the huntress and her deadly intentions.

A second slim form slipped from the tree line, her hands held low, palms open toward the deer as it stood immobile, mere feet from this new threat. It trembled, just a few leaping bounds away from the safety of the woods. Muscles jumped under its skin, ears and nose violently twitching but unable to make its body move away from the girl singing quietly before it. Sweet, liquid brown eyes locked with this new threat, breaking the gentle girl's heart with their endless innocence, but increasing her dedication to seeing this done correctly.

Her palms raised and the deer's breathing spiked as inevitability filled the air between them. A grunt broke the gentle notes coming from her slightly parted lips as her tender hands bracketed the sleek fur encasing its noble head.

"I'm sorry." The brunette whispered, golden swirls dancing within the dark depths of her curls. Her right hand slipped down its muscular neck, coming to rest in the elegant hollow at the center of its chest. For a moment, the world was silenced as she sought, and found, the steady thump of the creature's heart. Her eyes, red with suppressed emotion, dark with sorrow, met those of the girl across the clearing for a fraught second, then, catching an encouraging nod, closed with a snap of finality that was echoed by the sound of the deer collapsing, lifeless, onto the sweet grasses of the clearing.

"Whoo!" The blonde archer rose to her feet, arms pumping the air as she released a series of warrior trills into the air that were echoed by the calls of their companions further back in the wood. She danced lightly on her toes and twirled in glee as she unstrung her short bow and stowed it back in the carrier strapped tightly between the slim blades of her shoulders.

"What a prize!" She turned to her sister, the bright smile on her face reflecting the relief she felt that this wasn't the week they'd go hungry, eager to share their triumph.

But the other girl had gone.

"I thought you had gotten over this by now."

Tempest blew a strangled puff of air at the loose hair that had fallen from her braid and onto her tear-streaked face as she vigorously scrubbed at her tender palms. "No," she muttered around a clenched jaw, "I just got better at hiding it." The bell-like sleeves of her simple summer tunic dipped into the frigid mountain-fed waters of the stream outside their camp. The icy liquid dripped back down her arms, pooling in her lap as she knelt between the boulders littering the bank. Even though she knew the rivulets weren't blood, she couldn't help but rub just a little bit harder.

The soft bustling a hundred yards behind them, joyously muted voices bantering and teasing, reassured her that it was only her sister approaching. As much as she trusted the other girls of their little rebel band, she couldn't stomach the thought of them seeing her bled of strength. Her older sister, on the other hand, only ever seemed to see her at her worst.

"It is just a deer, Tempe." Dahlis' strong shoulders dipped in defeat as her arms fell from her hips. Unlike her younger sister, she had never had an opportunity to let remorse color her life, but it wasn't because she did not feel it. "We need to eat. You need to do better with this. It's not just our bellies at stake, it's our very survival."

With the reality of their circumstances pulling down the corner of her mouth, Dahlis reached inside the frequently patched pocket of her leather vest, leather provided by another deer in what felt like another lifetime. Her fingers dug around until she managed to grasp the drawstring of the tiny pouch she kept stored there. A few tugs freed it and, realizing her own hands were coated in layers of dried blood from her efforts to disembowel and drag their quarry back to camp, she used her teeth to pry it open and shook one of the treasures inside directly into her mouth. Peppered mint and the tang of citrus filled her senses, calming her building anxiety almost instantly.

"Here," she tossed the candy bag on the ground beside her sister and followed it with the towel and the change of clothes she'd tossed over her shoulder. She shamelessly began shedding the supple beige and green layers they donned when their travels brought them into the forest. "The mints may not fill your stomach, but they'll keep it from rebelling until you can start thinking of your own well-being once again and eat the damn deer." Her curt remark ended with a tiny squeak as she walked fearlessly into the cold, swift water. Even Dahlis, a warrior born and bred, though never truly meant to wield a weapon, wasn't immune to the pain of frozen toes. A string of under the breath curse words followed her to the center of the stream until they were suddenly lost as she submerged herself in the current.

"I may be weak, but I am not an imbecile." Tempest sighed, her head tilted back, catching a brief ray of sunshine that had made it through the canopy above. Her eyes were pressed tight, fighting the urge to relive those last few fraught moments of the deer's life, battling to push the fear and the surge of horror felt upon realizing its death was imminent from taking a place in her soul.

Because of her, there had been no blood. There had been no pain. No bite of flint in flesh. But, still, tomorrow would begin a new day bereft of a unique and cherished life. She'd barely been able to say her own name when she'd realized she'd been blessed with the ability to sense the life beating vibrantly just under the skin of those she touched. It was an indescribable feeling. The Essence of Life was beautiful, a symphony of energy and blood song, and, through it, she herself was Beauty.

Now, the healing power that filled her hands and called her heart forward with an undeniable need to ease the suffering of others, was nothing but a curse. It was one thing for a young girl to piece together the torn wing of an injured butterfly within a walled garden where nothing bad had ever happened. It was quite another to live a life even the most jaded of degenerates never suffered, forced to stand by when the soldiers sent to kill you lost their lives instead. The flutter of each of their souls being ripped from their bodies tore through Tempest's own, their pain echoing inside her, begging for relief. It wasn't a feeling she had ever been able to convey to her ever-practical sister. Dahlis often said pain was just another motivation to succeed, a way to prove to yourself that you were meant to be more than just an unfilled vessel.

Frankly, Tempest thought that reasoning was the only way her sister could accept her current situation, the belief that their strife was only temporary and that, if they held on, they would only come back stronger. One day, they would belong again. Their vessels, so to speak, filled with purpose.

Tempest might have the power to heal, but she was certain Dahlis' gift lay on the opposite end of that spectrum. They'd both trained with their father, as all Malorn heirs were expected to do, but while Tempest had excelled at the routine aspects of swordplay, Dahlis didn't just practice with a weapon, she led it in a deadly dance that was entrancing to observe. While Tempest had snuck away to relentlessly plague the Apothecary until he shared every ounce of his hedge healer knowledge, Dahlis had been winning mock battles against warriors twice her age, making their father an immeasurably proud man. Back then, it had been a point of honor to have raised his heir in the manner of their warrior forefathers, even when no battles loomed upon their horizon. Tempest, too, had been proud of her sister's flawless talent. It was a skill that had benefited them countless times since the downfall of House Malorn. And had led to enough injuries to make Tempest's own gift invaluable.

The cessation of aggravated splashing heralded the fact that Dahlis considered herself clean enough, or sufficiently tortured by the elements, to carry on with her day. Shivers wracked her athletic body, but she still managed to negotiate the slippery rock bed with grace while twisting her waist-length hair, ridding it of as much moisture as possible. Thrusting herself to her feet, Tempest tossed the towel to her sister before her elegant knees could clear the stream. Once, she would have turned bright red with embarrassment to see another human without a stitch of clothing to cover them. Once, Dahlis would have remained dirty rather than expose even an inch of her delicate skin to eyes that were not her own. After four years of each other's constant company in less-than-ideal living conditions, Tempest's only interest was to take note of the scars that she'd been unable to completely heal.

"How water can be so frakking cold in the midst of full summer is beyond me." Dahlis shivered, the curse word chattering past her clenched teeth.

"Mother would not be best pleased with your common soldier's mouth." Tempest couldn't stop the peevish words, even though she wished she could take them back the instant they escaped. Courtiers throughout the Kingdom of Hlyn had once praised her on her maturity and the kindness of her heart. Would they even recognize the petulant shrew she sometimes felt she had become?

"Perhaps not," Dahlis whipped the threadbare towel through her hair, making minimal real effort to soak away the moisture, "but she would be overjoyed that my warrior's soul has seen us alive thus far." A wet plop sounded like a sharp crack as the damp bit of rag slapped against Tempest's chest, leaving a cool spot against her skin that she didn't mind in the least, given the heat. She clutched it to her, silent, as Dahlis rushed to finish dressing.

"I'm heading to Fortuena for the evening." Dahlis' voice came muffled through the soft crimson cotton of her 'respectable' dress as she pulled it violently over her still wet body, tangling her damp golden hair somewhere around her arm and eliciting an angry mutter. "I'll be taking Monika with me but I'm sure the other girls would appreciate a little effort dressing out the rest of the meat." A final grunt and the dress settled snugly about her curves. She ran her hands down to smooth the sides as best as she could and then tightened the glittering gold and aqua belt that would hold her daggers. It had been one of the few possessions they had managed to retain in their mad dash for freedom.

"I didn't mean to run off." Tempest bent to retrieve the battered purse from where it lay at her feet, having no heart to sneak one of Dahlis' treats. She swung it back and forth in front of her nervously. She idolized her sister, always had, but she knew that every bit of pain and worry and responsibility Dahl carried on her shoulders wasn't hers to bear alone. Tempest, herself, was not exactly a slouch when it came to heavy burdens. "I will do my part, as I always manage."

"I know it's not on purpose." Dahlis abruptly stopped her vigorous attempt to fluff the wrinkles from her dress, her capable hands dropping limp at her side. "I just...worry." Her brow scrunched in a concerned manner as she struggled to express the feelings she normally kept reined in behind a stone wall of composure. "About you. About how you are going to survive this life we have been forced into when you're..." she shrugged tentatively, knowing Tempest would find what she said next hurtful, "as soft as you are."

"I said I'd finish the butchering, Dahl. Blood has never been a factor," stubbornness set her chin so firmly that Dahlis almost didn't hear the rest of her sentence, "just the spilling of it."

Tempest's eyes, a duller, more earthy shade of gold than her sister's, dropped briefly in embarrassment before regaining their prideful gleam. It was not in her to apologize for who she was. She gave the pouch a whirl and tossed it at her sister, immediately cringing as the clunky little bag bounced off the older girl's chest and lost itself in the frigid depths of the stream.

A few decisive steps brought the two girls together as Dahlis pulled Tempest in for a reluctant hug. With one small squeeze, she kissed her sister's forehead and then pushed her back an arm's length, her palms steady on the shorter girl's upper arms but her thumbs dimpled the skin, as if to imprint the importance of her next words.

"We cannot hesitate, Tempe. Our days of compassion and empathy are far behind us. When a kill is required, we make the kill." Her face was stoic, hard lines carved into cheeks that were once graced with the most glorious dimples in the realm, but her eyes, those unmistakable golden orbs that marked her as the Princess Heir of Hlyn, were glittering with unshed tears.

Chapter Three

"WAIT!" EVEN THOUGH HER personality was huge, Porta's voice was thin, which often led her to make extravagant gestures. Her hands flew about her almost cherubic face in a windmilling motion, prompting Tempest to grab the rough butchering blade the girl was waving recklessly about, prying it out of those tiny but tenacious fingers. Successful, she squatted down beside the freshly skinned buck and began sawing through flesh and bone.

It's just meat, she told herself. Sustenance. Survival. A blessing despite all the regret that congregated around her heart. She knew eventually the pain would leave, replaced with thankfulness and the return of her practical nature, but she rushed nevertheless to finish the task before her, desperate to be distracted from the dark thoughts lurking on the edges of her mind.

Aggravating Porta was an excellent way to do that. The girl was easy to rile and was as hilarious to watch as a mad kitten spitting in the face of a bull.

"You act like I'm a baby when you aren't much bigger than me." Her flailing arms found a place of defiance on her hips, her head cocking smugly, stick-straight black hair, which never stayed where it was supposed to, catching on her slightly chapped lips.

"I'm twenty, which makes me much older than you, both in years and experience." Tempest smirked and flicked a loose string of severed tendon at Porta, hitting her directly between her scowling brows. A sense of warmth filled her, and her smile was huge as Porta's own mouth opened in surprised shock.

"I'm not sure there is much truth to your experience statement." Verilee's calm voice drifted over from where she was methodically scraping the hide, her shoulders straining in repetition but a gently teasing smile on her face. Today, she had braided her fine blonde hair down each side of her freckled cheeks and tied the ends together in a knot at her nape that rolled back and forth hypnotically as she moved. The hide was staked in the dusty open spot between their tents, the lack of grass indicating they'd need to move camp soon. The intense heat beating down caused her to pause frequently to swipe at the sweat dripping off her pointed nose. At least she'd had the foresight to wear her sleeveless shift for her dirty work.

Born the fifth daughter of a minor baron in one of the more rural provinces, one could mistake the twinkle in her cornflower blue eyes as sweet innocence. If they didn't know better. "That is, if it's men we are talking about. I think you need to actually know a boy before you can claim to be a worldly woman."

"Hmpfh." Tempest huffed at her catty remark, smiling as she threw her an obscene hand gesture. The blonde might be more lax in the moral department than Tempest found comfortable, but she was a kind soul. In fact, she secretly admired that Verilee honored her body in the best way for her. Tempest could tolerate a little ribbing from time to time when it was in the name of good fun, and she knew Ver hadn't intended it to be anything else.

The youngest member of their group, however, was a different kettle of fish altogether. Tempest was bracing herself the moment Porta closed her mouth, swallowed hard, and opened it again. No one could get her back up in quite the same way. Dahlis would laugh and say it was Little Sister Syndrome and give Tempest the side-eye. Tempest called it Basic Brattiness and lack of proper discipline.

Porta hooted, "You've never been kissed?" She poked a blood-soaked finger into Tempest's shoulder, leaving behind a gruesome smudge that would take a whole bar of lye to remove. "Now, who is the pathetic child?"

"Still you." Tempest's tongue poked out of her mouth, proving she wasn't above being immature. Porta was the annoying younger sister she had never wished to have. More often than not, she was left to watch the girl while the older three hared off on their own daring escapades. It had ever been that way, though, even in the good times. Dahlis, Monika, and Verilee were three peas in a pod. Tempest had never felt slighted by them, not much, but growing up in the palace among strictly regulated tutors and lessons, the mere three years difference between her and Dahlis had seemed monumental at the time.

Luckily, Tempest wasn't the adventure-having type of girl and didn't mind being relegated to tending base camp and the little dervish within it. If she could just find a way to shut Porta's sassy and waspish mouth, she daresay she might even enjoy it.

Although, Porta's sassy wit often made Tempest miss her little brother. Her heart stuttered in her chest as his cherubic face flooded her memories. How she'd loved to hold him and twist her fingers through his golden curls as he told her the funny little stories he'd made up while trying to evade his nurse. His tales would center around brave princesses and knights that seemed to forever be the ones needing saved and never concluded until he could 'surprise' her with the real plot... which was, inevitably, that someone pooped where they shouldn't have. Out of everything she'd ever lost, she missed him most.

Ben would be eleven now.

"Twenty?" The whisper turned Tempest's head to where Dahlis was in the process of mounting her horse, her foot arrested halfway to the stirrup. A look of aghast horror on her face. "No, no, no, no...Ah, Tempe! I'm so sorry!" She dropped the horse's reins and slapped her forehead theatrically, causing her mount to side-step. "I missed your birthday!"

Canelope shook her mane from side to side, as if to express her disappointment, following it with a hearty snort of complaint. Tempest laughed. The white mare was frisky on the best of days, and it had been a few weeks since they had traveled farther than the edge of the forest. She was eager to stretch her legs and venture outside of the restrictive bounds of their small corral. She butted her head against Dahlis, not understanding why her rider was standing there with a glum face when they could already be in a full gallop somewhere.

Tempest shrugged. "It is only a day, Dahl. Something to mark one more year and one more wrinkle." She said it jokingly, hoping to put her sister at ease. She wasn't upset that her birthday had gone unnoticed. Back home, birthday celebrations had been an excuse for an extravagant party full of exuberant dancing, rich pastries and rare delicacies. A month of planning, a night of laughter, and then a week of bellyaches and excessive napping. None of which they had the time, resources, or patience for these days.

Participating in festivities in her honor also went against every molecule of her being. Even if the crowd was only a few, the attention would be horribly embarrassing for her. Her entire life had been spent in hiding the truest parts of herself, the secret magic that made her unique...and the one that made her dangerous. It was difficult to put the fear of discovery aside. Anyway, she didn't need Porta teasing her about her eternally reddened cheeks.

"Well," decisive as always, Dahlis turned and mounted the mare, settling into the saddle with the ease that many long days of practice had provided, "I can't be late to this meeting without possibly losing a valuable contact. Why don't you all get the meat put up, dress in something with less bloodstains, and meet us in Fortunea for a much-deserved birthday celebration tonight?"

Porta let out a squeal and leapt to her feet, dancing in place as only a child could do. "Really, Dahlis?!" her face lit up as a thousand sinister plans flew like lightning bolts through her mischievous little brain. There was a reason they didn't venture into towns often. That reason was partially due to one rambunctious and impulsive pre-teen. Tempest groaned under her breath. She didn't think she'd be doing much other than keeping tabs on the devious sprite. That prediction was solidified as Porta winked one of her brilliant green eyes and said, "Maybe you'll get that kiss tonight, Tem, if," she leaned forward, bowing mockingly at the waist, "you take that stick out of your butt!"

This time, it was Tempest's mouth that was left agape. Silence prevailed for a half a heartbeat before Dahlis began laughing uncontrollably. A breath later, a snort escaped Verilee, which she tried unsuccessfully to hide behind a red hand. She sat back on her heels, tears pouring down her freckled cheeks as a series of short hiccups cascaded into a laugh that wasn't much different than that of one of her father's donkeys.

Which, of course, made the two younger girls descend into their own bouts of hysterical laughter.

"What is so funny that you are all guffawing like street hooligans?" Monika stepped out of her tent. It was less dusty than the rest, with the edges crisply staked to the ground, and she obsessively smoothed the flaps back in place as she walked through. The girl herself, Dahlis' very best friend and her former Lady in Waiting, was less grubby than the rest of the gang. Her hair, a deep cinnamon hue, was carefully balanced and pinned to the top of her regal head, curls laying calmly and evenly spaced despite the humidity that plagued the rest of them. Her dress, a bright blue affair that wouldn't be out of place in the finest drawing rooms, had somehow survived several hard years relatively intact inside a saddle bag. Tempest sometimes wondered if Monika was hiding her own magic, some wondrous talent that removed wrinkles, dirt, and the stench of horse. There were, after all, more odd powers in this world.

"Porta is displaying her unladylike behavior," Tempest intoned in her most haughty voice, rising to her feet and stretching her back until it snapped with an uncouth amount of noise, "in the most appalling way imaginable." She pointed the knife at Porta, aiming for an air of condescension but smirking to assure Porta she held no hard feelings, "The poor bedraggled waif was expounding upon matters beyond her comprehension with the exemplary eloquence expected of a guttersnipe bent on bumfoolery."

"I don't know what you are saying but you are undoubtedly being a smart ass, Tem."

Tempest casually flipped the knife in the air, handily catching it in a showy display before she tossed it into the basket she'd stacked the sliced meat in. She'd take it down to the creek for a thorough wash in the freezing waters before they began the smoking process that would, hopefully, help see them fed through the winter. She toed a second, smaller basket, filled with scraps and unusable pieces of flesh, away from the main basket to help detract the flies. These unwanted slivers would be utilized as bait to catch the fish that would provide a welcome change from all the red meat and root vegetables that made up their regular diet.

"I'd rather be a smartass than a dumb one." Tempest remarked offhandedly, stepping past Monika to grab a towel. The pounding of small feet on earth was her only warning that she was about to be attacked, but a reluctant warrior was still a warrior, and it was the only warning she needed. She whirled, half-amused to see Porta flying at her with double fists filled with meat remnants and evil intention.

"Oh, no you don't!" Monika stretched forward to grab the girl's wrist, pivoting gracefully and redirecting the dripping handfuls of gore. Unfortunately, Porta tripped over her shoes, a hand-down from Tempest and a size too big for her tiny feet, and plunged, bloody meat and fingers first, directly into Monika's pristine abode. An audible inhale stole all the air from the forest, followed by an exhale that nearly whistled in its fury. Every eye darted away from the gruesome scene, choosing not to witness the inevitable dressing down that was about to descend on Porta's delicate head. One second passed in silence. Then two. The third brought with it salvation for their littlest rebel.

"I believe my horse," Monika's pointy chin lifted imperiously in the air as she gathered her skirts and turned away, "who is one hundred percent more ladylike than the lot of you," her eyes closed briefly as she took a steadying breath, "awaits me."

"Your horse has a dingle-dong, Moni." Porta pointed out helpfully from her prone position in the wreck of wood staves and canvas that was once Monika's palace in the woods. She was wiping her hands in wide arcs, leaving obscene red snow angel-like wing impressions to either side of her. Her eyes darted back and forth between the older girls and, despite the awkward pile of Monika's belongings buried beneath her, seemed content to stay where she was. Pretending not to hear, and refusing to see the destruction, the red head stalked off to collect her gelding, her precisely spaced steps nonetheless conveying the rage she was tamping into the toes of her slippers.

"Someone clean up that mess and then toss her," Dahlis pointed at the tangled heap of tent and girl, her finger bouncing up and down as she tried to hold in her laughter, "in the creek!"

"My pleasure!" Tempest rubbed her palms together, mischievous glee darkening her golden eyes so that she looked just as childishly demonic as Porta ever did. She jumped toward the jumbled destruction, causing the younger girl to scramble and squeal. Verilee sprung up from her work, cautiously approaching from the side to help corner the flailing dervish.

"Your pleasure, indeed." Verilee winked as she lunged for Porta. "That is another aspect of your so-called 'experience' that we will undoubtedly have to cover in a private chat sometime." Her strong hands, deft and quick from handling livestock the better part of her life, grasped the younger girl easily, holding her by the back of the neck and forcefully directing her toward the stream.

The pair picked their way sloppily through the underbrush, Porta complaining in her high-pitched nasally voice and Verilee applying guiding pressure as necessary.

Shaking her head, Tempest scooped up a few discarded towels, stooping further to pull a bar of highly scented floral soap from Monika's usually heavily guarded stash from a gap in the demolished tent.

"Maybe this won't be the worst birthday ever after all."

The husky timbre of Dahlis' chuckle, barely smothered by the fitful prancing of her mare, followed the Outlaw Princess into the forest.

Chapter Four

T HE VILLAGE OF FORTUNEA sat on a bare promontory edging out over the rock-strewn coast of the Parian Sea. A century ago, it had been a lonely outpost consisting of a few rugged huts tucked between the dangerous wildness of the Dunshyre forest and the sheer sweep of unscalable cliffs that made up the easternmost point of Hlyn.

Feeling much lighter after a quick scrub and fresh clothes, Tempest pulled her gelding to a gentle stop at the edge of the trees. If anyone were looking hard enough, they couldn't miss his dappled white and gray coat among the foliage, a fact that made her nervous but not cautious enough to trade him for another mount. Besides, Dahlis would never countenance giving up her precious Canelope who was whiter than high mountain snow. She patted his neck as he stood quietly, the epitome of patience.

"For the love of all kittens, Tem," Porta bounced up and down anxiously in the saddle of her long-legged mare, "it's Fortunea. No one," she leaned forward with a drawn-out groan of exasperation, the sort of frustration only a young girl can fully convey, "is waiting to get us. The scariest thing here is that bald goat-herder with that atrocious mustache!"

"First of all," Tempest whispered, "no one swears on the love of any feline, even the tiny ones. They have absolutely no capacity for softer feelings." She pretended to stretch slowly up in her saddle, peering past the last bit of foliage obscuring them from the village proper. In truth, she saw not with her eyes but was feeling the whirl of pure sensation pouring from the bustling buildings. Her magic wasn't foolproof and a lack of the excitable energy that she associated with danger didn't mean they were safe, it only suggested no one was actively harboring ill intent at this moment. She sighed and relaxed, nudging Obertroess forward.

"Secondly," she continued as they cleared the tree line, "Auogustos is a refined gentleman who makes the very best milked sweets."

"Well," Porta reluctantly averred, impatiently jabbing her mount with her heels in order to get past the constricting foliage and into the meadow. Her mare, a sturdy bay that was usually as unflappable as her rider was excitable, blew out a snort then yanked the reins out of Porta's reach, continuing on, undisturbed, at her own pace. The scrawny girl harrumphed and play-slapped the horse before pulling her legs up to sit cross-legged on the saddle.

She folded her haughty arms to match. "Auoggi is, of course, above reproach." She wiggled her pert little nose in the air before scrunching it, "But can you imagine if his facial hair fell in my candies?!"

Tempest shuddered, turning far enough in her seat to share a smile with Verilee, who was humming happily under her breath. "I suppose," she ceded, "you have a valid point."

"Damn straight."

"Porta!" Verilee admonished with a surprised gasp. Her mount, a somewhat fractious and entirely ugly long-eared mule, did a little startled sidestep at the sound but calmed quickly with a delicate pat on its neck. It picked its way quickly around Porta's mare, who had taken the opportunity to step off the path and munch on some wilted daisies.

"It's nothing you haven't said a thousand times, Veri." Porta strained to reach her dropped reins. "Don't come after me with your gentle manners just because we are around real people. That," she stated loftily, "would be extremely hypnocratical of you." She stole a glance under her dark brows at Tempest, seeking approval for her choice of word.

"Hypocritical, for sure." She pretended to mishear. "We wouldn't want to appear supercilious, now would we, Verilee, dear?" Tempest laughed, a happy feeling filling her truly for the first time in a long while. It was Fortunea, not the rabble-filled slums to be found outside Hlyn's borders. The only trouble awaiting them here would be caused by their own poor choices. Why shouldn't they take this one night to cut loose a bit? To forget that the shadow of the Warlock Emperor was ever encroaching upon them?

It was, after all, a night to celebrate the fact that she was now officially a grown woman. Her sardonic inner voice couldn't help but point out that she'd left her childhood behind long before her age allowed for it. She dismissed the thought. This was not the night for negativity.

"Hey," she pointed into the heart of the village where people were gathered around the town well in the growing darkness. "Isn't that Deik, Farmer Dennig's son?"

"Damn straight, it sure is!" Porta whooped, finally startling her horse into motion. With the flexibility of the young, she fell back into riding position on her worn saddle before her mare could go two steps. She began waving frantically at the poor boy who would, no doubt, have his ear talked off before the night was over.

"Don't press your luck with that mouth!" Tempest wagged a finger at her but instantly turned it into a shooing motion. "Get out of here! Go, have fun and please," she rolled her eyes, but the humor spilled forth nonetheless, "for the love of kittens, don't get in any trouble!"

Both horse and girl waited not a moment longer, all gangly legs and sudden energy focused on the fastest way into town. Polli Nan, the silly name Porta had chosen for her horse, was no dummy, and well-remembered the treats the young Dennig boy compulsively fed her while listening to Porta's tall tales.

"What a scamp! I fear we shall never make a proper lady of that one." Verilee's pale cheeks were dented with matching dimples, denying her attempt at displeasure.

Tempest snorted, "If any of us were ever 'proper ladies', it's far too late to go back now. And," she slyly pulled her horse aside to let Verilee pass. "If I'm not mistaken, that big sandy lump standing next to Deik sure does look like his older brother, Nance."

A feral, hungry smile appeared on Verilee's falsely gentle face, "Damn straight, I do believe you are correct." She was nearly purring.

Tempest rolled her eyes once again, their golden gleam picking up reflections of the fading sun. She smiled ironically at the older girl. "Ugh, already!" she laughed, "Begone!"

"Hiya!" Verilee and her mount quickly disappeared into the maze of buildings, their own pursuit well-engaged. Her mule, not as fast as a horse but twice as stubborn, began bugling its excitement as it kicked its awkwardly knobby hind legs in joy.

Tempest leaned back in her saddle, a cue for good old Bert to slow to a stop. She took in the peaceful, happy sounds emanating from people who knew no other life than that which their daily struggles provided them. She wasn't naive enough to think they didn't have worries to battle or dreams to chase, but their problems were the same as had been faced by generations before them...A washed out pier, a fallow field, or perhaps wolves within the far heather, eager to partake of a stray lamb.

The wolves that shadowed her weren't those of opportunity. They were beasts of intention, directed by a demanding master none of them could resist.

But that also was not a worry for today. She pushed off the feeling of doom that often found its way into her thoughts. Tonight, she would celebrate! Fragments of music began to leak into the meadow, punctuated with Porta's girlishly high-pitched squeals of glee. It warmed her heart while at the same time sending sparks of irritation dancing through her. With effort, she pushed her irrational exasperation away.

She was glad the girl could find some solace from their stress-filled existence, truly, no matter how brief. It hadn't always been so.

Tempest slipped from her gelding's back, loosening his girth and freeing the bit from his mouth. With a gentle hug, meeting the faithful equine's long forehead with her own delicately boned face, she turned Bert out to roam where he would.

Ever since Tempest had pulled the damaged little girl from the partially burnt hut that held the remains of what had been her family, Porta had tried to emotionally hold her at arm's length...with the same strength of conviction in which she held all her personal affronts.

A few months had passed with sour looks and hateful words but Tempest, dealing with her own unresolved feelings at losing a parent, chose to let it go. She could feel, even without the empathic part of her power, every ounce of Porta's undeserved hate toward her building until it simply became too much.

Looking back now, she felt a wave of shame consume her over the resentment she had felt toward the young orphan. At the time, though, all she could see was the fact that she had risked her life, as well as the safety of her sister, to heal a perfect stranger. One that morphed into a prickly little monster she could do no right for.

A season of tantrums and mean-spirited fights ensued before Tempest blew up and demanded Dahlis leave the ungrateful little twit in one of the orphanages scattered about the countryside.

It was one of the first times she could ever remember her older sister being disappointed in her although, she laughed to herself now, it seemed to happen more frequently as their exile went on.

'Porta is ours, Tempest.' Dahlis had said. 'A sister to us, in spirit and travail, if not in name. We cannot abandon her. We will not abandon her.'

'But,' her rebuttal had been weak, she had known this battle was over long before she had opened her mouth in complaint. The girl may have been plucking her every last nerve, but she would never have put her aside any more than Dahlis would. Still, the frustration was strong. 'She isn't mean to anyone else, only to me...the one that saved her!'

'Yes,' she'd said. 'You saved her.'

Tempest's confusion must have shown through because Dahlis sighed and reached across the space dividing them, tucking a flyaway strand of hair behind her sister's ear in the loving way she had done since they were children. The fire popped gently beside them as they sat on their lonely little log in the dark woods.

'You saved only her.'

Understanding hit Tempest hard in that moment, causing fury and empathy and sadness in a wild lightning bolt of mixed emotions to thrum achingly through her veins. On that chilly night of Last Month, someone had raided Porta's home, killed every-one she had ever known in her short life, and left her bereft. She hadn't been able to provide any details beyond quiet, shocked mumbles that shadow men had set the fires. Perhaps she'd never known who was truly responsible for that night. She'd needed someone to hate, and in an instant, Tempest knew the best way to heal her was to be her someone.

Her sour musings were interrupted when Tempest found her-self stumbling over a lumpy patch of vegetation that once had been a hayrick. Only years of intricate dance and swordsmanship lessons kept her from falling on her face. Across the field, Bert raised his head from the grass and snorted, as if laughing at her expense.

"What the vainglorious boggle?!" An offended voice emanating from the tussock of old hay startled her. A skittering of hooved legs threw particles of dust violently in the air and, through the force of her sudden sneezing fit, Tempest was able to make out at least five frantic goats making their way to the village in haste.

"Auoggie?" She coughed and wiped a hand over her face, won-dering how on earth she had missed approaching an entire man and a portion of his horned flock in what was basically a flat meadow. If he had been a minion of the Nightmare, she would have been a goner. "What on earth are you doing down there? Also, I don't think that is the proper use of the term vainglorious." She reached down to help him to his feet, not flinching when his frail but grubby hand wrapped around hers, the bones on the knobs of his joints poking imperiously at her softer flesh.

The man, dressed in faded cottons that were ripped, stained, and generally bedraggled, adjusted the brilliant blue satin tie fastened at his bare throat. He scooted around in a tight circle until he located his finely polished staff and slapped a ratty straw hat upon his bald head.

"Pshaw." Augoustos, the goat-herder spat. "It perfectly applies. You, interloper, are no doubt vain...thinking you can walk wherever you please. I," he twisted the tips of his monstrous mustache, "am simply glorious." His gap-toothed grin was truly marvelous, and Tempest just shook her head and smiled stupidly at him.

"Oh, girl," he exclaimed, wheezing a bit until he was able to dislodge errant bits of straw from his lips. "It's you...the Golden Goddess from the Depths of the Dunshyre Who Pretends She's a Brunette!"

A jolt of fear shot through her body and she froze, her eyes flashing around to see who was nearby. Unaware of the suddenly stiff body at his side, Augoustos cackled as he swiped at his eyes with the end of his exuberantly fancy tie.

"I's got a poetic soul, ya know?" He slapped his dirty thigh. "My own sweet wife, gods rest her ever-nagging soul, was always colorin' her hair some fancy shade. Bein' that there is no beauty witch in the woods, I'd say those roots are a dead give-away that it's time to hit the bottle again."

Tempest relaxed once again. She hadn't known Auoggie's wife, but she did recall there being a violently blue haired woman that had often tramped through the village yelling for 'that old goat'. She shook the tension from her shoulders. Dahlis was forever accusing her of borrowing trouble, just about as often as Porta reminded her that she was tragically uptight.

"I wanted to dye mine to match the meadow lavender, but my sister assured me it does not go well with either my skin tone or my personality." Not that the atrociously dank shade of brown she had chosen to hide her very noticeable hereditary natural color was doing anything to improve her looks either.

"Hmmm," he muttered through his hairy nose curtain, "that sister of yours is a pleasure for these old eyes but I believe she is too high strung for an old goatherd to hang about. Always planning and chatting in corners, that one." He gazed off toward the tree line blankly for a second, his jaw working slowly as he was lost in thought.

"Hey," he shouted suddenly, causing Tempest to clutch her heart once again, "them damn goats seem to have abandoned me. You wanna help me track their smelly asses down? I have fresh milk sweets..." his voice, though on the creaky side, was cajoling and oddly captivating. Tempest could see why a younger Augoustos had attracted someone as flamboyant and vivacious as his late wife.

"There's nothing I'd like more, Auoggie, but my dastardly sister is waiting for me. We are celebrating my birthday tonight." she added.

She could feel some of his energy fade slightly at her demurral. You didn't need healing magic to realize he was missing his wife fiercely.

"But," she slipped her arm through his, pulling him close enough to push a little bit of love at the lonely feelings shrouding his heart. "I would be honored if you'd be my escort tonight. Every lady deserves a handsome man to deliver her to a night of revelry. Possibly debauchery!"

"Debauchery, you say?" Auoggie's face lit up, his smile pushing the wrinkles closed around his eyes. "It would be downright unethical for me to allow your birthday to be filled with anything less!"

Chapter Five

"H aaarrrrr...haaarrr!" Auoggie's dry, abrasive laughter sounded much like a donkey's as he swung through the well-oiled hinges of what served for the doors of the Dirty Umbrage. The backswing of the frail strips of wood and leather caught Tempest's waiting palm in a stinging slap as she paused before following the old man inside. The smell of dank bodies and musky jars mixed uncomfortably with fragrant floral perfumes and pipe smoke in a dizzying assault on the senses.

Used to the natural scents of forest and horse, not to mention her own aroma - not too horrible thanks to the slivers of Monika's stolen soaps, the opening in the building gushed its unpleasant odor in her face, causing her to catch a surprised breath. Fortunately, there was no one standing near enough to notice her startled pause or to hear the choked inhale that worked its way from her throat to her bedeviled nose, where it puttered slowly out her nostrils. Thankfully, the interior of the small tavern was just as dark as it was dreary, so Tempest didn't worry that anyone might see the embarrassed flush riding her cheeks.

She took one last deep breath of the quickly falling night air, preparing herself for the night to come. Being raised as a princess and paraded regularly before the masses still didn't make entering a crowd of people easier for her, but it did allow the uncertain smile upon her face to appear welcoming. Her eyes adjusted much quicker than her nose had, and she felt her smile slip a little as she took in the number of people packed into every seat and crevice the Dirty Umbrage had to offer.

"'Ey!" Auoggie's gnarled hand lifted toward a gaggle of old men tucked into the far corner of the bar. An answering chorus of ancient 'Oi's!' filled the air, telling Tempest he had found his tribe of cronies. "Ah, Lass," he turned and squeezed her elbow gently, "it's me boys, all alive and in one place, no less. What a surprising treat!" Tempest's smile grew more sincere as the affection he felt toward his 'boys' suffused the energy around him with an irresistible radiance. Her magic surged in reaction, warming her heart and sending a tingle of power rushing through the tips of her fingers. An involuntary laugh slipped past her lips.

"Then why are you standing here? Go!" She gave him an impulsive hug, letting some of her magic seep through his ragged shirt and sink into his own heart, shoring up a few worn patches of muscle that were beginning to fail. A cloud of cackles and catcalls filled the air as Auoggie wiggled his hairy eyebrows and shot his friends a cocky thumbs-up.

And as quick as that, Tempest found herself alone once again. A sweeping glance around the gathered villagers, most dressed in pleasant shades of brown and cream, assured her that Dahlis and Monika, in their vibrant, once court-worthy dresses, were not there. Swallowing past the knot of anxiety building in her throat at the thought of being alone, she forced herself deeper into the tavern. The feeling of goodwill pervading the room was almost a physical caress to her senses. There was, despite the voice in her head, nothing to fear here.

Pasting a warm smile upon her strained face, she focused on the battered oak and stone bar and the woman bustling around behind it. She cautiously made her way past the small tables packed with bodies smelling of a hard day's work and the bounty of the earth. A handful of nods and a few softly murmured greetings brought her to the bar, and she rested her palms upon it gently. The surface of the wood shone bright despite the decades of calloused hands rubbing relentlessly against the veneer. Tempest let her magic drop into the memories of the long-dead tree, something she could only do with the oldest of inanimate objects. Ancient things, she felt, seemed to find another life when they had been filled with enough purpose. It spoke of dedication, of love, and of limitless patience. Much like the curvaceous woman standing behind it.

A massive amount of hair so light Tempest could only describe it as white, was pulled into a rumpled bun on the woman's head and tucked, unsuccessfully, into a bright red kerchief. It bobbed with her brisk movements, its glossy, almost translucent strands contrasting sharply with a face that hadn't quite reached middle age. She nearly oozed motherly practicality as she swiftly filled two tankards from a pitcher labeled 'goat' with one reddened hand while ladling stew from a steaming kettle wrapped in layers of damp cloth into a pair of serving bowls.

"Good even', milady." She greeted Tempest without turning around. "Jersika and Jerone," her voice raised smooth and vibrant, just loud enough to pull the attention of two young lovers canoodling at the edge of the crowd, "take this to that table of gigglers in the back, please?" She slid the food and drinks onto a cracked serving tray and passed it to a blushing girl that looked remarkably like her. A towel seemingly appeared from out of nowhere and she began wiping her hands briskly while staring down the young man. She lifted one surprisingly dark eyebrow, which was enough to get her point across without having to say one word. In seconds, his face began to flush from the neckline up and his energy shifted from the excitement of first love to a full-on squirm of inadequacy.

Tempest didn't know whether to laugh or to hide her face in sympathetic shame.

"Mom!" The girl's protest was half apology, half rebellion. She shifted the tray without spilling a drop, "Come on, Jer." The boy flinched as her small toes made contact with his shin and pulled him from the staring contest he was in no position to ever win. He managed to turn an even darker shade of red as he scurried off into the crowded room.

"He's a good boy, that one." The innkeeper said, shaking her head before putting her towel to use on the spotless bar. She turned the full force of her catty smile on Tempest. "Pretty sure I'll be welcoming him into the family way before he's ready. Gotta show him who's top wolf in this tavern, don't I?"

Seeing the way the girl had herded her beau away from her mother, she didn't see any trouble coming from that quarter. She didn't say this but nodded agreeably. Bright blue eyes ran over Tempest in a second's assessment and the rag disappeared as quickly as it had appeared.

"I'm Sayrin, Milady. What's your pleasure? The stew's passing flavorful today, if I don't say so myself."

"Oh," Tempest demurred, "I'm not a lady." Sayrin hummed agreeably, but her eyebrow lifted imperiously enough to indicate she didn't believe this for a second. It was Tempest's turn to blush, her fair cheeks taking on an unmistakable pink tinge.

"Well," she cleared her throat, her hands nervously patting the battered wood top of the bar, "the stew does smell delightful but...perhaps once my friends arrive? We are supposed to be celebrating my birthday."

"Happy birthday, Milady! You'll be wanting a drink then while you wait. Sit yourself down," she pointed a finger to a lone stool tucked into the shadows at the end of the bar, "and I'll bring you something nice. I've got a sweet rose wine I save for special occasions in the back."

Sayrin bustled away, humming a wordless tune loudly and joyously as she went about her work. Tempest, unsure of what else she should do besides obey the tavern keeper, sat down on the stool, wincing a little at the laborious creak it made as she judiciously arranged her skirts. She attempted to lean on a casual elbow as she waited but immediately felt a fool and folded her hands demurely in her lap. The wild thumping of her heart settled slowly as she became adjusted to the auras surrounding her. It helped that she could still hear Sayrin's melodic voice even through the battered wood partition dividing the dining area from what she assumed to be the kitchen, the sound grounding her amidst the cacophony caused by so many vibrantly dissonant bodies.

She knew her eyes would be almost glittering golden with all the emotions swirling through her body so she tried, as best she could, to keep them low as she peered about the room. Thank goodness, she thought, that she had inherited the thick, dark lashes common in her mother's people. They gave her enough of an illusion of safety that she could gather the wild, coursing magic trying to run roughshod over her body and ruthlessly tamp it back into the metaphorical box she caged it in.

A large cold fireplace took up the entirety of the wall adjacent to the door she had entered through, mirroring the length and worn appearance of the bar. Today, the hearth was empty of flame but, even through the crowd of jostling people, Tempest recognized several of the herbs drying upside down in its cold depths. Most were traditional plants used by hedge healers but at least two of them had more sinister properties. She considered that maybe Sayrin was more than she appeared to be. People had a way of surprising even her from time to time, which proved magic was far from foolproof.

"Ah, my Stars have been Blessed this day, to find such a visage of beauty and grace hidden in the shadows of this dumpy sludge pit." The masculine voice tickling the back of her neck startled Tempest, and she barely resisted reaching for the blade tucked away in the pocket of her skirt as she swiveled on her stool.

The man before her was as close to perfection as she had ever seen in a male. Thin but muscled, his hair gleaming as brightly as his smile, he arched a perfect eyebrow and gave her an elegant bow. He was undoubtedly more than pleasant to look upon...and he knew it.

"Milady." Sayrin bustled around the wall from the kitchen, the straight line of her lips and tight lines around her eyes indicating extreme irritation. She pulled her trusty rag from her apron with no wasted movement, her no-nonsense swipe clearing the condensation off the chilled glass of red wine she sat before Tempest. "And your...friend? Will *his graciousness* be having anything from my derelict establishment?"

"An ale, if you please?" The man pulled a bag heavy with coin from within his jacket and deftly palmed a silver piece, juggling it flippantly over his knuckles before dropping it onto the smooth wood of the bar. He lifted his hand from the coin in the same moment he gave Sayrin a cocky smile. "And keep the change for yourself, good lady."

"I'm no lady." Sayrin stated in a way that left no doubt and no room for further flattery from the young man. Her eyes slid to Tempest, hooded and with a veiled message she couldn't quite interpret. She took a few firm steps toward the back wall, pulling a dusty mug from a dark shelf and with an expert flip of the wrist filled it one-handed from the tapped keg, sloshing the amber liquid so it left a tiny puddle under the man's hand as he accepted the drink.

"I'm Wrone." The man's brief scowl was replaced with an engaging grin as he wiped the wetness on his cheery blue doublet and took a large swig. His throat bobbed as he downed half of the ale at one swallow. Tempest watched in fascination. She hadn't been sought out by many men in her life, certainly none as handsome as this confident stranger.

"And you are?" He questioned, leaning into her personal space in a way that surprised her but didn't alarm her. For all that it was unexpected, his presence didn't offend her. Quite the opposite. To be truthful, he smelled pleasant enough that she would gladly allow the closeness, if for no other reason than to keep the odor of the less desirable patrons at bay.

"Waiting for my friends." Tempest teased, taking a slow sip of her wine. Her eyebrow raised at the cool, sweet taste delighting her tongue and she lifted her glass to Sayrin in appreciation. She wasn't innocent to the pleasures of a good wine, but it had been a rarity in her life these past few years. The warm flush of the alcohol hit her stomach almost immediately and a sense of contentment filled her. With it, her courage seemed to blossom, turning her into a creature she wasn't familiar with.

"Ah," Wrone's bright blue eyes glistened with pleasure. He was, undoubtedly, a man who enjoyed the chase. "I have come across a lady most coy, have I now?" He tapped the empty mug on the bar, drawing Sayrin's attention and earning a tight nod from her from her position at the far end of the bar. Tempest couldn't be sure, but she thought she'd heard a growl rumble from the older woman's chest.

"You say coy," Tempest took another savoring sip, glancing at him through her dark lashes, "I say discerning."

"Forsooth! An admirable condition, to be sure." He accepted the second ale and rolled another coin across his knuckles before flipping it carelessly in Sayrin's direction. He turned away from Tempest with a nonchalant tip of his beverage, leaning against the bar and pretending to survey the crowded room. "I could be the veriest cad, intent only on besmirching your good reputation and stealing every tidbit of honor to your name. A name," he added with another quirk of his undeniably attractive upper lip, "you are so horribly denying me."

"...but," he continued, his elbow slipping back a few inches to brush against hers, "I could also be the most exciting night of your life." He had the audacity to wink at her.

Tempest laughed, her joy spilling forth from a well she thought had long gone dry. This was such good wine! A wild spirit seemed to overtake her, and she threw back the rest of her drink, her dimples deep grooves under the flush she could feel overtaking her pale skin.

"You have the utmost confidence in your appeal, sir! Perhaps I've been shortsighted to dismiss your efforts out of hand." She stood, the blood warm and racing through her extremities but they held her steady, nonetheless. She offered him her hand. "You have ten seconds to prove your worth."

"A dance?" He queried.

"A dance." She concurred.

His hand was cool and smooth as it enfolded hers, not unlike many of the courtiers she'd joined on the dance floor what seemed like a lifetime ago. That is where all similarity to her former life stopped. Chairs scooted loudly and villagers in muted colors grumbled, smiled, or heckled, depending on their level of inebriation, as Wrone decisively pulled her through the crowd.

To the music of an out-of-tune fiddle and a flute that had seen better days but was played with enthusiasm nonetheless, Tempest allowed herself to follow his lead in the bare few feet of space between tables as they pivoted about in an abbreviated rendition of an old country dance. A smile lit her face and color filled her cheeks as the other patrons began to clap and hoot as they gracefully dodged around tables, spilled drinks, and fellow dancers.

One last flourish and he twirled her into the dark shadows that lined the out-thrust stone of the massive fireplace. Tempest stumbled as the toe of her boot caught on an uneven floor paver, but Wrone swept her into his strong arms, his lithe horseman's body pressing her gently back against the wall. Her breath hitched in her throat as the sensation of another living heart beating so close to hers consumed her complete attention.

Never in a thousand years would she have imagined the excitement that filled her being the sole focus of those fiercely gleaming blue eyes. That she, the cautious - the dull - Malorn daughter, afraid of stepping outside the strict bounds that guarded her safety, could find herself being the object of attraction for, undeniably, one of the more extraordinary looking men she'd ever seen, was...thrilling.

"Impressed yet?" His long fingers trailed over her jaw as he tilted her chin, gently directing her closer as he lowered his head.

Tempest gulped. Not her most eloquent response but better than the squeaking, wordless answer she had swallowed down. She blinked rapidly, freezing in place as a deluge of thoughts, feelings, and indecisions flooded her in instantaneous succession before disappearing in the haze that overtook her as she closed her eyes.

His lips traced along hers, warm, smooth, seeking. Remotely, she could hear the hoots and catcalls filling the jovial air of the tavern behind his broad, shelter shoulders, but they didn't matter. The world didn't matter. Only this moment...these sensations...this instant of realizing that she'd always wondered what drew two people together in such a way as to make love possible.

It had ever been a mystery to her young mind. Why does a man choose war to protect the woman he loves? Why does that same woman lie despondent in her lonely bed, eager to be reunited with that one person who ignites her very soul? How did they know they had found their other half?

Wrone's hands dragged themselves away from her face and slowly tracked over her shoulders, their heat noticeable in their heavy drag across the fabric and down her arms. She could sense the pleasure he derived from towering over her much smaller frame, his need to dazzle her with his strength and virility. An eager rumble filled his chest as he adjusted his angle and tightened his grip on her elbows, his enjoyment of the kiss evident.

While Tempest felt...nothing.

Maybe, she considered, her mind following the movement of his lips as he pressed even closer, she felt some slight interest that this, her first kiss, was nice. Many girls she had known would have been ecstatic to share their lips with someone half as handsome. The sensations that had bombarded her were pleasant, overall, if not life changing. She could even see where she might enjoy the practice, once the shock of actually being kissed wore off.

When he rubbed his tongue against the seam of her mouth, however, her curiosity turned to unease. She may not have any experience with men, but she'd listened to Verilee's endless stories of passion enough to know that this wasn't it.

"I'm sorry." She pulled back, placing her hands between them on his chest and pushing gently to give herself some space to breathe. "I can't."

He dropped his hands and stepped back, the heat quickly chilling from his gaze. The light of the freshly lit lanterns suspended from the ceiling behind him left his face in sudden shadow, hiding his expression, even if Tempest had been brave enough to look at him. The stern grinding of his jaw could be heard over the languid plucking of the guitar strings as the musician tried to flag Sayrin's daughter down for an additional flagon of ale.

"That's unfortunate." He adjusted the sleeves on his doublet, shaking out the short bits of lace that lined the cuff, trying to appear nonchalant as he backed far enough away to give her an abbreviated and mocking bow. "I was so looking forward to a fun tussle tonight."

"I would never!" She gasped, affronted and shocked that he could think such a thing. Every shy molecule in her body burned away in an instant as she pulled herself up to her full height, her hands aggressively settling on her hips.

"Yeah, well..." he shot back, "you probably should." He stalked off toward the bar, not caring if he trampled toes in his quest to salvage the night with another drink. Over the sudden silence of people attempting to pretend they hadn't been shamelessly staring.

The flush riding high on her face had nothing to do with embarrassment and everything to do with the fury building inside her. For too many years she'd been careful. She'd been watchful. She'd been content to flee the only home she'd known because of a deadly bully she'd never met. She'd watched her sister's back, healing more near-fatal injuries than any gentle woman should have seen in her entire life.

She had excelled at being quiet, obedient, and unremarkably inconspicuous. No more! Her small feet made loud echoes as her boots nimbly ate up the distance between her and her nemesis. She slammed her fist down on the ancient wood in front of him, the bar nearly resonating with her rage.

"You have no right to speak to me that way, you...cad!" She may be filled with the heat of angry passion but that didn't enhance her non-existent cursing skills. He turned to look down at her, clearly unimpressed. Sort of, she mused, the way his kiss had made her react.

"Just because a woman is an unfeeling tease isn't a reason for me to entertain her presence after her usefulness is gone. Not," he smirked as he tossed down his shot of whiskey, "that you proved even the least bit satisfactory in the usefulness department."

"Hey, now!" Sayrin was suddenly looming over her side of the bar, flanked on either side by her wickedly-eyed daughter and a seriously intent Jer. "We treat ladies like ladies here, boy. You can take your filthy mouth and dirty coin elsewhere."

Tempest shot the innkeeper and her family a grateful look, thankful to know that, no matter how far she traveled, there were always good citizens to be found. These were the people she was fighting for. These were her people, the true heroes of Hlyn.

"Seems I've approached the wrong sister." His voice, so velvety smooth moments before, took on a snide tone that was no doubt truer to his personality. "But," he smirked, leaning out of her personal space as if he was the one who could not stomach the energy between them, "seeing as your precious Outlaw Princess is conveniently meeting her fate at the hands of Hlyn's Regent right this minute instead of embroiling me in her revolt, I thought I'd take a chance. Your frigid body, after all, isn't as cold as hers will be."

Tempest wasn't prone to violence, but she forgot that basic tenant of her personality as her fist shattered the traitor's nose. A surge of pain shot through her, echoed by the aching torment the intolerable ass was feeling. Her sense of empathy turned to perverse pleasure as the dark side of her magic fed off the satisfaction that filled her from knocking the smarmy smile off his face. Reaching behind her, she took the rag from the shocked innkeeper's grasp and wiped his blood off her knuckles with a casualness she didn't feel.

"See!" The dimple in her right cheek pulled her lips back in a gruesome smile. She winked at Sayrin. "Not so much of a lady after all."

"Bitch!" he glared at her, his flirty blue eyes now filled with hate. She smiled, not one whit sorry for defending her sister, and offered him the cloth. An evil laugh escaped her as he flinched and tossed an elbow between them to protect himself from another blow.

Tempest, feeling the villagers slowly standing to prevent the dastardly Wrone from following her, wasted no time in making her way to the door. She had to find Dahlis before it was too late.

Please, she begged whichever gods made it out of the Nightmare, *don't let it be too late*!

"Now that," Auoggie's creaky voice cut through the crowd, "was impressive!"

Chapter Six

"**N**IGHTMARE'S DAMNATION!" PORTA'S TINY body bounced off the door as Tempest pushed her way through. Her arm shot out, steadying the girl while she tried to catch her own breath. Adrenaline electrified every nerve in her body, and it took everything she had to not fall in a heap on the doorstep, a sobbing mess of fear and emotion. One thought kept bouncing around in the turbulent swirl running rampant in her head.

Dahlis was in danger.

Honestly, Dahlis was *always* in danger but, this time, perhaps Tempest could make a difference. Their entire lives had been a series of situations where Dahlis saved the day while Tempest hesitated, always too late and too cautious to be considered brave.

"Oh," Porta's clenched fists loosened as she realized who she'd almost been trampled by. She shook her arm free and attempted to push the rabid tangle of black hair out of her petulant face. "Tempest, you dunce, who has your panties in a wad?"

"I must find Dahlis and Monika!" Tempest spared no thought for Porta, who was beginning to sense the severity of the situation, although the jolt of additional fear that shook the girl threatened to spill over into her own well of worry. She couldn't be distracted though and, much like she had in the Dirty Umbrage, she locked her empathic power away deep.

She whistled shrilly into the gathering dark, her heart pounding loud enough to drown out Porta's wispy inhale. She almost didn't hear Obertroess' answering whinny but the thunder of mighty hooves on packed cobbles reassured her that he was coming. Heated curses followed his progress from those villagers unlucky enough to stand in his way. Even with the galloping of her own heart, Tempest prayed her big galoot of a horse didn't hurt anyone in his faithful quest to be by her side. She closed her eyes and swayed as a wave of unbidden rage accosted her from the inn behind her, so fueled with hate that it broke through her defenses. At least she hadn't killed that good-for-nothing traitor.

This time it was Porta who grabbed Tempest's arm. "What is it? What's happening?" Porta's voice cracked, but her grip was strong as her ever-dirty nails bit through the fabric of her sleeve, carving tiny bloody half-circles into her somehow still delicate skin.

"I haven't time to explain," Tempest opened her eyes, her hands firm as they bracketed Porta's freckled face. She bent slightly, touching her forehead lightly to the girl's, taking the brunt of her dread into herself and burying it deep in the miasma of panic clawing at her own stomach. "Dahlis was betrayed. I must find her."

She pushed away, bundling the bulk of her skirt into one hand as Obertroess slid to a stop in front of her. With efficient movements, she tightened his girth and shoved the bit back between his eager lips. She grabbed a handful of mane and pulled herself onto his broad, speckled back. Porta lunged forward, scrambling to hide the tears in her eyes as she grabbed at Tempest's horse.

"I'm coming with you!" Porta screamed, uncaring that a crowd had started to gather in the dim street. Stepping from the shadows where he'd been quietly watching, Deik, farmer Dennig's shy son and Porta's friend, spoke up.

"The golden lady left by the South Post Road. Ain't no turn offs nor double backs that way." He pointed to a small dirt trail Tempest could see disappearing into the heavy forest just past the tanner's stall on the edge of town.

"Dahlis would never forgive me if I put you in harm's way." She leaned down and gave the shaking girl a one-armed hug. "I need you to find Verilee and then you can follow." She pulled

Bert clear of the bystanders and turned to give Porta a reassuring smile that she in no way felt, but the girl was no longer there. Tempest caught the tail end of two slim sets of shoulders pushing their way through the gathered crowd before turning a grim face toward the looming forest road. She couldn't be too late. She wouldn't.

A jolt of resolution electrified her body, causing Bert to crow-hop and rear before bolting down the cobbled street. Villagers poked their heads out windows and doors as she passed, shaking their heads and anxiously questioning their neighbors in her wake. In only moments, she was clear of the buildings and shrouded in the dark provided by dense vegetation, all eyes disappearing as the forest closed around her.

All eyes except for one shrewd, menacing pair.

Norc of Thays, Acting Regent of Hlyn, appointed by Praxxys himself to keep order over the Malorn lands, stepped slowly out of the shadows of the tannery. His horse, a leggy bay more suited for a soldier than a lord, followed meekly behind him, snorting softly as Norc patted his neck.

"Let's get us a couple wayward princesses, shall we boy?" His voice was mellow and low although the gleam in his small, dark eyes was anything but. He was a man with a mission, charged by the most powerful being of their world to bring the Kingdom of

Hlyn to heel, and he'd see it through no matter the consequence. His directive had been to subdue the ruling family's bloodline, keeping them secured in castle Malorn to await the Warlock Emperor's judgment.

Norc had spent the last five years sending his finest men on this endless hunt, unable to leave the stronghold himself due to the sly machinations of the deposed Queen, but it was as if they had been chasing phantoms. The Malorn daughters, it seemed, had an equal abundance of luck and loyalty when it came to maintaining their freedom. Praxxys seemed to find humor in his inability to arrest the sisters, frequently asking for updates when, as he put it, he needed a good laugh. Frankly, Norc was tired of it.

When he had heard rumor of a traitor to the Empire willing to betray the royal rebels in exchange for a place in the Emperor's New Hlyn, he had locked the young Malorn prince in the dungeon, hostage against his mother's good behavior, and mounted his own excursion to end this menace once and for all. He'd felt that his own luck had changed dramatically when Dahlis Malorn and one of her lackeys were exactly where the traitor Wrone had said they would be.

Unfortunately, that hadn't been the case. He made a mental note to find the turncoat when this was over and reward him adequately. Oh, the unfaithful coward would get his gold. Norc was, above all things, a man of his word, but no one had said he'd escape his poor decisions unscathed. He had, after all, lived a portion of his life as an enemy of the Empire.

He and his men, dressed simply in the worn attire common to bandits and rogues, had barely entered the clearing and dismounted their horses before the princess had begun brandishing her sword. He hadn't expected her to surrender willingly but the extent of her competence with a weapon had astounded him. He was willing to admit he'd been a bit shocked when her opening attack disabled two of his men and put him on the defensive. Awed, even, until the moment her blade rang against his, sliding down its length and tangling in the guard with enough force to slam his hand into a nearby tree, releasing his hold on the sword.

Reigning in his surprise, he'd managed to pull his belt knife more out of instinct than skill, lunging forward and landing a glancing blow in her side. Brilliant red had surged to the surface of her crimson cotton dress, and he'd started to step back in satisfaction, sure the battle was over.

But the damn woman had kicked him in the face! He'd staggered back, tripping over one of his fallen soldiers as the rebel princess was helped onto her horse by her red-headed companion. A quick glance reassured him that none of his men had suffered more than minor injuries so, with a few terse commands, he had them mounted and crashing through the brush after the fugitives.

The princess had proved as wily as she was beautiful and destructive and, miraculously, their trail had gone cold less than a hundred feet from the clearing. As a life-long warrior and tactician, Norc couldn't help the glimmer of admiration that had mixed with his frustration.

But no more. She wasn't a woman to admire, no matter how fierce and resourceful. She was an enemy warrior begging to be destroyed.

Norc pulled his leather riding gloves out of his belt and slid them over his swollen knuckles, hiding his grimace of pain. Two of them were split open and had bled profusely, further igniting his determination.

They had lost the errant princess and her companion in the depths of the Dunshyre forest a few hours previously. Norc, however, was a man who always planned for contingencies. The younger sister had torn out of the village without a weapon or backup. Her soft face had been tight with worry, and he knew she would waste no time in leading him straight to his real quarry. It would be finished tonight, even if the result was less than what the Warlock Emperor may desire.

They had no need for two princesses anyway...he barely saw use for one.

Norc adjusted his leather tunic and pulled the short bow he'd bartered from a drunk hunter off his back. His wiry, battle-hardened body, although starting to show its age around the joints, was agile as he stepped into the saddle. He fitted a bolt into the bow, ready to fire from his off hand in a moment's notice, relying on his damaged dominant hand to steer his horse. A quick glance assured him his three remaining able-bodied men were grim-faced and ready for his command. He nodded in satisfaction.

They disappeared into the gloom of the forest.

Time seemed to stop, even though her heart raced.

The South Post Road passed in a blur as Tempest's entire world became the pulsing thunder of hooves on the dirt beneath her, the bunch and release of massive muscles powering them through the growing dark, and a prayerful litany dancing through her head that she would make it in time. What had begun as a wide, clear road, neatly paved with small chips of red quarry stone, had devolved after a mile into a rutted track just wide enough to safely permit a wagon to pass. Despite her worry, she had slowed Obertroess to a fast canter, her eyes vigilantly seeking any obstacles in their way.

Suddenly, the trees fell away, making room for a wide clearing. The incandescence from the rising dark moon, Myninn, dully reflecting the brighter light of Hyginn, barely broaching the horizon, bathed Obertroess' gray-speckled coat with an eerie glow. She sat higher in the saddle and the horse slowed of his own volition.

"Whoa, Bertie!" Battered grass ruined the pristine beauty of the meadow, interspersed with divots of earth torn by aggressive hooves and wildflowers in broken bunches trampled by uncaring boots. Instinct and experience brought awareness that this was more than the normal disturbance of wildlife.

Knowing she was getting close, Tempest let down the wall protecting her from the sensations of the creatures in the forest and cast about for the familiar essence that was her sister. At first, her mind got tangled in a confusion of frightened fauna, little hearts beating erratically as they recovered from their homes being invaded. Larger hearts, tethered to much stronger beasts, some violent predators in their own right, beat more with curiosity but were alert, nonetheless. People had been here recently, Tempest could tell. But, had they been her people?

She took a deep breath, filling her lungs and mind with calm, hoping what she was about to try would work. Much of her magic was trial and error, often heavy on the error. She exhaled peace and willed the poor forest denizens to forget their fears. Small noises in the brush and trees assured her that luck had been on her side as the beasts went on about their normal business of staying alive. Tears filled her eyes and she thanked the Brightness.

Obertroess whuffled and lowered his head as the soothing magic trickled back to Tempest, easing his body in the process. Dropping the reins, Tempest leaned forward and hugged his valiant neck, sending him an extra dose of strength and gratitude. A shiver wracked her slim body as she straightened. She weaved a bit in the saddle before catching herself and collecting the reins.

Weakness filled her body. Her magic wasn't inexhaustible, and she was quickly approaching a threshold she had never had to before. Gently pulling the life from the deer had taken its toll. Fire Forgers were known to 'burn out' when they surpassed their magical limits, suffering horrific scars that almost never healed. Water Weavers were often left 'dry' for days, even weeks, with some severe cases remaining a literal shell of the person they were before.

Healers were so rare that no one really knew what happened when they tapped themselves out - or they refused to talk about it. And the other thing she was...well, that was an unspeakable abomination *she* refused to talk about.

Another deep breath and she sent her senses out once again, sure, even without her magic, that Dahlis and Monika were close. Quiet consumed her, individual sounds and sensations surging and then falling away as she dismissed them one by one. A raven cawed, pulling her focus toward a solitary, lightning struck pine tree barely clinging to life on the edge of clearing.

She inhaled just as Obertroess snorted, catching the same scent she had. Blood.

She dismounted, barely catching herself as her unsteady legs tangled in her skirt. A hot muzzle insinuated itself under her arm while she gained her balance, reassuring Tempest that she wasn't alone. Together, they made short work reaching the tree, noting on their way the unmistakable signs of a recent battle.

Black wings shattered the silence as Tempest's shaking fingers touched the red smear, coming away wet and sticky. Her gaze was drawn to the bird peering down from the barren branches. It cawed again, hopping further out on the limb and tilting its head as if to see her better. Its eyes were an unnatural sky blue, and somewhat...familiar.

Tempest shook her head. The stress of constantly being on the run was finally getting to her. Surely, if there had been a body nearby the raven wouldn't be here watching her, right? Her father would tell frightening fire-side tales every Reaping-Season of birds that ate the eyes out of the corpses of unruly children lost to the Nightmare.

A memory of Dahlis squealing in laughter as Tempest followed her for days after hearing that tale with a giant, floppy hat surfaced out of nowhere. Tempest hadn't feared for her own safety, but she could almost feel, all these years later, the angst that had tied her stomach in knots as she knew, without a doubt, her bold and intractable sister would most certainly lose her eyes.

Perturbed by Dahlis' resistance to the physical protection she offered, Tempest had turned to the massive dusty library tucked away in the far reaches of her family castle. She had hoped to find a spell or charm of safe keeping, but those tomes far surpassed her fledgling mind. Her mother had found her weeping inconsolably, hat clutched to her scrawny chest, and after she'd expended all her gentle reassurances, had finally told her in frustration that scavenger birds preferred only the eyes of the dead.

It had been enough. Tempest didn't know anyone filled with more life than Dahlis. She was sure she was too brave and smart to ever be one of the sleeping cold she'd witnessed being sent into the Promise.

"You aren't a corpse eater, are you friend?" Her chuckle was, admittedly, a bit unhinged. The raven ruffled all his feathers, gave her a very reproachful glare for a bird, and flew off into the night sky, spiraling in ever-widening circles until he seemed to disappear in Myninn's obsidian glow.

She wouldn't find a corpse today, either. Dahlis was no less powerful and vibrant than she had been as a child. She certainly wouldn't be brought low by a devious charlatan, no matter how blue his eyes and chiseled his jaw.

With that certainty held foremost in her mind, Tempest reached out with her senses once again. This time her power was slower, more faint, less sure but...yes...

There!

Not more than a hundred yards into the woods she could feel them. Two women hunkered down in what felt to be a small cave hidden by an overgrown outcropping, the restless twitching of horses beset by flies creating tiny swirls of agitation at the edge of her senses.

"They are here, Bert!" Her fatigue forgotten, she dashed off into the trees, uncaring of the noise she made as she tramped over detritus, confident her horse would make his way through the dense foliage and around the small boulders littering the gradually rising slope.

A whistling whirring of air broke through her haze of excitement, bringing her quickly to a halt. As she skittered over the top of the last rise, she came face to face with Monika, her serious brown eyes focused with deadly intent as her slingshot circled in a violent halo over her mussed red hair.

Chapter Seven

"IT'S ME!" SHE SAID unnecessarily and tossed her hands in the air. A goofy grin split her face, but she'd never been happier to see the sharply beautiful edges of Monika's austere countenance. "There was to be an attack. I came as soon as I could!"

"An attack, really?" The older girl's biting sarcasm, along with a perfectly perfected eyeroll of disdain, went unnoticed as relief warmed every inch of Tempest's body. Monika's arm lowered and the slingshot slowed, dumping its pocket full of sharp stones harmlessly onto the ground. Her supple lips tilted slightly as she turned around, her version of a welcoming smile, in truth.

"I told you it'd be Tempe." Dahlis stepped gingerly out of the cavern, carefully advancing a few steps before plopping herself down in an abrupt drop onto a nearby fallen log. Her hand was pressed tightly to her side, attempting to prevent the blood from slipping past her fingers.

"You're injured!" Tempest hissed, catching her hair, the gold strands beginning to show through the bland brown she'd dyed them, on a low-lying branch as she pushed her way to Dahlis' side.

"It's just a little poke, Tempe." She attempted a laugh, but it ended in a grimace as she waved an unfamiliar short knife in the air, the last inch of its blade coated in her drying blood. Tempest batted it aside as she fell to her knees before her sister. "Although," Dahlis snorted, her pure golden tresses falling into her face in a snarl of disarray that still managed to be enchanting. "I should be honored to be stuck with the Imperial blade of the Regent of Hlyn himself."

"Norc of Thays?!" Tempest's jaw hung open just long enough for Dahlis to blow a puff of air into it, much as she had done to piss Tempest off when they were children. "The Warlock Emperor's minion himself deigned to descend from on high to come for us?"

"That gnadless flip Wrone set us up!" Dahlis groaned as Tempest pulled her bloody fingers away from the hastily wadded field dressing, delicately peeling back the rough edges of her dress, freeing them from where they had already begun to stick to her flesh. "When I get my hands on that wretched lying puff of dragon flatulence, he'll never use that pretty face to look at a woman ever again!"

"Well," Tempest picked the last bit of cloth from the wound, making eye contact and smiling as she firmly pushed her own palm into the bloody mess that was decidedly more than a 'little poke', "you won't be able to break his ever-so-noble nose. Someone did him the favor of making it a bit less perfect."

"You?" Tempest nodded. The liquid gold of Dahlis' eyes glittered with equal parts pain and pride. "That's my girl!" Searching the ground to retrieve her sling stones, Monika's non-committal grunt echoed with the equivalent of her own hearty 'well done'.

Pleasure competed with embarrassment to flood Tempest's cheeks a bright shade of pink as she pretended to focus on healing the wound. With the ease of much practice, she allowed the smallest tendril of her healing power to touch the essence that made up everything that was uniquely Dahlis, gently probing the injury to get a feel for where her magic was needed most.

Despite the frightening amount of blood saturating the front of the ruined gown, the blade hadn't caused any lasting damage, besides the fact Dahlis would need a new 'fancy' dress. It didn't take long to stop the flow of blood and coax the innermost layers of flesh to bind themselves back together, it was something they inherently wanted to do. Dahlis groaned again, this time in relief.

Tempest's dark lashes settled over her amber eyes. This next bit would take some effort. Bodies, she had discovered, healed much quicker when some of the injured person's own energy was involved. She reached for the magic again, this time pulling from Dahlis' innate power which had always felt like a deep, swirling pool. She found a well nearly as empty as her own.

"You've lost more blood than I had thought." She admonished, worry making her voice more accusatory than she had intended.

"It's blood." Dahlis' dark gold eyebrow rose to its most sarcastic height. "It came out. I did not think to ration it." She reached out with her mostly blood-free hand, tucking a stray dark-stained curl back behind Tempest's ear, her caring action belying her acid words.

"There you go again," Tempest quipped back, "not thinking." It felt good to be able to share banter with her sister, even when the circumstances were less than ideal. Sometimes, it was one of the few things to get her through a day. Monika cleared her throat as she stepped away to gather the horses. Her body language clearly saying without words that they should get on with the healing. The Malorn sisters shared a smirk before Tempest rolled her eyes and focused.

She needed help.

"This is going to hurt." It wasn't clear who it would hurt most.

She touched the ground, delving beneath the discarded and decaying leaf litter, past the bugs and worms and the life blossoming in the dense root network of the forest. First, it felt like she was wading through soft, gentle waves, the caress of the myriad and often overlooked essences in the dirt warm and loving against her senses.

Soon, the damp loveliness gave way to the sludgy sensation of life magic as it slowed, compressed against older layers of surplus power, begrudging the invasion in its quiet domain. She pushed harder, her stubbornness coming to her aid. In spite of all the times her mother bemoaned the trait, Tempest had been thankful for it more than once in the past difficult years.

She began to pant, her breaths coming shallow and fast, as her head began to thrum with a beat of its own. Ephemeral black dots began to dance across her vision and then she hit it.

Bedrock.

Salvation.

The stones of the earth had an immense power all of their own, seemingly inexhaustible but almost impossible to access for most mages. If she wasn't so drained from dealing with the trauma of the deer's recent death, she wouldn't have much trouble pulling from the depths. She had long felt that her healing magic came from the earth, although she had never been able to find any evidence to support the notion. One thing she knew for certain though, was that it wouldn't get any easier with her just sitting here.

Tempest dug deep into the stone. She pictured her hands as ghostly tendrils reaching into the rock, feeling out the tiniest cracks, filling them with the smallest bits of energy that she could afford to expend. Like a loyal friend, the natural energy of Telryuun ensnared and enfolded her own, mixing in a hug of welcome that brought tears to her eyes.

his was beauty. This feeling of completeness, of acceptance, of resolute devotion...it was strength personified bound with limitless love. Tempest breathed deeply, ecstasy filling her body.

Then she pulled.

Fire scorched her veins as she yanked the healing power from the very stone on which she stood. The land was willing to share its power with her, happy even, to have a purpose of good to serve, but earth was the most 'solid' magic, often intractable in its stubborn existence. It raced up her intangible spirit hands, into her physical body, jolting her with every inhale.

She began to shake, heat pooling like a dead weight in her stomach as the power settled inside her. Almost. Almost enough. She closed her eyes, teeth clenched tight to keep her jaw firmly shut. She would not cry out.

"Tempest?" Dahlis' voice was strained. She touched her sister's cheek, snatching her hand back when her fingertip began to sizzle against burning skin. "Tempest, stop whatever you are doing. Now!"

The power was immense. The depth of the presence inside her echoed within her soul. She could hear forever, feel the eternal vastness of the soil from which all life was dependent. She could sink into its warm embrace, ever loved, ever cherished, ever...

SLAP!

"What in the Ever-Loving Oracle, Dahl?!" Tempest cradled her face, fingering the cold spot that bore the bloody imprint of her sister's calloused fingertips. Her shocked eyes almost immediately began to roll up in her head as the force of the power she held inside her made itself known.

SLAP!

Dahlis grunted and held both of her hands tight against her middle. That second slap had needed more umph to be felt, tearing a bit of the skin that had just begun to heal. Tears streamed down her face, more from fear than pain. The sight of them, something that was wholly unfamiliar, drew Tempest away from the earth's seductive pull.

"Dahlis. I'm here." She scooted even closer, severing her tie with the ground beneath her. For a second, she felt bereft, unsteady and afloat. She put both palms against Dahlis' bloody side and, as swiftly as she could, pushed the majority of the borrowed power into healing her sister.

Dahlis screamed, stuffing a fist in her mouth at the last second to muffle it as best she could. Earth magic wasn't any easier to receive than it was to retrieve. Thankfully, only seconds passed before the wound had sealed, stitching the skin back together in a smooth arch that was as flawless as it had ever been.

Both girls slumped, holding each other up as they sat propped against the log, ragged breathing slowing to soft sighs of relief. Tempest began to laugh. Being able to channel so much power was a heady experience.

"That was..." she hesitated, not sure what emotion she was feeling. She settled for, "awesome."

Dahlis let out her own weak laugh. She would have said traumatizing, but her little sister didn't see magic the same way as she did.

"Dumbass. Don't do that again, alright?"

"Don't get yourself stabbed again and I won't have to...alright?" They shared a smile, each knowing they wouldn't be able to keep those promises. Tempest sobered. Today they had been lucky. Someday...they may not be so fortunate. Turning brusque, she tugged the bloodied edges of Dahlis' tattered dress into a ratty semblance of coverage.

"Thank you..." Dahlis stuttered to a stop, her whole body seeming to freeze as her head swiveled in the direction her sister had come, her trail easily visible through the dense underbrush.

"Oh, Tempest..." Dahlis' voice was small as she stood, pushing her sister's hands away and freeing her sword from its sheath, "what have you done?"

Dread filled Tempest as the sound grabbing her sister's attention began to reach her ears. The soft snorts of winded horses and the muted creaks of men shifting into position on worn saddles. She had led the Warlock Emperor's men straight to them!

Monika mounted her horse and kicked it alongside the sisters, dragging Obertroess and Canelope behind her stately palomino, Haiku. She offered Dahlis the mare's reins and tossed Tempest's at her, narrowly missing her face with the worn leather straps. Her slim arms reached for the stones she kept in a satchel close to her heart and, within moments, her slingshot was whirring once again.

"It's too late." Dahlis whispered. She stepped out in front of the horses, pushing Tempest toward the cave. "They have us surrounded."

"I didn't mean to..." Tempest felt the weight of the world pressing down on her shoulders. How could she be so stupid? In her rush to prove herself worthy of trust, she may have doomed them all.

Dahlis' hair glowed eerily, glinting golden even as the light faded. She held up a hand, cutting Tempest off. She pointed to the cave, silently waving her back.

"No, Dahl," Tempest pleaded. "I can help!"

"Just go, Tempe!"

Torn between wanting to cry and arguing for her right to stay, Tempest grabbed up Canelope's lead and pushed both horses back toward the cave entrance. She may not be as battle-hardened as her sister, but she'd received all the same training. She wasn't helpless. A wave of light-headedness shuddered through her body, making a lie out of her assertion.

A loud crack ricocheted around them followed by a cry of pain as an arrow lodged in Monika's palm. She clutched her hand and cursed as her slingshot dropped to the forest floor. Haiku danced sideways, barely keeping from crushing her leg between the saddle and a giant oak.

"No need to hide, little princess." Stepping from the shadows lurking among the silent tree trunks, a man seemingly materialized from nothing. His voice was surprisingly sonorous and fluid despite the waves of ill-intent oozing out of his soul. Tempest stopped in her tracks, watching warily as he fitted a second bolt to the small crossbow he cradled.

This, she knew without introduction, was Norc of Thays. The infamous monster who, under the geis of the Warlock Emperor, was responsible for slaying her father and imprisoning her mother and younger brother. A feeling unknown to her began to stir the darkness she kept suppressed at all costs. The feeling, she realized, was hate.

"Please don't put Trayvance and I," he motioned toward the solitary man stepping out of bushes behind them, "to the hassle of running you down, we are only two much put-upon men, you know. I lost the remainder, imbeciles, all of them, to some black-haired demon dervish disguising itself as a child."

Dahlis chuckled. From her position atop her mount, slowly pulling it around to face the second man, Monika snorted, her version of a belly-laugh. Each woman used the distraction to fill their free hands with knives pulled from the hidden pockets in their dresses. Tempest felt inadequacy hit her again as she flexed her empty hands.

"Ah," the man noticed the weapon the princess heir held. "I see you found my knife. That's not quite the fate I had intended for it."

"I'll be happy to return it to you." Dahlis drew back her hand, swift as lightning, and threw the knife he'd stabbed her with directly at his head. Quick reflex had him raising the cross-arm of the bow defensively and the knife skittered along the scarred wood, falling harmlessly to the forest floor.

Norc leveled his bow at Dahlis but she was already moving, following her throw with a fierce lunge and scything sweep of her sword. Long, golden curls seemed to flash through the air with a vengeance of their own, framing her face then retreating, as she pulled the force from her swing, feinting into a full spin just as he pressed the trigger, loosening the second bolt.

"No!" Tempest gasped, feeling the burn of flesh being ripped asunder as the arrow grazed Dahlis' cheek. Searing agony tore through her as her arm was jolted from its socket when the projectile embedded itself in the tree next to Canelope, showering the gentle mare's face with shards of bark. Whickers of fear echoed around them, as the normally staid mount reared. Her pain joined her master's, beating at the walls Tempest was hastily trying to reconstruct.

Gritting her teeth, she reached for the mare's halter, forcing her head down until she calmed. A few quick swipes of magic freed the splinters from her tender skin and eased the pain. Obertroess nipped at her shoulder, nervously shifting his feet and throwing his gloriously oafish head up and down aggressively, dividing his attention between the two men and alternating flattening his ears and baring his teeth.

"Hiya!" Monika bellowed suddenly, frightening her own horse into a full gallop in the restricted space. Within seconds, she had pinned the second man against a tree, buying her the barest of moments that she needed to dismount and pull her own sword from its place behind her saddle. Her skirts didn't hamper her as she darted under her mount's thrashing legs, taking a quick swipe with her knife and drawing first blood from the man's unprotected thigh.

She glanced back at Tempest. "I've got this one," she reversed the now bloody blade in her hand and tossed it into the dirt at the younger girl's feet. "Help your sister!" A slap on the rear sent her horse skittering off into the woods and she turned her attention to the man who wasted no time in slicing his sword at her middle.

The knife was cold in her hand as Tempest yanked it from the soil, the blood sliding free to feed the creatures of the earth. She watched her sister for a moment, in awe at the beautifully deadly dance happening in front of her as Dahlis and one of the Warlock Emperor's finest men weaved in and out of the dense foliage.

The mellow glow of Hyginn, the Bright Moon, began to filter through the trees, touching on the blades of both warriors as they lunged and parried, fleet and graceful of foot, even as Myninn's shadows fought for supremacy. Incongruently, Tempest thought about her childhood fixation with the beauty of the dark moon.

The two moons, it was said, battled each night to rule the evening, light and dark in an eternal war that was prophesied to shake the foundations of life itself. Tempest rather thought of them as lovers playing a game of cat and mouse among the stars, teasing each other with the very differences that made them unique, content with the chase and uncaring that the world they shone upon considered them doomed.

Norc leveled a particularly nasty underhand swing at Dahlis' head, jarring Tempest from her reminiscing. Her sister dodged it handily enough and laughed. This was a tactic their father had drilled into them with a single-minded ferocity. The best way to undermine an opponent, he'd said, especially one that was a match for you in martial skill, was to attack their insecurities and make them question why they ever thought they could engage with a Malorn Royal.

"Not a bad effort," Dahlis huffed as she returned with her own vicious thrust, "for a man with such tiny arms." While Norc outweighed her by far in pure muscle mass, he was several inches shorter, giving him a disadvantage in reach.

"Size doesn't matter, Princess, not when you are as good as I am," he had the audacity to wink.

Norc leapt handily out of her range, saluting her with a mockery of the gesture Maloran troops gave their commanders. His smile stretched to his ears when a growl deep in her throat revealed Dahlis' anger and her own weakness.

"Peasant!" The Outlaw Princess snapped, forcing her sword into his space in a furiously fierce attack. Fear clogged Tempest's throat as she watched the two evenly matched nemesis square off, thrusting and retreating in a dance only one of them would walk away from. She had worried for Dahlis' safety many times in their exile but only in an abstract way. Amongst all the warriors of Hlyn, she alone had remained undefeated. As their deadly dance wore on, Tempest feared they'd stumbled into new, un-welcome territory.

"Ha!" Finally, Norc's many years of battle experience triumphed over Dahlis' youth and agility. His sword locked close with hers, their guards nearly kissing as they struggled for supremacy. When the opportunity presented itself, as she stumbled over a hidden root, he took the tiny opening she'd left in her defense, throwing an elbow into her face and turning her cut cheek into a flowing river of blood. A second punch sent Dahlis staggering back and her grip on her sword loosened enough for him to disarm her.

Tempest ran forward, her fingers curling over the edge of the blade where it lay mere feet away from where Dahlis stood, defeated but unbroken. Her fear evaporated, anger filling the void and building to levels she'd never experienced before.

"Ah, ah, ah." Norc stepped on the sword, tsking at her as if she was a naughty child. Anger surged through her, scorching veins that had only known empathy with a fire that threatened to burn away everything good. Had he been so condescending as he ran his blade through her father's chest? Did he laugh as he caused the light to vanish in what was once a brilliant man? She raised the dagger Monika had given her. Her hand shook but...from fury, not fear. "You have no right to Hlyn, you murderous ass!" She spat. "Your precious emperor can go sit on his immortal thumb before he will ever rule the souls of *our* people."

"What?" He asked, feigning surprise. "Does the gentle lady have claws?" A snarl of impatience slipped through his chipped teeth as he kicked Tempest hard in the chin. Her head snapped back and her eyes began to water, her head suddenly pounding in tempo with her racing heart. Norc's wiry body was swift as he grabbed the her before she fell, yanking her to unsteady feet and sliding his dagger to her neck.

"I've taken enough ribbing over not putting down the Malorn revolt these past five years." He pointed the sword at Dahlis, his slimy hazel eyes, red-rimmed and intrusive, making steady contact with her own fiery gold orbs as he pressed an obnoxious kiss on Tempest's cheek. The reek of old whiskey and travel bread permeated the suddenly still air, adding to the sick knot of angst churning in her stomach. "If you want your sweet little sister here to see another day, I'm going to need you to call off your hound," he nodded at Monika who was retrieving her sword from the battered corpse of Trayvance, "and kneel."

"Bastard." She hissed, stunned. Her hands fisted at her sides as she sank to her knees.

"The emperor wants you alive for some unfathomable reason." He shrugged, as if he couldn't imagine a scenario in which that was a good idea. "But," he stroked Tempest's cheek with the edge of the dagger before pushing her violently to the ground. "I only need one of you to stay in His good graces."

He plunged the sword with both hands down at Dahlis, the evil grin freezing on his face as every muscle in his body seized.

His eyes rolled uncontrollably as shudders wracked him. Sweat began weeping from his pores and drops of blood pooled in his tear ducts then poured in viscous trails down his cheeks.

"Tempe, no...Not this way." Dahlis slowly reached out to her sister's form, splayed at Norc's feet like a virginal sacrifice. Her hands, hands Dahlis had often decried as too loving, too gentle, were wrapped firmly around Norc's ankles. Her chest heaved with effort. With tears.

"He took our father," Tempest growled through clenched teeth. Bloody trickles began to streak down her own face, her emotional pain so virulent Dahlis felt, once again, the loss of the Malorn King. "In return..." Her eyes lost their gold glow, deepening into a pit of despair so dark she could well have been looking into the Nightmare itself. "I shall give him..." She fashioned the last iota of her power into a shadow-hewn fist that she plunged into the depths of his chest, stopping his heart, slowing his breath...erasing every bit of self and soul, "Mercy."

Shock reverberated throughout the dark forest, tremors shaking the bedrock beneath them as the raw force of death fought to free itself from the bindings holding it within the Nightmare. Somehow, Tempest managed to draw it back into herself, the wisps of shadow melting into the pale porcelain of her exposed forearms, leaving black whorls etched into her skin. She rolled onto her back, bringing her hands to cover her face in horror.

Her chest heaved as she battled to contain the urge to release the wretched power once more.

"What are you?" Norc's last words faded as his final breath left his body, his eyes losing their gloss. They would carry their own echo forever in Tempest's memory.

"Sorry." She whispered. That is what she was, what she was cursed to be always. "I'm sorry."

Dahlis began to sob. She shook her head, unwilling to accept the situation in front of her. She'd tried, for so many years...she'd tried. She'd promised her father she'd keep her from it. She'd failed and Tempest would pay for her shortcomings, for *their* shortcomings.

Unless...

With sadness etched across every hard angle of her beautiful face, Dahlis stepped toward her sister with grim determination. She swiped a dirty, shaky hand across her eyes, leaving behind a smudge that spoke of grief and trial and obligation. Gathering her fortitude, she stalked up to the Regent of Hlyn's corpse and, without hesitation, slammed her sword blade into the burnt flesh above his heart. She twisted, tearing the flesh to hide the traces of her sister's sinister magic.

Then the darkness came for Tempest...and she welcomed it.

Chapter Eight

PAIN. DESPAIR. FEAR. ANGER.

A vague sense of movement lifted Tempest from the abyss wrapped soothingly around her mind. The sweet, sweaty familiar smell of horse brought her enough clarity to allow her to question her battered body, looking for the source of those emotions. She felt them often enough but, this time, they were not hers. They were his.

She shut down, unable to examine the memories beating at the edge of her consciousness. Instead, her eyes tightly closed to contain her building tears, she yearned for the silence to return. It, like the once peaceful years of her youth, proved elusive. The ropes holding her tight to Obertroess' mighty back shifted, their sibilant groans as they rubbed against the saddle in protest, filling her head with meaningless, harmless noise. She focused on their complaints, on the steady thump of her horse's tail as it shifted from side to side, screaming of his agitation at his unwieldy load. She was alive.

Euphoria.

That feeling was hers. She'd felt it before, coated in hatred and internal suffering. It was a feeling she loathed but craved with a morbid anticipation. It gave her the illusion of power, of strength...it made her feel the energy of life at a different, more visceral, level than she was used to.

It was what made her a monster.

Regret.

It was what made her hope she could be redeemed.

A swell of tiredness swept its greedy hands through Tempest, dulling the edge of thought once again. She welcomed its obliterating embrace but, before it could enclose her in its cocoon of nothingness, she fell into what had been the darkest of her memories.

She remembered the first time she had stolen a soul.

Someone was weeping.

Tempest clutched the Natural Magics book she had found moldering in the dark corner of the castle library to her small chest, fear and empathy coursing through her slim body in equal measure. If she was caught reading the forbidden manuals again her mother had promised to have the archives locked for good. As a voracious and eternally curious reader, that was a threat she did not take lightly.

A particularly heart-rending cry shuddered through the air and Tempest turned in her tracks. Someone needed her. She couldn't turn her back on such pain, even for all the books in the kingdom.

"Hello?" She pushed through the willows lining the crushed shale path that divided the pristine rose garden from the spring-fed koi pond. A sob was her only answer. Urgency grabbed ahold of her and she pulled her lace shawl from her boney shoulders, wrapping it tightly around the contraband book before stashing it among a few of the stronger willow branches.

She stepped through the foliage and her eyes were immediately drawn to the peaceful lapping of the water's edge. The fine cream lace of her pink day gown snagged on the broken reeds lining the shore but, even if she had noticed, she would not have cared.

"Dahlis?" Her voice was as small as her dainty frame. Worried creases crinkled the edges of her gold eyes and accentuated the fine sprinkling of equally golden freckles flitting across her cheekbones.

A bright blue puddle of silk surrounded her sister as she kneeled, keening despondently on the algae-speckled bank. Her long, bright tresses, the true gold of Malorn, were smeared with ruby red trails of blood. With a gasp, Tempest ran forward, uncaring when the squelching grasp of the mud stole her slippers, the wet debris of a millennia squeezing between her unprotected toes.

She half fell in the stagnant water as she grabbed her older sister's shoulder, finally able to see her face. Dahlis' perfect porcelain skin was marred with traces of blood rinsed in the salty flow of tears, her shaking hands stained with crimson.

"Einas."

For the first time, Tempest's eyes left her sister's ravaged face.

It wasn't her blood. It belonged to the black and white hound in her lap. Relief loosened every muscle in Tempest's body before a rush of sympathy filled her veins. The old dog had been Dahlis' loyal companion since before Tempest had been born. Tempest couldn't remember a time when he wasn't trailing Dahlis, sneaking meals under the table, or curling at her feet. To see him now, sprawled muddy and blood-soaked, an arrow still protruding from his side, was unbearable.

"I can help him, Dahl." Tempest offered. She dropped to her knees beside her sister and reached forward, petting the dog's faithful head. She wasn't supposed to use her healing powers, they were still new and unpredictable. Only her family knew she had them and she was under strict orders to never use them. If her father knew what she was thinking of attempting...

"He's gone, Tempe." Dahlis' voice was as flat as her eyes as the reality of the situation settled upon her. She leaned down and kissed him gently, smoothing his fur before she covered her eyes and began to cry in earnest.

Tempest's heart broke and, with it, any semblance of restraint. Resolutely, her petite hands gripped the arrow, yanking it from the dog's flesh before she could think twice. Almost instantly, she was bathed in what blood remained in his body. Bile climbed her throat, but she persevered, pulling the edges of the wound together and commanding it to heal.

Five torturous seconds passed. Then ten. Tempest's ribs burned as if the pit fires of Kolure, in the very bowels of the Nightmare, were kindling in her body. She felt each molecule of pain that wracked the dog as she forced first his ruptured vessel and then his soul back together. It was sloppy. She didn't know how to protect herself from experiencing his trauma as her own and the pain threatened to overcome her. But, after half a minute had passed with only the sound of her thundering heartbeat and Dahlis' sorrow echoing in her ears…it was done.

A whine broke through the desolation of Dahlis' sobs and Tempest's strenuous breathing.

"Einas?!" Dahlis' whisper was everything that was hope and happiness and faith. "He wasn't dead?" She questioned, ready to accept *the gift she'd been given. "You healed him, Tempe!" Her arms, already firm with fighting muscle, wrapped around her sister and she squeezed her with every tremendous ounce of love in her body.*

Tempest had brought him back from the dead.

And then, three days later, she killed him.

Dawn had long since passed and, still, Tempest refused to open her eyes. Her night had been plagued with fragments of dreams and figments of nightmare, all wrapped in a sweaty, hazy cocoon of unease. She was tired and sore and knew that her world had changed while she was struggling through the unnamed torments slinking through her unconscious mind.

Not to mention, she smelled. Like...dead squirrels in a barrel of fish guts stinky.

That thought had her cracking them open and taking a quick glance under the blanket, just in case. It wouldn't be the first time Porta had surprised her by smuggling something unpleasant into her bed. She lowered her heavy arms and a fitful sigh caused her dry lips to crack in protest.

No squirrels. No fish. No Porta.

She wasn't ready to face her new reality, even though the jovial whistling outside her window kept pounding an insistent tune of 'get up, get up, get going' throughout her entire being. If nothing else, she may pull herself out of the pretty floral-embroidered blanket's comforting embrace to commit an act of impulsive violence against the whistler.

She blanched. Not controlling her anger is what had gotten her shipped off to this strange, small room in the first place. Brilliant sunlight assaulted her as she peeled her eyes open further, her lashes caked with a sleepy crust. The space she was in was tiny, to say the least, a thin layer of roughly hewn boards and one small curtain covered window all that separated her from the noises of people well about their daily activities.

Two bunks were set into the narrow side walls, leaving enough space for two people to sit...if they were willing to have their knees touching. It was clean of cobwebs and all the unsavory things Tempest had gotten used to in her exile, but one deep inhale was enough to tell her that this room had once been used to store grain and was still, in fact, very much attached to a working stable.

In the distance, the bells of a worship tower called those inclined to their mid-morning service. Her pulse began to race and her eyes shot wide as the realization hit her. She managed to push herself into a half-sitting position as the world seemed to spin around her.

She was in Vyte.

Her mind spun in even greater circles. Vyte was the capital of Hlyn and the city of her birth, a place she never thought she'd ever be able to return to. Her feet found the hard-packed dirt floor and an ache ran through them at the sudden pressure, confirming her suspicion that she'd been unconscious. Her last vague recollections of a midnight ride strapped to the back of a horse faded quickly. How had she gotten here? Vyte was a dangerous place for anyone of Malorn blood, being under the heavy-handed rule of the emperor. Or, rather, the emperor's appointed regent.

A groan rolled into a mewling sob as her last memories bombarded her. She buried her face in her hands and let grief and regret consume her. Tears filled her palms in seconds, flowing through her shaking fingers and peppering her unprotected toes with warm drops of anguish.

Norc of Thays had been the Warlock Emperor's chosen man. Thanks to Tempest's thoughtless rage, Norc was no more. While he had been a vital instrument in killing her father and keeping Hlyn under the Imperial boot, his absence was sure to draw the wrathful eye of the emperor himself.

It had been five years since the Malorn reign had been ended by the Warlock Emperor's warriors. Five years in which they had been on the run, hiding and fighting just to stay alive in a kingdom that had once flourished under their rule. Interminable years in which Dahlis tried to reclaim their realm and free their mother and little brother from their questionable 'guardianship'. Years in which Tempest merely existed, content to be at her sister's side just so she didn't have to be alone.

Clarity swept through Tempest in an unforgiving rush, bringing with it not only the tragic events of the last few days but also the years she'd spent in blissful ignorance of her true shortcomings. A wail of self-hatred snaked its way out of the very center of her being, nearly silent yet heartbreaking in its intensity.

She had seen the grim look on Dahlis' face as she'd plunged her sword deep inside Norc's unbeating heart in an attempt to cover up Tempest's unthinkable crime. That was the moment, Tempest knew, that Dahlis had finally accepted that, despite all her love and efforts to protect her, to guide her…Tempest was little more than a monster.

Her power to heal was a wonderous thing, but this darkness lurking below the beauty? The depravity simmering under her porcelain skin and gentility, boiling just under the surface of her ingrained civility, was a danger that couldn't always be contained. Not when she, the vessel for two warring entities, was so...lacking.

She was a fool to think she could ever be anything other than a hindrance, not when she had been born with this curse upon her soul. Tempest had been young and clueless when she had twisted the natural order by raising Einas. What she had done to Norc...

She had known better. She just had not cared for anything beyond the rage that filled her at seeing the man who had been responsible for their father's death and was threatening to cause the same for her sister, standing so cock-sure before her.

Dahlis had spent half a decade trying to save Hlyn. In one action, Tempest had possibly destroyed it.

Her crying stopped abruptly when she realized the whistling had ceased some moments ago. Her survival instincts, something she did not know she had possessed before that awful night when Dahlis pulled her from their palace home, focused on the quiet footsteps that set the horses in the adjoining stable to snorting and flinging their heads. She reached for her magic, fumbling past her fatigue and straining against the barrier she had so easily surmounted before.

Something, she panicked, looking around her for a weapon, was blocking her from accessing her power! The door squealed on its leather hinges as it was flung inward, knocking violently against the wall and sending the timbers in the patched roof creaking.

"Hello, sleepyhead." A cheerful voice amplified the pounding in her head. "I thought you'd be lazy all day again." Relief swept through Tempest as she realized she wasn't alone, followed almost immediately with a spike of frustration as a heel of bread bounced off her forehead. "I brought you breakfast. Though," Porta cocked her hip and rested one grimy hand on its boney ridge, "from the looks of things, I should have brought a bucket of water to replenish your cry-baby tears."

Only by exerting an extreme amount of self-control was Tempest able to keep from chucking the bread back at the younger girl. Good thing, too, because at that moment the fragrant aroma of fresh rye hit her and set her stomach grumbling. She settled for drawing her eyebrows down in her dirtiest look as she ripped a giant hunk off the crust and shoved it into her mouth. Her voice was creaky and her tone dry as she spoke around her bite, pointing an accusing finger and not caring in the least about her unladylike behavior. The effort would have been lost on Porta anyway.

"Oh, the delight I feel at your face being the first thing I see after almost dying is overwhelmingly immense." If Tempest was good at one thing, it was matching sarcasm for sarcasm. She swallowed and wished Porta had brought water as the bread took its time working its way down her parched throat.

"Here." Porta pulled a crinkled envelope from the bodice of what appeared to be a worn but new-to-her polka-dotted blue linen dress. She threw it onto the wrinkled pillow beside Tempest and picked up a long, sharpened stick that had been propped against the head of the second cot. Her bright green eyes, always awash in equal measures of snark and sadness, took a quick inventory of Tempest and she seemed satisfied that her favorite adversary was awake and well enough to bite back. "If you had died, you'd probably look better." She waved her hand in front of her face, "You'd definitely smell better as a corpse."

Tempest couldn't disagree about the smell comment, so she merely shrugged her shoulders and made a crude gesture in Porta's direction. The younger girl laughed, returning the gesture with both hands, not in the least bothered when the tip of her makeshift spear caught on the opposite wall and splintered. She dropped it to the floor and unceremoniously kicked it under the cot that she must have been calling home while she was waiting for Tempest to rejoin the living.

"I'll go get you some water. Your emotional butt is gonna need it."

Whistling once more, she walked out of the room without a backward glance. Tempest watched her go, the poor excuse for a door swinging back into place to settle awkwardly in its crooked frame. Trying to take her time, she took smaller bites of her breakfast until the bread was gone. It helped to fill her stomach but did nothing to assuage the emptiness that had descended upon her when she saw the letter. She knew who it was from as well as she knew she wouldn't like what it had to say.

She brushed the crumbs from her hands and reached for the letter resolutely, unfolding it with care despite her immense trepidation. If she was going to bawl her eyes out again, it was better to have it done before Porta returned. Dark, sure sweeps of ink, in Dahlis' trademark nearly illegible scrawl made her eyes wet once again.

Dearest T,

I have failed you.

I wish I could be there when you wake up to apologize in person. As your big sister, I have always tried to keep you close, to protect you, I told myself...but, in reality, I was the one who needed you.

I know you never wanted this life. Truly, it's not what I would choose either had Fate not been so cruel. But it was and I did. I must. I would choose it a thousand times over because this person, so jaded and crass that our mother would never recognize her, is who I was born to be. The battles, the intrigue, the nights on horseback evading capture - these are the things that bring vitality to my spirit and validate my existence.

Justice for our people, revenge for our family, a good, safe life for you...this is what drives me. It is who I am and must be until the Warlock Emperor is defeated and Hlyn is free. But it has never been you and I am so sorry my selfish need to keep you close has...broken you. What you were forced to do, on my behalf, should never have come to be.

Yes, I'm sure you'll recognize the hustle and bustle of Vyte the moment you wake up. Who else knows the energy of the city of our birth better than you? It may seem that I am dumping you right in the mouth of the lion, so to speak, but I have the feeling you will be safer there, at least for the moment. You have your magic, and I have mine so, trust me, stay put and keep your head down and it'll all shake out just fine.

I know you won't listen but, please, don't worry if you don't hear from me for a while.

I'm going to fix this.

All my love,

D.

p.s. Please don't hate me for leaving Porta with you. She is NOT happy. Hide the knives.

Chapter Nine

"Guti." A whisper cut through the waning night, dragging Tempest from the depths of the confusing nightmare she'd been having. Slowly, the ephemeral strands that made up her dream dissipated, and consciousness forced her mind into unwilling alertness. She managed to contain a groan, but the unexpected voice echoing in the shell of her ear had surprised a snort out of her that she'd been unable to choke back. It may be too late to feign sleep, but that wouldn't stop her from trying.

"Hey, Gutra Twoshoes." The voice came again, this time accompanied by a poke of a boney finger in her shoulder and a warm exhale on her cheek.

"I'm not answering to that." Tempest rolled over in her tiny cot. She had nothing against getting up early but why Porta couldn't wait until at least moonset to start her incessant blathering was beyond her. She pulled her thin pillow over her head and followed it with a double handful of blankets. It didn't help.

"It's your name now." Porta laughed. Tempest wasn't sure if it was the darkness that surrounded them that gave her voice an extra sinister connotation or the girl's black soul itself.

"For the blasted love of all kittens, go back to bed, Porta!"

"I can't sleep. I need the outhouse."

Another poke, this time directly to Tempest's spine. She sighed and allowed the girl to pull the pillow off her head. She didn't want to be awake before the sun but, now that she was, the urge to pee hit her as well.

"I'll take you if you promise not to call me that again." She felt it was a more than magnanimous offer.

"If you don't take me, I'll squat right here on the floor." Porta obviously didn't agree.

Porta began to jiggle back and forth next to the bed, nearly vibrating in her urgency. Within the last few seconds, her need must have escalated to the point she no longer thought teasing Tempest awake was funny. She pulled Tempest's blanket off, leaving her shivering in her thin shift despite the extreme warmth the coming day was sure to bring.

Tempest was too familiar with the younger girl to not take her seriously. Some battles, she reflected as she sat up and motioned Porta to back away so that she had space to put her legs, were lost well before they were fought. She shuffled her toes over the hard-packed earth, now fragrant with fresh reeds she'd gathered herself, searching for her thin-soled slippers.

Porta was nearly jumping up and down. "Come on, Guti!" She couldn't help but throw one more provocation in, especially since she knew she had won this round. Again.

"My name is Tempest. T-E-M..." She trailed off as Porta unceremoniously skipped out the door, letting it thump loudly in the near silence of the sleepy Lower City. A trio of disapproving horsey snorts followed her exit, and Tempest was perversely happy she wasn't the only one awakened so early.

"Seriously," Tempest took a moment to give the agitated horses gentle nose pats as she walked through the stable, sparing a glance at Obertroess where he snoozed on, unperturbed, from his cozy corner stall. "I wish you could have given me a prettier fake name while I was struggling on the brink of a horribly tragic ending to my life."

"Missed opportunities and all that...blah, blah, blah." Porta swung the heavy outer door wide and surprised Tempest by holding it for her. "We look nothing alike, but Dahlis said I should make sure people thought we were blood relations and that I should never, ever, reveal our true names. So, we had to become Liala Butterberry and Gutra Twoshoes or face certain and immediate death." She carefully closed the door, making sure the latch held even in her rush. Every farm girl knew the importance of keeping a shut gate locked.

"With that reasoning, as my 'sister' shouldn't we share the same last name?"

"Nah." The street before them was bathed softly in the light of the second moon, Myninn. Tempest took a moment to reach out with her senses to insure they were, indeed, as alone as it seemed. Besides the sickly glow of the drunk that had passed out next to the main steps leading into the Evermore after last night's festivities, the courtyard was empty. Porta's small hand grabbed her wrist and began to pull her across the stone yard that separated them from the outhouse that served several of the Lower City businesses. "We are only half-sisters. Your father was a slow-wit who walked in front of a wagon full of dead puppies."

"Ouch. That's dark."

"Yeah, tragic, really." Porta released Tempest and raced the few remaining steps to the privy. The slamming door muffled her next words, but she spoke loudly enough to cover the sound of her relieving herself. Mostly. "I tell people you are very much still affected by his demise to explain why your face looks like that all the time."

"Why are all the puppies...wait!" Tempest couldn't help thumping her fist against the closed door. "What does my face look like, exactly?"

"You know. Like you are constantly smelling something bad or only ever eat sour things." The door sprung open, nearly flattening Tempest's nose. She rolled her eyes, aware that, if it hadn't been before, her face was surely reflecting her disgust now. She stomped past Porta, ignoring her grin, and made quick work of finishing her own business.

"Will you please go back to bed now?"

"Sure." Porta skipped back toward the stables just as the sun cleared the edge of the horizon. She pointed that pesky, sharp little finger up at the chimney of the Evermore Inn where a wisp of smoke began to curl. "It looks like you've got a morning meal to make though, Guti Twoshoes!"

Tempest groaned and went to see if she could wake the drunkard before the breakfast rush arrived. He, she was sure, hadn't bothered to make it to the outhouse. Her daily nightmare, it seemed, had just begun.

Tempest looked up from the table she'd just cleared, her red knuckles buried in a sudsy rag. The tune she'd been humming as she worked faded from her lips as she saw the giant of a man that stepped through the always open door of the Evermore Inn, a scraggly white terrier tucked under one beefy arm. An expletive replaced the song when she saw what, or more accurately, who, he dragged in behind him with his other hand.

"I found a depraved vagabond wandering the streets. Would you like to take custody and improve my day?" The intimidating constable, not waiting for an answer, broke into a smile and nodded at the tavern keeper, Dax Marcoyne, who was equally as large and twice as gentle, who had been busying himself by polishing his prized ale horn collection.

"I don't think I'll claim her until after you tell me what she's done this time." Tempest dried her hands on the section of her apron not filled with the bric-a-brac she'd acquired while waiting tables during the busy lunch hours. She gave the girl a pointed look, raising one of her eyebrows high. It hadn't been the first time Porta had been dragged into the Evermore in shame for disturbing the peace.

The constable lifted the little dog up in explanation. Tempest felt pity for it as it was obviously malnourished and mangy. Judging by the dry length of tongue hanging out of its crooked teeth and the way its eyes rolled independently of each other, it was also horribly inbred.

"What?" Porta tried to shake Meryl's burly hand off her scrawny arm to no avail. "The lady shoved the pitiful fluff and a fistful of smallcoin at me. If she didn't want me to make my own decisions, she should have opened her flabby painted lips and told me exactly what she wanted. I think," she sniffed, no doubt as snootily as the fancy lady, "I did a fine job in my interpretation."

Tempest's golden eyes met Meryl's baby blues and they both shrugged at the same moment, laughing. There were just some arguments you couldn't even begin to dispute. He released her arm and stepped back, waving at his uncle who was drawing a flagon of ale for him at the bar.

"We are just fortunate," Tempest ruffled the top of Porta's already tangled black hair, eliciting an aggravated shriek as the girl pulled violently away, "you didn't pocket the money and sell the dog to the butcher."

"Hmpf." Porta puffed out her cheeks in frustration and folded her freed arms over her thin chest. "That bugger wouldn't give me anything for him. He shrank to nearly no meat after I had shaved him."

The burly constable shook his head and joined his uncle, leaving the girls standing idly by the open door. Tempest took a quick glance around the empty dining room, turning away from the men so that only Porta could see her expression.

"You need to stop taking risks like that, P." She said quietly.

"I beg to remind you that you should be addressing me as Liala, a refined young lady experiencing a most egregious destitutivity." Porta attempted to flatten the hair standing haphazardly around her dirty ears. How on Telryuun did the girl get so filthy? Refined lady, my rear, Tempest harrumphed.

"You've found the Lower City library and some free time, I see." Tempest remarked, her delicate pink lips quirking up on one side, a dimple denting a cheek that was just starting to regain some of its former plumpness. "Although an extra hour or two with a dictionary wouldn't go amiss."

At the bar, Meryl laughed uproariously at something his uncle had said and tipped the ale mug back. The tiny dog on his lap stood on its back legs and managed to control its wobbly tongue well enough to catch the few drops of golden brew that escaped down the sides of the glass.

"I bet Meryl is a good kisser." Porta elbowed Tempest in her hip, seeking to change the subject. She didn't like being admonished, least of all by someone who she thought had earned the name

'Guti Twoshoes' honestly. "His hands are all manly and his arms are beefy. Helpless girls like that stuff."

Tempest gasped in feigned shock. "Miss Liala! You are too young to be thinking of a man's kisses, sister dear."

"Eww." Porta fell out of character for half a second before throwing her pert nose back up in the air. "I would never think of gracing such a churl with the taste of my lips. I, after all, am a fine, upstanding lady." She gestured toward the bar. "Have you not seen my little, useless mutant dog-thing?"

Both girls broke out in hilarious laughter, bending at the waist and hiding their toothy grins behind their less than ladylike scrubbed red hands. It felt so good. It had been so long.

"Eeek!" A high-pitch scream destroyed the jovial atmosphere. With reflexes finely honed over the past five turbulent years of living on the run, Tempest shoved Porta behind her and reached for the knife she no longer carried.

Dax and Meryl, the former soldier and the current one, lurched to their feet, attention focused on the kitchen door-way. Meryl's aforementioned large hands must have squeezed the little white varmint too hard because it let out a yip as ear shattering as the scream.

"Ungrateful mutt!" Meryl shook his hand, the pitiful excuse for a dog flying through the air before landing, somehow, gracefully on its spindly legs and running out the door without a backward glance. Five mangled red puncture wounds appeared almost immediately.

"Who brought that rabid thing into my establishment?" Juli Marcoyne, mistress and renowned songbird of the Evermore Inn, stepped out of the hot back kitchen, her tremendous breasts leading the way. Sweat glistened on their rounded cream tops and dotted her hairline, pushing her sometimes frizzled hair into delightfully attractive curls. Simultaneously, three individual fingers pointed unerringly toward the youngest person in the room.

"Well, I never!" Porta popped off. Tempest giggled a bit at her affront as she left the doorway to retrieve a fresh towel and a clean pitcher of water. For some reason, the girl had decided her Liala Butterberry persona was pompous as well as prim, although she wasn't very successful in keeping her true brash self under control. Her soft-soled shoes hit the floor a bit too heavily as she strode toward the bar, more a clumsy tromp than the imperious walk she thought it was.

"My poor, innocent baby nephew!" Juli leaned a bit forward to peer at Meryl's injury but refused to come any closer. Her checks took on an extra flush and she dragged her signature black lace fan from its place on her perfectly padded hip. She began to fan herself in as elegant a manner as possible while using her free hand to pat her giant of a nephew awkwardly on the back.

"Is that a tooth?" Porta's voice was excited as she leaned forward and pinched the tiny, yellowed fragment from Meryl's palm, leaving a bloody trail running across his roughened skin.

"Oh!" Juli fanned herself more ferociously as she wrapped an arm around Porta's thin shoulders and pulled her close against her side, bustling her out of the room with a brisk strength that couldn't be denied. "You must come away from here, miss. These things are not for youthful eyes and," she paused to wink at Tempest over her plump shoulder, "I think you've had enough excitement for one morning."

Disgust turned Juli's beautiful face pale as she noticed Porta turning the gnarly tooth over in her hand and poking it with a dirty finger. A swift sweep of her fan sent the tooth flying and a low growl in the woman's throat made Porta choke down the complaint she was about to air.

Porta grumbled but allowed Juli to escort her away from the scene of the crime. She knew the next few hours would be filled with listening to the older woman's stories of her own misspent youth while 'sampling' the newest delivery of baked goods. Both Marcoynes, staunch Loyalists and two of Dahlis' most trusted supporters, knew Porta's tragic backstory and tended to coddle the girl whenever the chance permitted. Dax wasn't any better and as he trundled off after the pair like a puppy hoping to get treats of his own. Tempest knew at least Porta's afternoon would be pleasant.

She sighed as she looked over the recently vacated tables she still needed to clean. With the afternoon rush behind them, she'd probably have a few moments to get off her feet as well.

"Here." Tempest placed her fresh supplies on the bar and took Meryl's hand in her own, pulling it closer to her face to pretend to examine it. In truth, she had already used her magic to assess the damage and found the wound to be little more than surface scratches. It was also surprisingly clean considering the relative ick factor of the attacker. "Let me clean this up a bit."

Tempest dragged the wet cloth across his large hand, clearing the skin of blood and saliva. Mostly saliva. So much saliva. She looked up as she felt him stiffen and discovered that he was cursed with the same ability to blush a brilliant red as his aunt. She felt a responding rush of blood to her own cheeks.

He certainly was big, she thought as she wrung the rag into the bowl and set it aside. Damn Porta for suggesting he may be attractive, boyfriend material. She wasn't in the market for a man to protect her. Who would protect him from her? She, after all, was the real villain of this story.

"There." She stepped away, pushing her curls nervously back into the bland kerchief she kept them bound under. "All better. I didn't even have to amputate." Her attempted joke was lame at best, but Meryl laughed all the same. It was a wonderful, heartfelt sound, Tempest thought. Her smile was genuine as she pushed the dirty bowl and towel under the bar. She couldn't help but quip, "We can't have Auntie's precious little man fighting off Hlyn's monsters with only one hand, now, could we?"

"I certainly need two functioning arms to pass the upcoming inspection." Meryl flexed his fingers, surprised that the tiny puncture wounds were already nearly invisible. Good. He didn't have to come up with a valiant tale to explain the injury to his fellow constables. He could only imagine the razzing he would get if the truth were known.

"Inspection?" Tempest reached for his mug, intending to refill it but he waved her off. "I wasn't aware the Regency cared about the state of Vyte's constables."

Stepping away from the bar, Meryl took a quick look around the Evermore before turning back to her. His voice was a low grumble as he leaned closer. He locked his thumbs casually in his belt, but he looked a bit nervous, as if he were afraid to be caught gossiping with her in the empty tavern.

"I'm sure the truth will be around by the end of tonight's supper rush, but rumor is Regent Norc is dead." He straightened and tugged his uniform coat down on his hips, patting to make sure his short club and street sword were firmly in place. He saw Tempest's heart-shaped face blanche white and cleared his throat as she stared blankly at him for a second too long.

"Well," he shifted away and sketched a low bow, internally cursing himself for mentioning something as horrifying as death in front of such a gentle, soft woman, "I must be back on shift. Thank you for the healing." He bowed awkwardly once more and set off for the door quicker than the ugly dog-creature had.

"Wait!" Tempest stammered, her hands falling limp at her sides. "Who will the people look to if Hlyn doesn't have a regent?" she asked, her heart creeping into her throat. Maybe, she thought, this was their chance. Perhaps all of Dahlis' hard work and their mutual sacrifice would finally find the success they desperately craved. This may be the first step in freeing their people from the tyranny of the Warlock Emperor.

Meryl stopped on the stoop and poked his head back through the door. He smiled reassuringly, "Not to worry, Miss. The constables are always about if you need us, and the emperor is sending his own First General to act as Regent of Hlyn. Vyte will be more secure than ever."

He nodded respectfully one last time and stepped back into the streets of Vyte. Tempest stood silent. A thousand thoughts flitted through her mind, circling chaotically before they slipped away unacknowledged. Feelings of fear, of pain, of intense anger ratcheted through her, ripping into her composure and leaving holes in the very fabric of her soul.

It couldn't be. The rumors must be wrong!

Hlyn was a small kingdom, proud but inconsequential in the overall scheme of things. It was a tiny speck in the greatness of Telryuun. Why would the Warlock Emperor send his best man to rule it? An unmatchable, emotionless warrior bound, sworn, and dedicated to eradicating the Glorious Empire's most dastardly foes. A man as powerful, it was whispered, as the emperor, but soul-bound to the Dragonbone Blade to serve as an eternal, vengeful shadow bound to his master's every cruel whim.

A whirlwind of hatred churned inside Tempest, lighting fire to every synapse, igniting every vein with molten hot anger, building into a tornado of violent fury that wasn't her own. A voice filled her head, sardonic and cruel, as it spat:

Roryn T'Yanil. The Bled. The Bonded...The Scourge of Salvadon.

She closed her eyes, sorting through the rage and hate filling her, pushing it to the back of her mind until only her own uncertainty and fear remained. A sick giggle echoed inside her brain, then the voice attempted to soothe her angst, brushing delicately along the veins it had burned with a cool, ghostly caress.

Hello, Beauty. Have you missed me?

Norc wasn't gone after all.

Chapter Ten

"**Y**OU KNOW MORE THAN anyone, Father, the pain an immortal life brings."

Praxxys knelt slowly into the soft grass lining the edge of a freshly filled grave. Moisture soaked through the knees of his breeches, but he paid it no mind. His eyes, so gray as to appear a startling silver, danced away from the second grave, this one an empty, gaping hole, eagerly waiting its tribute. Next to it, an intricately carved casket rested, its lid open to reveal the fine white silk that made a plush bed of its interior. Silk that matched perfectly the dress that his dear Everlain wore.

"Do not do this, Evi." He fought back the tremble of dread that threatened to shake the hands he laid on his daughter's heaving shoulders. Silent tears streaked down her delicate face as she looked up at him, the light and the dark of the twin moons etching swirling shadows under her sharp cheekbones. "Tomas would not want this," he plead. "He loved you as much as I love you. It would have devastated him to know what you have planned."

Everlain gently pulled away from her father, undisputedly the greatest man in any kingdom, and leaned her slender back upon the waiting coffin. She drew her knees up to her chest, wrapping her arms around them in the innocent way she'd done since she'd been a child.

They sat in silence for a moment. Everlain contemplating her choices and Praxxys furiously plotting ways to make them for her. Smiling oddly, she reached out and plucked a tiny white daisy from its precarious place in the dirt threatening to crumble into the gaping hole she was determined to rest in. She twirled it once, then twice, before slowly pinching off each of its dew-wetted petals. She handed its empty stem to her father.

"It's not just Tomas." Her voice was strong, for all its softness. "My womb is as dead as my body should once have been. Never shall I hold a child of my blood and cherish them, to raise them as you raised me."

"I can fix this, Dearheart." Praxxys crawled forward, pulling her close to him, squeezing her harder than he possibly should. His desperate hands shook her slightly as he tried to reassure her...tried to reassure himself. "Whatever we need to do. I need you here with me, Everlain. I am nothing without you."

"It wasn't my choice to stay. It wasn't my Fate to stay." Everlain rested her head on her father's shoulder, her generous red curls

spilling over his chest and tickling his nose as he kissed her head ever-so gently. "You were born of gods. They meant for you to be eternal, to bless the world in ways they no longer could. You will be fine. You have always been fine."

A shudder shook her thin body though she was able to hold back the pained cry that clawed at her soul. "I am a thief, a thief of life, of time, and it hurts so much, Daddy! What I am…is not meant to be." She pushed out of his embrace, her fine-boned face and luminous gray eyes as serious as they were resolute.

The knife she pulled from the satchel at her side was simple for all its cruelty. Carved from an ancient ebony ash tree and bound in stone and vine, it was the antithesis of the Dragonbone blade burning in rage at his side. It was Mercy where his knife was Damnation.

"Where did you get that?" His voice was rough. Pain unlike anything he had ever experienced before welled up inside him. His eyes filled with the tears he had thought dried eons ago. The unassuming blade she held pulsed with the energy of the earth, with solace and forgiveness and the sibilant hum of a river over time-worn rock.

Maybe, if he had known of such a power all those years ago…

No. His rage, even then, was already too great to leave him any other path.

"Then I shall join you!" He plucked the Heartwood blade from her pale hand and, without hesitation, plunged it into his worthless heart. A flash of red and gold blasted across the meadow. Praxxys opened his eyes, desperate to see flesh and blood rent asunder and his soul preparing to depart. Instead, Everlain sat calmly, the wooden blade in her frail grasp once more.

"This ending was meant for me, Father. Much as that one," she pointed her finger disdainfully at the Dragonbone blade resting at this hip, "is the harbinger of your Fate."

He lurched to his feet, anger replacing his fear. His big, hard-knuckled hands tore at his hair and his jaw clenched hard, his teeth grinding together discordantly. How could he convince her to remain at his side? If she wanted a child, he would find her one. By the Nightmare, if she wanted a dozen, he'd get them for her!

"You took my Death away from me." Her words were quiet, accusing. His heart broke as he realized it was the only time she had ever shown her disappointment in him.

"What is it you want, Evi? How can I ever atone for the wrong I have done you?"

Standing, Everlain walked to where Praxxys paced, the Immortal Emperor reduced to a weeping, broken man. She gave him her gentlest smile, a warm kiss on the cheek, and curled his reluctant fingers around the Heartwood blade.

"Give it back."

Praxxys jerked upright, his legs caught up in the fine furs lining his bed. Reflex had him reaching for the Dragonbone blade, but he could feel it across the room, safely settled into the golden sheath that helped bind its power. His hands were shaking as he covered his face. He hadn't had that dream in a long time.

Why was he having it now?

He groaned and massaged his aching temples with his fingertips, kicking his feet free of their encumbrance and shifting to the side of his mattress. He pulled the bed curtains open with a violent twist of his hands. He needed very little sleep and it irritated him to have his rare moment of bliss so disturbed.

On the sill of his open window two ravens perched, eerily quiet, watching him. He'd seen them many times over the years, one the white of snow, the other the hue of the Deep Nothing. They hadn't flinched when he had bolted upright but a swift toss of a pillow at the casement had them cawing and flapping indignantly out into the gathering dawn.

"Stupid shills!" he mumbled at their departing backs. The damn unnatural things seemed determined to spy upon him in the most inopportune moments. He suspected they were leashed spirit creatures bound to report on him to their master or, more likely, they were just drawn to the tortured souls inside the blade.

Either way, their magic signature was so minimal as to be nonexistent. He'd been inclined to let them linger. With the remnants of the dream riding him, though, they were lucky to have left with their lives.

The sun was making its presence known, creeping through the bank of windows on the east side of his tower room. The weak light caught on the golden sheath housing the Dragonbone blade, sending a glare of illumination cascading about the room and annoying him further. He gave the blade a dark, scowling glare of his own.

The cursed knife wasn't the source of all his problems, he wasn't self-delusional enough to believe that, but it was the bane of his existence. He could feel it pulsing softly, even bound in gold, though the sheath at least dampened the voices. It was hungry.

So was he. His stomach growling, Praxxys left his bed, forgoing the robe slung across the foot in favor of letting the chill air soothe away the fevered flush of the night that had gathered on his skin. He paused in front of the window so recently vacated by those dastardly ravens and breathed deeply as the morning broke over Noxia below.

He was the Eternal Emperor, unquestioned ruler of the Glorious Empire. He controlled lands he had never seen, people he would never meet. It was more than he had ever set out to achieve.

Once, he was nothing more than a father. Once he was nothing less than completely beloved.

His mind circled back to his dream and Everlain's words. Why remind him of his greatest regret at a time when he was preparing for his greatest triumph? He missed his sweet Evi. Her loss was an endless ache resonating in the otherwise empty center of his soul. For the millionth time, he cursed the gods who gave him his daughter and then took her away.

Nevermind them, he turned away from the window. He had made himself a son. One who could not beg for death.

Praxxys took mere moments to prepare himself for the day. He dressed in a fine but simple suit, pressed crisply as was his preference, but not so ostentatious as to send the dignitaries he would see today mewling at his feet. He rather wished they still remembered him as a humble king and did not cower the way some of them were wont to do. Such behavior got boring after a while. Not to mention, reassuring them he wouldn't kill them outright was time consuming.

He wasn't done conquering the known world yet. He still had one more task to complete. Remnants of another dream filtered through his psyche. Not a dream provided by the Morphi, but one borne of meticulous research and planning. Before the dual moons swallowed the sun, he would see his ambitions fulfilled.

He toed his muddy boots, discarded haphazardly the night before, away from his wardrobe and pulled out a pair of shiny low-cuts. He tossed them on the floor and stepped into them, tapping the heels to settle them more firmly on his feet. A couple of passes of his hands dislodged the tangles from his sinfully dark hair and he was ready for the day.

His hand closed reluctantly on the Dragonbone blade, but he strapped it to his waist without hesitation. The servants couldn't safely clean the room if it was left behind and, truth be told, sometimes Solay's taunting voice was the best company he had over the course of a day.

He hurried down the seemingly unending stairs, curling down to the base of the tower and out into the castle proper. Servants scattered as he approached, bowing low or sending him warm smiles, depending on which tales they chose to believe about him. His useless courtiers would not be up for hours, but he knew the one person he did want to talk to would already be breaking his fast. He threw the doors to the Grand Hall wide, and his stomach growled again as the smell of morning pork and biscuits assailed him.

As he had expected, only one person sat at the table, his back to the roaring flames crackling in the wide fireplace. The man looked up, his handsome face young yet harsh in the soft light. He stood quickly as the emperor approached.

"Roryn!" Praxxys greeted the Scourge of Salvadon with a mellow smile and a clap on the shoulder. "You're still here, son? I would have thought you'd have half a continent behind you already."

"My apologies, Eminence." The Salvadonian prince bowed stiffly. His hair, Praxxys noticed disapprovingly, was pulled into a warrior's braid in the style of his people, the shaved sides laying bare the blue and black dragon tattoos he'd earned upon his entry to manhood.

It was a barbaric look Praxxys had tried for years to change, but no amount of compulsion through their bond could convince the stolen prince to alter it. As a compromise, while he was at court, Roryn wore his hair down, the long black strands covering his glaring rebellion. The emperor allowed this, however reluctantly, because he didn't actually want Roryn to be his mindless puppet. No matter how irritating he found his personal grooming choices.

"What's with this Eminence crap? Feeling a bit formal today, my son?" Praxxys accepted the plate prepared by the Steward of Kitchens and sat himself at the foot of the table, close to his Bonded. He scooped some gravy onto a biscuit and popped it into his mouth before he was fully seated. He was a soldier much longer than he was royalty, and some habits were too ingrained to put aside. The expedient consumption of a good meal was one of them.

Roryn's steely gray eyes were ironic under the ebony eyebrow he arched. His whole demeanor screamed insolence and derision, expressions Praxxys both hated and admired in his Second-in-Command.

"We can't all be morning people, Praxxys. Is it not enough that you rule the world with absolute power? Must you accost me, in particular, with a good mood and chatter so early?"

"Considering you have been up longer than me, an immortal demi-god with no real need to rest, perhaps we should examine who the real morning person is in this situation." He speared a salty slice of breakfast pork and shook it at the other man knowingly.

"Well, there are morning people," Roryn raised his steaming mug of caff in a salute to the man who had drained him of every ounce of his innate power and held his very soul in the palm of his hand. Or on his hip, as it were, "and then there are mourning people."

"Truth." Praxxys swallowed his pork, wishing this Steward of Kitchens could be immortal when he moved aside a second biscuit to find three more perfectly cooked pieces of his favorite meat. Good help was so hard to find in some lifetimes. Speaking of which...

"I'd like to commend you for the spectacular defeat of Kalonia. Its jewel mines will be a fine, well, jewel in my crown."

"It was a slaughter that could have been avoided if any of their lower lords had stood above the rest as an acceptable Regent of the Realm." Roryn's sharp cheekbones became razor-taunt with the force of his disgust. The tail of his braid brushed over his shoulder as he shook his head in frustration. Praxxys' curse on him may have curbed his wilder emotions, but idiocy still left a bad taste in his mouth.

"Nevertheless. You always have my best interests, and those of the Glorious Empire, in mind. It burdens a ruler to worry that his generals aren't as loyal as one might wish."

"Not that you have given me a choice in the matter, Excellency. Who knows where Salvadon would have stood in your graces had I been left in the Golden Lands." Unbidden, his sun-bronzed hand rubbed at the red, angry scar puckering the strong length of his right forearm. It throbbed horribly in this close proximity to the bedamned blade. Thankfully, after a quarter-century of servitude, it only bled when he sought to fight the dark power of the curse or to deny one of Praxxys' dictates.

"You were wasted among your so-called people, Ryn. I, better than anyone, should recognize a man who was born gods-touched."

The younger man scoffed. Many of Salvadon's inhabitants were so blessed. It was why they chose to exist in such a dangerous homeland. The Edge of the World provided many opportunities to live a life built of equal parts challenge and beauty. Men such as he found themselves unfulfilled, unhappy, and prone to corruption in the 'civilized' world.

"Do you miss that life, truly?" Praxxys pushed his plate away, his appetite gone as he considered the son he had stolen for himself. An heir powerful, cunning, and, at least while Praxxys drew breath, immortal. "I have given you a greater purpose upon this world. All the battles a warrior can desire. Wealth. A fine horse. What more can you want?"

"To choose the wars I fight and the souls I sever? The opportunity to have laid my mother in her grave as a loving son should have? To defend the T'Yanil name with the honor of my forefathers? To sire an heir that would continue the bloodline should my brother's progeny not thrive?"

Roryn took a cautious sip from his mug, unconcerned that his words could be construed as traitorous to the most powerful being in Telryuun. To him, it was a forthright answer to an honest question. The fact that he was being deprived of these pivotal moments seemed unimportant. In some way, it was. If Praxxys had wanted an emotionally savvy slave, he shouldn't have bound his soul to an inhuman creation.

"I am done with this conversation." Praxxys stood abruptly. Three swift strides had him standing before the roaring flames and he stared at them for a few furious breaths, his head braced against the mantle. The details of his dream flooded him with remembered despair and grief. His hands curled into fists with a ferocity that brought blood to bear as the manicured half-moons of his nails dug mercilessly into his palms. The coppery smell flooded his nostrils at the same moment the Dragonbone blade began to hum at his side.

Damn insatiable thing.

With several centuries of practice, Praxxys calmed himself in a heart's beat. He stood upright, sweeping his hand over the fire and extinguishing the dancing flames without a hiss of resistance. He turned to place his hands on Roryn's shoulders. If his grip was more painful than apologetic, it couldn't be helped. It was, after all, the way of warriors to never admit their shortcomings.

"Tell me of your plans for assuming the Hlyn Regency." He began to pace, his arms locked stiffly behind his back and his well-polished shoes ringing loudly as their steel-soled bottoms struck the cobbled floor.

Sighing heavily, Roryn pushed the last half of his caff away. They didn't have such a brew in Salvadon and if he had grown to love anything Noxian since he'd been pulled away from his homeland, it was the bitter sting of the dark liquid on his tongue. He stood, retrieving his broadsword from the back of his chair and fastening the holster low upon his slim hips before speaking. The hesitation was another small defiance Praxxys had become accustomed to over the years.

"I had hoped to ride in with a show of force, though I don't expect much resistance. Our intel suggests that there are many staunch Loyalists in Vyte but they have not gathered a sizable standing army as of yet. However," Roryn pulled a rumpled missive from his pocket, "I was notified this morning that a rather virulent illness is traveling amongst the contingent we have stationed here. I've ordered them quarantined and sent word for Eighth company to join me in Vyte when they are done securing the Kalonian border."

"A most prudent action for a most wise general." Praxxys praised, nodding his head to convey his complete agreement. He stopped his pacing, stroking his bare chin in contemplation for a moment before turning to Roryn.

"This may prove to be fortuitous for us, actually. Norc's demise leaves us blind in that corner of the Empire. It wouldn't hurt for you to go in before the Eighth arrives and do a little observing of your own."

"That was my thought as well. Norc wasn't a well-loved regent. It shouldn't be hard to ascertain where his death is being celebrated the most and that is where we will find our rebels."

"I need the Malorn heir brought to me alive and well before the Eclipse." He seemed to reconsider. "At least alive and not liable to expire before she has served her purpose. If her edges are ruffled, I would not mind. I hear her personality is exceptionally sharp."

"What of the other princess?"

"Norc, the Bright have mercy on his ever-loyal soul, no matter how incompetent he proved to be, had brilliant spies. The second princess is weak, a mouse beside a lion, he'd said." Praxxys waved his hand in dismissal. "I care not what you do with her. Leave her free, take her head, it matters not. The power I need is dark and deadly, the sort to be housed within a daring rebel, not a wilting flower of a maiden."

"As you will, it shall be done." He bowed low enough to set the glass beads woven into the base of his braid clacking against the floor.

"Roryn?" His back no longer ridged, the Warlock Emperor seemed to have withered in both intensity and vitality, his arms loose and despondent at his sides. If Roryn had to assign a feeling to his stance, he might have said confused. "Have I really brought you no pleasure in this life?"

"I am sorry," Roryn's voice was flat, although a faint echo of regret could be heard. "I no longer remember how that emotion feels."

Chapter Eleven

"WHY, I HAVE NEVER!" Juli flounced through the narrow doorway of the kitchen, her vibrant red and gold cotton dress catching on the ragged splinters hanging tenaciously from the ancient wood frame, pulling the material tight around her ample curves like eager, grasping fingers. An impatient wave of her hand down her hip separated her from the wood but didn't slow her or ease her irate expression.

Looking up from the vegetables she'd been cutting into even, stew-sized chunks, Tempest held in her sigh. She loved working in the tiny kitchen of the Evermore Inn, tucked out of sight and quarantined from the chaotic energy of the town. She crawled out of her simple cot in the granary behind the stables every morning with an eagerness to feel the satisfaction of a 'normal' life the labor provided. She reveled in the sensation of not having a purpose greater than that of serving others. No illustrious lineage to uphold. No expectations of perfection.

She was...happy.

Seeing the angry flush of red working its way up Juli's already somewhat florid neck and into her cheeks told Tempest that was about to change. Gently, she set her knife down, sliding it out of sight under a bunch of dirt-laden carrots. The fuming woman before her stopped abruptly, picking up the dented iron pan Tempest had been using to collect her discards. She shook it with both white-knuckled hands before tossing it violently back down in place. A smile quirked the corner of her flustered cheeks, as if she were picturing herself ripping the head off whatever customer had made her so peeved.

Tempest leaned away from her table, using the time it took for Juli's frantic breaths to slow to stretch her back and calmly push the tendrils of her hair back into place in her neat bun. A few frilly fronds from the discarded carrot tops catching on her fingers proved her previous attempts to straighten her locks had been horribly unsuccessful. She tried not to think of the state of her once glorious hair, recently redyed a flaccid and unremarkable brown, as she examined her boss from under her lashes.

Juli Marcoyne was a lively, buxom example of womanhood and was normally as jovial as she was beautiful. She took pride in her curves and in the milky smooth turn of her cheek. Her hair was always twisted onto the very top of her stately head in gorgeously gleaming curls of red, seeming to dance back and forth with each precise sway of her generous hips. She was often found laughing and teasing customers, both new and old, as she made her rounds of the Inn. In truth, she had her choice of flirting options in any room she entered. Her beauty was a major draw in their hidden corner of the capital city of Vyte but, if that wasn't enough to earn her more tips than any three of the other barmaids she employed, the woman could sing like a goddess.

She was so excitingly engaging on nearly every level that even her husband, the staid and ever loyal ex-horse soldier, Daxtyr Marcoyne, was captivated and unbothered by her harmless flirtations. Most evenings, he could be found leaning against the bar, slowly wiping and refilling tankards, always with an enraptured smile transforming his war-battered face as he watched her shine.

Having listened to her many a night since she'd left her sister, Tempest thought that Juli's voice had a healing power of its own. It had soothed her on the occasions nothing else would. On the flip side of every 'gift' though, was a downfall. Juli might be able to channel her joviality to cheer up a weary traveler or brighten a dark winter night, but if her rage was ever brought to the surface, it could prove to be a situation in which a grown man would be wise to run. Tempest felt a thrill fill her at the prospect of going toe-to-toe with the enraged enchantress and she bit her lip to hide the smile that threatened to break free. As much as she hated living on the run, she did truly miss the small moments of excitement.

Like the time you sucked the soul from my very chest? Norc's voice whispered sinisterly in the back of her mind. Tempest pushed it away. The longer she ignored him, the stronger he got, but that was a problem for another day.

"I knew you didn't care for kitchen work, Jules," she taunted the innkeeper, "but abusing the cookware is very uncouth."

Juli's blue eyes zeroed in on Tempest, as if just realizing she was there. Three loud, fierce breaths filled the space between them before the older woman began to laugh uproariously. Juli was one of the few people the Malorn heirs trusted with their true identities, mainly due to the heroic efforts she and her husband had made to uphold the realm in the last few weeks of the war. But while Daxtyr was deferential in every bone in his humongous body, Juli didn't see anyone as having any more right to be esteemed than her, be they royalty or not.

She shoved the iron pan across the scarred wooden table, this time more playfully. She scooped up a few handfuls of the scraps that had scattered in her fury and tossed them into the offal bucket they kept stored by the open exterior door a few steps away. A squeal from deep in the stable indicated Squirt, the resident pig, had heard the distinct sound of scraps hitting the metal and would be around to clean up momentarily. They were lucky that the Evermore was situated at the edge of the city with no buildings littering the greenspace between it and the wall to block the summer breezes that trundled down from the snow-capped mountain.

Not that the breeze benefited Tempest all that much, she mused as sweat gathered delicately on her temples. The giant cauldron of perpetual stew the Evermore was famous for sat over a fire that hadn't been allowed to go out for three years. It was one of Tempest's jobs to ensure the conglomeration of meat and veggies stayed at a steady bubble. The rumor was that the last person to let the flame falter had to leave the Evermore in shame.

Though she figured the real truth was that he'd needed an excuse to follow his dream of joining the constables and could find no other way to gain his aunt's permission. Juli may have run Meryl out of the kitchen with his tail metaphorically tucked between his legs, but she'd also packed him three of her famous pies and the fuzzy sheepskin blanket she'd stolen from Dax's side of the bed.

More than her figure was soft and generous.

"Is that dog-thing back?" Tempest asked. "I told Porta not to feed it anymore." She picked her knife back up and grabbed a basketful of beets to chop. They were, in her opinion, the secret ingredient in making the famous stew taste just a little more like dirt.

Juli pulled out her signature fan and began cooling herself as she propped one hip against the unlit oven. Her elegantly padded backside brushed up against the loaves of yesterday's bread and sweet buns stacked precariously on top of the iron monstrosity. She sighed dramatically, "If only." She tapped her fan on flat stomach, a habit she had when she was feeling contemplative. "I have actually grown somewhat fond of the little idiot."

Tempest choked back a laugh, causing the older woman to realize the way her words sounded.

"I meant the dog," Juli said in her most contrite tone, "not Porta!" She fluttered the fan on her midsection again, tilting her head and arching an eyebrow. "Although," she mused, "the feeling does apply to the girl to a slightly lesser degree."

"Anyway," she twisted to the side and pulled down one of their less-than-perfect serving mugs and clutched it between her breasts. "I was training that beautiful brat," she paused to roll her eyes, "sorry, I can't call her that sweet-sounding name without snorting." She made a sound much like Obertroess would make when Tempest offered him oats that were not sweetened first by a pint of honey. "I was having her seat the late lunch patrons and work on her smile," she shook her head in consternation, "that child has the most curmudgeonly scowl...when the most handsome man I've ever seen outside of a dream walks in!"

Tempest paused. Juli never gave much credence to good looks that weren't her own. "I'm liking how this story is proceeding so far. If you tell me she is suffering muscle twitches from using her face the way it was meant for a young girl to use, I'll be absolutely giddy."

"That would be rewarding," Juli winked, both fully knowing they would jump in front of a wagon to save the little minx. Realistically, it would be a wagon pulled by a pair of goats, not necessarily something horse-drawn, "but she's holding up a pleasant facade like her life depended on it."

Tempest's shock was real. It took her a moment to pull her jaw back off her chest and resume her chopping.

"So, tall, dark, and delicious walks in and, naturally," she gestured grandly with the mug, "I pushed that skinny stick of skin, hair, and frowns behind me and offered him my best table near the bar. Honey, I swear I just about swooned when he turned those eyes on me...but not in a good way. He reeks of danger and mystery."

Tempest mock saluted the inn owner with her chopping knife to her temple, "Just like the Evermore's perpetual stew!" Juli's expression was supremely unamused. It was an upspoken joke that Juli could sing and bake, but any other meal was outside her purview. Tempest choked back her giggle and cleared her throat.

"So why are you positively vibrating with aggravation? One would think such a paragon would have you flustered in an entirely different way."

"That man barely gave me a glance before he ignored me and went to sit in the back corner." Her fan began to flutter at a more rapid rate. "Why, that is the spot I reserve for the town drunk! I can't remember the last time I even swept under that table!"

Tempest held back the snide comment that wanted to leave her lips. She doubted Juli had ever swept under any of her tables. A fact that worked wonderfully in her own favor. Without floors to sweep and beets to cut, Tempest would be a poor ex-royal on the run with no roof over her head.

"So," Juli continued, "I followed him." She hummed low in her chest, "The view, I tell you, my girl, was worth his little disrespect." Her fan paused, resting on her shoulder as she lost herself in her memory, her eyes drifting half-closed in pleasure. She shook herself abruptly as she heard Dax's guffaw loudly as he served one of the regulars at the bar. "Anyway, he seats himself, pulls some papers out of his satchel, and demands 'whatever's edible and a cold mug of mead'."

"We've had gruff customers before." Tempest reminds her.

"And then," Juli's face began to redden once again as remembered angst flooded her, "he told me to shoo!" She bent a bit, her height normally holding her a head above most women, so that there was no way Tempest would miss her flustered incredulity. "Like a fly! I have a mind to put a little something extra special in his soup."

"I've got to see this man." Tempest grinned ear-to-ear, put her knife down and wiped her hands on her apron. She grabbed the tankard from Juli and topped it off at the keg they kept in the kitchen for when the stable hands needed to quench their thirst. It wasn't cold, but lukewarm was better than topped with spit, which was what her boss had no doubt intended to serve him.

"Wait one second, missy!" Juli reached out and grabbed Tempest by the apron strap before she could slip out the kitchen door. She hauled her back and twirled her so that she came face to breast with the older woman. Juli licked her fingers and slicked some of the flyaway curls back from her face, pulled the corner of her own dress up and swiped it furiously over the sweat trails glistening on Tempest's face and neck. She leaned her back and gave her a swift all-encompassing glance before finishing her tidying by popping two of the buttons off her bodice...not unlatching them...actually pulling the bits of bone and thread hard enough to separate them from the fabric. One button pinged against the big iron pot and an inelegant plop made Tempest afraid the other had irrevocably become part of the stew itself.

"Oh, that's not bad!" Juli said approvingly, batting Tempest's hands away when she tried to pull the gaping fabric back together before the sweat on her chest could be noticed and scrubbed away too. She knew she was probably scowling more fiercely than Porta, but she was really at a loss on what else to do. Juli was a run-away carriage pulled by six mules and Tempest didn't know which way to jump.

"Stand up straight, a lady who knows her worth always leads with her best assets. Remember, your smile can calm the most irritable man, but your hips would do better to excite him. And for the sake of all that is Bright, do not give him that horrid fake name you're saddled with! A man wants to be able to call out in passion without sounding like a moron."

"If he's so cold, why are you pushing me at him?" Tempest felt amusement fill her. As a young princess on the verge of her debut, her mother had forced her to endure endless lessons on deportment, grace, and, yes, even flirting. The first two were easy given her prior physical training, but engaging in small talk intended to entrance the opposite sex? Her interest had been nil and her ability decidedly deplorable. She had absolutely no intention of wasting her time trying to succeed at doing so now.

"Some men are intimidated by so much womanly sustenance." A flick of her fan encompassed the entirety of Juli's, admittedly, amply luscious form. "You are the second most scrumptious woman in Vyte and, frankly, if you don't mind me saying so, your highness, you are wound tight...*and battling the immortal ruler of the entire known world!* It wouldn't hurt to have a little fun while you can. Not to mention," a twirl of her wrist was all that she needed for her fan to portray her level of studied nonchalance, "I am married."

"And I'm married...to a cause." Tempest pointed out.

"Enslaved to a fading dream, more like." Juli was callous in voicing her opinion and Tempest couldn't even be mad at the statement. She wasn't sure if what she and Dahlis were doing was necessary or even wanted by the people of Hlyn. The Warlock Emperor had conquered them as completely as any empire ever had, but he hadn't destroyed them...yet. "Not to mention," the older woman smirked, "bound to babysitting a tiny harridan that never gives you a moment's peace."

"Wait? Porta, I mean, Liala, is out there with him now?" When Juli said Porta needed training, what she really meant was that she needed a complete personality make-over, one customer at a time. A spike of anxiety had her running out of the kitchen. Something told her this man wasn't someone who would appreciate a mouthy minx practicing her non-existent charm on him.

Her golden eyes flicked around the room, taking in the other patrons in a glance before settling on the table in the furthest corner of the inn. Tucked between the massive stone fireplace taking up a good portion of the front wall and the ornate staircase leading to the sleeping rooms above, it was a small table and was often overlooked in favor of the statelier tables that were grouped for optimal social interaction. From a security standpoint, Tempest realized it also provided the best opportunity to see people coming into the dining area before they had a chance to see you. Juli was right. This man was used to danger and either commonly caused it or was running from it.

He was also sitting bolt upright in his chair, a pained, but curious, look on his chiseled face. Tempest didn't have to guess why. Across from him sat Porta, her black hair pulled back in a braid that should have made her look prim and proper but only served to accentuate the ferocity in her green eyes.

"How many kids do you have, and did you marry their mother? Guti has standards, you know." She shrugged her tiny shoulders as she pushed a crumpled bundle of silverware folded into what was once one of Juli's prized linen napkins across the table to him. "I don't know what those standards are, but I figure you look like the type she'd probably kiss. Your hands are big, and you don't smell like a goat's underbelly. That's important, you know."

"Oh my! Liala!" Even with embarrassment flooding her face a bright red as she crossed the room in quick strides, she managed to recall their stupid cover names. She slapped her free hand over the girl's mouth but pulled it back in disgust when Porta's wet tongue slid between her fingers. "Eww."

"What?" Porta looked confused but determined to get the answers she needed. "Donwel the blacksmith has four bastards, that he knows of, although he calls them by-blows, and has never been married. I've seen three of them and they are really ugly. Mischel Stewart, the baker's wife, says they wouldn't have turned out with crooked eyes if the man hadn't been fornicating outside the bonds of marriage." She shook Tempest's hand off her shoulder and angrily scooted her chair back. "I was just making sure if you kissed this one, he wouldn't make you raise any bug-eyed by-blows." She threw her hands in the air as she stomped away. "See if I care if my future nieces and nephews look like Morti." Tempest shuddered, guessing Morti was the name Porta had given the dog-thing. No, she wouldn't want her children looking that way either.

"I'm sorry about that. She was raised in a forest. By wolves. Really, really stupid wolves." She glanced back over her shoulder to make sure Porta was truly leaving. The girl sulked to a spot behind the bar, propping her scrawny arms on its polished top and returning to her trademark scowl. One hand reached out to grab a handful of shelled nuts from the community bowl and the other flashed Tempest a crude gesture.

The man grunted and casually went back to flipping through the sketches he had laid out in front of him. From what she could tell from her position, they were rather crude portraits labeled with names and locations. Juli was right, but not in the manner she'd intended. He would be a good distraction from her hum-drum existence. As someone who had been living a secret for five years, she could smell one a mile away. It might be fun to see if she could discover his. She attempted to engage him in conversation once more.

"If she offended you, I offer you my sincerest apology. She has taken an uncomfortable interest in my love life as of late."

"I'm sure," he muttered, casual disrespect and disinterest coloring his every word, "as a barmaid in an establishment such as this, your love life would be all varieties of interesting."

"Excuse me?" Tempest gaped for a breathless moment before a surge of Malorn rage coursed through her body. Only by sheer will and much practice was she able to squash it down. Had this insufferable moron just insinuated what she thought he did?

"Liala?" She called out loudly. "Can you have Juli dip out a bowl of the special stew for our guest, please?" The evil snicker behind her back had her smirking.

She slammed the tankard on the table in front of the ungrateful man, causing his eyes to flicker up in surprise. His beautiful, serious, soul-entrapping eyes. Why, of all the men she'd ever met, whether they be princes or paupers, did she feel pulled to discover his secrets? It was more than obvious he wasn't interested in her any further than how fast she could bring his supper.

She didn't miss the ease with which his hand descended to the blunt-hilted dagger riding high on his sharp hip bone. She hadn't noticed the blade in its unassuming blackened leather sheath when she'd walked in, but she was paying attention now. His clothes, while showing the signs of wear that extensive travel caused, were of fine quality and were a few cuts up from merely functional. The hat that was pulled low over his head, obscuring all but a thick tail of the blackest hair, was relatively new, the black felt still sharp in its creases. Whoever he was, he had never been a simple soldier and the calluses on his palms were those of a warrior, not a farmer or merchant.

The clearly defined arch of his noble nose and sharp blades of his cheeks would catch eyes anywhere he went. Even hiding in this shadowed corner, he would be noticed. He was stark beauty personified but the perfection of his face and the lithely muscled lines of his body only made up a fraction of his allure.

This, she knew, was a very dangerous man.

And yet, the irresistible ebb and flow of his aura flooding this secluded corner behind the hearth had her every sense arching and her aching to get closer...to understand the puzzling confluence of power that was rushing under his skin. It was unlike any she'd felt before. In fact, her anger melted completely in the wake of her curiosity.

She knew she'd been standing there a second too long, a moment more than was socially acceptable so, blushing slightly, she pulled a damp rag from the belt of her apron and attempted to mop up a spot of mead that had slid down the side of his mug to pool in the scarred wood of the tabletop.

"My thanks." His voice was deep and calm as his back straightened, the crisp linen of his shirt rasping against the rough field stones that comprised the outer wall. A shiver chased across Tempest's shoulders, and she nodded to cover the motion. His right hand slowly edged away from his weapon and proceeded to gather his packet of sketches, shuffling them gently so as to not fray the edges or smear the charcoal. His fingertips were deft as they aligned the pages, although those silvery eyes were locked on her every move.

"Well then," she stuffed her wet rag in the pocket of her apron and untied it before balling it into a lump and tossing it into the empty fireplace, "I hope you have a Bright-blessed day, sir, and enjoy your meal. Dax?" She waved at him on her way out the door. She knew two sets of curious female eyes would be watching from the shadows of the kitchen. "Tell Juli I'm taking the afternoon off to do dirty barmaid things."

The big man gave her a confused look, his normally jovial smile falling off his face as he took in the strange man and her stiff shoulders. He reached for the club he kept stashed under the bar but hesitated when she gave him a toothy smile. He ended up waving weakly at her and went back to his conversation with the regular.

The heat outside the Evermore slapped her across the face and she darted into the shade of the stable, taking a moment to adjust after the relative cool of the inn. How had she let her legendary control slip away so easily? Porta must be riding the highest cloud of pleasure right now, knowing that the cold fish she traveled with had finally lost her composure. That, more than anything, convinced Tempest to take a deep breath and put thoughts of the handsome stranger behind her.

The Brightest save me from innocents! Youth is wasted on the weak. The now familiar snarky voice turned Tempest's stomach and destroyed any calm she had begun to gather.

Go away! She dared address the demon lurking inside her. A devil, admittedly, of her own making.

Someone, he accused, *woke me up with a flood of girly feelings. I thought I'd join whatever fun was about to begin, but instead I find you propped against a smelly stable bemoaning your piddling struggles and empty loins.*

If you don't shut up, Tempest directed her anger at the spirit swimming around inside her brain, *I'll find a way to kill you again!*

A throaty chuckle was her only answer. With Morti appearing from nowhere and trailing at her heels, she stomped off to enjoy the rest of her Nightmare-blasted afternoon.

Chapter Twelve

I'LL BUY TWO APPLES *if I want to, corpse.* Tempest's irritation only increased after she left the inn. Obertroess had refused to leave his oats and the comfort of his stall, foiling her plan of getting outside the city walls for a much-needed ride. She'd flicked a handful of hay at him, which he joyfully attempted to lip out of his long unkempt mane as she stalked out into the sun for a long walk around Vyte. It would do her good, she decided, to get out on her own. No sooner than she had thought it, Norc had butted into her consciousness, deciding to 'stick around to watch her childish tantrum'.

Why are you so dull? He bemoaned now after she had spent the last quarter-hour carefully picking through the contents of the Orchardmaster's finest wagon. Any of the apples would have been adequate but she was having too much fun revenge-tormenting the ghost.

What is boring about fruit? I happen to like apples and find them a rewarding treat for all the hard work I put in around the

Evermore. From his position under her arm, Morti began to wiggle, determined to get his broken stubs of teeth on her fingers. Tempest shuffled him so he was facing the other direction and squeezed her elbow just enough to temporarily cut off his air supply. She would have let him down, but he'd already gnawed on two horses' legs and the spoke of a wagon wheel while it was in motion. The tiny thing, like Norc, was a menace that she now felt responsible for.

Norc's sigh was so lusty she wondered if his soldiers had ever guessed just what a drama queen he was. *You are, quite literally, the murderous second-in-command of a thieving band of villainous traitors, seeking to dethrone the rightful ruler of the Glorious Empire. Can't you at least steal the produce and keep my unlife a bit more interesting?*

Tempest rolled her eyes, ignoring her own dramatic streak. *Well, if you think shopping for scrumptious and healthy staples isn't gratifying, why don't you try some silence?* Taking a deep breath, she slammed walls of power up around where she'd guessed he was nurturing his essence...or whatever it was unbodied spirits did for fun...and waited. Ten seconds passed, and then thirty with no annoying whisper creeping into her mind. Finally!

Digging six shiny smallcoin from the pocket sewn into her skirt, Tempest handed the money to the rotund salesman who had been watching her like a hawk. He tilted his moon-like head so his beady blue eyes could get a better look as he counted them. She laughed and curtsied to him in her finest courtly manner, knowing her mother would have been as pleased by her form as she would be disgusted with his insolence in counting the coin in front of her.

The glazed look on his florid face as he tucked the coin into the pouch hanging under his belly clearly communicated that he found her baffling but was too polite to call her out. He shrugged his shoulders and turned back to smile at an elderly woman making a perfunctory examination of his goods before shoving them into her market basket. He must think Tempest really liked her apples.

She could feel the satisfaction of conquering a new magic skill lighting her face and putting an extra twinkle in her eyes. Nearly bouncing with pleasure for having locked Norc away, even if only temporarily, Tempest skipped back toward the Evermore, darting into the dim alley that would take her to the fenced lot behind the stables. Her eyes were still adjusting to the darkness provided by the ancient stone walls squeezing in around her when she found herself abruptly face-to-chest, and chest-to-washboard abs, with a very hard male body.

The zing of recognition that ran through her and brought all her senses rising to high alert left her in no question of whom she had collided. As quick as that, her day turned dreary once more. But below the bad luck, she had to acknowledge that the excitement Norc yearned for was here now in full force. She said the first thing that came to mind.

"How was your stew?"

The man reached out his left hand to steady her, cupping the skin of her elbow in a firm caress that somehow, despite the callouses lining his fingertips and the grip keeping her from falling, remained gentle. His thumb traced the tender curve of soft skin exposed by her rolled-up blouse sleeves. Her breath caught.

She was desperate to reach out to him. To use her magic to explore the energy coursing through his body, arching across the space between them, electrifying and bringing a frozen clarity to the dimly lit alley. But...something held her back. Some instinct that told her he was more than just a battle-stained warrior. That his secrets may be as deadly as her own.

She yanked her arm out of his grasp and stepped back, her violent movements causing her apples to fall from her hand to the dank, wet stone ground. *Shit,* she mumbled as she bent to chase them, wiping the grime on her overskirt with a grimace. So much for her perfect apples! Though Obertroess, she decided, didn't deserve even the wormiest of fruit. It was his fault, after all, that she was now stuck in this uncomfortable and unsettling situation.

"I take it that my actions at the inn brought you some discomfort?" He touched the brim of his dark hat briefly in the barest of gentlemanly gestures as he pulled his gaze from her backside.

"Being called a whore often is upsetting." Tempest snapped, taking two steps back and brushing her hands down her chest as if she was attempting to wipe away something dirty. She had intended to make him feel shame for touching her so inappropriately, even if it had been entirely accidental, but that plan backfired tragically. She squeaked in mortification as the jagged nail of her right pinky caught the frazzled fabric of her shirt and sheared off a third button. His silvery eyes did not miss the opportunity to dip into the crevice she'd further revealed in her attempted spite. The corner of his mouth tipped up in a devilish smirk.

"I meant no offense. In my experience, women lacking so many buttons are often a master of more than one trade."

"In your experience," Tempest's embarrassed fury evaporated and she found it a challenge not to smile, "of having so much experience, maybe that makes you the whore."

This time he gave her a deeper bow, conceding the point immediately. "Since you have such an aversion to being so titled, I would be happy to call you by the name your mother once gave an innocent babe in the cradle."

Tempest considered. Even though she found Juli's advice fraught with fault, there was no way she was telling anyone, much less a man so handsome and intense, that her name was Guti Twoshoes. Damn Porta for the hundredth time! "Ben."

"Ben?" He made a show of eyeing her exposed cleavage. Despite the fluster that was building in her from being so close to his magnetic heat, Tempest managed to nod. "I daresay I have never heard of a woman so obviously blessed with beauty and grace with such a masculine name."

"You asked for the name of one of my mother's children. You didn't specify that you desired mine." Her voice bordered on breathless, she couldn't help that, but the stubborn streak running hard as steel up and down her spine wouldn't allow her to soften toward him completely.

"I see you're not the forgiving type. That's unfortunate, since I'm not the sort to give up easily. Perhaps we can agree to a truce?" He leaned closer, the fingers of his left hand gently pushing the strands of hair gathered at her cheek behind the pale, sensitive shell of her ear. "Is there anything," his voice was a gravelly whisper, chasing chills across her skin, "I can do to make you forgive my dastardly tongue?"

Tempest jerked her head back, afraid the dye would bleed onto his fingers and expose the full glory of her golden curls. It wouldn't take a genius to discover her identity after that, and this man was too crafty not to make the deduction immediately. There was only one family in Telryuun that could lay claim to this particular blessing from the Bright.

His words caught up with her, the very mention of his tongue bringing back fireside stories of passionate nights that Verilee had told the other girls after they had thought Tempest and Porta tucked safely asleep in their blankets. Her pulse began to run rampant under her pale skin, the blue veins of her wrists thundering in time with the salacious thoughts coursing through her head.

If half the things Verilee had described were possible...maybe Juli's suggestion had merit. She tilted her head back to look him full in the face for the first time. Her eyes devoured the hard planes and rough crevices, the scars as well as the flawless glow that seemed to echo from his soul. She found her hands lifting of their own accord, lightly touching the travel-worn shirt over his well-muscled chest.

He seemed just as entranced, his attention locked intently on her lips. He bent his head, moving slowly to cup her chin, giving her plenty of opportunity to draw away. His strong fingers burned a claim into her in a way she didn't fully understand but accepted without question.

She didn't move. The world seemed to disappear in that moment as the loud calls of merchants bled into the joyous sounds of buskers singing for smallcoin and disappeared in the haze that seemed to envelop her. Tempest's breath trickled in bare gasps as his mouth brushed hers.

"Tell me you want this, little barmaid. That it's my touch and not my money you desire."

An angry yip punctuated the air, startling enough sanity into Tempest that she finally registered his words. With a violent jerk, she tore herself away, running a shaking hand over her lips and realizing she'd dropped the damned apples again.

Roryn straightened, half-pulling the small blade he kept tucked into the back of his belt as he sought out impending danger. Not finding any threats, his eyes found the barmaid once again and he took an involuntary step back, sending the mare behind him dancing as what he thought was a dead rabbit slung under the girl's arm began to struggle and squirm until it was facing him. He, a man who was afraid of nothing in this mortal world, shuddered. Weeping rings of raw skin accentuated two wobbling brown orbs that seemed to be glaring into his very soul, while drops of gleaming saliva streamed in anticipation from the mouth of a creature that certainly looked dead but...wasn't?

"What in the Nightmare's Unclean Exithole is that thing?"

"That, my fine, arrogant fellow...is your penance." Tempest, her mind no longer drowning in the urges of her body, shoved the mutt into the soldier's arms, leaving him no choice but to accept the smelly pink and putrid burden as she turned and stomped her way past his mare.

Chapter Thirteen

The feelings that had swept through Roryn evaporated as the girl gave him one last sour look and passed out of sight around the corner. An itch, a reminder of sensations he barely remembered experiencing, lingered along with the scent of her. He inhaled deeply, seeking to retain the moment just a heartbeat more, but the curse of the blade reasserted itself, burning away all feeling except for the throbbing of the scar hidden under the bracer on his forearm. He felt blood begin to trickle from the wound that never quite seemed to heal and carelessly flicked the wet warmth away as it dripped from his fingertips.

"Well, girl," He addressed his snorting palomino, "looks like I've got you a snack for later." He took the scraggly white sack of bones with its giant, unstable eyes and shoved it into a half-empty saddle bag, hoping it wouldn't contaminate the last of his travel rations.

The mare, whom Roryn had unimaginatively named Horse, gave a mighty shake of her head and tried to nip at the growling burden strapped to her back. She reluctantly stepped out of the alley when her master tugged on her lead but paused to look back every few steps, the whites of her eyes exposed, as she tried to decide if the creature posed a mortal danger or just smelled like it.

With the midafternoon sun beginning to disappear behind the taller buildings lining the well-tended stone roads of Vyte's Market District, the people began to appear in force. Roryn noted that most were well-dressed and there was a decided lack of the poverty common in other realms he'd helped to conquer. Here and there, he saw indications that the people had begun to suffer under Norc's somewhat haphazard rule, but it only took a few minutes to realize that the past five years had caused no real harm to the city's infrastructure. The citizens of Vyte were proud and undefeated by their subjugation, determined to cling to the quality of life provided by Malorn rule for as long as they could.

If it were left up to him, the deposed heirs could have Hyln. Their bloodline had provided a strong rulership from time beyond memory. Their only mistake had been in thinking their small but elite standing army could face a demi-god and survive. Much, he reflected, as the Salvadonians had believed in their sanctuary at the Edge of the World.

In truth, Roryn suspected Praxxys had grown bored with the endless slew of campaigns and conquests in the past handful of years. He had disappeared often as of late, leaving the running of his assets to sycophants and scheming toadies. And, Roryn scoffed, causing the wound under his bracer to burn in warning, forcing the responsibility of maintaining the empire to one dumb general who couldn't die no matter how hard he'd tried.

Overthrowing Hlyn wasn't about gaining more land and influence, not after the initial war that saw their king dead and their princesses running for their lives. Every instinct he possessed told him that his appointment to regent was more than Praxxys wanting to ensure the complete dominance of the Glorious Empire. Although he wasn't sure of his master's true intentions, it could only be about the thing for which Praxxys truly cared.

Power.

The Malorn heiress, in particular, had drawn the Warlock Emperor's interest. From experience, Roryn knew that wasn't attention anyone voluntarily sought out. She possessed a unique magic, thus Praxxys wanted to possess her. Somehow, it had become Roryn's duty to see it was done.

Roryn picked a random apple off the cart as he passed, tossing the merchant a goldbit. "See a bushel of your finest is sent to the Evermore, would you?" He didn't bother to stick around to see the man's awestruck nod when he peered at the shiny coin in his puffy palm.

Once he cleared the cluttered Market District, the cobbled road widened, and the horse-drawn conveyances turned into a more refined class of foot traffic. The inns and forges and taverns slowly gave way to grocers and haberdasheries and then a residential district with increasingly larger houses. Horse whickered as they passed the last block of homes, more like little palaces of their own, and the smell of fresh grass filled the air.

Ahead, on a rise above the city, surrounded by communal fields and decorative public gardens, stood Castle Malorn. Made of the same white stone that formed the protective wall around Vyte, the castle had been a symbol of the grace and charm of the reigning family for centuries. Roryn was unimpressed. Even before the curse had stolen bits of his soul, it had been hard to awe him. He'd grown to manhood in the largest building in Salvadon, some would call it their royal residence, but it had been made of the same wood and thatch as every other home in their village. It had been more than enough for a people who saw strength in muscle and bone and not in stone and gold.

His eyes searched for and found the smaller cluster of buildings that would house the services necessary to keep the castle running smoothly. The clank of a hammer drew his silvery gaze, and he abandoned the path, leading Horse through the flowers and shrubbery in that direction knowing that the stables would be close to the smithy. He debated remounting her for the short distance up the hill, but a sharp bark changed his mind. Could the little demon spawn read thoughts? He shuddered but continued picking his way on foot.

The castle staff could be seen hurrying about their tasks as he approached the outbuildings. Each person wore a pleasant look upon their face, passing around smiles as bright as the stone castle towering over them. If any of them had been distressed by the passing of their former regent or worried about the next one arriving, they didn't show it. An unscratchable itch began to form on the back of his neck, a sure indication that his innate sense of decency was fighting with the influence of the Bladesouls. Roryn turned the mare toward the dark opening that, from the sweetly rich smell of feed and horseflesh, would prove to be the stable.

Stepping inside, his eyes took a moment to adjust but the happy whinny in his ear told him all he needed to know. Horse was never happier than when she was around her own kind. When he allowed himself to think about it, he knew he had been doing her a great disservice by keeping her as his mount this past decade. Roryn was a loner, always had been. His faithful mare deserved better than the existence he'd chosen. Maybe when he moved on from this place, it would be alone.

"Whooowee, gollyjig!" A shadow leaped down from the loft above their heads, ignoring the ladder put there for sensible people to use, and landed a spare few feet in front of them. Horse jerked her head up and down but more in excitement than startlement. A shaggy head complete with a pale, befreckled face appeared out of the shadows, the slim body of a boy following.

Roryn shoved his dagger back into its belt sheath. Stupid, fearless Vytians! Norc should have brought the battle to their door and taught them some caution instead of meeting the King of Hlyn and his army on the field of honor, far away from any civilian casualties.

The stable boy took the mare with a smile, "Ain't she the most purtiest critter, now iddint she? I'm Noser, by the by." He patted her cheek, earning a snuffle of her black muzzle against his unruly bush of ginger hair. It was Horse's version of a hug. Roryn stood back and watched for a minute to ensure she'd be in good hands as the boy briskly released the girth and began to pull off her saddle.

"We'll get your fine lady cleaned up, fed, an' settled, mi'lord, just you..." The boy stopped with a stutter as a growling tornado of fury seemed to erupt inside the saddle bag. Roryn smiled cockily and folded his arms as the kid froze. Seeing he would get no help from the fine gent, Noser set the saddle on the ground and with more caution than sense, stuck a finger under the flap and lifted the corner just enough to see inside. He jumped back, wiping his hand on his hay-strewn pants as if to avoid contamination. "What in th' everloving eye of th' white raven is that?"

Roryn laughed, pulling his hat from his head and tossing it in the barrow of fresh shit behind him. Now that he was no longer trying to hide his identity from the people of Hlyn he was more than relieved to be rid of the hot, itchy thing. "I have no idea. It's yours now though."

"You're th't one, huh? New regen'?" Noser eyed the vivid blue dragon tattoo revealed as Roryn pulled his Nightmare black hair back into its customary braid. He scratched at his own untamable mass of frizz before coming to a decision. He was quick as he darted forward, his fingers nimble as he untied the violently shaking bag and yanked the saddle away and onto his slim shoulder. "Well," he toed the leather satchel away from the marc and pulled her further into the stable, nearly stumbling in his haste, "I ain't carin' who you be, mi lord regent sir, I ain't takin' that thing. I'm a stableboy, not a monster tamer."

Roryn's humor slipped away faster than Noser had. He cursed the nameless girl for leaving him with the rodent-dog even as a bolt of lust took him by surprise. Once again, his scar throbbed in response. What was it about that soft spitfire of a barmaid that affected the souls of the Dragonblade so?

He'd denied Praxxys' demands before and the resulting pain had been debilitating, entertaining the idea of a quick tryst had never set it off. Why the curse thought having a bit of fun with the girl was a betrayal was beyond him. It hadn't happened often, since the curse dampened many of his impulses beyond the need to serve the empire, but he had found physical solace in female arms on and off throughout the years without punishment.

Scooping up the now quiet saddle bag, Roryn shrugged it over his own broad shoulder, thumping it hard enough to settle the tiny demon, and left the cool comfort of the stable. He slipped unnoticed through the common courtyard and followed a gaggle of giggling maids through the serving door into the kitchens.

Any one of them, he thought, would be happy to assuage the need the Evermore chit had kindled in him. A deep, warning growl sounded...much too close to his ear...but instead of thumping the temperamental beast into submission, Roryn found himself in agreement. None of those flighty flips would ignite the fire in quite the same way as she had.

The kitchens of Castle Malorn were enormous. His own childhood home could easily fit inside this one space. Every inch of it was filled with busy people rushing about and tending to their duties, all with that irritating smile of contentment on their face. Was there not an unhappy person in this entire realm? Roryn stalked away, the bag bouncing against his back and woofing with each step.

He chose the widest door and went through it, following the lamp-lined corridor deeper into the castle proper. After many twists and turns, he pushed aside a heavy door carved with the rose crest of Malorn. On the other side he was met with the stern gaze of a crisply dressed elderly gentleman, his mouth turned down in a severe frown.

"This entrance is not for public use." He tried to wave Roryn back the way he came. His stiff gray hair, slicked back at the temples to cover his thinning crown, did not move with his brisk gesture. "You'll be pleased to seek the common areas for your common endeavors." The man's speech ended with his nose stuck further in the air than should be possible.

Finally, Roryn's relief was palpable, a sour being suited to his own personality! This was a man he could understand.

"Ah, then I made a wise choice on selecting it seeing as I have never been called common in the entirety of my life." He turned his head just enough that the dragon tattoo picked up the sun streaming through the floor to ceiling windows bracketing the large door where they welcomed their important guests. He could hear the man gulp as the realization of whom he addressed filtered past his indignation.

Roryn tilted his own chin higher, the stubble hazing his jawline somehow adding to his royal visage instead of detracting. He shifted his burden and offered it to the older man as one of his station would be expected to do.

"I'm sorry, your grace." The man gave a nervous bow, taking the proffered saddle bag without hesitation, but holding it at arm's length as it began to make a sound not unlike that heard during the death throes of a wild boar. "I was not made aware of your arrival."

"Please do not address me as such. General T'Yanil will suffice." Roryn cracked his neck and flexed the sore muscles in his shoulders as he took in the glittering crystal chandelier lighting the foyer and the marble main staircase that was the focal point of the entry. The opulence in this room made him squirm. "It is," he muttered, "the most common of my purposes."

"Quite so, General, sir." The man handily ignored his sarcasm. He beckoned to a slight girl with rosy cheeks and bouncy brown curls who stood stationed patiently at the foot of the grand staircase. "Take this to the Regent General's rooms, please, Meyloni." The girl rushed forward and attempted to curtsy while grabbing the bag, which was easily half her size.

"Please don't take that to my rooms, Meyloni." Roryn passed her the smaller satchel he always carried slung over his shoulder while traveling. It contained his documents, drawings, and the sigil ring Praxxys insisted he carry to seal any written correspondence between them. He motioned to one of the footmen at attention near the formal entryway. "You may take this to my room, Miss Meyloni. He," Roryn lifted the saddlebag away from the girl and handed it to the young man, "may take this directly to your master of the kitchen."

The creature took that moment to pop its ugly head out of hiding, its hideous nose, complete with wiry hairs and flopping tongue, wrinkled the skin on its bare forehead as it attempted to sniff its potential new home.

"What in the Bright's Salty Navel is that?" The girl squeaked, her blue eyes wide on the creature the footman was now dangling at the very edge of his reach. Roryn laughed, though it took him a moment to remember and savor the feeling of true humor.

"I've been calling it the Death Nugget."

"You intend we eat it?" The older man seemed aghast, the white streaks of his full eyebrows meeting in bafflement. He'd heard the new regent was from the unknown wild country at the edge of the known world but, surely, they still had taste buds there?

"Sorry," Roryn was anything but, however his mother *had* taught him the manners fit for a prince once upon a time, "I did not catch your name." He arched one black eyebrow impossibly high, a talent that used to drive his older brother insane.

"Hartfello Loxlei, Master of the Keys, at your service my Gr ace..er, General, sir." The man stuttered, his eyes glued to the raggedy, nearly toothless thing attempting to chew its way out of his saddle bag. Roryn didn't blame him. He was of half a mind to burn the entire satchel even though it contained the majority of his meager belongings.

"I'm here to spread the emperor's reign, good man, not rampant disease. No one is expected to eat that thing, but I thought the Kitchen Master might have some concoction suitable to bathe away its smell." Everyone in the room looked at him as if he were crazy. Maybe he was.

"What?" He raised his palms, feeling the touch of embarrassment pinking his cheeks. "It was a gift."

Hartfello Loxlei was the first to break out of his shocked stupor, expediently shooing his understaff back through the door normally reserved for the less common denizens of Castle Malorn.

"Your rooms, General T'Yanil?" He was austere elegance once again as he made his way up the grand staircase, trusting his new regent to follow. The Master of the Keys began a droning monologue on each feature of the castle as they passed. Beyond memorizing the layout of the hallways and public rooms in case a battle broke out within the walls, Roryn didn't bother to listen. The Second King's Third Wife's favorite settee, covered in silk imported from the high reaches of the mystical island of Tanburr held no interest to him. He didn't believe it to be of interest to anyone with a heartbeat.

After an interminably long time, and several barely repressed yawns, they arrived in the lush west wing of the palace. They passed many closed doors before ending up at a stately double door at the very end of the hall. As his title suggested, Hartfello Loxlei pulled a ring of keys from his belt, thumbing through them before separating out a larger key with a scrollwork pattern. He opened the doors with a flourish and stood back. "Your room, sir."

More than ready to report back to Praxxys and find himself a bed, Roryn stepped through the doors in eager anticipation. Almost immediately his mood turned as sour as Hartfello Loxlei's face. Every inch of furniture was covered in white fabric or white paint, accented copiously in gold. He turned around, a grimace pulling his entire countenance into a strained pucker.

"Are all the rooms so," Roryn waved his hand, searching for the right word to describe something so anathema to his warrior's upbringing, "fluffy?"

"The Malorn family private chambers were decorated according to their individual tastes, your...er, General T'Yanil. Which were decidedly less ostentatious than what is provided for our esteemed guests."

"I'm assuming this was Norc's chamber?"

"He did prefer the best Castle Malorn had to offer."

"Not to remind you of your tragic past," Roryn really didn't care what painful memories he left the man to deal with. The Master of the Keys seemed the sort that loved being reminded of his disappointments, "but you are short two princesses. Perhaps one of their rooms is less..."

"Fluffy?" The man provided helpfully, already shutting and re-locking the doors. "This way, please."

Another ten-minute tramp up and down halls and stairs, this time in blissful silence, led them to a secluded turret tower facing the peaceful line of trees that marked the beginning of the massive Dunshyre forest making up the greater portion of Hlyn's north and eastern borders. Roryn stepped down the three steps into the expansive chamber and felt like he had come home.

"This room belonged to our most beloved second princess, Tempest Anyabella Rutherstan Malorn. She wasn't fond of hordes of people encroaching on her rest and preferred a simpler environment in which to escape the trials of royal expectations." Hartfello made his way to the sconces hanging at regular intervals around the walls, lighting each one with a snap of his fingers. Surprise touched Roryn, not something that was easy to do. He would have never thought the cold man capable of the rage necessary to fuel fire magic.

The light wasn't necessary with the bank of windows circling the room, broken up only by the quaint fireplace opposite the entryway, but Roryn was thankful for it, nonetheless. The long inner wall provided space to the left of the door for a heavy wardrobe and dressing area. To his right, an enormous bed sat upon a dais, covered in faded blue velvet and shimmering pearl sheets. More than a dozen matching pillows in varying fabrics lay fluffed and ready to accept a sleepy head. Those, Roryn shook his head at the odd fancies of women, would have to go.

"I'll leave you now, sir. Meyloni will have had time to refresh your belongings and will bring your evening meal unless you prefer to dine in state?"

"A tray will be more than adequate. My thanks." Roryn patiently waited for him to back out the door, ignoring his bows. The click of the door latching into place was the finest music to his ears. Alone at last. Hartfello Loxlei was correct in assuming he valued his privacy. It had been too long since he'd felt even a semblance of it. For so long he'd been surrounded by the eyes of those wanting something from him, it was a blessing from the Bright to have even a mote of relief from the pressures of leadership.

There was only one last duty he had to perform before he could truly relax.

Roryn unlatched the bracer covering his right arm as he approached the small dining table situated so that it captured the best light the rising sun had to offer. He let the metal cuff fall, its heavy silver edge scoring a gouge across the otherwise pristinely polished cherry wood. With a bare sigh, he dragged a dirty finger through the dark blood seeping onto pale skin untouched by the sun. He didn't care about a possible infection. Unlike the Dragonblade scar, any inflammation would heal. Eventually, he always healed.

His boots were muffled against the soft rugs as he made his way to the long mirror adjoining the wardrobe. He captured another drop of brilliant red blood on his fingertip and used it to draw a sigil, one Praxxys taught him before sending him on his first campaign, onto the cool surface. He saw his own reflection staring back at him for a brief moment, dark circles under eyes that were no longer familiar, before it blurred. The magic was fast, searching throughout the known world for the master who had created it. When it cleared, solidifying into the reflection of another room and of another man, Roryn closed his eyes and prayed that the Bright would sear the resulting image from his memory.

"I am not going to ask why you are naked."

Praxxys strode away from the mirror where he had just finished drawing his own sigil to answer Roryn's call. The younger man averted his gaze, only turning his attention back when the Warlock Emperor had reseated himself in the massive hide-covered chair propped close to the roaring fireplace.

"I was hot." He stated, sweeping his open palm across his taut stomach to wipe away a trail of sweat. He flipped through the book he had been carrying and sat it carefully on his lap, his finger trailing slowly across blood-red lines of ink while he hummed happily under his breath.

"A smart man would put out the fire, Praxxys."

"The book is made of putrefied fyrewyrm hide. It only opens when it reaches a certain temperature." Praxxys responded in an absent manner, clicking his tongue against the roof of his mouth. He drew in a sharp breath, freezing half-way through a paragraph. Then, seemingly satisfied with what he had found within the pages, he slammed the pale blue book shut, tossing it into the flames without a thought.

He reached beside him for the large bowl of cool water the servants had been replenishing all afternoon with a relieved sigh. With great relish, he lifted the large porous sponge soaking there and began to squeeze it with his powerful fists. Sparkling beads of water drenched first his satiny black hair then ran across the sharp planes of his face, caressing his shoulders and mighty chest before pooling below his navel.

"Ah," he smirked at Roryn, savoring his disgruntled disapproval, "that is better." For all their wild ways and penchant for danger, the Salvadonian people were rather...prudish. Water sloshed out of the bowl and onto the floor as he dropped the sponge back into it with a careless tilt of his wrist. "I assume you have reached Vyte and have the Hlyn well under control? I'm bored senseless here in Noxia and the wyrm skin was the most fascinating part of that book. Perhaps you can share some tales of ruthless beheadings or wrongly incarcerated children?" He propped his noble chin in his hand, resting his elbow against the multiple layers of fur protecting him from the hard arm of the chair.

"The people are content, other than a grumpy butler and one quarrelsome barmaid." Roryn loosened his belt and laid his scabbarded sword and sheathed dagger more carefully on the small table.

"No secret dissenters plotting to spill my Nightmare-rotted innards?" The Warlock Emperor sounded hopeful, but Roryn merely shook his head.

"Damn. Whyever did I bother to conquer Hlyn? It sounds like a dreadfully lame place for an evil overlord." Praxxys sat forward in his chair with a suddenness that had Roryn's hand itching to grab his blade. "Any news of my false-hearted Malorn princess?"

"Even though I have just arrived to take my regency in the palace, my time in Vyte has not been wasted. My sources say she is near. In fact, Eighth Company should arrive any day now to help facilitate her capture."

"Well done, my son!" Praxxys beamed, his smile eerily pale as the sun dropped below the horizon in Noxia, leaving his silhouette backlit by the fire.

Roryn's tense shoulders relaxed a fragment, followed immediately by his usual sense of self-loathing. He knew the emperor's praise should not comfort him. He did not ask, nor ever desire, to be an eternal slave in service to the mightiest throne in Telryuun. The Salvadonian prince that always lurked just below his skin, in the sacred places the souls bound to the Dragonblade couldn't touch, hated the pride that filled him at Praxxys' warm approval.

But he felt it just the same. And Praxxys knew. The Nightmare damn him, he always knew.

"Perhaps the quarrelsome barmaid would be game to participate in an activity more heated than an argument? You'd do well to seek such a fiery distraction to fill your undoubtedly boresome nights in Hlyn." The Warlock Emperor tried to divert the river of morbid apathy that was sure to flood Roryn. As he had many times since his unwilling indenture, the younger man allowed it.

"I daresay the sight of your hairless ass has shriveled my manhood indefinitely."

"Hmpf." Praxxys laughed, although his energy was no longer filled with fatherly good humor. "Then you'll have extra energy to find the girl and bring her to me before the moons swallow the sun. That, if you haven't guessed," his Brightest-blessed eyes glowed silver in the gathering dark as he waved his hand, dismissing the magic that held their connection through the mirror. His voice echoed stonily on his last words, "is a command."

A flood of agony shot through the torn flesh of his right arm, reminding Roryn that, despite the Warlock Emperor's teasing manner and insistence on calling him son, he was still a mercurial immortal whoreson. He grabbed the wound, gritting his teeth through the worst of the pain, blood seeping through his fingers and leaving hot splatters on the white marble floor. He staggered up the low steps of the dais and tore a pristine white sheer panel curtain from the canopy, twisting it around his arm to slow the bleeding. Feeling exhausted and defeated, Roryn threw himself back on the bed.

A sad, shaky inhale filled his lungs as he pushed all his conflicting feelings - rage, fear, pride, lust - deep inside the dark, broken shell that had once been a beloved brother and son. He closed his cursed eyes, a bedamned silver to match those of his conniving master. His soul, he knew, was irrevocably bound to the swirling inferno that was the Nightmare's last tenacious hold on the world.

He was lost.

Yet, he was not alone.

The gentle, yet spirited, smell of strawberries among the clover wafted from the pillow under his head, easing him into the darkness with a welcoming embrace. The whispering flap of a raven's wing as it landed protectively on his windowsill providing his lullaby.

Chapter Fourteen

Summer in Hlyn was a test in tenacity. Having just left the crisp vortex of cool air funneling down the IronRock mountain pass that separated them from the rest of the continent, the Outlaw Princess and her 'court' struggled to stow their extra layers of clothing as the humidity of the valley slapped them in the face. The shining white stone of Malorn Castle was a glowing beacon on the horizon.

Home.

Equal portions of hope and sadness battled within her heart, as it always did when they were so close to the city of her birth. The warm feelings of pride swirling and drowning in the angst that filled her at the thought that she would never walk those narrow streets or laze about in the decorative gardens again. Not in peace.

Dahlis finally got her blanket rolled tightly enough to strap to the back of Canelope's saddle and made quick work of binding it behind her. The water from her canister was still delightfully chilled and she gloried in its crisp, pure taste, coursing coldly down her throat as the hot sun kissed her face in welcome. She, for one, loved all the differences that combined to make Hlyn one of the wealthiest kingdoms in Telryuun. With its south border lined by mountains, the plains plateau to the west ending in sheer cliffs that dropped into the Byyrin Sea, and the north and east surrounded by the impenetrable Dunshyre forest, people from every race and background sought safety and thrived within its protective embrace.

Almost unseating herself as she leaned far to the right, she passed the flask to the blonde beside her who took a giant swig with a nod of appreciation. Verilee capped it and tossed it to the redhead bringing up the rear. Throat moist once again, she took up the conversation she'd been having before the spitting snow of the pass had left them tight-lipped and shivering.

"Do you think he'll support Hlyn in upholding the Malorn claim to the throne? The Warlock Emperor isn't exactly forgiving of traitors." Verilee pulled her feet out of her stirrups and crossed her legs in front of her, balancing easily on her mule's broad back.

Dahlis wished she could do the same. They'd been riding for hours now and every muscle below her waist was practically begging for relief. She rolled her shoulders and cracked her neck. The muscles of her upper half weren't exactly happy either.

"Many alliances have been solidified with the promise of a Malorn marriage in the past." Monika stated simply. She had a way of seeing the most efficient solution to just about any situation. It made her an excellent advisor and tactician but a terrible conversationalist at court. Dahlis gave a noncommittal hum, trying to think through all the pitfalls and advantages.

"Once we reach the safehouse I'll have an opportunity to think this through a little more thoroughly. I feel there is an angle I am just not seeing yet." She dropped her reins, knowing Canelope would stay true to the course they had chosen, and unwrapped a tie from her wrist. The wind had started to pick up, sweeping in the lush smell of hay that had been bathed in a good rain and dried slowly in the sun. It was another welcome scent, but it made seeing through her gloriously golden curls an aggravating hassle.

The ache beginning to build in her temples, combined with the weariness plaguing her soul made it very hard to think. "Anyway," she picked up the lead again, patting the mare on her sweaty white neck, "I am not overly convinced I'd make anyone a good bride, much less for a bull-headed narcissist like King Vray. No doubt we would be arguing every moment that he isn't preening before his mirror."

"Tempest would be a great asset for this one, Dahlis." Monika's statement bordered on heartless, but Verilee slowly nodded her agreement. A sick feeling gathered at the back of Dahlis' throat, mixing with the guilt and sadness she carried when it came to her little sister.

"I don't want to involve her." Not yet. The pang of her headache increased exponentially with the sour feeling in her gut. She didn't have magic in the same way that Tempest did, but no one could fault her instinct for survival. Change was coming. Five years of running from the past was coming to an end, an end she couldn't yet determine. She wasn't ready. "How about we discuss it over Father's 20-year port when we're settled in the old hunting chalet?"

Verilee smiled. She never overly felt the effects of alcohol, but she did enjoy the taste and camaraderie a glass brought her. "The ramshackle ruins of your family's burnt-out palatial mansion can hardly claim the name chalet anymore."

"Well," Dahlis laughed, her voice husky and jubilant despite her exhaustion, "the cellar remains intact and that is all that really matters, right?"

Verilee saluted her and smirked in agreement. "My princess is always right. Though I'd rather be anticipating a soft bed and a hard man."

Monika, her braid painfully tight, nary a hair daring to fall out of place, relaxed enough to let out a little snort of air, causing the other girls to giggle, knowing without seeing that the brilliant redhead was rolling her eyes.

Dahlis shook her head but smiled, nonetheless. It would be good to rest for a few days in relative peace. The chalet may now only be a ragged husk of what it once was, but it was within a day's hard ride of Vyte...and of the sister she had been feeling a growing need to check in on. Though if Tempest was in any mood to see her was another thing. Her sister was civility and grace personified but she was also the most stubborn and unforgiving chit to walk Telryuun when she felt slighted.

An itch began tickling the skin on the back of her neck and Dahlis immediately froze, her instincts kicking in and a full-scale burning flush tightened her spine. Danger! A quick scan of the fields surrounding them showed nothing but tall golden grass, rows of well-tended summer grain, and the shimmering cut of the Torynce river that divided it all. Her gaze shifted to the silent mountains behind them and her stomach dropped into her toes.

There! She stood tall in her saddle, focusing her golden eyes on the dust cloud filling the horizon. It wasn't large enough to indicate a troop of any real force, but it was also throwing up twice the dust of their own party.

"...she will undoubtedly agree with me." Her friends were still arguing in the way of boon companions without a care that they would actually hurt the other's feelings, although their voices were muted in the cloud of alarm that rushed through Dahlis' body. Monika glanced her way when she failed to respond, her slight smile transforming in an instant to a fierce frown.

Verilee's head swiveled to follow, taking in the line of horses in full gallop behind them. While their uniforms were a dark blur from this distance, the brilliant Rampant Dragon shields of the emperor's elite were more than apparent. "Shit!"

"Bright Blast our luck!" Monika laid her heels into the sides of her gelding, blasting past Verilee's startled mule who lurched into a clunky run, braying in annoyance as he attempted to lay his teeth into the offending beast. The slim blonde managed somehow to keep her seat and, within a breath, had her feet firmly back into her stirrups.

Canelope whinnied in alarm a half second before Dahlis leaned forward in her saddle, highly attuned to her master's posture and intent, she was in full stride before there was any need for a set of heels to her ribs. They quickly became a blur of white and gold as they chased across the wide dirt and shell road that bisected the very center of Hlyn. Dahlis peered under her arm and saw the distinct outline of eight...maybe, ten...men mercilessly whipping their mounts and gaining ground. Realization filled her the same time that Monika's voice broke through the heavy drumming of their horse's hooves on hard-packed earth.

"We'll never make it to the Midhlyn Bridge!"

"Then we fight!" Dahlis pulled Canelope's head down, slowing the mare abruptly and turning her in a tight circle to face the oncoming soldiers.

"Dahl!" Verilee's strained voice echoed along with the heartbeat in her ears. "The Coldwater Clench!"

Dahlis balked, the thought of taking their fight into the icy waters of the mountain fed river bisecting Hlyn and through the narrow gorge was horrifying. If they managed to escape the deadly rapids and get the horses past the sharp shards of rockfall lining the river's bank, they would emerge within clear view of Vyte.

The chance of all three of them making it out unscathed was slim, but it was possibly their only chance. And it provided an opportunity to ambush those hot on their heels that they wouldn't otherwise have. Dahlis didn't think for a moment that they weren't the intended target. She was just surprised it had taken them this long.

Cool shadows touched her face and she looked to the sky. Two ravens circled overhead, one black and one white, swooping and intertwining before racing away toward the rocky crags that bracketed the river and began the stranglehold that gave the Clench its name. She wasn't superstitious but it was an omen that was good enough for her.

"For the Honor of Hlyn!" Dahlis cried, echoing the battle call that was just as much a part of her as her own name. She raised her sword high in the air and spun Canelope toward the rocky split in the ground that would even the odds or commit them to the Nightmare. "Hiya!" She screamed, leaning close against her horse's neck, urging every last iota of speed out of the loyal mare.

It seemed that only seconds passed as the three outlaws drove their horses onto the narrow trail that disappeared into the stark white marble crags. Cold spray blasted them from where the river was forced to narrow against the small gap that provided its mouth into the Mesiayl Valley. They had taken this path a few times in the past five years, but it was never a fun experience.

Canelope slowed to a walk, tossing her head up and down in protest but stepping out gently onto the ever-changing sandbar that lined the south side of the Clench. Monika was studiously evaluating the flowing level of the water rushing past them, trying to estimate where the best place to ford the river was this time. Her gelding, Haiku, was steadily trudging along, his nose practically glued to Canelope's flashy white tail.

"Nightmare eat you, nag!" Dahlis turned in her saddle to see Verilee struggling with her reins, slapping her mule repeatedly with the loose ends as he refused to come one step further into the narrow crevice. "Pestilence!" She yelled his name, fear high in her normally gentle voice. She looked behind her and froze, all color, even the prominent line of freckles on her cheeks, fading from her face.

"Leave him!" Dahlis screamed. She attempted to turn her mare, but the narrow path wouldn't allow her to pass Monika and her mount without one or both of them falling into the deep and churning river.

"Go!" Monika unceremoniously loosened the ties to her bedroll and tossed it onto the stretch of quickly narrowing sand. "I'll take her up with me. Just get out of here!"

Dahlis heard a pair of raucous squawks above her and resolutely nudged Canelope into the freezing waters. Verilee would not soon recover from leaving her prized equine friend behind, but he would provide the distraction they needed to buy just enough time. If they were fortunate.

Deep chuffs of pain worked their way out of the mare's throat as the icy embrace of the Torynce closed around her chest. An answering mewl left Dahlis' tightly clenched teeth, frozen before it could fully become a sound. A giant splash heralded Haiku's leap into the water, Monika misjudging the depth in her bid to hold Verilee tight on the saddle behind her.

"Bright's Hairy Balls!" She moaned as the cold hit her at the waist. Dahlis had to smile, despite the situation. The redhead didn't lose her composure often, but the uncommon cussing meant that she had removed all stops to her temper. The emperor's soldiers were in for a surprise when they caught up!

Luckily, it was close to the end of summer in Hlyn so the river was running low. Their horses charged forward, gamely digging their hooves into the sandy river bottom and plunging through the rapids in great strides. Canelope surged forward three more body lengths and warmth began to bathe Dahlis' skin as they picked their way through strangled brush and out through a break in the rock. Never had she been happier to leave the Cold-water Clench behind her.

Haiku's light gold body stumbled into view, his legs shaking as the burden of carrying double caught up with him. Both girls jumped free, Monika slapping the gelding on the rear to send him running. Her slingshot was already in motion as she took cover behind one of the piles of rubble that marked the rockfall that had created the path through the Clench.

Verilee, having grabbed her bow from the boot of her saddle before leaving her mule, jogged slightly uphill and jabbed her arrows calmly in a row before half-drawing the tension. Her position put her behind where the men would be forced to emerge but, thanks to five years on the run, she had lost all compulsion to fight fair. An arrow in the back almost always worked better than one in the stomach.

Dahlis dismounted, shoving Canelope in the direction Haiku had taken. She knew they wouldn't go far but she needed them well out of the line of fire. She took up position, her sword held low before her, in the clearing north of the entrance. Any soldiers that survived the initial crossfire would be forced to meet her one by one.

They waited.

An echo filled the small canyon as the soldiers bottlenecked behind the grumpy mule. His screeching brays of indignation amplified the cacophony of noise as men shouted and bellowed at the cold. At least one screamed in horror before the sound was swallowed by the forceful rapids.

One heartbeat passed, then two.

Dahlis closed her eyes and said a quick prayer to the Bright, seeking out the pre-battle calm that had always filled her in the moments before she was forced to fight. She didn't crave the spilling of blood the way some warriors did, but it was her purpose, the calling of her bloodline to protect her people. If she failed in this, who, then, was she?

All at once, three men came rushing past the rocks, their horses dripping wet and fighting the reins. In quick succession, the front two went down, falling under the hooves of the third mount, causing it to buck and throw its rider into the mess of blood and broken bones beneath him. A second arrow from the hill pierced his throat and ended his thrashing.

Then the Clench seemed to spit the last warriors out, their horses well-trained enough to jump the jumbled pile of dead and dying with impressive agility, given the half-frozen state of their muscles. The two front men rushed toward Dahlis, their swords at the ready and their faces grim. A smile lit hers, turning the beautiful planes harsh. She bashed her hilt against the leather buckler protecting her arm. "Come fight me you mindless thralls!" she taunted.

Verilee's arrow missed its next victim as a sudden gust of wind lodged it into his saddle instead of his angry face. He charged up the small hill with unbelievable speed, raising his sword before she could bring her own weapon to bear. Thankfully, Monika's stones were even quicker, and a small but fierce pebble brought him tumbling down the slope just in time.

The clang of metal meeting metal rang out over the valley before Dahlis was even aware that she was in motion. It was like that sometimes. If she gave her movements over to the battle, if she let instinct guide her, then it was like the gods of war possessed her body. It was, perhaps, her very own brand of magic.

The fugue that came upon her had saved them in many skirmishes. It had certainly put fear and caution into Norc's handpicked men. Today though, she thought as she felt her muscles slowing and her swings became heavy swipes instead of just an easy extension of motion, it may not be enough.

The two men lingering just behind the protective screen of the rock, warily watching for more airborne missiles coming at them suddenly screamed and bolted forward, their horses half-rearing, trying to turn to face the danger closing in behind them.

A raucous neigh echoed down the cavern, ending in a horrible noise that could only belong to one bedamned creature. Pestilence's ugly face preceded his equally battle-scarred body into the valley. He stood for a second, head held high as if to survey his domain, before laying back his massive ears and moving into his signature jolting, gangly run. The calvary, so to speak, had arrived.

The obstinate mule was on a rampage. He kicked and bit his way through the men unlucky enough to be on foot. Even the mounted captain of the troop did not get spared his wrath as the heinous brute charged, butting the smaller horse in the side with his brawny chest and trampling both man and beast mercilessly under his dinner plate sized hooves.

As if they had trained in this maneuver all their lives, the three girls disengaged from their separate battles and began to run. The emperor's men, distracted by this new and imminent threat to their lives, gave little notice that their quarry was escaping. Nor did they wonder how they would explain this failure to their general. They were focused on surviving a demon the likes of which they'd never fought before.

Two sharp whistles brought Canelope and Haiku to their sides, Dahlis and Monika wasting no time swinging onto their backs. They danced nervously as a low-pitched whoop that grew in volume left Verilee's slender throat. The shadows of night had begun to surround them, but her smile was visible in all its glory. It was immediately followed by ground-shaking thumping as Pestilence gave up his vengeance to return to his master.

"I guess I won't turn him into mule jerky after all." Verilee gave the bastard, now bugling his dominance and showing his yellow teeth in victory, a brief hug around his ugly neck and pulled herself into his saddle.

They left the emperor's most elite soldiers behind, bleeding and cursing in the growing dark, and urged their tired mounts into a gallop as they left the opulent gates of Vyte behind and surged toward the treacherous depths of the Dunshyre forest. Dahlis did not spare a glance for the castle glowing with a brightness all its own, so temptingly within reach. She did not let the memories, or the responsibilities, or the regret touch her as she led her small entourage, the two moons slowly replacing the light of the sun on her back.

Someday, she would come back.

Someday, she would come home.

Chapter Fifteen

"T HERE HAS BEEN A ruckus, My Lord Regent."

Eighty-three. That was the number of times Roryn had rolled his eyes this week. Who knew that being an agent of the ultimate domination of an empire would be significantly easier than running one household?

"I told you not to call me that."

"My apologies, Sir Regent General, if it appears I am not inclined to pay much mind to your preference. I am, after all, a simple Master of the Keys serving the Glorious Empire to the best of my meager ability."

Roryn sighed and tossed his handful of carrots into the trough before Horse. He'd been in Vyte for just short of a week, but it had been enough time for most of the castle denizens to lose their fear of his nefarious reputation. Hartfello Luxlei, in particular, had decided he could exert the power of his position in the household to make snide, bordering on disrespectful, comments with impunity.

And the diabolical Scourge of Salvadon let him get away with it...because he found the uptight man irrationally amusing.

The stiff Master of the Keys cleared his throat and straightened his already impossibly erect spine, side stepping slightly so that he stole the very last of the sun's light from the dimly lit stall on which Roryn had been leaning. This had been the first evening he'd had a free moment and he'd been contemplating sneaking off for a late supper. Perhaps he would seek out an out-of-the-way inn where the barmaids had little control of their tongues? Ones that, perhaps, tasted sweeter than any wine served throughout the known kingdoms. Not, of course, that he'd been thinking of some insolent serving girl.

Irritation blossomed. It wasn't Luxlei's fault he was feeling like a caged werecat, but he felt the urge to pounce on him anyway. After all, the passive-aggressive self-aggrandizing peon was not *that* funny.

"What is meager is your ability to get to the point. Tell me, Harti," he stressed his own apparent ineptitude at remembering names, "what has so disturbed the ambience of this fine realm as to bring you so diligently to my side?"

Luxlei hmphed and straightened every starchy point on his black surcoat. Seriously? Who in their right mind wore wool in this heat? The fact that the man wasn't sweating profusely drove Roryn absolutely batty. He held up his hand.

"Wait. Before you accost me with any of your inane chatter about propriety or discretion or the abhorrent length of a maiden's skirt these days, tell me," He turned quickly and pinned the glorified butler with his deadly gaze, "what is your power? Don't be coy, I know a man of your stature has one."

Roryn was surprised when the older man began to blush. "That's neither here nor there, your eminence, may I remind you of the ruckus?"

"You most certainly can. After you divulge your main magic. I've been informed your fire forging is your secondary talent."

A full minute passed in which Hartfello Luxlei debated whether or not it was time for him to retire. Then he seemed to fold into himself, the stiffness melting out of his shoulders and spine with a giant sigh of submission. He began to move his slim hands in an intricate dance, swirling and dipping them around each other with delicate grace. Roryn watched, intrigued, as the movements became more rapid, more fluent...entrancing.

An audible pop filled the air as Luxlei ended his flourishing by holding his cupped hands mere inches from the general's face. Slowly, he opened them to reveal...a glittering bubble.

"Tada." He deadpanned.

"What does it do?" Roryn reached out and poked it. The jelly-like surface reflected light in beautiful rainbows as it gave softly under his finger. Luxlei's face turned redder, if that were possible.

"You asked about my magic. I answered. Can we proceed with the ruckus announcement?"

Roryn just folded his arms over his chest and arched his eyebrow.

"Fine!" The older man clapped his hands shut with a brisk motion, splattering the bubble between his palms. Globs of glitter danced off the tips of his fingers as he shook them clean. "It's a bubble. It does nothing and serves no purpose. Ha!" His exclamation left no doubt as to how flustered and stirred up he was. "Just as an emergency declaration does when one is not allowed to declare it!"

"It takes that much effort to make the one?"

"It is possible to mass expel in a more impressive manner, of course. I merely was being expedient while preserving a notion of propriety in this entirely useless display of magic." Luxlei folded his still sticky hands together piously in front of him.

"Wait…do you fart bubbles?" Roryn's voice was a mix of disbelief and laughter. He physically had to reach up and pinch his lips together behind his own hand to keep from guffawing in a fashion entirely unsuited for a regent.

"Now," Luxlei bowed stiffly, obviously clenching to preserve his dignity, "I will be retiring to my chambers for the remainder of the evening. If you would like to ensure the injured men that have arrived under the emperor's banner survive, I suggest you'll find them lingering in the Lower City Barracks." Luxlei wobbled off into the dark toward the castle without waiting for a dismissal, cursing violently under his breath.

Roryn echoed his sentiment and threw open the door to Horse's stall. Looks like he'd be taking that night ride after all, just not in a manner he'd prefer.

Vyte had many guardhouses sprinkled throughout the city, fully staffed with the eager second sons of the country hoping to distinguish themselves and provide honor for their families. Even though times of war were few and far between throughout their modern history, they were once a nation of esteemed warriors, much as the Salvadonians had been. How Praxxys had subdued them with barely a fight was a question Roryn had never discovered a satisfying answer to.

Though crime and aggression were nearly nonexistent in Vyte compared to the other large cities he'd traveled through, each constable accepted into a guardhouse had been vigorously trained and had to pass a rigorous set of tests to make a placement. They even held regular competitions between guardhouses to showcase their martial skills. The warriors of Vyte may be complacent, but they were not without tremendous skill.

The only thing keeping those men and women from joining the ranks of an outlaw army in support of a Hlyn free of the Glorious Empire was the fact that the princess had not yet called for them. When she did, the Nightmare would be sure to witness a great deal of bloodshed. All of this rushed to the fore of Roryn's mind as he stepped into the ornate foyer decorating the Lower City's Market Street Guardhouse.

"First General!" The sharp salute from the desk officer was gratifying after this week's dealings with Luxlei and his ilk at the palace. The young man stood erect, stepping away from the massive desk carved with the rose sigil of Malorn, and giving a deep bow. A glittering line of gold trophies stood sentinel behind his strongly muscled back. Roryn gave a crisp salute back, setting the man at his ease.

He was inordinately pleased to be recognized on sight. Not because he craved the notoriety, but because it signified the Hlyn soldiers were just as well-informed, intelligence-wise, as they were well-trained in the combat arts. If they were his troops, they would be undefeatable. The fact that they were only nominally under his command did not lessen his appreciation of quality training. Hartfello Luxlei aside, Hlyn was shaping up to be a kingdom to envy.

"I was told several of the Empire's soldiers are being treated here. I'd like to be escorted to them immediately."

"Yes, sir, First General." The man led the way to the single wooden door and opened it with a swift sweep of his hand over the elaborate lock. Roryn hid his surprise at seeing a metalist using his talent so transparently, as if it was of minimal value. In the army of the emperor, he would be an advanced soldier, using his power at the front lines to direct spears through the hearts of his enemies, earning untold accolades and war prizes. Here, he rode a desk and unlocked doors.

Expecting more lavish accouterments, he was further surprised to see plain wooden walls hung with the occasional worn tapestry or badge of honor from decades gone by. Each simple door he passed was left open, easily accessible to all. An officer's hall, a mess hall, a large room filled with training equipment and one with neatly made bunks where those on shift could choose to stay if they did not live close by. The final room in the hall was the only one with a closed door. This time, the desk attendant turned the knob, pushing inside slowly so as to not disturb its occupants. He stepped aside but did not leave.

"General T'yanil!" There were a dozen beds in the spacious room, five of which had occupants. One man sat on a chair beside the bed of another, slowly dragging a wet, cool rag over the forehead of his compatriot. He stood, tossing the rag into a large bowl being traded out for a fresh one by a bowed old woman with the bone-strewn necklace characteristically worn by the hedge healers in this region. Roryn returned his salute briskly as a few of the other men struggled to sit upright.

"At your ease, please." He said quietly. He nodded his thanks at the guardsman and grabbed the chair next to the man he recognized as the captain of the Eighth. "Dougan." He greeted.

The man had a large moon-shaped cut sewed closed on his cheekbone, but it was red with gathering infection. He grimaced as he placed his heavily wrapped foot on the floor, the bloody bandages on it and wrapped around his chest gave clear signs that they had met a truly dastardly enemy.

"Who did this to you, Captain?"

"Me?" The man huffed then clenched at his side as a wave of pain shot through him. "I was attacked by a mule."

Roryn looked at the other men in the room, each in various states of disrepair. "You were all attacked by a mule?"

Dougan laughed, although it was a weak effort due to the spasm it sent shooting through his broken ribs. "No, First General, sir. Well," he admitted, "three of us were laid low by that steel-footed denizen of the Deep Nightmare passing itself off as a mule, but the rest are casualties of the Outlaw Princess." He coughed and Roryn pushed lightly on his shoulder, assisting him into a prone position. "I saw her myself. A beautiful sight, to be sure."

Oddly, the other men in the room, the conscious ones at least, nodded in agreement. Roryn filled the small bedside cup from the pitcher of cool fresh water left beside it and offered it to his captain. He waited for the man to collect himself before he continued his story.

"We came upon them fresh off the pass. Three girls, First General, barely even old enough to claim full womanhood. We knew it was her, right away, given her golden hair. It gleamed with the sunlight even from as far as the mountain." He took another sip, weary and aching but able to hold himself up without undue effort. "We followed them through the pass and into a cut in the river. They ambushed us and, unfortunately, we lost two men before they set that Nightmare beast on us and escaped."

The First General was at a loss. There was true admiration in the man's voice, even mixed as it was with sorrow for the deaths of his men. The unhealing gash under his bracer throbbed, reminding him he had no sympathy for enemies of the Empire and no loyalties other than an undying devotion to the Warlock Emperor.

"Did you see where they went?"

Dougan nodded, setting the glass with finality on the blanket beside him. "Yes, they entered the Dunshyre forest by the Cliffsend Trail. My sources say it tapers off not far into the woods. I hear there used to be a small sea-side cliff village used as the summer home destination of the Vytian elite, but it is in ruins now."

"Don't worry about her, Captain. I'll see to her capture myself." Not that he particularly cared to see another royal enslaved the way he was. Praxxys, however, he thought as blood began to seep through the bindings of his bracer, would have it no other way. He changed the subject, standing and looking around the dimly lit room. "How are your men?"

"Madam Bluxlin and a sawbones have been in, but a fever has set in for a few of us. Mostly some broken bones and bruises." He pointed to the glaring wound on his cheek, "That Bright-blasted mule had hooves as big as my head and as dirty as a Borarian whore. I'm afraid the infection is settling in me as well. You'll be down a few more soldiers before the night is through."

Silence coursed through the room as those men still awake turned blank stares to the ceiling. None of them would bemoan their fate, although a few eyes were wet as their thoughts turned to the family they'd left back home. Roryn knew they served the empire for the same reason as he himself did...they had no real choice to do otherwise. Rage snuck its way out of the far crevice in his soul where he kept it hidden. He couldn't escape Praxxys, he didn't even know if he wanted to anymore, but he would do whatever it took to see these men live.

"We need a Healer. Not an old woman washing wounds with rotten leaves! Why haven't you called for one?" He turned an accusing stare on the unfortunate old woman. She calmly dumped her bowl of water into the sink at the far end of the infirmary and took her time drying her gnarled hands on her apron. Her eyes were sharp, the light green orbs surrounding her dark as night pupils seemed to cut straight through Roryn.

"Oh?" Her voice was strong, easily crossing the distance between them as she reached into a voluminous pocket, pulling out a handful of carefully dried herbs which she crushed into another bowl. "How many Healers does your precious Warlock Emperor have? Perhaps you should ask him to lend us his?"

"Everyone I have met in Vyte has some level of magic. You're telling me not a one of them can heal?"

"Seems to be, I ain't telling you anything." Madam Bluxlin reached into another pocket of her apron, withdrawing a worn stone and nonchalantly began grinding her leaves into powder that she dumped into a tumbler of waiting water. Never once did her piercing eyes leave the Salvadonian and Roryn had the distinct feeling she was as resentful of Noxia's rule as Luxlei, just not as good at hiding it.

"I know one, Sir." Roryn broke away from the witch's gaze. The metalist at the door rubbed a spot on his hand nervously, as if he was unsure he should admit the fact. "Well, I think she is the real deal."

"Excellent. Can you bring her here...?"

"Meryl. Sir." He cleared his throat and shifted back and forth on his large feet.

"Yes, Meryl. What is it? I must warn you, I am about out of patience." Out of patience and getting crankier by the moment. The unhealing wound beneath his bracer was throbbing painfully, the curse echoing in every vein. Painful in its reminder that his quarry was just a horse ride away and this delay was not in the emperor's best interest and, thus, wasn't important. "Just spit it out."

"She'll be free to go afterward, First General Regent, sir?" Meryl's cheeks were tinged pink as he stepped outside of his comfort zone by questioning a superior. Nevertheless, his tight stance and steady eye contact confirmed he wouldn't be condemning the girl to a life of forced servitude to the Empire.

"Does no one in this Infernal Darkness you call a city understand the meaning of treason?"

"Yes, sir. Sorry, sir. She's...she's just..." His throat cleared once more and he squeaked out, "special."

Roryn's growl woke the unconscious man, causing him to start thrashing and moaning. Five long strides had the new regent of Hlyn at his bedside, helping to restrain the man. There was a swift shuffle behind him and the hair stood up on the back of his neck for a second before a cup was thrust at him.

"For the pain and fever." The woman's voice was gruff, and she began to mumble about evil minions not being of the same quality as they had been in her day. She picked a piece of chalk out of her bodice and began to draw a large circle on the wood panel. When it was completed, she spat on her hand and slapped it dead center. A shimmer started and quickly became a swirling vortex that the woman quickly disappeared into. A wet slurp heralded the closing of the portal and every man in the room stared blankly at the wall for a second.

"You must have pissed her off. She usually waits for the door."

"Go get the Healer, soldier!" He yelled, patience officially nonexistent.

"Sir, I..." Meryl's feet had led his body toward the exit without his volition. Still, he hesitated.

Eighty-four. He'd have to have the Healer examine him. There is no way so much eye-rolling hadn't caused him some degree of brain damage.

"I promise I will not lay a murderous or enslaving finger on your precious girlfriend. You just better hope she is what you say she is! Otherwise, I may find myself inclined to take your insolence out on her.

Chapter Sixteen

"**D**OES THIS SKIRT MAKE my butt look big?" Porta swirled the hem of her frilly blue taffeta dress in a semi-circle around her, pulling at some of the bows littering the front. The contrived grimace on her face didn't detract from the pleased smile hiding behind her eyes. Their time in Vyte, it seemed, had dulled the girl's edges, both literally and figuratively. It would take more than a few regular meals and a safe place to sleep to make anything about Porta soft, however.

"A dress full of ham shanks couldn't make you look less stick-like." Tempest shoved the post of one of Juli's least ostentatious earrings into the space where her plain silver studs had been and winked at Porta in the mirror. They were both feeling pretty in the borrowed and altered gowns Juli had insisted they wear for 'The Performance'. She'd even brought in extra help for tonight so her 'girls' could enjoy a night of dancing and revelry.

Her own dress was a sleek confection of red silk, perfectly fit to accentuate every curve Tempest hadn't realized she possessed.

If confidence and seduction were something one could wear, this dress would be it without question. Straightening from the mirror, her eyes caught on the flesh pushed uncomfortably into prominent display above her neckline. The white creaminess of her breasts seemed almost to glow against the sultry brilliance of her dress.

Huh, she thought, those were new.

"At least I'm not sticking out of the top of my dress like I have two pork butts strapped to my chest." Porta whistled and snapped her fingers in quick succession, her version of a standing ovation. "If you make it down the stairs without those unbalancing you and sending you tumbling to a painful death, you will probably make some poor gentlemen hungry for bacon." Tempest turned in a huff and tossed the dress' matching silk purse at Porta's head in a half-hearted attempt to get some respect. She wasn't mad though...they did look nice.

"Don't think I didn't notice you stuffing your bodice with Juli's honey rolls."

"I don't need boobs yet. I wasn't using the space for anything else, may as well save some snacks for later." She snagged another bun off the tray and shoved it down the front of her dress. "See? I'll even pack one for you since you are all out of room."

"Uh huh." Tempest had been hungry plenty of times in the past five years, but she was never so starved that she would eat bodice buns. Especially since, knowing Porta, there was no telling what else she had shoved down there before the rolls.

Looking around the small dressing room built into the corner of the extensive apartment that made up the third floor of the Evermore Inn, Tempest spotted the brush Porta had tossed on the settee and picked it up. She gently pulled the long black and red hairs out of its bristles, letting them drift out the open window and into the street below, then began to run it through her own, brown-tinted curls.

"It was nice of Gustavia to take in these dresses for us on such short notice." She said, speaking of the friendly seamstress that ran a shop down on Market Street and was Juli's very best friend. Tempest fingered the silk at her hip and did her own brief twirl in front of the mirror. The material clung to her chest, stomach, and thighs and belled out slightly below the knees, creating more of a 'swish' when she moved versus the 'swoosh' of Juli and Porta's gowns. "She did a really good job. Even in the palace my clothes were never so elegant."

"Gussie's a hussy."

"Porta!" Tempest gasped then scrambled to readjust her cleavage after the sudden movement.

Thin shoulders shrugged. She grabbed a second roll and began to nibble on it, sending crumbs rolling down her front as she opened her mouth to defend her opinion. "It's not her fault, really. If her parents didn't want her to be naughty, they shouldn't have given her a name that rhymes with hussy."

"That statement doesn't follow any rules of logic."

"Neither does your face."

"Girls!" Juli appeared in the curtain-covered doorway that led into the bedchamber she shared with Dax. "Stop your Bright-blasted bickering. I swear the urge to join in and begin caterwauling myself is almost too much to resist. You know I must preserve my vocal cords for tonight's performance."

Juli's glorious red hair was piled into a towering coiffure studded throughout with sparkling diamonds. The mound of curls, combined with her stiletto heels, made the already statuesque songstress absolutely impressive. Every inch of her curvaceous body was swathed in a vibrant yellow fabric designed to catch, and keep, every eye in the room.

"Oh!" Porta dropped her skirts and ran over to circle Juli, her blue gown pressing insistently into the older woman's as she stood on her tiptoes. She began to twist her own simple braid into a lump on the top of her petite head. "How'd you get those jewel-things to stick in your hair? They are so pretty."

"You'll keep your grubby hands off my diamond hairpins, brat. They were a gift from the Queen." With brisk movements, she pulled a small container of faux sapphire pins off her vanity and popped a few of them in place to secure the young girl's braid in a soft loop over her pixie-like ears. She surreptitiously slid the remainder of the container into one of the blue dress's pockets, knowing how much they'd be cherished when Porta found them later.

"It's not stealing if I ask first." Porta said, once again using her non-logic. Juli let out a lofty sigh and turned sharply on the pointed heel of her gleaming snow-white pumps. Matching diamonds glittered at her neck and wrists, with tiny fragments sewn into strategic swirls throughout her skirt.

"Come along." She swept out of the room and Porta's thin body, swallowed as it was in too much fabric, trailed close behind. Tempest ran her hand through the brown curls she'd left loose, soft and shiny despite their dull color. She hadn't had a proper cut in a long while, so the tresses spilled down her back to pool in the shallow indent above her buttocks. One last look in the mirror showed that she carried her own special shimmer in the random gleam of golden locks that refused to submit to the indignity of the dye.

She yanked the fabric panel partition closed behind her and followed Porta's chatter through the bedroom, past the living quarters, and through the final door at the top of the staircase. The joyous sounds of a full house below warmed her heart. She didn't normally care for having so many souls packed so close together, but each one pinged against the protective shield she had wrapped around herself with little explosive fragments of joviality. Tonight promised to be one of those rare nights of happiness that she would cherish during the trying times to come.

"Maybe Meryl will take pity on you and ask for a dance." Porta turned to look at Tempest over her shoulder, batting her obscenely long and dark eyelashes. Juli hesitated long enough to rap the girl's fingers with her bone-handle fan as they reached once more for the pins in her hair.

"My sweet Meryl is busy guarding the kingdom and won't be coming tonight, more's the pity." Juli transferred the fan to her left hand and gripped the handrail, her steps regal as she descended. She was already wearing her stage face, as she liked to call it, equal parts untouchable elegance and steamy sin, and a loud cheer shook the very walls of the Evermore as friends, neighbors, and strangers alike caught sight of the songstress.

"Good luck, Juli!" Tempest's call was lost amid the cacophony of howls, claps, and whistles.

"I'm going to go sit behind Gussie and see who she sneaks out with. Maybe if he's all pimply and stuff I can blackmail her into making me a handbag to match this dress." With a maniacal chuckle Porta disappeared into the crowd. Despite her being the smallest person in the room, Tempest had no trouble tracking her progress through the inn as she elbowed, pushed, and cussed her way to the table behind the seamstress. Tempest shook her head, but it was a movement filled more with fondness than despair.

To her left, Dax was busy filling tankards and piling them on the trays that were quickly taken away by the girls they'd hired in for the night's festivities. It was early in the night, but the poor things were already shifting from foot to foot and rolling their necks to loosen their shoulders. The pockets of their aprons were heavy with smallcoin though, ensuring they would be eagerly waiting to be hired for the next performance. She began making her way behind the bar, but Dax smiled and shook his finger at her.

Tonight's concert, he'd told her earlier, was intended to honor the day they had opened the inn. They couldn't say it out loud, but if it hadn't been for the support the King and Queen had given them all those years ago, the Evermore would have stayed a dream. Both he and Juli had made it a point to insist she enjoyed the night. There would be no work for her.

She waved at him and sent a curtsy of thanks in his direction. She scanned the packed building and slowly worked her way closer to the door. It was stifling hot in here already and that would only get worse as the night wore on. If she was lucky, a nice breeze off the mountains would be funneled into the entrance from time to time. It would be a shame to perspire on such a beautiful dress.

She tucked herself against the back wall to the right of the door, the gaudy gold and blue wallpaper at her back reminding her very much of the dresses Juli and Porta wore. She ran her hands down the slick fabric covering her stomach and was thankful that her borrowed dress didn't blend in with any of the Evermore's decor.

"Hey!" She protested as someone ran into her elbow, setting her teeth jarring with the force in which her head bounced off the wall. She turned to the clumsy intruder with fire in her eyes that quickly transformed to pleasure as she saw Meryl standing in the doorway with a harried look in his eyes. Evidently, he had forgotten how huge of a crowd his aunt drew with her special events.

"I didn't think you could make it tonight!" Tempest reached for his wounded hand before stopping herself. He may not want everyone in the Lower City to know he'd been injured. It wasn't like she needed to check his wound either. If there was one thing she was confident about, it was her ability to heal the bites of tiny demons. "Your aunt is going to be ecstatic!"

Realizing he was being talked to, Meryl looked down, his face blank for a second as he took in her appearance, trying to place where he knew her from. Tempest smiled. She was sure she looked nothing like the barmaid he had met a handful of times. "Miss Twoshoes! I'm sorry, I didn't see you there. I'm actually not here to watch Juli, I…"

The first soaring notes of Juli Marcoyne's voice stopped every breath in the room as all other sound, and, it seemed, even time, stopped for one brief heartbeat. Whatever worry or fear or heartache had come into the room was suspended as hope, love, and brotherhood found a foothold in every gathered soul. Unbidden tears filled Tempest's eyes as she was flooded with emotion.

Just as she felt she couldn't contain the sensations flowing through her, charging her magic and electrifying her every nerve ending, the music stopped. Almost as quickly, a bevy of cheers filled the air. Mugs were lifted and a round of applause threatened to shake the Evermore off its foundation stones.

Meryl leaned down, his mouth only inches from her ear. Tempest struggled to understand what he was saying but the crowd was still deafening. She shook her head, pointed to her ear and shrugged. Juli swept her hands and the crowd, many of them veterans who never missed a single show, went silent at the cue.

"I am here to see you." Meryl's shout echoed about the suddenly quiet room. Suggestive chuckles turned Tempest's cheeks bright red, turning into unabashed guffaws of good humor as she grabbed his big arm and yanked him out of the Evermore.

"I freaking told you!" Porta's yell of victory followed them out the door.

"For all the Light of the Bright!" Meryl cussed as the relative peace of the Lower City enclosed them. Stars could be seen over the roofs of the surrounding buildings and the two moons set low, barely visible over the high wall protecting Vyte. "Sorry," he turned to Tempest, embarrassment written all over his face. "I didn't mean to shout. I..."

Tempest was bent in half, laughter shaking her shoulders with its ferocity. Seeing his masculine face tight with horror as she ushered him out the door had immediately transformed an awkward moment into absurdity.

"Yes," Meryl stood straight, folding his arms over his chest. "Ha, ha. Have a laugh at the big bungling idiot daring to wear a guard uniform. Are you quite finished?"

She tugged her dress back into place as she straightened, fighting to stabilize her breathing. The laughter felt so good, even if it had been partially at her expense. Poor Meryl looked properly aghast at her reaction, but she couldn't help riding the wave of delight still echoing off of the people inside the Evermore.

"I apologize, Meryl, I'm not laughing at you, I promise. And please don't call me Miss Twoshoes. It's an absolutely horrific name."

He cracked a smile, but a seriousness lurked behind his eyes that sobered her. Now that she was paying direct attention to him and wasn't in a room filled with exhilaration, she could feel him nearly vibrating with anxiety.

"What is it?" She asked. This time she didn't hesitate to grab his hand. "I can tell something is wrong."

"I have a big favor to ask of you, Gutra." He swiped his free hand through his hair and shifted a bit away from her. As sure as she hated that name, she knew he was as hesitant as he was desperate.

"Your aunt and uncle have helped me out more than I can ever repay. Of course I'll help."

"That's just it. I know Dax and Juli are Loyalists and, I'm pretty certain, you are too. What I have to ask may be in conflict with those beliefs. I don't want you to hate me or be hurt. I don't even know why I promised him..." His voice trailed off as his thoughts went internal. From the dark cloud that took over his face those thoughts must have been intense. She dropped his hand, and his eyes shot to her.

"Wow. You really may be a big bungling idiot. Spit it out and let me decide."

"You know," he cocked his head to the side and gave her an appraising look from under his lowered brows, "I never believed you were related to that little black-haired minx, but I am starting to see the resemblance."

"Be careful," she wagged a finger in his face, "those are fighting words, and I have access to every bowl of perpetual stew you eat."

"Do you have the power to heal?" He had finally taken her advice and spit it out, surprising her for a moment into silence. "There are some seriously injured men down at the guardhouse, a few of them not expected to make it till morning."

"Yes." She admitted quietly, looking around to make sure they were truly alone. "I'll do what I can for them, but you understand it's not something I want known? It could cause me a tremendous amount of grief. Healers tend to disappear when people in power hear about them."

"I won't be spreading it around. I wouldn't have mentioned you at all but knowing how my aunt and uncle feel about Princess Dahlis, I thought it was best."

"Wait! What does she have to do with this?" Fear coursed through Tempest. She could feel Norc shoving against her shield, insistently knocking, kicking, and punching against it. She pushed back harder, taking a deep breath and strengthening the cage she kept him in. She grabbed Meryl's arm and began walking toward the street, tugging at him to hurry. If Dahlis was in trouble, they couldn't waste any time.

"The injured men are Noxian Elite. The princess and her compatriots are responsible."

Tempest stumbled for a second in her heels but righted herself and continued on, bunching her skirt around her knees so she could walk faster. He was correct. The emperor may not care if those men died but he would use their deaths as a reason to increase the patrols searching for them. It would only be a matter of time before he found them all.

And then what? Whatever he would do to them wouldn't be good. Not after five years of defiance.

Chapter Seventeen

"**T**HE PRINCESS ESCAPED UNHARMED? And the others?" She gulped. She didn't want to ask. She had to know.

"Evidently, they were unscathed...thanks to a mule."

Tempest laughed under her breath, relief filling her along with an urgent need to save the enemy soldiers. Stupid, stubborn Pestilence saved the day, that had to be a first. He had bought Dahlis some time, she could do no less.

"Ah," she could feel his eyes on her back, questioning her silence. "I suppose a well-trained ass-assin is a good thing to have at your side?" A weak laugh left her lips and she couldn't help but grimace at the effort.

"I hope you heal better than you joke." He touched her shoulder lightly, pointing at the small, dark red door she'd almost walked past. "There."

The door opened before they could turn the handle. A harried young man with wild red hair and an eye-catching spray of freckles greeted them. His uniform was a mirror of Meryl's except for the yellow band sewn onto the upper arms with 'cadet' scrawled in large black letters. "Guardsman Meryl! The Captain of Outer Watch Post requires your presence, sir. Immediately," he added. The Adam's apple in his thin neck bobbed erratically.

"Fucking shit." Meryl looked at her and shrugged in apology. His cussing wasn't the worst thing she'd ever heard but it was sweet of him to be concerned. He cleared his throat, but no words came out.

"Go," she said, "I've survived this long on my own."

"My aunt would kill me if I didn't escort you back to her door. I'll return before you're done here. I promise."

The cadet just seemed to notice her presence. His watery blue eyes dipped to her chest, setting fire to his cheeks while his throat continued to bounce spasmodically. For his peace of mind, she ignored him completely. She was here to heal soldiers, not a boy who was three heavy breaths away from passing out. She turned toward the only other door in the room, striding forward as fast as her balance would allow in her spike-heeled shoes. She stopped abruptly, staring blankly at a door that had no handle.

A big arm brushed her side as Meryl reached forward. She barely saw the faint scar on his hand as it danced intricately over the wood. A click sounded loudly in the small room as the door unlocked from its frame. Tempest's mouth formed a perfect circle as she looked up at Meryl in surprise.

"Metal magic? Impressive." Her praise had him turning red again. The man wouldn't make a great spy, but she didn't need spies. She needed friends.

"The infirmary is behind the door at the end of the hall. You'll be OK?" He pushed the door open and stepped back.

"Of course. I'll see you at the Evermore for lunch this week?" She felt she needed to have a long conversation with Meryl to feel out where his loyalties lay. He may call himself a bungling brute, but she knew without a doubt he'd be a valuable asset to the cause. If he was amenable.

He nodded and she slid through the door, already feeling the pain of the warriors inside. She lowered her skirts and smoothed them as she stalked past several open doors. Before she knew it, she was one wooden panel away from her sister's victims.

The thought gave her pause. Were these men worthy of healing? They represented an emperor that had lost his sympathy for humanity ages ago. Did that make them wrong, or just pitiable?

Who would she be if she started deciding who was deserving of her gift?

The door squeaked on its hinges as she pushed it wide. Her magic thrummed under her skin, but it wasn't her healing energy reaching out, ready to assess her patients. It was that other all-consuming feeling, the one she had grown to crave. The one that made her uncertain and wary. She slapped on a smile and stepped confidently into the room, cussing softly through her gritted teeth.

"I really must be the unluckiest girl in the entirety of Vyte."

"You?" Roryn knew his jaw was hanging slack, not a good look for the Scourge of Salvadon to ever assume. "You're the Healer?" He shook his head, and she watched the tail of his braid swing slowly with his disbelief. Her compulsion to touch it was mind-boggling. It was just hair, she told herself. If her mother would see it, she wouldn't hesitate to label it as not very dignified hair, what with the stiff dark strip stretching from his forehead to the base of his neck and the shaved sides revealing gaudy blue dragon tattoos.

Warning signals started shooting through her mind, crying desperately for her attention, but she had no ability to pay them any heed. He was wearing a crisp but casual white shirt left to hang loosely against the sharp jut of his hips. Black trousers with pressed pleats ran down the strong length of his legs, the hems decorated with tiny bits of golden horsehair, and ending in…two open-toed leather sandals?

She mentally shook herself, the sight of his nearly bare feet enough to break the crazy hold he had on her.

"And you are the ass-rabbit pulling me away from a rare and much-needed night of revelry." She curtsied, spreading the red flare of her skirt around her in a display worthy of a king's daughter. The irony that she clearly intended with the movement was lost on Roryn as her breasts shifted forward, practically spilling over her bodice. Her words took a second to register.

"Ass-rabbit?" His well-shaped lips curled into a smile.

"Can we just get on with this? I have a dance to attend, and these men are getting bored with our discussion."

"Oh," the man with the head wound said giddily from his bed, "do go on. I'm not quite sure which of you is the rabbit and which the ass, but your eyeballs are gyrating like loose children's marbles and it is excessively amusing."

"Madam Bluxlin was here, hmm?" Tempest arched an eyebrow and left her nemesis behind, carefully looking at each man as she walked past their beds. "She takes great pleasure in making her patients loopy. I must say her concoctions leave no room for pain."

"The pink fox that left through a hole in the wall?" The man's question went unanswered as he giggled and fell back onto his pillow with a goofy smile.

"Please," Roryn gestured and pulled a chair close to the grinner's bed for her, "why don't you start with him."

Surprisingly, she didn't argue. Neither, though, did she take his chair. She seated herself carefully on the edge of the bed, tucked up close against the soldier's side. She reached forward, smiling as she brushed her fingers lightly over his flushed forehead, pushing a few sweat-darkened hairs back into his hairline.

Roryn's knuckles turned white as he gripped the chair's back. "Do you have to touch someone to heal them?" He couldn't contain the grit in his voice as a surge of irritation filled him.

"Do you have to touch someone to kill them?" She spat back while still smiling sweetly at her patient. Although there were no outward signs of his injury, Tempest's magic was immediately drawn to the swelling gathering under his skull. Left untreated, he would fall asleep and never wake up.

"Not always." Roryn said shortly.

"Well, me neither." She admitted, "but it certainly makes it easier." Tempest touched her lips to the soldier's forehead. It was an unnecessary gesture, but the low growl from the tattooed bully staring so intently at her brought her an obscene rush of pleasure. She didn't know what his problem was…he was the one that had accused her of immorality, why should he be surprised that she'd not hesitate to touch a man in pain? But she did find she enjoyed needling him.

With a big, tall shadow seemingly stalking her every move in the infirmary, Tempest made quick work of clearing away bruises, fusing bones, and closing lacerations until only the captain of the guard remained. Like any man of integrity, he had insisted his men be healed before him. She felt satisfaction that she hadn't withheld the full extent of her power in healing these men. They may be the emperor's men, but that did not mean they were truly her enemy.

"That's an impressive wound, Captain." She sat back on her heels beside his bed to examine the gaping gash across the entirety of his cheek revealed by the bloodied bandages. It had the distinct crescent moon shape of a very large hoof. Pestilence was unruly but she had never thought him dangerous until this very moment. She'd have to start sneaking him extra carrots to keep on his good side.

"You seem fairly lucid after being in Bluxlin's care." It would have been better had he been insentient. This was more than a simple laceration and would be very painful to heal.

"When Masyn began babbling about three-headed goats nibbling his toes, I told that witch to take her potions elsewhere."

The valiant man attempted to smile, the skin of his cheek pulling into a traumatic grimace. Tempest didn't hesitate at that point. She touched his temple with two fingers as her other hand pressed the free-hanging flesh back into place. Blood seeped down her arm, pooling in her elbow briefly before disappearing into the redness of her skirt. She gritted her teeth as the captain's agony leaked through her defenses.

She tried to assume his pain, but he was fighting her, somehow knowing what she was doing and unwilling to let her absorb some of his burden. She marked his bruised face in her memory. This was a man worthy of saving. A true gentleman that her father would have been honored to welcome into his personal guard.

"Stop that." She admonished. She yanked her hand away from his cheek for a second and lightly tapped it with a gentle slap. It worked to distract him, and she was able to pull his pain away completely before resuming her healing. The cheek was the greatest of his injuries, but she soothed a sprained ankle and a slight concussion before letting her hands fall into her lap.

Excellent work, girl! These men will live to hunt you and your sister down like the churlish ingrates you are. Tempest wanted to ignore Norc's soft, pleased voice but it echoed her own uncertainty, slipping easily past her guard. Her lips tightened, carving deep unsettled creases in her cheeks where there should have been dimples of satisfaction at a job well done.

Should I remind you the emperor is the one who invaded our land? You killed our father. I don't understand why you hate us so.

Seriously? Norc spirit let out an eerie cackle. *I'm dead because of you. I don't know what you do for fun around here, but I can verify being inside you is lame.* Tempest saw a shadow image of him in her mind, waggling perverted eyebrows. She shivered with disgust, much as he had intended.

If you were truly dead, I would certainly be in a better mood. She slammed the wall back into place, her frustration lending her the strength to bind him once again.

She stood, her silent conversation with Norc leaving her too frazzled to be mindful of her fatigue and swayed dangerously in her heels. Before she had even realized, two steely arms wrapped around her from behind and she felt herself being pulled against a chest harder than the bare ground that had been her bed for years.

"Easy, there." His words tickled her ear, the gruff tone setting fire to...well, she didn't need healing magic to sense exactly where this particular illness was centered. If the spark of awareness running up and down her spine was any indicator, his body was experiencing its own corresponding flash of heat. "You are truly amazing. I've never seen someone heal like that." His words of praise caught her off guard. "Let me take you home."

Tempest's breath stuttered in her lungs and her confused senses battled for a moment before reason reasserted itself. "Meryl will be waiting for me. He brought me here and has promised to return me."

"Even though it seems you are on more-than-familiar terms with the guardsman, I must insist."

She shook off his hold and stumbled forward, not stopping until she had put the captain, his bed, and his footlocker between them. She dared to meet his eyes, hot blue diamonds scattered in their snowy gray depths with her own warm golden gaze.

"That is completely unnecessary. I'll be on my way now, without your heavy-handed presence, if you don't mind."

"I said I will escort you. You'd do well to listen, girl." His eagle-sharp eyes lost any fragment of blue as cold silver bled through his irises. He took a menacing step in her direction. Tempest gulped but calmly continued to walk away. Rule number one of being a Malorn princess was *Show No Fear.*

The captain reached out swiftly, grasping his commander with an autonomy unexpected of one of the Emperor's Elite. "Don't hurt her, First General T'Yanil. The ravens are never wrong." With those cryptic words, his eyes rolled back into his head and he slipped into a deep, healing sleep, his fingers locked firmly around Roryn's wrist.

Tempest had frozen with her hand on the door. All the blood rushed from her head and her knees began to shake. The hair. The tattoos. Fear coursed through her but she somehow managed to grasp the knob and pull it open, slipping through the hall until she stopped, trembling against the metal-locked outer door.

T'Yanil. First General. He was the Scourge of Salvadon? This strangely charismatic stranger was the emperor's most trusted man and the new Regent of Hlyn? Next to Praxxys himself, Roryn T'Yanil was the man most likely to bring death and dishonor to her family. It couldn't be true.

But she knew it was.

Damn Meryl and his big bungling blue eyes exhorting favors! She couldn't wait for him to return. What if T'Yanil figured out who she was? She could tell, from the glimpse she'd stolen before leaving the infirmary behind, that the soldier's words had intrigued him. She had to get away.

Now.

Darkness suffused her blood and for once she didn't hesitate. The death magic filled her with self-hatred even as it danced on her delicate fingertips, like little electric lightning bolts jumping from each of her short, soap-worn nails. She let them build, her palms beginning to glow, flashing white and red and white again. Pain arched between her hands, zinging up her elbows and touching her heart. It enfolded her softest emotions. It engulfed every good intention she'd ever held. It strangled her empathy.

It...felt so good.

"Argh!!" With a violent slash, she slammed her hands against the door, the cursed magic eating away at the integrity of the metal rods inside, making them fragile and burning the wood that had held them steady for a century. She closed her eyes, breathing hard as two black hand-shaped outlines appeared in the panel above the lock. If seen, they would be a dead give-away that she wasn't who she claimed. She didn't care. She was done in Vyte.

A crack sounded as the iron failed and the door swung wide. Rage still running high, Tempest paused to pull off her heels, slapping them down on the pristine desk and leaving an ash smear in her wake. She dared the new regent to come after her. He didn't know who he was dealing with. Norc hadn't. Malorn princess rule number two was *Take No Prisoners*.

She stepped out into the night.

Chapter Eighteen

T HE FORMER QUEEN OF Hlyn was not a happy woman.

Roryn groaned as he left the stable to see her standing still and straight at the rear entrance to the formal gardens. Mirabel Malorn was the epitome of class and good breeding and had never been less than pleasant, even though his very presence had to be a painful reminder of her husband's death.

Her still-dark hair had been let down from the stringent coif she kept it in during the daylight hours and was bound into a loose braid that caught and reflected Hyginn's pale light. Even the dark moon seemed to favor her, softly bathing her skin in a caress of shadows and wiping away the crow's feet and worry lines exposed by harsher light. Despite her beauty, an essence of sorrow lingered in her eyes.

She reminded him, in a way, of his own mother.

"Walk with me?" she asked. Her voice was quiet and unassuming for one who had been born to rule, but it had not yet failed to get his attention. Once she had that, he'd realized almost instantly, she was very good at getting whatever other concessions she desired.

"It is very late, Your Highness." Roryn attempted to prevaricate. He wasn't in the mood to pull punches, either metaphorically or physically, and despite her frail appearance, he wasn't sure he could win an all-out battle with her, even if he wanted to try. He had a pretty good idea of what she wanted to speak about and there was no hope it would be a positive experience for either of them.

After leaving the Noxian Elite safely asleep in their cots, he had stalked out of the Lower City Guardhouse with an unsettled feeling that was as unfamiliar as it was unwelcome. In his unbound youth, he had been passionate and hot-headed to the degree that his brother had often bemoaned his reckless impulsivity. Although he had perhaps been the bane of Tarwyn's existence, his people had celebrated him as being one of their fabled Firehearts, elemental warriors that, with extensive training of both mind and body, were capable of controlling the very essence of the sun.

Praxxys had changed that with his curse. The dark magic that bound him in unwilling service to the emperor took away not only his autonomy and the prowess of his magic, but also dampened every emotion, every need, and every desire that did not directly serve the Empire. The Warlock Emperor had not only stolen Roryn's future, he'd taken his flame.

For the past quarter of a century, he had not even cared. The curse hadn't dulled his mind, but it had erased every morsel of empathy, every drop of pleasure, every fond memory that had made him a true prince of Salvadon. He didn't enjoy leading endless armies in a seemingly aimless quest to unite the known world, but someone had to rule them. Why not Praxxys?

Under his metal bracer, the wound on his forearm eased, the lack of pain telling him the magic that bound him was pleased at this logic. It was proof that he, himself, had not changed. The curse had, letting bits and pieces of the Roryn from before slip through the cracks. There was only one new aspect of his life that could account for the change.

That girl, no simple maid, it seemed, but a healer of court-worthy talent, was responsible. She was claiming entirely too much of his attention at a time when Praxxys was giving him too much of his. If the curse was sentient enough to realize her worth to the empire, and sometimes he swore he felt a canny presence lurking in the dark shadows that held him tight, she would be the next 'asset' to the empire to be forced into servitude. Oddly enough, that was something he didn't want.

What he wanted was to keep her for himself.

Like the trifant worm that lived in the swamps of Salvadon, she had crawled under his skin with a ferocity that should concern them both. A fire was building within him once again, but it could only lead to an inferno of agony. The thought doused him in a heavy deluge of reality, sobering him as well as the curse ever had.

"I understand." The woman in front of him stated in her gentle voice. "As I am no longer a reigning queen, however, please call me Lady Mirabel." She made little sound except for the slight brush of her long skirt against the stone as she turned toward the castle, but desolation rolled off her in waves even he couldn't ignore.

"Wait." Roryn's exhale exploded in the otherwise silent night, but it was an expression of surrender, not anger. "Please." He angled his arm toward her and offered his escort through the night shrouded gardens. "I may be a bastard of the worst sort, but my mother raised me to be a gentlemanly bastard."

"We are all the worst sort at something, Regent T'Yanil."

"Where I was from, we had no true titles. Certainly not something so stiff and unpalatable as Regent. I'd prefer if you'd call me Roryn." He cleared his throat, feeling unaccountably uncomfortable. "Hlyn was blessed under Malorn rule and that was due to more than just the late king's influence. I can't imagine you having a fault deep enough to be considered a failure."

"Oh," she turned her pale face up to him, completely unafraid to be walking arm in arm with the man who had caused the death of many in the name of an empire he'd never sworn to serve, "I would have thought it obvious that I have little aptitude for being patient."

Despite her declaration, they continued to walk in relative silence, their lightly shod feet softly rasping as they walked along the crushed shell path. The wind picked up, dancing through the shrubs and long grasses surrounding them, carrying with it the last haunting notes of a song without words. The muffled clapping and hoots of approval tapered off, marking an end to a night's revelry deep in the soul of Vyte.

Roryn felt calm begin to settle into his muscles as the sounds of a city existing in peace began to soothe away his vexation. At the edge of the greenspace, meticulously tended to replicate the wildness of the landscape outside its gates, Vyte was dotted with the gentle glow of lamps, their golden illumination broken by the occasional shadow of a carriage making its way slowly across the cobbles.

"You've heard of the attack outside the gates, I assume?" Roryn stopped beside the stone bench a few feet from the still water of the largest of the decorative ponds. He had found himself gazing upon it from the windows in his tower room far above, its placid depth dotted with lily pads in full bloom, the perfect backdrop for retrospection. He swept his hand down, indicating she should sit. Lady Mirabel shook her head, refusing his offer. Instead, she broke the brown flower top off a cattail and began to slowly strip it, letting the fluff fall through her fingers.

"Hartfello had said there was a ruckus." As a confidant of old, he'd actually had more to say on the matter, but that wasn't knowledge she felt obliged to share. If Dahl and Tempe had been in that skirmish, and her mother's intuition told her they had, then she needed to know if they had survived. She held out hope that someday they would be reunited, whether as a free country or under the emperor's heavy hand made little difference to her. In the meantime, she ached for any news of them...no matter the source.

"Two men dead and another handful grievously wounded is more than a mere scuffle."

"I'm sorry to hear your men are suffering," she really wasn't, but her mother had also raised her to avoid being a bastard, "but what about the girls? Have they been injured?" The second she waited for his response seemed to be one of the longest in her life.

"They were last seen hightailing it into the Dunshyre. As hale and hearty as notorious outlaws get, anyway."

"What will the emperor do?" Roryn had to lean closer to hear her whisper. He considered his response before speaking. He wanted to tell her that he'd seen two very different sides to the emperor, and they constantly seemed to be out of balance with each other. He'd known Praxxys to be benevolent and considerate to those under his protection. He'd also seen him randomly choose the nearest unlucky soul to feed the blade when it was hungry. He had experienced each first hand. The emperor cared...until he didn't.

In the end, the curse held his tongue.

"It's no secret he has plans for Princess Dahlis, although I am not privy to those particular machinations. Only two of his soldiers died, neither under the princess' blade. I'm inclined to think he could be bargained into leniency. Which might not have been the case had the Healer refused to tend them."

This time Lady Mirabel sat, relief stealing the strength from her legs. She tossed the loose handful of torn vegetation into the lake when his words caught up to her. Surging to her feet, she moved as fast as the warrior she was rumored to have once been.

"A true healer?" She interrupted him, being so bold as to clutch his unguarded forearm, her manicured nails leaving half-moon indentations in his skin. "Not that charlatan Bluxlin?"

"If I were to admit to knowing the location of a healer, it would put her in danger. I will only say, I am not easily impressed. Today was a rare experience." He watched her carefully, his lashes hooding his eyes. Her face, normally as stoic as it was refined, was alive with expression.

A thousand thoughts marched through the former queen's head in quick succession. Was the healer in Vyte Tempest? Why had she been left behind when the other girls escaped? She hadn't seen either of her daughters in five years, would she even recognize the young woman she'd become? If she hurried, could she see her youngest daughter before she disappeared again?

Her brain froze on that last possibility. She had sent her daughters off in the dead of night when she'd gotten word that Hlyn had fallen. Benevolence had been a small child at the time with a broken leg that she'd refused to let Tempest heal. She had intended to follow them in a borrowed carriage, but Norc had shown up and sealed the gates before she could arrange it. It was her fault they'd been separated...but if they could convince the emperor to forgive their crimes? If they could finally come home?

"I need to see this healer right away." She demanded. Her feet were swift on the path as she hurried back toward the castle, trusting him to follow. A flush decorated her fine-boned face as she scooped her skirts up, only stopping once she had reached the heavy door of the stable. Without waiting for his assistance, she began pulling at it, opening it inch by squeaking inch.

His hand folded around the iron handle, and she stepped back to let him draw it open. He did no such thing, waiting for her to look at him. "Well?" She stomped her foot in impatience and Roryn got his first glimpse of what he thought was the true queen of Hlyn.

"As I said," he was intrigued by the hint of panic running under her plea, "it is late. Perhaps I can arrange to contact her tomorrow."

"Please," her slim, chill hand reached out, barely grazing his forearm before being retracted, "there is no reason for you to attend to this personally. If you'll tell me where to find the healer, I will go myself. Tonight."

"You do not look ill, Lady Mirabel. In fact," his eyebrow arched though the gesture was lost in the gathered dark, "you look quite lively."

"It's Benny." Her shaking hand cupped the base of her throat. "My son, Prince Benevolence. He...he has a wasting sickness," she turned to look at him, but her eyes were pinned to a place just above his shoulder. "I didn't want anyone to know, but if I can see the healer, I must."

"As Regent, however unwanted, I am responsible for you and your son's welfare." He pretended to be weighing his options. He didn't believe for a moment that the thick boy he'd seen playing with the hounds in the courtyard was in any imminent danger of death by starvation.

A tick began at the corner of her mouth as she finally met his gaze. He could swear she was biting her tongue and wondered if it was simple stubbornness or something more. Whatever caused her angst, instinct prodded him to play along. He bowed respectfully, although it was much shallower than was strictly proper and pulled the stable door wide.

"I'll get my horse."

Chapter Nineteen

"**A** KITTEN WILL BE welcome at camp. I'll teach it to be the fiercest of rat killers."

A teeth-jarring screech filled the air, startling Tempest enough that she almost dropped the steaming pouch of perpetual stew that Juli had foisted on her. She'd tried to leave it behind but the older woman, with tears in her eyes, had insisted it would provide them with all the nutrients they needed to survive the horrors of the deep forest. If nothing else, the smell would keep predators at bay.

She meant well, Tempest knew, and she would miss many things about her stay at the Evermore Inn. The stew was not one of those things.

"I thought we had decided after Morti there wouldn't be any more pets."

"If I had Morti, I wouldn't need something to eat rats now, would I?" At first, Tempest had felt bad about foisting the rabid dog-creature onto a stranger, but since discovering that she'd literally given him to her worst enemy, she felt much better about the decision. She steadied the sloshing bag tight against her body and flung an empty burlap bag at Porta.

"I'd be worried he'd be committing acts of cannibalism. I'm still not certain he was a dog."

"I don't know why we can't wait until morning to leave." Porta's whine echoed across the empty courtyard between the Evermore and its stable. She was still wearing her fancy party dress and took a moment to pull up the top skirt, wrapping it around the kitten gingerly in an attempt to tame its flashing claws. Once it was subdued, still except for an ongoing low growl promising a painful death, Porta shook open the sack and began to dig the rolls out of her corset one by one. After a humid night of vigorous dancing, Tempest decided she might prefer the stew after all.

"You are seriously asking why we need to flee a city run by our second-greatest enemy?" Tempest drew in a deep breath as frustration threatened to spill over into a verbal battle she would have no chance of winning. Porta wasn't smarter than her when it came to winning a disagreement, but she was definitely more stubbornly tenacious that her viewpoint was right, even when it wasn't. Anyway, Tempest knew the real reason the girl was making a fuss.

"He didn't seem so bad." Porta's lip extended in a full pout. She'd been without a true home for almost as long as Tempest. The Evermore Inn, and Juli in particular, would be hard to leave behind. "His face was more unhappy than it was mean. Maybe he'll just trap us in the Palace with the rest of your family."

Tempest stopped, grabbing Porta's shoulder and waiting patiently until the girl turned her moss-green eyes to her. Her long lashes were damp, proving that sometime between when she'd ushered her off the dance floor with the bad news and when Tempest had cornered a triumphant Juli to express her goodbyes, the girl had found a moment for her softer emotions.

"I need to know that you're with me on this, Porta. You know," she kept her voice soothing and steady, the way she'd treat a skittish horse, "you can stay here. No one will think less of you for wanting that." The girl yanked out of Tempest's grip and stalked toward their back-of-stable room, her legs making strides longer than they should have been able to manage. She let out a forced laugh that was matched by an equally loud hiss from her folded skirt.

"You would be dead within a day if I didn't come along to save you." Porta's cocky smile was back in place. "Remember the time I rode Polli Nan to your rescue when you were stuck in the middle of that stampeding herd of goats?"

Tempest pushed back her sweat-dampened curls, grimacing as her hand came away with a faint brown stain. The heat was causing the coloring to streak. That could be problematic if she didn't find the supplies she needed to redye it, but it was an issue for another day. She had enough to worry about.

"I seem to remember that you unlatched the gate that released said goats and that I had to stand between you and a group of angry shepherds determined to paddle your rear."

"You must be misremembering, Tem. It's OK, that happens when you're old, I hear."

Porta hopped the last few steps to the stable and disappeared inside. Relief filled Tempest followed by a flood of worry and guilt. Being hunted and on the run was no place for a child but, in some ways, Porta had left her childhood behind long ago. The truth was she'd miss her little 'sister' if they ever parted ways, and wasn't that the most selfish feeling she could have?

Tempest lowered the pouch of stew and rested it against the rough wooden side of the building. She took a second to stretch her back and pull the bodice of the red dress as far up her chest as it would go. Now they just had to grab their horses and the saddlebags stowed under their cots and they could leave. She wished she could talk Porta into changing into their riding leathers but maybe it was better to ditch the dresses once they were well on their way.

"Going somewhere?" The deep masculine voice stopped her before she'd cleared the stable's threshold. Excitement and fear lit the dark areas of her soul as she spun around.

Porta's startled breath echoed abrasively loud to Tempest's ear, but the scourge of Salvadon's expression never changed. A quick flick of fingers behind her back warned the girl to stay out of sight. The slight scuffing of her taffeta skirts as she stepped further into the darkness was loud in the cavernous building, forcing Tempest to step fully into the courtyard to face the man who was destined to be her enemy.

"It's not like you've left me much choice. My kind can't develop roots if we don't want them to be planted in a powerful man's garden." Her steps were strong and sure as she came forward, even though she was almost quaking inside.

A crash sounded in the shadows of the stable that made her cringe, startling her enough that she was nearly standing toe-to-toe with him before she realized it. Porta always made everything harder, even when she wasn't trying to.

Tempest squeaked unintentionally as Roryn T'Yanil grabbed her arm and shoved her behind him. A short knife was in his hand before she had even caught her balance, leaning heavily into his back for an instant too long. The scents of clothing freshly laundered in the palace mixed with an intoxicating fragrance of masculinity flooded her nose, leaving her with old memories of clean blankets on cool nights and new urges she didn't dare put a name to.

"Let go of me!" She whispered. Or did she scream and the noise was muted from the sound of her heart beating out of control in her chest? Her attention seemed to narrow to the point where his hand lay protectively against her rib cage, pressing her firmly into his fiery flesh. Was every man capable of causing this reaction or was it his unique magic? She felt woefully uneducated when it came to the opposite sex. She should have paid Verilee more mind instead of covering her ears.

"A bit jumpy, are we?" He joked, but his eyes were still locked onto the dark space, intense and shining, as if he could see clearly, not only what lurked in the dark, but also what truths resided in her heart.

"I was about to get my horse and go, if you don't mind releasing me." She tried to shift away, but his hand merely trailed down her side, grazing the rise of her hip before he unerringly grabbed her wrist.

"Maybe I should take a look? Seems to me a girl like you would never find herself alone. There could be a man full of dark desires waiting to grab you."

"Maybe he's not inside." She shot back, a zing of pure lust streaking through her when he looked down with the wickedest of grins upon his face. Roryn lowered the dagger, and his eyes fell to the plump swell of her lips. Tempest gulped as she found herself unintentionally leaning back into the raging energy swirling surrounding him. Instinct took a strong hold on her, pulling her weight onto her toes in eager anticipation, as she realized he was going to kiss her.

And she wanted him to.

An ear-shattering caterwauling pierced through the veil of passion that had captured her right before a tiny gray ball of fury came hissing and spitting out of the building. Roryn straightened and Tempest took the opportunity to yank her arm from his grasp, shaking as she put one breath of space between them, then two.

Porta would be heartbroken to lose her assassin-in-training, but her quick thinking in releasing the dervish had most likely saved her from capture and saved Tempest from a decision she would undoubtedly regret. She was obviously in no position to make any life-changing decisions. Her eyes were drawn to his hair, pulled back in a tight braid that accentuated the black and blue inks decorating his skull. An urge to reach up and trace the patterns was almost too much for her to resist.

"A girl like me?" She breathed, jolting as his words hit her. Anger replaced the confusion and wanton ache building inside her like a fall into the glacial waters of the Torynce. "I'm sure I'll be overjoyed to hear what you mean by that."

"A girl like you." He stalked after her as she took several steps backward, the practical heels of her riding boots reverberating hollowly on the cobbles. She wondered if her heart would ever find a normal beat again. "Beautiful." One step closer. "Seductive." She could feel the heat that surrounded him like a blanket enfolding her, encouraging her to come closer, to be near him, be with him...if only for a little while.

A snort sounded and a curious puff of air lifted her hair as her retreat was halted by the broad side of a horse. One hand crept to her throat as the other felt behind her, searching for anything she could use as a weapon but finding nothing more than the mare's soft underbelly. Damn this stupid dress and its lack of concealing pockets! If he was set on hurting her, she only had one defense. One she had sworn to die before using again.

Then, his body boxing hers in, his face inches from her own, he tipped her chin gently upward, forcing her to meet his gaze.

His heat engulfed her, radiating from his silver eyes flecked with vivid blue streaks. She drew in a shaky breath when his thumb traced the bow of her lip, entrancing her. Every nerve ending was electrified and focused solely on him as a single word sounded against the corner of her mouth.

"Mine."

His upper lip tasted her lower one, a bare brush, not even a kiss, merely a promise. His words registered and, before she could examine the consequences, she sent every bit of force she could build into a solid punch to his kidney.

"Umph." She knew the hit hadn't caused any damage, she doubted he had even felt it, but it served its purpose as he drew back in surprise. She darted past him and gained a few steps toward escape before his iron grip manacled her wrist once again.

She didn't fight him, it would do her little good as it was rumored that his strength had been preternaturally enhanced by the Warlock Emperor's spell work. Having felt the rigid intensity of his body against her own, she was inclined to believe it.

Fortunately, her mother had taught her that there was more than one way to win a battle. She forced every tense muscle in her body to relax. She planted her most vexing smirk on her face and laughed. "I belong to no man, least of all you."

"Delusion is a common female affliction."

Alright, now she was going to hurt him. She balled up her fist but relaxed it as a playful smile lit his face, emphasizing that he had once been a carefree boy her own age. It was a revelation that had her catching her breath again. Was the Scourge of Salvadon...teasing her?

As much as she'd love to explore this aspect of him, and maybe find a true reason to place a well-aimed kick to his manly region, she could feel Porta's agitation building in the stable behind them. She wouldn't stay still long, and Tempest couldn't jeopardize her safety just because she was having fun bantering with the enemy.

"Why are you here?" Her question was blunt but had the desired effect as he released her hand, sure she wasn't an immediate flight risk. His disappointment was palpable that she had given up so easily. "I know you didn't seek me out merely because the opportunity to taste my lips was too tantalizing to resist."

His eyes began to glitter in the dark, the warm blue tones overtaking the chilly silver. "As to that, you might be surprised." She swayed unintentionally toward him, a spike in his energy drawing her in despite herself. She shook her head and took another step back as his smile turned knowing. Forget shielding herself from Norc's ceaseless chatter, she needed to find a way to protect herself from this man!

He sighed. "As much as I'd love to show you exactly what those lips can do to a man, you are correct. I need you to come with me."

"Not a chance." Tempest left no wiggle room in that statement. She didn't trust him and, if the yearning plaguing her was any indication, she couldn't trust herself.

"You'd leave your prince to suffer?"

"You, sir, are most certainly not my prince."

With an easy show of grace that left her in no doubt of how strong this enemy of hers was, Roryn grabbed her and in one fluid motion lifted them both onto the patient palomino's saddle. His arm pinned her tightly against his chest, her backside pressed indecently against the soft fabric covering his iron-hard thighs. Tempest gulped, speechless, as his fingers settled on the bare flesh of her own thigh, exposed wantonly by the high slit cut in her dress.

"We shall see about that."

Chapter Twenty

"I'M NOT GOING IN there with you. It would be like a sacrificial maiden walking willingly into the dragon's mouth." Tempest stood outside the giant double doors of the room that had once been her parents' bedchamber. Undoubtedly, it had long been claimed for the use of the Regent, and she had just, without much complaint, walked herself directly into the maw of the monster.

"I'm under the impression that you would not do anything I asked willingly." He reached over her shoulder and rapped on the door. "Fortunately, I'm not the one you're here to see."

Not even a full second had passed before one of the doors swung open and Tempest was confronted with the presence of the mother she hadn't seen in half a decade. Her knees went weak and only through sheer willpower did she remain unmoving. The chance to catch a glimpse of her or of her little brother had been the only thing keeping her compliant as they had moved through the deserted halls of the palace.

Mirabel Malorn stared hard at her youngest daughter, her eyes devouring each feature, cataloging the changes and accepting that every slight, visible scar hid a dozen inner wounds. Minute expressions of sorrow, sympathy, and regret chased across her stoic face, nearly indeterminable except for the miasma of feeling flooding Tempest's magical senses. Finally, her examination landed on Tempest's red dress and lurid display of cleavage and the sad emotions began to mix with disappointment and horror and guilt.

Tempest nearly broke as her mother's response dimmed her joy. She had always sought her mother's approval, to the point where Dahlis had often teased her about her almost obsessive need to be the 'favorite' child. What her sister never understood was that Tempest had been born knowing she was second. Second in line for the crown. Second in beauty, grace, and martial aptitude. Second, sometimes third, in any affection her parents spared her.

Being a proper lady was the one area in which Tempest was inherently better than Dahlis. Like the fine linens and pristine marble stone of her birthplace, this was another aspect of her former life that had been irrefutably taken from her by the Warlock Emperor's rule. The only thing left to her was her stubborn pride. Which was another category in which she came in second...but she didn't begrudge Porta that win.

"Your Majesty." She bowed low, keeping her hands folded timidly in front of her and her eyes lowered deferentially. She could feel Roryn studying her and had to fight the urge to turn her head and stick her tongue out at him. The past five years must have bored her silly if she found provoking one of the world's most dangerous men fun.

"Please," the queen drew the door back, her skirts billowing gently in welcome, and motioned them inside, "come in."

Tempest felt out of sorts as she preceded Roryn into the chamber. Every drape, pillow, and wardrobe sat as they had on that fateful evening when the queen had flown about her chambers, packing jewels and coins into discrete purses she hoped would see her daughters to safety. Even her cosmetics cases and toiletries were arranged precisely as they always had been. It seemed, for a moment, that nothing had changed for her mother in the last five years. She could tell from the sadness clinging to her mother's aura, however, that was far from the truth.

Her father would never be part of this room again.

"Where is the prince?" A quick glance upon entering had alerted Roryn to the fact that they were the only three people present. If the prince had been here recently, there was no evidence of that fact.

"The prince is sleeping." Her offhand manner clearly conveyed she wasn't concerned for her son's safety. Roryn cleared his throat, wondering what was actually behind the request to see the healer. He wasn't obtuse, in most circumstances, and things were not adding up in a way that satisfied his curiosity.

"You said he was gravely ill, which is why I agreed to bring the healer."

"Well," Lady Mirabel's eyes were focused on the face of the younger woman before her. Roryn felt that she barely realized he was in the room. She blinked hard, seeming to come to her senses, "actually, it was a female problem I was needing addressed but I didn't want to burden you with the details. You may leave us now, if you please."

Roryn snorted, bringing the former queen's icy attention to him. "I do not please. As the guardian of your safety, I'll stay to ensure it."

"Very well." The queen stared him down as she began to unbutton the blouse tucked primly into her skirts. Roryn's snort turned into a cough as he choked on Lady Mirabel's audacity. His cheeks took on a slight pink hue and he turned quickly, stalking to the open balcony doors and stepping just outside them. Tempest had to bite back a smile at seeing him so flustered.

"If you could lie on the bed, your Majesty?" Tempest followed, sitting beside her on the bed close enough to feel the comforting heat radiating from her body. "Where are you feeling poorly?"

"Is he watching?" Her mother's whisper brought back the memory of the times they'd sneak into the kitchens to steal sweet buns from under the head baker's eagle eye.

"No," Tempest turned slightly, catching him at the edge of her vision as he stood looking out into the dark night at the kingdom that was now his, "but I've no doubt he has the hearing of a Fyrfox."

"I can fix that." The queen made a brief circle with her hands, cupping the air and then releasing it with a brisk closing of her fists. How had Tempest forgotten this small talent of her mother's? She'd often been the recipient of it as a child when she'd proven too rambunctious to sit still in the throne room. It didn't halt all sound around them but anyone outside the shield would only hear muttering that they wouldn't quite be able to decipher.

"I feel some discomfort in your stomach," Tempest continued to run her hands over the queen but found no cause for alarm. "Is that where you are ill?" Surprise hit her hard when her mother grabbed her hands and held them tight against her chest.

"I'm fine. I just wanted to see you. I needed to see you, Tempe." Tears filled both of their eyes before the queen turned her head. Tempest choked back a sniffle. Now was not the time to give in to her softer emotions, no matter how long she'd denied them.

"I've missed you and Ben, mom." A tear slipped free, running down her cheek until it fell, disappearing into the red-framed abyss of her cleavage. "And," she whispered, "father."

"Baby girl," Mirabel's use of the pet name for her youngest daughter slipped out, nearly causing them both to break. "You have no idea what I've been through, waiting each day for news of your capture. Praising the Bright each night when it didn't come. Although," her eyes flicked over the red dress in distaste. "It appears I should have been more specific in my prayers. I have a feeling I do not ever care to know the lengths you girls have gone to in order to survive."

"This is one of Juli's made over. I've been staying with her in the city for a few months now." She smiled reassuringly but couldn't help the imp that made her add, "My normal wardrobe is a tattered pair of boy's pantaloons and a peasant's blouse. Which, may I say, is much more comfortable than this contraption." She poked at the corset encircling her ribs, tapping out a quick rhythm on the hollow bone.

"The time away has changed you, made you stronger. Even I can feel that." Mirabel drew in a deep stuttering breath, as if she was hesitant to say what she felt needed said. "That's good, Tempe, you'll need that strength. I am going to ask you to do a big thing."

"Whatever it is, Mother, you know I will do it."

"That prissy regent this one replaced," She gave a sharp nod toward Roryn, "had thought the emperor would be amenable to an alliance between our two houses." Norc stirred uneasily and Tempest grimaced in pain as she had to forcefully wrestle him into silence. "I need you to convince your sister to give up this futile quest for the freedom of Hlyn and come home to face what future we can scrape from this mess."

"You mean...?" A hiss left her throat at the realization of what her mother was asking.

"Marriage, yes." A hard look took up residence on the queen's face, erasing any trace of tears she may have wanted to shed. "An alliance, a truce, a peaceful resolution through the bonds of matrimony...you aren't stupid, Tempest Anyabella. You know this is our only recourse."

"I may have changed, Mother, but Dahlis hasn't. Her every waking moment is devoted to preserving the honor and integrity that make us Malorns. She won't agree. She'll see this as selling herself to the enemy."

"If you can't get your sister to do it," Her voice was firm, stiff in the way that left Tempest in no doubt that this was a royal command. "Then you shall marry him and do what must be done to ensure his forgiveness for her brash foolishness."

"I shall not!" Tempest's outburst caused the bubble surrounding them to pop and she stood, embarrassed as she hastily straightened her skirts. The queen gaped at her for a moment before she sat upright, a frown tight upon her face as she slid her arms through the robe laying at the foot of her bed and yanked the ties hard around her still slim stomach.

Heavy footsteps drove a wedge between both women as Roryn's eyes darted questioningly between the two. "Everything alright here, ladies?"

"That will be all." Mirabel did not spare a look for her child as she poured herself a glass of water from the pitcher on her bedside table, but Tempest saw her hands shake. This had not been the reunion either of them had planned. "Thank you, I am much improved."

Sketching out the bow that was expected of her, even though the queen kept her back carefully to them, Tempest rushed for the door. She pulled the handle with her own trembling hand, barely hearing the queen's parting words as she left the rooms she'd always been welcome in as a child.

"You'll see the girl is compensated and returned to where she belongs, My Lord Regent?"

"Of course, Lady Malorn." Roryn inclined his head as he closed the door behind him. Her thoughts jumbled and steeped in anguish at disobeying her mother, Tempest began walking down the corridor that would most quickly take her out of the castle, completely forgetting the danger at her back.

"Where do you think you are heading, my pretty healer? I have some questions for you." Roryn's hand slipped to Tempest's side, startling her as his long fingers grazed the underside of her breast. He pivoted and guided her back toward the queen's chambers, though he didn't stop as they passed them. His arm was strong and sure at her back as he chose one of the smaller hallways that would, eventually, lead them directly to her old bedchamber. Trepidation froze her in place, but he didn't hesitate as he scooped her up and threw her over his shoulder.

"Put me down you brute!" She pounded on his back, to no effect. His long stride quickly ate up the distance and before she knew it, they were outside the very room where she'd spent her youth reading and daydreaming. "Release me this very instant or I'll...I'll scream!"

"Only if you are a good girl." His chuckle was dark and though she wasn't sure of his meaning, her body seemed to understand, growing electrified as his hand brushed against the round globe of her buttocks. She squeaked and renewed her assault, grabbing at the sleek braid dangling between his shoulders and yanking as hard as she could.

"You told the queen you would take me home."

"I told her I would see you put where you belonged." He pulled a key from his trouser pocket and slid it into the lock, pushing the door open and bending to keep her head from banging against the low frame. A quick click confirmed he had relocked it behind them. Only then did he set her on her feet.

She should be scared but what she felt instead was a mixture of inevitability and anger. She stalked away from him, her hands propped dangerously on her hips, fuming as she took in the small details in the room that revealed the mark he had made on her personal space. His boots lay discarded on her hearth, his jacket tossed upon the feminine sofa where she'd spent endless days dreaming of a future where she would bring glory to the Malorn name.

"Who are you to decide where that is?" She lost what little temper remained as she picked up the book laying spine up on the bed, the inner pages splayed indelicately. *A Mystery of Endeavors,* she read the title. The bastard was reading her favorite book!

"Who are you," his stride ate up the distance between them until she found herself pinned against the footboard, "to deny this feeling that connects us?" He plucked the book from her hand and dropped it carelessly on the floor. "The bond that is growing stronger hour by hour, pulling me to your side whether I want it or not?"

Tempest's fury transformed into a different kind of heat as his chest met hers. Her hands came up between them, fisting in his shirt, but she did not push him away. His arm came around her, burning the flesh exposed by the low back of her dress and she groaned as his pelvis pressed against her oddly churning stomach, forcing her backward onto the bed.

"What...what are you doing?" She stuttered, as his calloused warrior's palms ran down the inside of her arms, pushing them up above her head and holding them fast in one hand. His intoxicating eyes were half-lidded, his breathing heavy as he trailed his lips over the underside of her jaw. A low growl escaped him as his eagerly questing mouth made its way down her neck, sucking gently at the pulse beating out of control just beneath her skin.

"Showing you where you belong." His knee parted her thighs, shoving her skirt impossibly high, making her squirm as the fabric of his pants rubbed the delicate inside of her legs. His free hand danced across her collarbone, slowly tracing the pale mound of her breast before his fingertips slid under the scant fabric. She moaned, arching against him as his palm brushed her nipple.

"I...I don't..." She was lost. The sensations surging through her body were so new, so electrifying, so...all consuming. She felt like this part of her had lain dormant until he'd come along. Until he'd found her.

"I'll stop when you tell me to," he promised.

She trusted him.

She just didn't trust herself.

He was everything she'd ever dreamed of, but he was also one thing she hadn't. He was her enemy. Maybe he didn't realize it, but she certainly did. No matter the urges coursing through her, could she put that aside? There was no future for them.

But, did she have much of one anyway?

Could she, for one brief moment in time, make her own choice? Follow the urges of her own body without consideration for the fall out? Would her mother disapprove? Without doubt. Would her sister be disappointed? Yes. In the big scheme of things, he was her enemy. But at this moment?

He was a man, hot and hard between her legs.

Perhaps the only man that would ever ignite the fire she hadn't even realized she could kindle. A flame that might never be fed again but would rage like an inferno in her memories. Memories she'd earned for all the cold nights and lonely trails of the last five years. Memories that would comfort her in the stark, hopeless days to come.

She tugged her arms, and he released them immediately, bracing himself on his elbows as her hands plucked frantically at the buttons of his shirt, fumbling until she could slide them inside, the first willing touch of her skin against his.

"Roryn." Her whimper drew a moan from his throat, sending a bolt of lust ricocheting between them.

It was the sound of her surrender.

Her victory.

His mouth descended on hers, as if to steal his name from her very lips. Or...perhaps to seal it there, hers to keep forever. To own. To use as she chose. With an instinct she didn't even know she possessed, Tempest's tongue slid against his upper lip, begging for more. He surged against her in shock, rocking past the boundary he'd set for himself and rubbing his length against the very core of her.

"Brightest Be Damned, woman!" Roryn broke their kiss, panting as he tried to distance himself as the dam holding the curse in place weakened, flooding him with feelings he thought long dead. He pulled back, taking in the flushed excitement clear on her face and the fear and need standing hand-in-hand in her vivid eyes. Such a lovely, unique gold, they entranced him in a way he'd never felt, challenged him in a way that engaged every molecule of his worthless being.

Unable to help himself, he kissed her again, gently this time as she trembled beneath him. He cradled her head between his palms, his hands tangling in her loose curls as she pressed up against him, her breathy moan of excitement setting fire to his need to possess her.

He pulled back, shifting his weight to the bed beside her, breathing deeply through his nose to restore his control. His thumb brushed her temple, trying to calm her and give himself a moment. A streak of brown marred her forehead, and he looked at his stained hand in curiosity, sure the dirt hadn't been there before.

"What's this?"

She froze, terror erasing the lust from her body.

Tears inundated her almost golden eyes, chipping away at some of the hardness encasing his heart. He ran his spread fingers

through her tresses, his gut clenching as more of the dye transferred to his hand, revealing an unmistakable gleam of gold.

"Will you tell me your name?" His voice was low, certain. She
turned her head away, but it was too late. Her almost golden
eyes. Her manners, both too refined and too wild to belong to
a simple maid. Her profile, so reminiscent of the queen they
had just left.

"It's Tempest."

He felt the words more than he heard them as they cut like
an icy blade through their passion. Dread battled with pain as
the curse hit him with a vengeance, tearing a bloody welt in
the blade-wound almost as fiercely as the truth of her heritage
seared his heart.

"Tempest? The unwanted sister." His horror was obvious as
all the puzzle pieces fell into place.

It was nothing compared to the shame that filled her as his
words registered. She had known it all her life, had feared it
was the truth, but to hear it coming from his mouth? An
empty ache built in her chest, and she expected anger to fill
the hole, but...there was nothing. She couldn't blame him for
knowing the truth of her, though the words ripped through
her vulnerable heart, nonetheless.

"Tempest Anyabella Rutherstan Malorn, Second Heir of Hlyn. Outlaw, rebel, maid, disgrace."

Her hands were tentative as they bracketed the creases in the hard planes of his cheeks. Her tears were silent tribute to memories gone before they'd ever had a chance to be examined in the light of day, salting his lips as she placed hers, soft as a butterfly, upon them one last time.

An apology. A goodbye.

"What am I supposed to do now?" He asked gruffly, mostly to himself. He closed his eyes as if the sight of her caused him pain. Tempest drew back, touching a trembling hand to his temple, sliding it back over his blue dragon tattoo.

"Sleep." She whispered, her magic plucking at the web of conscious thought running like a beautiful kaleidoscope within him, calming it, quieting it.

She slipped out the door, leaving him and her heart behind on the bed.

The imposter! Norc's unvoice screamed inside her head, an edge of insanity coloring his usual ironic tone with urgency. *You almost parted your legs and accepted the seed of the very miscreant that caused my downfall! You should be shoving a blade into his opportunistic heart instead of contemplating allowing him a stab at you instead! I'd always figured the Malorn Royal line was filled with tender-hearted weaklings, but I never thought they'd harbored a moron in their midst!*

Tempest let him rage as she snuck, unnoticed, from the palace. Thankfully, the stable was empty when she entered it. Her smile was weak as she met the placid gaze of the gentle palomino picking at the hay before her. The mare whickered a soft greeting and stood motionless as Tempest saddled her and urged her into the night.

Do you have no spine, chit? No words of defense you wish to spout at me about true love or some such lackwit notion? She had no argument for him as she happened to agree fully. She had been stupid.

And, if given the chance, she would be again.

Chapter Twenty-one

"Excuse me, your General Eminence!" Hartfello Loxlei threw himself bodily before the double doors of the informal dining area as Roryn approached. The Master of the Key's stoic face reflected bold courage despite the shiver that chased up his rigid spine. At another time, Roryn might have found his boldness amusing, but a bleak darkness was riding him hard, and he was in no mood for the older man's drama. "Lady Malorn is very insistent on not being disturbed as she breaks her fast with her son."

"Get out of my way, skrull! *Her Majesty*," he snarled the title like it was an epithet, "will see me with or without your body decorating her floor. Move!"

Loxlei's puffy lips wobbled but he stood his ground, whether from bravery or from incapacitating fear was unclear. Roryn's frustration of waking up alone was amplified by the vengeance of the curse needing to find the girl that could ruin the emperor's carefully laid plans. Roryn felt a little out-of-sorts himself, shame filling him as he recalled the foolish, unthinking words he'd muttered last night.

She'd confessed what had to be her deepest, darkest secret, and he'd mindlessly repeated Praxxys' hurtful nonsense. He was no better than a skrull himself. Each time he thought of her beautiful face running with tears, a foreign ripple of regret touched his heart, followed by the burning jolt of the curse ripping through his blade-wound.

The door flashed open and Lady Mirabel graced him with a regal nod. "Come in, please, Roryn. Hartfello, could you take Benni back to his chambers?" She gave her golden-haired son a gentle kiss on the head as he passed her then reseated herself as if she didn't have a care in the world.

Her choice in using his given name wasn't lost on Roryn and he was reminded once again how a soft body could hide a sharp wit. He clasped his hands behind his back and rocked on his heels as Loxlei escorted Benevolence Malorn out the door. The boy gave him a considering look that had Roryn believing, without a doubt, that somewhere between here and the royal suites, he would ditch Loxlei and circle back to cause some mischief. A laugh caught in the back of his throat - *Ben*. The girl had given plenty of clues to her identity. He'd just been too obtuse to see.

"Lady Mirabel." He sketched a bow, still aggravated but having lost the edge of his anger. "You failed to tell me that you are on quite familiar terms with the healer." He picked a grape off the bunch abandoned on the boy's plate and popped it in his mouth. "Nor did you inform me that said healer was a notorious traitor to our Emperor."

"She's my daughter." She didn't bother to deny it and began nonchalantly applying a thin layer of butter to a toasted slice of bread. "What would you've had me do? I've read of the Salvadons and their renowned honor. I highly doubt you are so far gone to that curse as to be without any. I am surprised you found her out, my little Tempe can be quite resourceful when she chooses."

"It's amazing what secrets a woman will spill when she's under a man who knows what he is doing." He pasted on his most villainous smirk, struggling not to flinch at the additional disservice he was heaping upon the girl that may have stolen his heart. "The only thing she didn't tell me was where she was running off to when she slipped out of my room this morning."

She appeared to have little concern for her daughter regarding his crass insinuation, not even blinking to indicate she had understood his implication. Instead, she studied him intensely, very much the fearless, emotionless queen she'd been rumored to be.

His scowl didn't intimidate her, but the considering look in her intelligent eyes gave him pause.

"I assume you've already torn apart the Evermore Inn?" He nodded. Not only was she long gone from the city, but so was Horse. "There is another place," she admitted, taking a dainty bite of her bread and chewing it slowly. "I will tell you where to find my girls, but you must promise me something."

"The safety of both of your daughters is in the balance." Anger boiled within his veins, incensed on Tempest's behalf even though he'd treated her as poorly as anyone. "It would behoove you to tell me anyway. But," he folded his hands over the back of the chair opposite hers, his knuckles growing white against the mahogany, "I'll entertain your request."

"I have heard a rumor that the emperor may be amenable to an alliance of marriage. I would have you approach His Eminence on behalf of Hlyn and offer Dahlis in exchange for his grace and forgiveness. If she proves difficult...give him Tempest."

"No."

"No?" She seemed a bit ruffled at his vehemence.

"Praxxys has no need to wed either of your daughters, even if he had the desire to do so. He is the Warlock Emperor and won't bargain for an alliance. If that were something he wanted, he'd merely take it. Besides," he shrugged his shoulders, "it's not the Outlaw Princess' hand he desires, it's her magic."

"Dahlis doesn't..." The former queen grabbed her goblet and took a deep sip of its contents, buying herself a few seconds to think. "What purpose can she possibly fulfill that he doesn't have the power to accomplish himself?"

"The emperor's mysteries are his own. Whatever he wants of her, she will have no choice but to give it."

"Can you give me your word to protect them?" Her voice was strong but, somehow, lacked her previous conviction.

"I cannot deny the emperor." The back of the chair cracked under the force of his grip, shattering his veneer of composure. The thought of bringing more sorrow to a life already plagued with strife and uncertainty was anathema to the man he used to be, to the man he'd always be. "But I will not leave her to face him alone."

She sat still, staring diligently at half-slice of bread laying innocently in the center of her gold-rimmed plate. She tapped her knife on it twice, a nervous habit her own mother had tried to beat out of her years before.

"There is an old royal hunting chalet on the coast, about a day's ride into the Dunshyre. You'll find a map in the King's Study."

The door clicked softly behind him with a finality that sent a jolt through her implacable spine. The former Queen of Hlyn stacked her used place setting carefully next to that of her son. She wiped the table assiduously with her napkin, propped her head in her hands, and began to sob.

"Bright Bless my poor, sweet babies."

"Whoa, girl." Tempest pulled Roryn's stolen mare to a stop beside the small creek that marked the half-way point between Vyte and the ruins of the hunting chalet that had been her father's favorite place to go when the strain of being king became too much.

They'd ridden as hard as she dared through the deepest part of the night, and the mare had gamely kept up a steady lope for hours after the sun began to warm the treetops. While Obertroess was a king among horses, she'd never ridden a mount so willing to please as the golden mare. She was a true trooper, so much so that Tempest had taken to calling her that.

"You're such a fine lady, Trooper. What do you say we take a little rest?" The mare whickered in agreement and flared her nostrils at the smell of fresh water. She patted the mare's flank and loosened her boots in the stirrups. Her red dress was bunched uncomfortably around her waist, the sides split indecently with the help of a knife she'd found on an unguarded workbench in the stable and a little desperation.

Tempest could not wait to stretch her own legs and have a few moments while Trooper drank to rub some of the ache out of her buttocks. It had been a few months since she'd had a proper ride. She did miss the freedom, but not the side effects. Her stomach chose that moment to growl, reminding her that she hadn't eaten in over a day. She reached back to dig through the saddlebags that had been slung over the wall next to Trooper's stall, hoping there might be some hard tack or jerky inside.

She drew back the flap and shrieked as she was attacked by a pale ferocious shadow. Its teeth raked against her hand, and she snatched it back, digging deep into the cleavage exposed by her stupid red dress, trying in vain to pull her knife free. Her shriek turned to a scream of fear as Trooper bolted, bucking and stomping to free herself from the screeching fleshy pink monster that had to have been born of the Nightmare itself.

The horse finally succeeded in shaking the creature from her back but, in doing so, Tempest also lost her seat. She felt weightless for a moment as she flew through the air, she even had time to contemplate the choices she'd made to bring her to this end as time seemed to still. Bright be Damned...she was going to die a virgin!

She fell hard, her hip slamming into a rock protruding from the edge of the stream. The air left her in a puff as she landed flat against the dirt path, the back of her head ricocheting violently with the impact. Sound ceased and the world froze, and, for a brief second, she stood on the precipice between the Nightmare and the Promise.

A frightened bugle brought the world cascading back with a vengeance and frantic stomping mixed with an eerie, whining howl, fractured the peace of her near death. The decreasing crack of saplings being broken, and the hiss of brush being bent suggested she was alive and made one thing perfectly clear...the palomino was long gone.

Her next realization was that her relief at being alive wouldn't last long. Her eyes were screwed shut, refusing to look upon the beast that would eat her, but she could feel the hot puffs of its laborious breath on her face. Then...it yipped.

"Morti?" Tempest was incredulous as a tiny thump on her sternum preceded the wet drag of a tongue across her cheek. At least she hoped it was his tongue and not one of his obscenely protruding eyeballs. She threw an arm over her face to protect herself and groaned as the little dog-creature joyfully pranced over her prone body with its teeny needle-sharp claws. "Brightness strike me dead, how in Telryuun did you get in that saddlebag?"

The dog didn't answer, which was a good thing, or it would have meant she had suffered greater damage to her head than she had thought. He just stared at her expectantly with one bulbous eye as the other tracked the path of two ravens flying high above a break in the trees. She considered just lying there and giving up but, after most of the pulsating pain ceased, decided she'd rather not end up within easy reach of Morti if she truly did become a corpse. He switched both eyes to her and gave her nose a long, leisurely lick as if to savor the possibilities.

"Uck!" She flicked his little body off her chest, pausing to shove one boob back into the gaping front of the dress that had somehow been ripped in the fall, and rolled slowly to her hands and knees.

She closed her eyes and concentrated, using just a touch of her magic to take away the worst of the aches. Healing herself was a tricky endeavor. If she repaired too much damage, she burned through her own energy, which created more problems than it solved. She could take energy from the forest around her, like she had when she'd closed Dahlis' wound, but it had never set right with her to cause suffering in order to heal her own.

Convinced she'd live after all, Tempest tied her hair back with a loose strip of fabric torn from her dress and pushed off from her knees. She stood for a moment with her arms wrapped protectively around her chest as she evaluated her situation. It wasn't ideal, but she'd been in much worse circumstances.

She wasn't as familiar with this densely wooded portion of the Dunshyre , they'd tended to avoid being this close to Vyte, but she remembered there being a small fur trapper's shack not far from where she stood. If she were lucky, it would provide some protection from the night and a place to build a fire. At worst, she would have Morti to battle the rats that were sure to be living in its walls.

First things first, she would drink as much water as she could hold. That should help tame the growl, for a little while, and give her the strength to resist eating Morti. Once they reached the shack maybe she would find that some benevolent soul had left a tin of beans lying about. There was no harm in dreaming, she thought, then laughed at how easily she had fallen into old habits.

"Come on you little...whatever you are." She tucked Morti under her arm, facing him backwards so she didn't accidentally look down and see his face, and, with a stomach full of water, began the long trek that would surely take her into dangerous territory.

Which was where she flourished best, after all.

Chapter Twenty-two

"The Nightmare Eat You, Morti! Stop defiling that poor thing's corpse!"

Tempest grabbed the nearest rusted tin from the pile she'd kicked together to clear the cabin floor and chucked it at the overly excited little beast. He made eye contact with her and yipped proudly, as if inviting her to join him in his macabre celebration of victory. It took three more cans before he jumped off the body of the rat he'd killed. His face was tragic as he slunk under the bed, dragging the poor thing behind him and out of her sight.

Porta would be pleased. Morti was a natural at rat elimination...and, it appeared, was dedicated to learning the finer nuances of necrophilia. Tempest was just happy not to have to watch his deviant escapades any longer, although it had made her lose any appetite she'd had.

She turned back to the small fire she'd started in a discarded kettle and fed it another handful of sticks. The fireplace itself was a mess of broken brick, the chimney clogged with a decade's worth of bird nests. She let her mind wander as she watched the smoke trail slowly fade as it was pulled out through the cracks in the shack's broken window.

The tattered roof and vine-shrouded walls of the cabin fell away as she finally had time to digest her mother's words and formulate a plan to convince Dahlis to give up her quest to return a Malorn to the throne of Hlyn. Even if she was willing to return to a life within the walls of Vyte, she was absolutely sure her sister wouldn't agree to give herself to a man she despised.

If it came down to Tempest marrying the Warlock Emperor, would she be brave enough to face the unpredictable wrath of a man who had saved the world from the Nightmare only to plunge it into another dark fate? Would she be content to live out her short life, too soon an old woman bound to a man who never aged? Could she give up any hope of love in order to make a truce with a man who may someday forget she had ever existed?

Against her better judgment, a chiseled face filled her mind. Roryn T'Yanil. It was a strong name, although an uncommon one, and she thought she liked it very much. She had the better part of a day to consider, and then dismiss, his harsh words.

It was actually the least hurtful response he could have had to the news that he was eagerly kissing the second most wanted outlaw in Hlyn. She giggled a bit as she thought about the hit he must have taken to his manly pride for thinking she was a harmless healer who moonlighted as a lady of the night in her free time!

If he only knew!

If he only knew...the painful knot of sorrow returned to her throat. He could never find out. If he discovered the true extent of her magic, if the Warlock Emperor ever did, she was as good as dead. They might keep a healer around, chained in a fancy tower at their whim, but the other thing she was...the horrible things she could do?

No one could ever fully trust that beast not to turn on them. Not even her mother had been able to fully embrace her, and she only suspected the true monster residing inside the golden beauty of her second child. Only Dahlis had ever been able to love her. Mainly because Dahlis harbored dark secrets all her own.

The sound of rhythmic bumping and breathy squeals shattered her musings.

"Son of a Headless Sea-Possum, Morti! That's it!"

Tempest grabbed the corner post of the bed and yanked it a foot away from the wall. Fresh pine needles and fragrant borderberry leaves drifted to the floor, the result of her trying to make the bare frame a little softer and better smelling. With a grimace of disgust on her face she leaned into the open space and lifted the mangled body of the rat away from the disgusting dog-thing.

"That's enough fun for one night. You'll get dehydrated and end up deader than you actually look."

The dog whined and followed on her heel as she stalked to the door and yanked it open. She drew her arm back and then froze as the face from her daydreams stood before her. Behind him stood one of the black-maned white chargers that the Hlyn royal stables were known for breeding...and the palomino. Relief at seeing her unharmed quickly evaporated under the deluge of feeling that swamped her. Unsure how seeing him should make her feel, she went with mild disinterest.

"What are you doing here?" She remembered she was dangling a dead rat by the tail and took a second to swing it as far into the brush as possible.

"I was thinking about coming in," his intense eyes fell to the doorway by her feet, "but I'm not sure your company is enough to compensate for having to breathe the same air as that thing." Morti took offense at his nod and began to growl.

Roryn felt shy and hesitant now that he had found her. Chasing her into the forest had seemed the right thing to do, his only acceptable course of action, but facing her now, with the truth of her between them? She wasn't a bar wench or a healer he could bargain with, she was descended from a royal bloodline more ancient than even his own.

More than that, she was rumored to be every bit as fierce with a blade as her sister, even if she was sometimes hesitant to use it. She was feisty and compassionate. Soft and ungiving. She was everything he didn't know he'd wanted in his future. In Salvaldon, he'd been too young and reckless to care about tomorrows, much less worry about who would spend them at his side. When Praxxys had bound him and pulled him away from everything he'd ever known, locking him in an eternity of darkness, he only wished there would, someday, be no tomorrow. Pain exploded in his arm and a tiny grunt left his mouth as he ground his teeth in resistance.

He was unworthy, a slave, a murderer. In the past twenty-five years, he'd come to terms with that. If she rejected him, he couldn't imagine how broken he'd be. For a man who had never felt real fear, he was terrified of how much she'd made him feel in so little time. He stood, staring at her as unabashedly as she was staring at him, and couldn't help but nourish the tiny spark of hope blossoming within him. She hadn't stabbed him yet, except with those beautiful, unmistakably golden eyes.

"Can I come in?"

"That depends." She stood aside, a smile lurking at the corner of her mouth. "Do you intend to kill me? Arrest me? Tie me out as a sacrifice to the hungry forest dragons?"

"I don't intend any of those things but the night is early." A dimple dented his cheek and she was lost. He could call her unwanted, but that was not the way he made her feel.

"I suppose as a notorious bandit I can," she cocked her eyebrow at him imperiously, "and will, defend myself."

"As a man who is seeing more of your breasts than he deserves, I'll agree to anything you say right now." He laughed as she looked down at her exposed chest, the tear from her fall gaping inelegantly.

"Oh!" She clasped it together as he stepped forward, a blush painting her bare flesh with a glow that made his breathing hitch. He was barely over the sill before a stiff arm against his chest stopped him in his tracks.

"Did you bring any food? I have decided that is the price you'll pay for a roof tonight."

Roryn looked over her shoulder at the broken cabin, barely suitable for a rat, much less a princess. He had done this to her. If he hadn't chased her off with his callous words she would never be here, hungry and bruised in the middle of a forest known for its deadly creatures. He sketched her a low, gentlemanly bow.

"I don't have much but if you are happy with canned beans and hardtack, I packed the finest."

Tempest grinned widely, dropping her hand and throwing the squeaky door wide. Her stomach growled. "Bring it all! I'll stoke the fire."

Who was he to get between a woman and her meal? Roryn grabbed Horse's reins and that of the stable mount, leading them around the back of the cabin and securing them in the tiny lean-to there. Luckily, there was dry hay left in the enclosure and enough fresh rainwater in the trough to last them until morning.

He patted Horse's side and took the saddles off each, shouldering his bags easily. The mare had been standing near a creek where it was obvious there'd been a struggle. She must have bolted off into the brush, leaving her rider, but like the good mount she was, she had eventually returned. If it hadn't been for her, he would have never seen the nearly invisible trail that shot off into the woods and led to this cabin.

She was waiting for him when he returned, her face bright and expectant as he handed her the food. She eagerly shoved a biscuit into her mouth and had two tins of beans opened and balanced at the edge of her small fire before he had fully examined his surroundings. He studiously ignored the dog-thing staring at him from beneath the bed and was not going to ask how it had gotten here.

Neither one spoke as they watched the flames, nibbling their way through every piece of hardtack, saving the last of it to scoop their beans. At last, she sat back, rubbing her belly in satisfaction. Her eyes turned to him.

"You never told me why you are here."

"Is it not obvious?" He shrugged his shoulders as she continued to stare at him. "I'm here for you. Praxxys demands I bring your sister to him. He has some mad plan that involves a spell he says will change the world and redeem him. It will only work if he performs it during the coming eclipse, with the help of magic only your sister can provide."

"That is what you will do, then? My mother said..."

"Praxxys is many things, in search of a wife is not one of them." He said shortly.

Tempest sighed as she stood, wiping the crumbs from her hands onto the tattered remnants of her dress. "Well. I guess that's that. I'm too tired to escape until morning so...goodnight."

He was at her side in a moment, gently cupping her elbow and turning her to face him. Her disappointment was obvious on her face, and it sent a bolt of self-disgust straight to his gut. "I couldn't care less about Praxxys and his silly spells." He told her, lifting her chin so he could see those beautiful eyes as he tried to explain. "Your family has made Hlyn a country to be admired, and I've seen plenty to know. He'd do well to keep a Malorn on the throne. The simple fact of the matter is I am Bound to his will, with no choice but to bring your sister to him."

He pushed the loose curls from her face, pleased to see that most of the brown dye had left it, leaving her unique brilliance fully on display. She should not have to hide who she truly was. "I will do everything possible to see that she doesn't come to harm."

"I will make a promise to you, as well. If it comes down to a confrontation with the Warlock Emperor, I will be at my sister's side."

"No." He drew his hand back, emphatic. "Praxxys will do to you what he did to me...or worse!"

"This discussion is going nowhere." She stepped around him, pulling his bedroll from the pile of saddlebags and throwing it at him. He caught it against his chest and gave her a baleful look, letting her know he was far from done with this conversation.

"Here you go! My hospitality extends to providing you with the best accommodations the Hovel House has to offer." She started kicking trash, forest debris, and the remains of broken

housewares toward the sides of the room. Morti barked erratically, dancing around in the approximately seven-foot space she'd
cleared.

"I'm not sleeping on that floor, Tempest. I know you are mad at
me," he dropped the bedroll onto the leaf-strewn platform that
would serve no other purpose than to keep them a foot above
the cabin's floor-dwelling pests, "and rightly so, but I had hoped
you didn't hate me."

She didn't hate him and that was the problem. She didn't have
time to delve into the ramifications of sharing the bed because a
stream of red on the back of his hand caught her eye, causing her
to gasp in horror.

"You're bleeding!"

"It's nothing." He flicked his wrist toward the pile of refuse
now shoved haplessly against the wall, sending flecks of blood
spraying over the old cans and bottles.

"It's quite a bit of something. You are getting blood all over my
bed!"

He unbuckled the silver bracer that hid the evidence of his
indenture to the Dragonbone Blade and dropped it onto the
wobbly three-legged table at the bottom of the bed. He rifled
through his saddlebag and pulled out a roll of bandages, swiftly

wrapping it around his forearm. He shook out his bedroll next and spread it over the leaf-strewn frame with a flourish.

"There. No more blood."

"Too bad there isn't a healer nearby that could put an end to your suffering."

"Tempest," sadness filtered through the darkness gathering around them. Even the steady glow of her tiny fire seemed chill on his face. "This is no simple wound. It is a curse made with the Warlock Emperor's darkest magic." He pressed the bandages tight as a wave of agony tore through him. "Even thinking about undoing it causes it to punish me. What if it were to hurt you, too?"

"Life is misery. The only thing that makes it not so is our willingness to change it."

He thought about her words for a second and hope began to burn inside him, a much hotter conflagration than the curse could ever manage. "Do your worst."

She laughed, "I always do." She pushed him back until his knees hit the bed, feeling power of a different sort surging through her as she mimicked his action of the night before. She didn't have clean linens or water to treat him, so she settled down beside him, carefully cradling his wrist and elbow against her chest. Her eyes closed as she let her magic delve deep.

Immediately, a dark force lashed out at her. Warning her away with a sentience that was surprising. He was right. This curse wasn't a simple spell. It was a living creature all its own. She was confident she could defeat it, eventually. First though, she'd have to understand it, and that would take time. For now, she would heal him as much as she could.

He gritted his teeth, but a hiss of pain escaped, nonetheless. He knew the curse would throw everything it had at him in order to fight back, she wasn't the first healer he'd seen, but never had it been so unbearably intense. That was a good sign. It meant whatever dark magic swirled inside him was scared. It meant this seemingly fragile woman really did have the power to defeat it. Another wave of agony ripped through him, this time centering in his chest. He began to pant, his fists clenched as his entire being feared it was being torn asunder.

On top of the raging pain Tempest could feel through the link she'd created between them with her magic, stabbing like icicles violently through her core, she could sense his hope dying swiftly under the curse's influence. This wasn't working.

"Don't think of the pain. Focus on me." She crawled onto his lap, letting her fingers toy with the buttons at his collar, freeing them and sliding her hands inside, distracted by the firm jut of his collarbone against her thumbs. His fists immediately unclenched, his muscles loosening as his hands spread over her hips, then lower until he was cupping her ass.

"I take back what I said about not touching your patient." His groan rumbled enticingly through both of their chests, pressed so tightly together. "You may put your hands anywhere you'd like, Healer."

She took the initiative and while her hands wrapped around his bandaged flesh, her mouth came down upon his, sliding sideways so that her tongue could find its way inside. A murmur of excited encouragement sent a thrill coursing through her and her magic surged, wanting to lose itself in the empty chasm where the bare remnants of his own power existed, to meld with it, fill it, absorb him into the very essence of herself. She felt emboldened to deepen the kiss, letting out her own growl of pleasure before remembering her purpose.

She pulled away from his kiss but did not complain as his lips continued, kissing the corner of her mouth and descending down the column of her throat, sucking sweetly at the pounding pulse there. She squeaked in surprise at the rush of lust that raced through her veins, lighting every part of her on fire. She took that strange, intoxicating power and, mixing it with her own, shoved every ounce of her magic into the wound in his arm.

His teeth replaced his tongue, scoring her flesh unintentionally. He would no doubt be horrified to see what he had done, but she welcomed the pain, in this moment she needed it. It kept her tethered, gave her solid purchase on a slippery slope, as the curse came awake. It tried to lash at her but she would not give quarter. She healed where she could, her magic darting just out of the reach of the darkness, letting it chase her, spreading the goodness of her healing inside it in tiny touches before she slipped away once again.

She was exhilarated. She was euphoric. She was...tired.

She was in trouble.

"Tempest!" A voice, faint. Intriguing. Irresistible. "Come back to me."

She pushed at him weakly, but he pulled her hands from his arm, locking them in the space between them. A kiss warmed lips that had grown cold, drawing her away from the echoes of power still vibrating in the small space. Roryn hovered over her, pressing her into the bed, his pelvis tight against hers. "Sit back, I'm not done."

A relieved laugh left his beautiful mouth and he lowered himself so that his entire body covered the length of hers. It was, quite literally, the best thing she had ever felt. His lips nuzzled her jawline, edging up to the fragrant spot just below her ear. A shudder wracked her body. "Mmmm..." he mumbled, "It feels good to me."

She moaned. She was feeling more than good, too.

"Is this what you want, Tempest? Am I what you want?" He nipped at her lower lip, pulling it into his mouth before pressing butterfly-soft kisses across it.

"I think...yes."

Roryn placed a light kiss on her lips, lingering a second before he pulled back. He slid his body to the side and rolled her away from him to face the wall before throwing himself down on his back beside her.

"What?" she groaned, too confused and tired from the energy lost in healing to fight him.

"Let me know when you know 'yes'." He started tracing circles on the exposed skin of her back with his fingertips, calming her...and himself. "For now, go to sleep, Tempest."

She thought a minute, but her mind was sluggish, drowning in the unexpected sensations still swamping her body. He was right. If she was considering sleeping with the enemy, perhaps it would be better to find a way to make him an ally instead?

"Can I say yes to cuddling?" She mumbled. In answer, he wrapped his muscled arms around her and pulled her tight to his chest. He couldn't help placing a protective kiss behind the pale shell of her ear.

"What about that thing?" Roryn's head twitched to the left, indicating Morti who stood with his little knife-tipped paws stretched to reach the edge of the bed, tongue lolling hopefully.

"Absolutely not." She yawned. "He sleeps on the floor."

Morti huffed, his liquid eyes turning fierce in the dark. The rattle of his toes across the floor was the last thing Tempest heard as sleep overtook her.

Whatever bit of goodness left in the creature that once held the name Norc of Thays was lost as rage wrapped tight about his soul. He had been generous with the Malorn twits, though they didn't know it, risking his Emperor's disapproval and wrath as he let them slip through his fingers time and time again. They had been no threat, not against his tenure as Regent of Hlyn, but look what his benevolence had brought him!

Betrayed! Stabbed in the back by that dark Malorn whore! That dirty trull passing herself off as lady healer, so clever in hiding the murderous shadows that were just as much a part of her as her lauded compassion. Diabolical!

He had been fooled along with the rest, allowing her to drive this body merely because she'd had it first. No more! He'd sat silent as she continued to plot against his beloved Emperor, even chuckled as some of her antics struck him as plucky and inspired. Shacking up with the emperor's pet war dragon, though? That was beyond the bounds of what he would tolerate.

Norc had pulled himself out of the gutters as a child, fighting and scraping, pillaging and murdering his way to a reputation that caught the emperor's eye and secured him a place within the ranks of his favor. Another decade of plotting and subterfuge, of alliance and treachery passed before his true worth had been seen by the Eternal Warlock Emperor. Years spent groveling, of proving his faithfulness...years alone with no friends and no lover to soften his heart.

She'd refused to share this vessel with him but eagerly gave herself to the emperor's golden boy? The man who had done nothing to deserve his power except to be at the right place at the right time?! Who was Regent where Norc was...nothing? He was no longer content to linger as an observer to his unlife. His revenge would not be denied.

With his death, he'd made her a murderer. Now he'd make her a traitor.

Chapter Twenty-three

"He's got her!" Porta was screaming before she'd managed to pull Polli Nan to a complete stop. She had long ago lost her grip on Obertroess' lead, but he had followed her, nonetheless. Her strident voice filled the brush-dotted meadow as he continued on past her at full gallop, headed for the modest barn they used as a stable.

Porta leapt off her poor, frothing mare, stumbling as her thin legs hit the ground. Dahlis was there in an instant, cupping her elbow as she stowed her sword in the sheath slung across her back. She had been on guard duty, slouched behind one of the half-walls that made up the ruined portion of what used to be the chalet's foyer when the pounding of hoofbeats had jolted her from her quiet thoughts.

"Tempest?" Dahlis' golder than gold eyes shone fiercely in the early morning light, noting her sister's absence and calculating a dozen scenarios as to why she wasn't on her horse's back, liking none of them.

"I don't know if she's dead or not. Dahlis, it's all my fault! I got lost in the dark and now Tem might be a burned-up corpse like all the others...because of me!" Her screams were frantic, devolving into a mixture of tears interspersed with unintelligible cursing.

"She's not dead, Porta." The girl's fear was inciting her own, "I need you to calm down and tell me what is going on! Who has Tempest?"

"The stupid Regent! He took her to the palace last night and she never came back. I waited for her on the forest path but she didn't show up! If I hadn't given her a hard time about leaving he never would have caught her!" Porta's wailing broke Dahlis' heart but she refused to believe her sister was gone. She'd feel it if she were.

"He wouldn't kill her, P." She pulled the girl against her, letting her bury her little pixie-like face in her shirt while she sobbed, rubbing a comforting hand through her knotted black hair. The loud creaking of a door pulled her attention to the side entrance of the crumbling building to see Verilee and Monika rushing their way.

Verilee's bow was strung but loose in her hand, her arrows bouncing haphazardly in the quiver she'd not taken the time to properly tie down. She was bleary-eyed and wearing her thigh-length summer undershift, her blonde hair still mussed from her bedroll. She stumbled in her hurry, but regained her balance with her next step, throwing a hand back to press the jostling arrows firmly against her back.

The other girl was as put together as it was possible to be this far from polite society. Monika had found an airy green summer frock that managed to make her look both lovely and helped her to become invisible in the tall grass, young trees, and ragged bushes that dotted the land surrounding the old hunting mansion. Her favorite accessory, her sling, was held ready in her hand as her eyes went immediately to the tree line, alert, as always, for unexpected enemies.

"What is going on, Dahlis?" Verilee pulled Porta into an embrace of her own, renewing the tears and the babbling. Now the girl was howling some nonsense about a cat?

"The Regent has captured Tempest." Dahlis' stomach sank as the truth of the words settled firmly in her mind, igniting her rage as well as eliciting a healthy dose of fear.

"What do you need us to do?" Ever-practical Monika was already mentally packing her horse. Taking action was where she was most comfortable, and she knew her friend wouldn't disappoint. Some days Dahlis thought she had followed her into the life of an outlaw not merely because of her loyalty, but because she never had to look for adventure when she was at the side of a rebel princess.

"Verilee," She decided abruptly, choosing her plan not by its probability of success, but by how it sat with her gut. It had worked so far. "I will write a missive for you to deliver to the Warlock Emperor's nearest emissary. Maybe I can buy us some time. I know it is asking a lot, but…"

"It's done, Dahl. Don't even think I have any hesitation about delivering it straight to the front doors of the Noxian Palace itself, or I'll start thinking you don't know me at all." She winked, "Besides, those Noxian soldiers sure do look fine in their uniforms."

Dahlis engulfed both her and Porta in a giant hug. Squeezing until the younger girl quit crying and the older one quit her giggles. "Thank you. You know I never doubt you."

"Monika," her voice turned brisk, "I'll need you to hit up our allies and gather them for a strike upon the capital, if it becomes necessary."

Monika's smile was eager as she gave Dahlis a nod. When the princess took a step toward her, the red-head's expression went flat and she waved her hands in front of her body, clearly blocking any attempt at physical contact.

"What about me?" Porta had dried her tears but was standing aggressively within the protective circle of Verilee's arms.

"Porta, the pantry is stocked..." Dahlis began.

"I can't stay here. I won't stay here." The girl yanked herself out of Verilee's reach, folding her arms stubbornly over her chest. When her lower lip stuck out in an angry pout, Dahlis knew she would not be reasoned with.

"Your horse is blown." Monika stated matter-of-factly.

"And no one is getting that big white brute away from the feed trough any time soon." Verilee added.

All three turned to Dahlis as one. That was what they were, she thought, smiling sadly. One gang, one family. One silly group of trusting, faithful imbeciles that were going to get themselves killed out of loyalty. She sighed.

"She can come up with me. Canelope can easily bear our weight, and I'll need whatever intelligence she has gathered on the workings of the city and palace. We've been away too long to trust in our memories."

Monika nodded and grabbed Polli Nan's bridle, intending to cool the mare and turn her out before she saddled the fresh horses. She would have them ready and be mounted with her own pack before either Dahlis or Verilee could get their bags together.

"You think you can take orders without questioning them?" Dahlis asked the younger girl. Porta unfolded her scrawny arms, nodding eagerly. A howling dervish took that opportunity to pop its head out of the top of her blue dress, flat-faced and evil-eyed, it growled as it inspected the women standing gape-mouthed around it. "Porta, what is that?!"

"Tempest said I could have it."

"I highly doubt that." Tear tracks streaked and matted his fur and some of the sympathy she felt for Porta transferred to the tiny kitten.

"Well, she's probably dead and it's too late to ask her, huh?"

Dahlis grabbed the hissing bag of gray fur and bones. She held it at arm's length, a look of distaste on her face as she thrust it at Monika. She thought it was the most adorable thing she'd ever seen, but it was important to set boundaries when it came to Porta. There was no telling what she'd try to drag home next. "Can you leave a pound or so of jerked venison in the barn for this fella?" She whispered. Monika cracked a smile as she snuggled the kitten against her cheek.

Dahlis headed for the door at a walk, already composing the words she must say, as Porta sprinted for the door. "Will you grab my saddlebag while I write the letters?" Her request was absent-minded, but she caught Porta's eager nod. "Hey!" She yelled at the girl, "change out of that ridiculous dress!"

"Eat toenails!" Porta shot back then must have realized she wasn't talking to Tempest. She threw her hands over her mouth in horror, her green eyes peeled wide, then disappeared into the chalet as Dahlis' laughter filled the air.

In no time at all, the letters were written, which didn't surprise Dahlis as she had composed them over and over again in her head in the course of the past few years. The dark chalet seemed somber as she stood back from the butler's desk that had some-how inexplicably escaped the fire that wrecked the remainder of the front section of the building. The grand staircase, a much smaller but no less regal version of the one in the palace in Vyte, had been a favorite place of hers to sit. She didn't see the gaping wound of a past tragedy, she saw the possibility of future trips to a rebuilt existence with her sister at her side. Hope, like the happy memories she had of this place as a child, lingered in its halls. One day, by the Bright, the echo of laughter would reach the darkest corners once again.

She sighed. Those were dreams for another time. The future of more than just a disheveled old building in the woods was in the balance. Dahlis could feel herself getting antsy. She'd been dangerously content in her exile the past few years. The opportunity to finally be able to fight back was both terrifying and exciting.

"Where is that girl?" Dahlis growled in frustration, hollering Porta's name into the depths of the abandoned hall with no response. She poked her head out of the destroyed entry door. Monika and Verilee sat fidgeting on their mounts, their movements mimicking the nervous energy of their horses. Her long legs ate up the space between them and she handed off the sealed missives before she could change her mind. Dahlis waved at them, "Go on ahead and the Bright Bless you that we meet again soon."

They gave her formal half-bows from horseback as they kicked their mounts into motion, tearing off toward the forest paths that would lead them to a very different fate than that awaiting either of their princesses.

Dahlis pulled Canelope to a stop as a flash of warning hit her, appearing as an irritating tingle in the tips of her fingers. She had no true magic, certainly not comparable to what Tempest had been blessed with, but whatever this 'gift' of hers was, magic or instinct, it had saved her many times over the years. Ahead, the trail wove around a blind corner, preventing her seeing any oncoming enemy, but the sudden silence of the birds overhead was enough to convince her of the danger.

"Porta." She whispered to the girl asleep against her back and shook her with the hand she'd been using to hold her onto the horse. "Shhhh." She murmured as Porta's bony frame shifted against her, one of her wicked elbows digging into Dahlis' spine as she pushed herself upright.

Dahlis moved her hand to the bow in her lap and quietly withdrew an arrow from the quiver strapped to the saddle under her leg. Without making a sound, she notched it and tapped the end of the bow twice upon Canelope's neck, signaling the mare to lower her head. She could feel Porta stiffen behind her as the first thuds of heavy hoofbeats reached their ears.

The outlaw princess drew in a deep breath, her focus pinpointed to the spot where a man on horseback would get an arrow to the chest if one was required. A shuffle out of step alerted her to the fact that there were two riders, not one, and she laid a second arrow across her lap. She loosened her boots in the stirrups, prepared to fire then pull Porta into the brush. Hopefully, a second arrow would be possible in the confusion.

"Halt!" Dahlis called out when the man came into view. His face was stern, hard planes, and even over the distance between them, she could feel the intensity of his blue gaze. That, combined with his black as Nightmare hair pulled high and shaved on the sides to showcase matching dragon tattoos, left her no doubt who stood a mere half-dozen yards from her arrow. The sword he held ready at his side indicated he'd heard them as well and hadn't hesitated in his approach. This, more than anything, sent a bolt of fear through Dahlis.

"It's that connivating bastard who stole Tempest!" Porta's scream echoed through the forest, causing Canelope and the palomino he rode to flatten their ears. The black-maned palace mount was less disciplined, crow hopping and pulling on the lead tied to the man's saddle.

"Conniving?" He arched a single eyebrow. He made a show of spreading his hands and returning his weapon to the scabbard tied down firmly behind him.

"Don't correct her. You have no authority to do so and it wouldn't help anyway." Dahlis' bow was up in an instant, arrow fully drawn and ready at the notch. "Where is my sister?"

"Whoa!" Roryn lifted his hands slowly over his head. "I mean no harm. We both have the same goal here. I don't know where Tempest is."

"Liar!" Porta climbed down, quicker than any squirrel, and grabbed a rock off the path. She chucked it at Roryn and followed it up with a short stick and an acorn. "I saw you take her to the palace and she never came back. I know you were trying to put ugly bastard babies in her belly!"

"Porta stop. You'll hit that poor horse." She took her eye off her enemy for a brief second, completely stymied by the accusation. "Bastard babies?" She shook her head, knowing Porta well enough to figure out this was one of her wild suppositions. Most likely. Tempest did have the unfortunate habit of unduly admiring people who could lift just one eyebrow.

"She ran early this morning. I was hoping she'd made her way to you by now." He smirked at Porta, "While your bastard baby theory sounds intriguing, you'd be wrong to ever imagine Tempest could bear a child that is less than perfect."

"My sister is no one's fool. And neither am I." She kept her arrow trained directly at his heart, worried that maybe her sister was a fool. The man was way too comfortable using her name for a supposed enemy. Her fingertips had stopped tingling, making her think that perhaps he was no longer the danger she had anticipated him being. Still, she hadn't stayed alive by taking foolish chances herself. "Porta, there is a set of iron cuffs in that right bag."

"Step down from your horse, sir." She motioned with the bow as Porta giggled and dug through the satchel. He dropped his reins and dismounted smoothly, keeping his hands visible the entire time. She wasn't sure if he truly wasn't impressed by the fact that she could kill him before he could lift that deep crease in his cheek into a charming dimple again, or if it was all a ploy to set her at ease.

"I realize you have no reason to trust me but, if you could speed this up, that would be great. I'm worried your sister has gotten herself in some sort of trouble. When she ran this morning, she didn't take either of the horses." He held his arms stretched in front of him as Porta darted in and slapped them into place then kicked him violently in the shin before climbing into his empty saddle. She nudged the palomino around him but lined the spare mount beside him.

Dahlis kept her deadly arrow trained on him but rolled her eyes as she caught the girl's dastardly smile out of the corner of her eye. Porta waited until he had one foot in the stirrup and then dug her heels into the poor mare, sending her jolting forward and pulling the other horse behind her and causing the Regent to bounce twice on one leg before he was able to boost himself into the saddle. They surged past Dahlis and she chuckled as she followed, taking the tension off her bow but keeping it within easy firing reach.

Chapter Twenty-four

T HE FACT THAT TEMPEST was on foot was a bit worrisome, but she could take care of herself, Dahlis had no doubt about that. It was quite possible that cutting through the forest bracken would prove a quicker route than that she would have had to take on horseback. It was the kind of thinking she'd come to expect from her quiet sister.

As they backtracked along the path that would take them back to the chalet, Dahlis studied the man in front of her. She'd grown up on stories of the exploits of the foreign warrior bound in eternal service to the emperor. Not much had been known about those from the Edge of the World before Praxxys had conquered them and had stolen their prince, but they had been rumored to be fierce predators in a land filled with monsters.

The tattoos scrawling from the side of his temples then high along his thickly braided hairline gave him an alien appearance that both intrigued and repelled her. She could picture him as the heartless killer and ruthless commander from the tales she'd heard at her father's knee but, seeing him now, riding easy in the saddle before her, all she saw was a calm man of an age seemingly with herself, content to wear the chains handed him by a woman who should be the last one he gave control to.

Perhaps she should be worried that he had relinquished his freedom so readily? Was he so powerful that he had no fear of her advantage? Should she even now just shoot an arrow into his unprotected back? Oddly, she felt none of the concerns she should be considering with such a deadly adversary would be necessary with him.

She was more than a little confused that she didn't sense any ill-will toward her bubbling beneath his skin like a pustulent case of deceptive intent. Aside from the chiseled body of a life-long fighter and sinful looks worthy of a god, he appeared to be...almost normal.

The trees had thinned, giving way to the acres of overgrown pasture they would have to traverse to reach the chalet. Dahlis urged Canelope forward, locking eyes with the man as she pulled alongside him but still far enough out of reach to feel she could have a comfortable conversation. Not that conversing with a notorious warrior that had long been the enemy of her people could lay claim to being anything near comforting. He lifted his manacled hands to his forehead in a cynical, impudent salute.

"Care to tell me why you were traveling with my sister in the first place?" If he made some cock-a-mamie story up about them being desperately in love, she'd know he was lying. Dahlis wasn't a romantic and, though Tempest had a soft heart, she was just as practical and twice as loyal. It wasn't impossible that her little sister had fallen into love, or more likely, she tilted her head and considered how he sat his horse, had found herself fully engulfed in a case of lust. Dahlis just thought it was improbable that the man known as the Scourge of Salvadon, the cold right hand of the Warlock Emperor, had done the same.

"Do you want the story to start before or after I accused her of being a whore?"

"Oh, I must hear what she thought of that assumption!" Glee lit her golden eyes and Roryn was struck by the bloodthirsty urges shared by both sisters under the thick veneer of their ladylike demeanors.

"Long story short," the smile he shot her was self-deprecating, "she wasn't impressed and threw a rat at me. Then I coerced her into healing my men." Here he cocked that eyebrow again, "Men that you and your little group of bandits nearly killed."

"Um, good for her?" Dahlis didn't feel shame at wounding them. They lived in a kill-or-be-killed world, after all. That said, she took no pride in it either and was relieved Tempest had been able to save them.

"After that, I tracked her down and abducted her." He shrugged, almost apologetically.

"I told you!" Porta pumped her fist in victory before pointing it, center finger held rigidly vertical, and her meanest glare at their prisoner. He turned his charming smile on her, but she was patently immune to the lure of a charismatic man. He sighed, looking back at Dahlis with a frown.

"Actually, I took her to see your mother before I manhandled her and attempted to lock her in my bedchamber...which was actually her bedchamber, I suppose." He looked up at the sky, his luminous eyes reflecting back the clouds chasing through the blue above. She waited patiently for him to think through his thoughts. "Anyway," he was back to laughing at himself, "I finally caught on to the truth of who she was, and..."

"And?" Dahlis prompted, but she was smiling as well.

"She put me to sleep and snuck out the door."

Dahlis began to laugh, feeling the humor in her lean stomach. Porta was cackling from her place at the head of the line. Even the Scourge of Salvadon spared the situation a chuckle. He'd been anything but pleased at the time but...Tempest had changed him. Her healing hands had helped lessen the curse and, even if he was not certain she'd yet broken it, the girl herself was responsible for the light he now saw shining in his future. It had pierced the soul of darkness inside him, and he knew without question that he would never be the same empty shell of a human he'd been after leaving the Golden Lands.

"Phew!" Dahlis wiped the tears from her eyes and swallowed another laugh as she tried to catch her breath. "She used to do that to me, too! We'd be on our way to weapons practice and she'd stop me somewhere between the royal suites and the courtyard, leaving me snoring on the floor, so that she could impress our father with her timeliness."

Porta twisted around in her saddle, looking indignant. "Is that why I used to take four hour naps every seventh day?!"

It was Dahlis' turn to look at the sky.

She swore she could hear Porta grinding her teeth from three horses away. She definitely didn't mistake her huff of fury or miss when the girl jabbed the mare with a heel, sending them loping through the grass and forcing Roryn to turn forward, grasping the gelding tight with his knees.

Maybe this was a chance to learn more about their enemy. Maybe this was her moment to end the strife between Hlyn and the Glorious Empire. If she could convince T'Yanil to intercede on behalf of the Malorn claim to the throne, perhaps she'd be the next Malorn he escorted into the Pale Palace. He seemed a decent sort of man, if you could discount the fact that he had probably slaughtered nearly as many people as the emperor, at least in this lifetime.

A yipping bark pulled Dahlis' attention away from the man's broad back. Before she could think to call out, Porta jumped from the still trotting horse and ran to scoop up what appeared to be a rabid raccoon, smiling from ear-to-ear as she planted kisses on its...head?

"What in the Brightest's Backside is that?" Disgust ran through her. If they didn't find Tempest in time, she'd have to put Porta down to prevent her suffering from whatever evil was afflicting that corpse-like creature.

She dismounted and pulled the bridle down over Canclope's pearly forelock. She approached Roryn T'Yanil's horse and did the same for it, keeping a wary eye on him as she passed. "Please stay mounted." She didn't know if she was asking or giving a command and grimaced internally, hoping he hadn't noticed her softening attitude. His eyes cut to the thing in Porta's embrace and then rolled as if he was acknowledging the fact that he had the worst luck in Telryuun.

"I'll be more than happy to."

"This is Morti! Tempest said I could keep him." Porta turned toward Dahlis to show her the wriggling ball of happiness barely contained within the protective circle of her arms, but her eyes widened impossibly. Dahlis began to turn.

"I most certainly did not." She heard her sister's voice in her ear right before something bashed into the side of her head. Frantic yapping and girlish screeches echoed alongside the pain, amplifying it to an unbearable degree. When a blackness darker than the Nightmare came for her, she was more than happy to take its hand and follow it into the Nothing.

Chapter Twenty-five

"SHHH, SWEETNESS, BE STILL." A masculine voice whispering in her ear woke Dahlis from Darkness' soft embrace. She groaned, peeling her eyes open slowly as she started to become aware of a ferocious pounding thrumming through her skull. A curtain of stringy black hair obscured her vision, but she could see well enough to surmise that she hadn't had too much to drink and had fallen in with a guileful rogue.

It wasn't a man tempting her to silence with his gentle purr and satiny words. It was a stern admonition from the man straddling her thrashing sister, pinning her to the ground not five feet away, his bound hands held just wide enough to cover her thin shoulders.

"Tempest? What...?"

"She hurt you!" Porta was holding Dahlis' head in her lap and somehow licking her cheek? Ugh! No, it was that plague-infested quadra-ped who was making sweet love to her auditory canal, dulling the words being forcefully uttered by the current regent of Hlyn.

"A measly bump on the cranium is nothing compared to what the emperor will do when I deliver her to him! I'll finally get the recognition I deserve, and I will be restored to serve at his side!"

"What did she say?"

"She's been talking nonsense since she knocked you out." Roryn looked over at her, his eyes flicking immediately back to Tempest's strained face, when she began to buck wildly underneath him. "And she is really mad at me."

"Get your pestilent junk off my pelvis, Usurper!" Tempest's body flexed with more strength than anyone in the clearing would have credited to her slim frame, nearly shoving Roryn to the side. He slid his legs under her thighs, holding her more firmly in place as the muscles in his arms began to bulge.

"Fuck...Fuck!!" Dahlis struggled to her feet, her hand sifting through the blood-matted hair at the back of her head. She turned to Porta as the girl scampered over to help hold Tempest down, her small hands pushing firmly against Tempest's sweaty forehead.

"How long has she been dealing with this?" Her fingers came away coated in red but the wound itself wasn't the worst she'd ever suffered. It slowed her thoughts just enough to make them feel like poured honey on a chilly day. Although that could also be the panic begging to take control. She began to pace, ignoring the dizzy feeling that swamped her when she turned back toward the struggle too fast.

"I dunno." Porta changed the angle of her pressure so that she was hovering, bony elbows locked, and staring down into Tempest's angry, almost glowing eyes. "She's always been weird, but this is a new weird."

"That's not my sister." Dahlis declared, stuck between folding her hands protectively across her chest or using them to rip at the man forcing Tempe to remain still in the dirt. This wasn't his fault directly, but she wasn't feeling too much like being discerning with her animosity at this moment.

"Oh, you've got that right." Tempest's body went still, the fight leaving her so abruptly that Porta lost her grip and fell back onto her frilly bottom. "Your precious sister was a waste of space. Believe me when I say I'll make much better use of this vessel than she ever did." A wicked smile appeared on Tempest's chapped lips. "The amount of power in here, untouched, untapped." An oddly exuberant inhale had her eyes rolling up into her head, chasing an eerie shiver that seemed to emanate from the depths of her being. "Ahhhh..." Her exhale was throaty and froze the blood of everyone watching. "It's incredible."

Roryn looked at Dahlis and the trepidation in his gaze more than matched her own. They were warriors, prone to act first and ask questions over the corpse. This was beyond the realm of anything they knew how to manage.

"I'll enjoy seeing just what I can do with so much potential at my fingertips," the creature inside Tempest promised. "At least until the Emperor in his Benevolent Glory restores me to a proper, masculine body. In the meantime, she owes me this much."

"Norc of Thays?" Dahlis questioned, although she already knew.

"Didn't that incompetent fool get himself killed months ago?" Roryn was confused and Dahlis didn't blame him. This was definitely surreal to her...but who else could it be? How? She had no clue, but his next words confirmed her suspicion.

"Norc of Tempest, now." His laughter was gut-churning in her sister's dulcet voice.

"No. This cannot be." Dahlis dropped to her knees and grabbed Tempest's chin, forcefully turning her head to face her. "I do not know how you are accomplishing this, knave, but I will not allow it to continue. Leave my sister. Leave her now!"

Tempest's golden eyes closed, and a peaceful expression took over her face as her body went limp beneath those holding her down. A heartbeat. Two. A full minute of quick breaths passed before Dahlis dared take her hands away, sitting back warily on her heels.

"Did you kill it?" Porta's voice was tiny as she reached a fingertip out and poked Tempest in the side of her head.

A sudden jerk freed her right arm and a jolt of fearsome strength filled it as it clipped Roryn on the jaw and sent him rolling. Porta squeaked and scrambled backward, her eyes wide, as Tempest...no, Norc...surged upward, the dagger from Dahlis' unguarded thigh sheath held firmly under Dahlis' chin.

"Incompetent, huh?" His snarl twisted Tempest's beautiful face into a farce of what it once was.

"Please don't hurt her," Dahlis' throat bobbed as emotion filled it. "What is it you want?"

"Gods! You are as stupidly trusting as her. No wonder Hlyn was so easy to conquer. All it took was one dead king and you're all ready to turn over and take whatever shows up with the sweetest promises." He spat dismissively in the direction where Roryn was stealthily getting to his feet, sliding slowly sideways to try to tackle her from behind. "That's enough sneaking, Pretty Boy." The knife touched the pulse in her neck, and Roryn straightened, holding his bound hands high. Although the curse was only a weak mumble deep inside him, it was adamant no harm came to the princess heir Praxxys wanted so badly.

"Tempest." With effort, Dahlis tamed the tremble running through her, but she couldn't control the tears leaking from her eyes. "Tempe, please. Don't let this happen. Be strong, sister, like I know you are."

"Shut up!" The blade drew a thin bloody line across her neck. "Stand up with me, now. Let's find us a pretty horse and be off, huh?" Norc fisted Dahlis' hair around Tempest's hand and gestured with her pointed chin to Porta, "You, waif. Get us a fresh horse from the barn. That gray speckled brute looks well-fed enough to carry us to the emperor easily."

Dahlis' nod sent the girl running to comply. Hopping like a mange-afflicted rabbit, Morti was hot on her heels, yipping joyfully.

"Now." Norc's satisfaction was so extreme as to almost be giddy. "Get down on your knees you maggoty foreign pretender."

"Such hurtful words. You'd do well to temper them before you end up wounding someone with their edge." Roryn lowered himself reluctantly as his eyes followed the trail of blood now racing down the once future queen's sternum.

"Oh, you are going to find yourself more than wounded. With you gone, the emperor will need me more than ever."

"You aren't man enough to put me in my grave." He pointedly looked at Tempest's nearly exposed chest and gave his cockiest, most infuriating grin. It died almost immediately as Norc giggled.

"True, but it will be much more poetic when I tell the tale that you died by much weaker hands than mine. It seems the Outlaw Princess will get her revenge after all."

Tempest's foot slid through the tall grass and her toe pushed the bow that had fallen there in front of Dahlis. "Pick it up." Norc commanded, his knife wavered as he pointed the tip a bit to the left. "The arrow is there."

Dahlis did as she was told, her muscles loose and waiting for her opportunity to strike. Norc had the upper hand by holding Tempe hostage, but he couldn't possibly think she'd willing travel with him, docilely allowing him to deliver her to her greatest enemy. She fitted the arrow and pulled it taut. If she shot the arrow to wound only, she may have time to swing the bow and disarm Norc.

"Make it a killing shot, your highness," he seemed to read her mind, "or your little sissy here will suffer from a rather fatal tummy ache." The dagger abruptly left her neck and was point-deep in Tempest's abdomen, a steady trickle of blood running down the blade, coating her hand. "I'm in full control of her power so there will be no miraculous recovery."

"You'll be dead, too!"

"If you had failed to notice, I'm already dead. It's not exactly stimulating riding around in here all day with your sister's uninspired thoughts. Which," Tempest's lip curled in disgust, "I must say, have turned rather disgustingly prurient lately."

Roryn shrugged his broad shoulders, catching Dahlis' eye. "Do what you must. Just promise me you'll take care of Tempest. There is no better thing for a man to die for than love."

"You love her?" Dahlis gaped as she watched Roryn shake his long hair off his shoulders, the light of the sun reflecting off the metallic ink outlining his dragon tattoos. He nodded, gave Tempest one last, lingering look, then fixed his intense eyes on the heavens above.

"May the Bright Bless that my death makes me worthy of seeing her one day in the Promise."

"How touching." Norc sneered. "Fire!"

"Please." Dahlis begged, her fingers shook against her cheek as she drew the fletching near her ear. "We can do this some other way."

The knife slid deeper.

"I owe her this much just for being an ass," Roryn said. "You both will have a better chance to survive this if I'm gone. Eye or heart, Princess Dahlis. Make it count."

"I choose heart." She dropped the bow and, with all the force she could muster, plunged the arrow into her own stomach.

"No!" Someone screamed. Tempest grabbed her head. Red blood looked black against the silk of her dress, its tatters dancing in and out of the viscous stream like willowy children at play. She fell to her knees, bending in on herself as the world around her paused.

What have you done, Norc? Terror ran like ice through her veins as she caught glimpses of the past day. Falling asleep beside Roryn, waking to feel the rage of years sifting through her soul, slipping silently out the door of the hovel and attempting to coax one of the horses away from their shed. They had rebelled at being taken so he had left them, using Tempest's own memories to guide him past the dangers of the forest. Hours spent lurking along the tree line and then crawling through the tall grass. All the while her...his...mind had been a tumultuous mess of hate and euphoria. Joy for the prestige bringing the outlaw princess to Praxxys would bring him. Hate for...everything else.

What needed to be done, fool girl! All my life I've fought and clawed to get where I am. You have no idea what it means to have to crawl your way out of the gutters of this cesspool. You have all the power in the world and choose never to take action.

Action? Nearly killing everyone dear to me in order to turn my sister over to an eternal being that has no use for either of us beyond feeding our souls to the evil magic he tends so assiduously? The emperor has no capacity for empathy. He only seeks to take, never to give. He would steal everything from you as surely as he has taken it from me.

What is a sister, anyway, except for another mouth to feed or another competitor seeking your glory? You'd have done better without her. Without all of those needy, puling hangers-on holding you back, you could have had any-thing. Everything!

If that is what you think, my sorrow has doubled for you.

What would you have me do, now? The angry mass that was the devastated soul that she had torn from the world when she killed Norc seemed to shrink, swirling in on itself before settling into a barely pulsing ball.

Nothing, she took control of her body, all her thoughts and feel-ings, and she created a prison deep inside her, lining its walls with the warm memories of sisterly hugs, childhood victories, and wild rides through midnight fields strewn with flowers, simply to feel the joy of the double moons on your face. She wrapped him inside, leaving, as a final gift, a glowing spark of the hope that had kept her sane in the past years. *You've been through enough.*

Chapter Twenty-six

RORYN SURGED TO HIS feet, ready to pull the blade from Tempest's hand. She was curled in on herself and he tried to gently peel her hands away from her knees. The knife fell onto the ground and he tossed it over his shoulder violently enough to lodge the steel to the hilt in the dirt.

"Careful." Dahlis warned as he sat Tempest back so that he could examine her wound. His fingers probed tenderly around the edges, coming back sticky but not tremendously wet. Satisfied, he tore off his shirt, tearing it into strips before binding it tightly around her middle. Tears streamed down her dirty cheeks as he picked her up, cradling her against his chest.

"What about you? Do you need help?" His eyes dipped to her waist.

Dahlis pulled up her shirt, showing the protective corset she wore underneath. The point of the arrow had barely made it through the leather, leaving nothing behind but a bloody scratch and a ruined shirt. She dug into her pant pocket and pulled out a key. She stepped closer, not quite trust in her eyes, but grudging respect. She unlocked his cuffs and pulled them clear.

"Would you really have let me kill you?"

He shrugged, the boyish grin on his face telling her nothing. "*Would* you have killed me?"

"Hmm." She answered, noncommittally. She moved to wrap the irons over Tempest's wrists. "Just until we know for sure."

"Don't." Roryn shifted out of her reach. "It's her."

"Are you sure?" Dahlis wanted to believe, she truly did. But she knew her sister's truth, not merely the shiny parts she would show a suitor. If that is what the man holding her so tenderly was.

"I'll bet my life on it."

"That was intense!" Porta popped up out of the grass behind them, a sword too heavy for her arms dragging along behind her. Morti the dog-thing was chewing on the dirty tip, occasionally stopping to push the grass and soil around his fetid mouth with his surprisingly pink tongue.

"What took you so long? I expected you here to rescue us a full five minutes ago." Dahlis took the sword with one hand and began to walk across the meadow, motioning Roryn to follow.

"Better late than never. It's not my fault the only weapon near that big stupid horse was this giant sword. Why, I almost pulled my arms off to bring it to you." Porta wiggled her bare arms in the air, mere pale sticks against the stark blue sky. Dahlis noticed she'd been smart enough to strip down to her shift before trying to sneak through the field.

"It's Tempest's sword. Surely you aren't that much weaker than her?" Dahlis balanced the longblade on her palm by the hilt and made a show of twirling it effortlessly before her. It was a trick their father had taught them to improve dexterity and finger strength. Dahlis found it focused her attention to the point she could ignore the conversations she didn't want to have or the feelings she was in no mood to contemplate.

"Well," Porta stooped down and scooped up Morti, squeezing him tight to her chest. His eyes bulged a bit more than normal, but he didn't fuss. "I am more the brains of the operation sort. I'll leave the menial work to the big-shouldered broads." Dahlis reached back and popped Porta on the head softly, a reminder to watch her tongue.

"It's important to know your limits," she said, "and I have reached mine." A forceful sigh left her as the shadow of the chalet engulfed them. "Oh, Wise and Resourceful Porta, would you be so kind as to snag some clean clothes and water from the kitchen?"

"Sure thing!" She darted off into darkness.

"Wash your hands before touching the linens and leave that ugly beast in there!" Dahlis thought to call after her. The last thing she needed was to catch a disease while cleaning up her scratches.

"He's not ugly. He's...uniquely proportioned." An indignant yip echoed her shout.

Dahlis was solemn as she turned to examine the man holding her sister. From the tattoos curling along his hairline to the well-delineated muscles revealed by his absent shirt, his entire aura spoke of a man used to living life on the edge. He practically reeked of all the warning signs she'd learned to recognize: Dangerous. Feral. Fearless. She was still half-tempted to drive an arrow through his heart. A good leader learned to delegate though, so if any heart-rending was to be done, it would be Tempest's burden to bear.

"How is she?"

"She's awake." Roryn shifted his arm so that he could rub the tear streaks from her face. He said nothing more as his eyes roved over her, searching for answers to questions he didn't know if he could speak out loud.

"Please, put me down." Tempest's voice trembled but he did as she asked, carefully letting her feet fall, steadying her until she was confident her first step wouldn't send her plummeting to the ground.

Dahlis sat down on one of the large stones that had fallen away from the burned wall. She propped her back against the shattered frame that had once held the stately entrance door in place. She watched, unblinking, as Tempest approached, slowly reaching out to touch the bloody spot she had inflicted. Dahlis couldn't help her flinch, and tears began to roll unchecked down Tempest's face once again.

"I'm sorry!" She worried at her bottom lip, further splitting it and breaking Dahlis' heart. Tempest had always been softer than they could afford to be. Had she coddled her too much? Sheltered her when she should have been showing her the hard realities a little closer? She sighed. It didn't matter. She loved her sister as she was and if she was required to sacrifice every bit of her own softness to preserve her little sister's, she would do exactly that. She owed her that much for dragging her into this life.

"It's not the first time you've brained me, Tempe, though I hope heartily that it is the last." She held out her hand, pulling her down to the stone beside her. Out of the corner of her eye, she watched the Salvadonian as he hovered, eyes falcon-focused on Tempest.

"I am so sorry, Dahl. I don't know how he took control."

"You should have told me what was going on. I could have helped somehow." Dahlis' jaw was tight, the dimple jumping under the strain.

"How was I supposed to do that? You dropped me at the Evermore and ran." She drew in a deep breath, letting it out and, with it, all of her frustration at being the useless little sister that always needed saved. "Anyway, I thought I could handle this myself. I...liked living in one spot for a while, you know?" She said with a good dose of guilt. "Porta was doing well there, too. Juli was even giving her smiling lessons!"

They both shared a laugh and the tension between them broke.

"He's gone?" Dahlis questioned finally, hesitant to say his name.

"Not gone but locked away. Quiet for now."

"Are you going to heal me, or what?" It was her apology and Tempest recognized it as such. She lifted her hand eagerly to Dahlis' head, in her own wordless apology. Her eyes shut and she leaned in, enjoying the mini-hug of being pressed against her sister's side. With a smile on her face, she reached for her power.

Only to come up...empty. Confusion twisted her face and she tried again. The dark swirl of her death magic came eagerly to her call, more than happy to fill the well that had held all her light.

She sent her senses out, seeking, searching, but…all her goodness, all her healing?

"I…" Tempest fell back upon the grass, her hands shaking violently and terror turning her face a stark white. "It's gone!"

Dahlis choked back a surge of fear as her sister's alarm triggered her own. She latched onto Tempest's cold forearms, stooping to catch her madly rolling eyes. "What's gone, Tempe?"

"My magic." Her gaze was hollow, lost, so, despite the trepidation swirling within her, Dahlis pulled her tightly into her embrace, rubbing calming circles on her back. "My healing…it has disappeared!"

She trembled as Dahlis held her, shock filling her body. Roryn crouched behind her, his hand firm against her back as her head began to loll weakly on her neck. "You've been through the wringer today, Tempe." Dahlis nodded at Roryn and he took an unresisting Tempest back into his arms. "Rest for now. We will figure this all out when you wake up, alright?" She smoothed a few errant curls back, trailing her fingertips over Tempest's too-cold cheek.

"Her room is upstairs. Come." She ducked into the dark, not seeming to need a moment for her eyes to adjust. "Be careful on the first stairs, they lean a bit." Dahlis was brisk as she ran up the grand staircase, trusting Roryn to follow. She yanked her loose hair back, ignoring the pain it caused, and bound it in a tail behind her. She cracked her knuckles viciously and gave him a quick glance over her shoulder.

Roryn surmised she was one of those people who couldn't sit still for very long. Those life called in many directions, and they feared missing the adventure each opportunity provided. Though she wouldn't like the comparison, the Outlaw Princess was very much like the Warlock Emperor in this way.

Roryn's eyes had adjusted, and he took his own opportunity to take a closer look at the near-ruin the girls had chosen as their safehouse. The hunting chalet was simple when compared to the luxurious castles Praxxys tended to keep splayed across the breadth of Telryuun, but what he could see of it in the light streaming through the stained-glass scenes of deer and dogs high overhead was appealing.

"This way." She pointed right and trudged down a long hall, her feet stirring the dust in the deep red carpet. Another stained glass lit the end of the corridor, casting an enchanting mirage of golden swirls across Dahlis' skin as she stopped before it, fiddling with the handle of the last door in the hall. Roryn's eyes widened as the glass pieces coalesced to form the figures of two small golden hair and amber-eyed girls. They were dressed to match in long royal blue gowns and could have been twins except that the taller girl's hair was unforgivingly straight and the shorter's held a rambunctious curl.

"This was your home." He realized.

"Yes." She said as she pushed the door open on squeaky hinges and rushed about pulling curtains wide. She turned down the bed next, the simple white linens stark against the otherwise opulent decor.

"Put her here." Roryn reluctantly shifted her onto the bed, straightening her arms and legs with gentle hands. Dahlis elbowed him aside and climbed onto the bed beside Tempest. She waved him off. "There is a sleeping shift in that wardrobe. Grab it for me?"

Feeling very out of place, he opened the dresser door and found the simple white gown hanging beside a sprightly flowered dress. A man's white shirt and a pair of doeskin breeches rounded out the contents of the cabinet. Not a very substantial wardrobe for a princess.

His fingers touched the soft cotton of the short shift and a wave of essence, strawberries and clover, scented the air as he pulled it free from the hanger. He couldn't stop his long inhale as the unique smell that was Tempest's alone filled his senses. It was at that moment that he realized he was lost. The Scourge of Salvadon was irrevocably in love.

The sound of ripping jerked him from his revelation, and he turned back to the bed in time to see Tempest stripped to the skin, Dahlis' movements efficient as she removed the soiled and tattered evening gown, tossing the pieces to the floor behind her.

"Maybe I should go fetch that black-haired munchkin?" He shielded his eyes and tossed the shift down on the bed. He cleared his throat uncomfortably, hoping she wouldn't notice the red stain of embarrassment painting his cheeks.

"It's nice to see a man with a little modesty," she laughed, "but I need to clean and stitch her wound and can't do that without seeing it."

"I can't help but feel Tempest would be very not alright with this situation. I'll be more than happy to go help the waif with the supplies."

"We call her Porta and she is probably standing outside the door now listening in when she should be minding that the water boils quicker." The patter of small feet retreating down the hall-way brought a genuine smile to Dahlis' face, one that shone brightly in her impossible eyes.

"Here." She covered Tempest with two sheets so that only her stomach, the blood crusted wound showing up brightly against her pale flesh, was exposed. "Sit." She pointed across from her. "I may need you to hold her down. She's not a slouch when it comes to handling pain, but it's also rare that she has to deal with her own."

"Healing causes her pain?"

Dahlis nodded, her smile falling away. "The Malorn bloodline comes with many blessings, but our curses are just as numerous. Tempest's curse is more than equal to the power she's been given."

She used Roryn's torn shirt to dab at some of the blood along the edge of the wound before continuing, "As a child, she used to scream for quite a long time after a healing. My mother and father became so upset that they forbade her to use her power ever again. That's when she learned to hide the pain."

"Here are the towels." Porta whistled as she jogged through the door, warm water sloshing from side to side, spilling out of the bowl as she sat it on the bed. She peeled the clean squares of cloth off her shoulder one-by-one and attempted to fold them neatly.

"Did you learn nothing from a summer spent living at an inn?" Dahlis asked, grabbing the top crinkled ball of fabric and shaking loose before she dipped it into the bowl. She didn't bother to ring it out as she ran it across the bloody mess of flesh, causing pink rivulets to run down Tempest's sides.

Porta shrugged, "Folding is a waste of time. I'm a warrior, not a washerwoman." She crawled carefully onto the head of the bed. "Is she gonna wake up soon?"

"Tempest is tough. There doesn't seem to be much fresh blood here so," her hand paused and she bent closer, "that's odd."

"What is it?" Roryn's deep voice rumbled darkly as a thousand scenarios of woe entered his mind. "What's wrong?"

Dahlis dipped the cloth again and scrubbed it hard across Tempest's stomach. Roryn immediately grabbed her hand, pulling it forcefully away. His fingers tightened painfully over the delicate bones in her wrist but Dahlis merely grunted, "Look."

There was no wound. A red line and a few drops of blood were the only signs she'd been injured. Surprise flitted over both of their faces, followed by relief.

"She said lost her healing." His confusion was clear.

"She cannot use it, but it doesn't mean it isn't there."

"You think Norc did this?"

"That," she shrugged, not really worried about the finer details as long as Tempest was fine, "or her body healed itself."

"So, she's just taking a nap?" Moving stealthily, Porta wet her finger in her mouth and then slipped it into Tempest's ear.

"What in the Bright's Rancid Buttcheeks?!" Tempest screamed as she came awake, flailing her arms and landing a good smack across Porta's chin. An accidental slap, but deserved, nonetheless.

"Your ninnies are hanging out, Tem." Porta began giggling uncontrollably and jumped off the bed, running out the door before she could get another smack.

Tempest looked down to see all her naked glory on display and then she began to shriek. "Who took my Nightmare Damned clothes when I was helpless? Was it you?" She pointed an aggressive finger at Roryn, poking him painfully in a naked bicep. Her other hand grabbed frantically at the sheets around her. He held his palms up, all innocence. Luckily, he'd cast his eyes to the ceiling before he'd been caught staring.

"Calm down, Tempe." Dahlis moved off the bed and scooped the shift off the floor where it had been tossed in the kerfuffle. "If he hasn't seen them already, something tells me he will soon."

"That sounds like a promising idea to me." Both girls ignored Roryn's quip, so he slid backwards off the bed, giving them some space. He leaned against the wall beside the double set of windows and looked down upon the horses milling about outside the barn though his attention was focused on the conversation behind him.

"What happened?" Tempest muttered, feeling the fool. Once again, she was showing the weakness that seemed to follow her like a bad dream. She gathered her shift against her chest and pulled it on as quickly as possible.

"Well, I'm not sure what you remember so...You bonked me on the head, tried to cut my throat, stabbed yourself in the belly. Then I stabbed myself. You did some sort of mind-wrangling with the ghost of Norc and locked him up. Then you cried like a baby because you realized what an ass you were for hitting me. Then you passed out because you couldn't access your healing power."

"You're not hurt badly?" Tempest looked Dahlis over closely.

"Not even a headache." Dahlis lied.

"What about me?" Her hand ran along the raw line marring her abdomen. "I remember the knife going in..."

"You weren't as injured as we had feared." At this, Roryn made eye contact with Dahlis over his shoulder but didn't say anything. She raised her eyebrow at him in challenge and he gave her a slight shrug. He wasn't sure exactly what her game was by not telling Tempest about her healing, but he wasn't enough of a fool to get into an argument over it until he knew what he was fighting against.

"We need to discuss our strategy, Dahl." Her eyes cut to Roryn, as if unsure whether she should trust him or run him through. Just last night he was promising to deliver her sister to the Warlock Emperor. What was he doing standing so nonchalantly in her bedchamber? More importantly, why wasn't Dahlis sticking her sword in him?

"I'll fix a broth. Then we'll talk." She stood, pushing firmly on Tempest's shoulder until she was laying down against the pillows. Like a mother hen, she tucked the blanket around her, much as she had on cold winter nights when Tempest had snuck into the crown princess' room so they could read to each other from the titillating romance books their mother would never approve of them having. "For now, rest."

"Uh," Roryn straightened as Tempest's fierce golden eyes locked on him. "I'm going to take care of the horses." He scrambled from the room, causing Dahlis to put her hand over her mouth to stifle her laugh.

"For a cold-blooded killer set on chaining us to a heartless emperor, I rather like him." She kissed Tempest's forehead and left the room, shutting the door softly behind her.

Tempest sighed and buried her head in her pillow. She kind of liked him, too. Right now, though, she wanted a nap more than she wanted to get a better look at that sleekly muscled chest.

As sleep pulled her under, she felt the raging death magic singing deep inside her, the now unchecked power sending feelers out along her veins, filling her dark corners and laughing with glee. The end, she could feel, was coming.

Was it ready for her?

Chapter Twenty-seven

V OICES LURED HER OUT of her dreams.

Cracking her eyes open, Tempest was lost for a moment. She'd half-expected to wake up in her little back-of-the-stable cot, sore from tossing and turning on her straw-filled lump of a mattress. Instead, she snuggled the freshly laundered blanket close to her face and breathed in the memories of other blessed mornings she'd awakened in this room.

Even though they rarely got to spend time here together, Dahlis always made sure her bed was aired out and the linens pristine...just in case. It was one of the many things that made her honor her sister above all others. She didn't follow Dahlis because she thought her cause was just. She stood for her because she knew no one would be a better ruler for Hlyn. If Dahlis took care of her people half as well as she did her little sister, she would surely be a queen of legend.

A yawn caught her by surprise but she rode it out, turning it into a full body stretch that loosened her overworked muscles, a tiny twinge near her navel the only souvenir she carried from the morning's harrowing adventure. She sat up and scooted off the bed, dangling at the edge before she let her feet slip to the floor, her toes testing the cool wood and finding it swept free of the dust and debris of an nearly abandoned structure. Of course Dahlis had taken care of that, too.

She felt remarkably good.

The sun was coming in low through the windows so, thankfully, she hadn't wasted the entire day lazing in bed. She threw open the door to her wardrobe and took out the floral dress, pulling it over her head and smoothing it down her hips, noticing it was much tighter than the last time she'd worn it. The light green cotton, dotted with pink flowers, wasn't one she would have chosen for herself, but she loved it because she'd gotten it as a gift of gratitude from a woman whose child she had saved.

A wave of regret speared through her. Would she ever be able to heal again?

The mumble of voices and a chitter of laughter drew her to the open bank of windows as she was braiding her hair. It wouldn't stay tamed for long but she had to at least make an effort to appear somewhat ladylike. Not that anyone would mistake her for anything other than a half-wild harridan.

Far below, Roryn began singing a dirty soldier chant she'd heard many a time as she waited tables at the Evermore. They'd started a fire and arranged some rough-cut deadfall for seats. Dahlis was leaning toward the flames, turning something on the spit, while Porta danced, her arms flopping like she was some odd bird experiencing a seizure.

His voice was smooth and tempting, much like Roryn himself. The gods truly had put all the best parts of a man together when they made him. It was no wonder Praxxys had chosen him as his personal guard and advisor. If she were an all-powerful overlord, she'd be content to have him at her side for an eternity as well.

She couldn't contain her smile as he began her favorite part of the song, the refrain that shamed the naughty barmaid. Her toe couldn't help but tapping and she hummed along. When the moment came to shout, 'Bella Badnews', they sang Gutra Twoshoes instead. Tempest's gasp was lost in the howls of laughter and her eyes immediately went to Roryn. He was staring right at her, his teeth bright in the gathering gloam.

Bright's Blessed Toenail! They were telling stories about her!

"Whatever Porta told you, she's lying!" She yelled out the window.

"Am not!" Morti's bark punctuated Porta's denial and his back legs scratched at the ground in his own aggressive statement.

"Come down, sleepy britches!" Dahlis waved something in the air. "We have meat."

Tempest nearly ran around the room, searching for her boots. Her stomach began to grumble violently and she realized she'd only had one pitiful serving of beans in the past two days. That was no way to live. She tripped over her feet in her haste, grabbing the window frame to keep from falling to her death.

"Where are my shoes?" She called down.

"Sorry! I washed them. Meet me at the kitchen door?" Tempest was scurrying down the stairs, sliding across the humidity-dampened foyer tiles, and hopping from foot to foot in the doorway before Dahlis had a chance to show Porta how to turn the spit to keep the meat from burning. She tugged the boots from the dead branches she'd had them suspended from to dry and loped over to her sister's side.

She dropped the boots inside the door and with a flourish presented Tempest with a chunk of something that smelled absolutely delicious. "Here, this first. I know you have to be starving."

"Fresh rabbit?" Tempest popped the entire bit in her mouth. Her eyes almost rolled up in her head from the sheer pleasure of eating the savory meat. "When did you have time to set snares?"

"Turns out your man can hunt more than the enemies of the Emperor." Dahlis leaned casually against the side of the house, watching Porta closely as she batted out a tiny fire that had singed the fluff of fur on Morti's tail.

"He's not my man." Tempest murmured as she swallowed the last bite and licked the grease from her fingers. Eager to get more of the rabbit, she had her slightly damp right boot on and laced within seconds.

"Then you won't mind if I take him?"

"Don't you even dare!" She straightened, a scowl puckering her face.

"Ha!" Dahlis shoved Tempest in the shoulder, knocking her off balance so that she had to take a second stab at pulling on her left boot. "I knew it! Don't worry, he's not my type. Much too wild for me. I've had enough of anything with a hard edge. A nice soft gentleman who makes me breakfast and rubs my feet sounds about perfect."

"A soft gentleman who will bore you silly in a week?" Tempest's smirk slipped as stepped outside. She watched Roryn roll another log close to the fire, stopping it an instant before it hit the still-smoking dog-thing. He wiped his hands on his pants, chips of wood and clumps of dirt marking his strong thighs. He sat, patting the space beside him as he caught her looking. He winked. "Pretty sure he is everyone's type and knows it well."

"Nah." Dahlis' dismissed the thought. "He's too solitary. That man has been alone for a long time. You know," she tucked a stray curl behind Tempest's ear, "you have my blessing to be as wild as your heart desires."

"I don't know, Dahl. My heart has never beat this wildly."

"That's how you know it's real." She grabbed her sister's hand and led her toward the fire. "Come, let's get something in your stomach besides butterflies."

With the rabbit devoured and the broth Dahlis had made settling pleasantly in their stomachs, their minds, reluctantly, turned to the choices they each had to make in the coming days. Decisions that could affect not only their own future, but that of Telryuun itself. It was a sobering thought and their laughter slowly died as the flames turned to coals before them.

Dahlis tossed the piece of bark she'd been fiddling with into the dark behind Morti, causing the mutt to turn in a tight circle before yapping at the 'monster' that must be lurking in the tall grass. "Have you fed your kitten, Porta?"

"His name is Lax the Destroyer and he hates me. I put him in a punishment box until he loves me again."

"What in the Everloving...? Go let him out now!"

"How will he learn if he doesn't have time to reflect? Tempest puts me in the punishment box all the time." She pointed accusingly at her tormentor, sitting thigh-to-thigh on the log with a bemused-looking Roryn. Tempest groaned and put her face in her hands while Dahlis stared at her in disapproval.

"Just go save that damn cat, P." She fished a handful of rabbit bones from the edge of the pit and passed them to the girl. "Give him these and have Morti kill a rat or two for him. Tempest says he has a taste for them?"

Tempest peeked through her laced fingers as Porta and her sidekick ran past. Her braid whipped Roryn in the face as she swung toward where Dahlis sat, brow lifted nearly to her hairline as if she couldn't wait to hear this explanation. Cheeks pink, she tried to defend herself. "I swear it's not a real box, Dahl. You know how Porta prattles on and on?! I just wanted one moment of peace. So," she shrugged, "I may have told her my magic could create an impenetrable shield around her that would prevent anyone from hearing her until she was properly apologetic."

"Hmmm." Having been on the receiving end of Porta's chatter, Dahlis was more than a little intrigued and didn't have it in her to pretend to be upset. "Tempe, you may just be a genius. A slightly fiendish one, but a genius nonetheless."

"Speaking of diabolical, we should talk about the Emperor's plan for us before Porta gets back." She could feel the warmth of Roryn's leg against her backside and her face flushed a deeper red.

"What's your stake in this?" Dahlis looked directly at Roryn, her chin at an aggressive tilt that was all too familiar to Tempest. If his answer didn't line up with Dahlis' plan, only the Bright could protect him.

Suddenly, Roryn shifted behind Tempest, bringing one leg over to straddle the log, trapping her between his thighs. She gulped as his chest rubbed against her back. Luckily for her slipping sanity, he'd found a replacement shirt somewhere. His muscled forearm appeared before her and she was enveloped in a curtain of intense heat as his other arm wrapped around her. He pointed to the angry red scar that he had once hidden religiously under his metal bracer.

"Long ago, twenty-five years if one were to count such things," he told them matter-of-factly, "a silly, prideful boy was trapped into a contract he could never hope to break. Praxxys stole my freedom, tore me from my people, and changed the course of my life indefinitely. He ripped me to pieces. Turned me into a creature without love or compassion." He sat back but his arms remained on the legs bracketing Tempest's, his hands lightly cupping the outside of her knees. "Then he gave me a purpose."

Both girls remained silent as he continued. "Nothing in this world is completely evil or all good, and so it is with the Warlock Emperor. He treated me well despite all the tragedy he brought me. He saves as many people as he enslaves, raising the poor, desolate places by allocating resources from the stronger countries," he paused, "like Hlyn."

"We haven't seen any major changes in infrastructure or finances." Dahlis hesitated, "It is one of the reasons I haven't led a real revolt. I can't justify the lives of our people just because I miss palace life."

"He's been..." Roryn rubbed his head, mussing his midnight-black crest, "distracted."

Dahlis and Tempest shared a look. "What are our chances of getting an audience with him," Tempest asked, "and negotiating our freedom? You told me he would not consider an alliance of marriage. What else could we offer?"

"I am not against uniting Hlyn under the banner of the Glorious Kingdom," Dahlis declared, surprising them. "If we were given some autonomy in the distribution of our assets."

"Unfortunately, I'm not sure that's possible. Praxxys wants to bind you to him, as he did to me. Using your magic under the power of the eclipse is, according to him, the only way to ensure his spell is successful."

"But Dahlis doesn't..."

"What spell?" Dahlis interrupted, signaling Tempest to silence with their secret fingertip to chin gesture.

Roryn shrugged and his hands slipped up her legs, one settling on her thigh as he wrapped the other casually around her waist. "I have no clue. He's been tight-lipped other than to say it will be world-altering."

"That doesn't sound promising." Dahlis tilted her head to the stars. For the first time she could remember, she truly felt defeated. She was tired. Tired of life on the run. Tired of fighting a battle no one else truly believed needed to be fought. The truth was, she needed Hlyn much more than it needed her.

"I want to help Hlyn, but I am not sure if I can defy Praxxys if he gives me a direct order. The curse may have weakened but it's not gone. If we had more time..."

"But the eclipse is in two days." Dahlis finished for him.

"And I can't heal you." Tempest's forlorn voice added.

"You already have." He whispered into her hair, causing a shiver to ricochet up her spine.

Dahlis smiled sadly and Tempest already knew she was plotting a course of action that she couldn't be talked out of. There were many ways to describe her sister's temperament, and self-sacrificing martyr had always been at the top of the list.

"Well, kids, this has been fun, but the dawn will come soon enough and with it some hard decisions. Porta," she called to the girl skipping happily toward them, Lax snuggled under her chin and Morti dragging behind, his few teeth locked tight on the hem of her dress, "you can sleep with me tonight."

"But Tempest will get cold without me." Her pout extended across her piquant face and spread along every inch of her spare frame.

"I very much doubt that will be the case tonight." She stood, wrapping her arm around the girl's shoulder and attempted to lead her away but Porta was having none of it and shook herself free.

She gave Roryn an imperious side-eye, looking at him up and down. "You know my expectations." She said mysteriously. The Malorn sisters shook their heads, but Roryn merely nodded solemnly.

"So it shall be, waif."

"Wonderful!" Her green eyes actually sparkled and a true smile lifted her lips. She tossed her ratted hair and squeezed Lax hard enough to make him hiss as she grabbed Dahlis' arm and led her away. "Sweet dreams then."

Chapter Twenty-eight

SILENCE ENSHROUDED THEM AS the echo of feet on stone coupled with Porta's never-ending chatter faded into the depths of the kitchen. A late-burning limb crackled in the fire before flaring out.

"What was that all about?" Tempest asked.

"Confirming a promise that is too gracious for the likes of me, but one I fully intend to find a way to fulfill." He refused to say more, just smoothed the curls on top of her head, tucking a few behind the curved shell of her ear and leaning in so that his cheek rubbed lightly against her own, the slight brush of stubble beginning to grow out capturing every bit of her attention. How something so simple could ignite every nerve-ending in her body was beyond her conception.

"That tickles," she breathed.

"Mmmm," he replied, using the hand on her stomach to urge her closer. She resisted for a half second before she melted back against him. The hem of her skirt rode up as his hand clenched in reaction to the feeling of her curves aligning to his hard planes. He kissed the corner of her mouth, running his open lips across her cheek and touching the tip of his tongue to the tender spot where her jaw met her neck. "How do you like this?"

A low moan as she tilted her head was her only answer. It was enough.

He moved her braid to the side, exposing the exquisite line of her throat. His hand trailed down its sun-kissed length, trailing his knuckles across the top then down the side of her breast. The modest cut of her dress teased him, hiding what the red dress had so blatantly displayed the day before. He massaged her slim hips, pulling her in closer than she thought possible as he kissed his way down the side of her neck, sucking gently where it met her shoulder.

"I want your mouth, Sweetest."

She turned in his arms, eager to forget the future under the heat of his caress. Her hands slipped behind his neck, threading through his silky hair, and she surged against him, taking him by surprise as she readily gave what he asked, sliding her mouth against his. It was his turn to moan as her tongue touched his tentatively, running along the seam of his lips.

She wasn't unsure, the thought sent a bolt of need straight to his groin, she was savoring. Though it cost him every bit of control he had, he held her gently, letting her take the lead. When her hands slid down his shoulders and slipped inside the collar of his shirt, he nearly lost his mind, trembling in anticipation of feeling her narrow fingers dance across his skin.

"That's my girl," he encouraged, cradling the heart-shaped perfection of her face in his large hands, "touch what you want to touch.' He deepened their kiss, stroking her tongue with his playfully. "Taste what you want to taste."

"I want..." her palms left his chest and disappointment slowed him as she pulled his hands from her face. "I want..." It was her turn to tremble as boldness consumed her, "you to touch me."

"Here." She set his hands on her chest and arched into them.

A growl escaped him along with his inhibitions, "Fuck." He lifted her onto his lap, sliding her legs behind him so that her heat met his own, binding her close with an arm behind her ass. His mouth slanted aggressively over hers, his tongue taking what she offered, giving more than she ever dreamed. She burned hot against him and welcomed his hand as he slid it into the neckline of her dress and cupped her breast.

"What have I ever done that the Bright has blessed me with you? Fuck, woman. You are perfect."

A thin cry of need shot through Tempest, and she locked her ankles behind his back, desperate to feel that hard, insistent part of him against the throbbing sensations flooding her. She thrust against him, making him moan, causing her to quiver with a need she didn't fully comprehend. How could any mortal understand this?

Surely this feeling was as close to the Promise as anyone could get?

"Roryn." She moaned his name, knowing who she needed even if she didn't know why. Her hands dipped to the waistband of his pants. One button and a single zipper were the only things keeping her from the secrets she needed to discover. Did she dare?

All her thoughts slipped away as his mouth left hers, trailing down her neck and across the top of her breast. Her breath left her as his tongue darted out, licking her aching nipple. She jumped, surprised at the deluge of feeling that one touch elicited, and knocked them off balance.

They slid off the log, landing side by side in the dirt. She broke the kiss, looking around somewhat stupefied at their position before meeting his gloriously blue eyes above her. He was the first to laugh. She soon joined him, and it was the most wonderful sound he had heard in his forsaken life.

"Not my finest effort at wooing the woman I love." He smoothed her hair back, enthralled by how it glowed golden against his skin.

"Love?" She froze.

"You're familiar with the word? It means adore." He kissed her shocked mouth, running his thumb across the plump rise of her bottom lip. "Treasured above all others." He stood and helped her to her feet. "Can't live without."

"You don't mean that." She stared up at him, trying to read his face in the low light of Myninn.

"I don't say things I don't mean."

"Then you *can't* mean that." Her eyes were so serious as he cupped her cheek, pleased when she leaned into his caress. She might be having trouble accepting his words, but her actions suggested she was not rejecting him. It was more than he'd ever dreamed of deserving.

"Tempest, I'm not asking you to feel the same way. Love is not an exchange, it's a gift in which the Bright blesses the giver. In Salvadon, we don't offer our hearts to others with the expectation that they will never break it. We have a saying in my homeland, 'A foolish man protects his heart within the love of another, but a wise man feeds the flame that warms them both'." He pulled

394

her tight against his chest, savoring the way she fit against him so perfectly, tucked under his chin, her arms low on his waist. "I may be many things but, hopefully," he kissed her head, and she could feel the smile on his face, "I am not a fool. I will love you while I can, where I can, and however you will let me...and my life will be all the better for it."

"Who knew you were more philosopher than warrior?" Her attempt at humor was weak as she poked the hard-as-granite planes of his stomach with her finger. She sighed, turning pink when she realized it came out more dreamy than frustrated. "What am I supposed to do with that knowledge?"

"Anything you want." He loosened his hold on her, giving her some space. "Or nothing at all."

"I think," she stepped away, her fingertips brushing down his arm until her delicate hand slipped into his, grasping it tight as she pulled, "I would like to go to bed now."

He squeezed her hand to let her know he understood her trepidation and wasn't offended by it. He'd lived the past few decades of his life in a gray haze of ennui, feeling little and caring even less. Never had he dared think of a future where he would find love. Never would he have considered the Bright would find him worthy of it. It may be Praxxys' noose around his neck, but it was his hands that carried the blood of countless souls.

Even as a young, reckless man, full of passions and rash spontaneity, he'd never thought that holding the hand of one woman would mean so much...would mean everything...to him. He had been telling the truth when he said the decision to love him was hers, but the man he had been in Salvadon would have thrown her over his shoulder and done everything in his power to convince her that she loved him back.

Yet, here he was, allowing himself to be guided through the dark kitchen of a burned ruin by a slip of a woman who was used to making life-saving decisions but was vacillating on the one that mattered most to him. He was proud that she was treating her love with the value it deserved.

The front foyer carried a much different, almost magical feel at night. If one could ignore the gaping wound that marred the entrance, the remainder of the room appeared untouched except by the passage of time.

"How did the chalet go to ruin, anyway? The fire damage seems pretty isolated."

"Dragonfire." She was distracted, giving him a concise answer but not a very informative one. It seemed almost as if she was desperate to get up the stairs as quickly as humanly possible. He hoped he wasn't the reason for her haste. Then her words hit him.

"Wait." She stuttered back a half-step as he came to an abrupt halt just short of the carpeted landing. Her eyes were alight in a way that intrigued him, starlight dancing within their golden depths, and he almost forgot what he had intended to say. "You mean real dragons?"

She nodded, wordlessly urging him on once again. He followed as she turned to the right, taking him toward the wing that had once housed the princesses and the little prince.

"Living dragons?" He asked again, looking at her askance. Dragons had been extinct for a millennium, perhaps more. They had beasts they called water dragons in Salvadon but they were not the same. The last known dragon had been sacrificed, in time before memory, to create the blade that Praxxys carried.

"Sometimes they come from beyond the Byyrin Sea, though it is rare now. This chalet used to be the Grand Palace but the Malorns of that era rebuilt in the interior of Hlyn because of the dragon raids. The Pale Palace is centered on a convergence of ley lines which makes it easier for someone with shielding powers to defend."

Roryn dropped his hand, questions racing through his head like a surge of fire in a dry field. "Tempest, there are no surviving dragons. There haven't been for a long time."

"No," she left him standing there and continued walking backwards to her room, lifting her brow questioningly, as if she were wondering why she had to explain something any child should know, "the last attack occurred about fifteen years ago. My father was one of Vyte's most talented shield magicians, so he didn't worry much about bringing us here on hunting holidays. That changed the night one almost stole Dahlis away. We didn't return to the chalet after that...but neither did the dragons."

He shook his head, astounded by this piece of world-changing history that she shared so nonchalantly. Dragons had been nearly idolized in Salvadon. Legends told that the Salvadonian royals were actually descendants of the people who had loyally served dragonkind and that some of their inherent magic was given to them by the dragons themselves. "That is a story I would love to hear."

"Another time, maybe?" Her clasped hands were white knuckled in front of her and for the first time, he noticed the extent of her unease. She gave him a wobbly smile and turned away, her steps brisk as she continued down the hall.

"Which room is mine?" He gestured to the three unoccupied chambers lining the hall. She stopped in front of the last and swung the door wide.

"This one." She looked at him over her shoulder, holding her breath, then stepped inside.

"Tempest..." He groaned, all thought of dragons and impossibilities gone. Unable to control his feet, he followed her. She was standing next to the mussed bed, fiddling with the disheveled blanket as she tried to tug it into some semblance of neatness. Part of her red dress lay on the floor and she picked it up, nervously running the swath of fabric through her hands.

It was the sexiest thing he'd ever seen. He must have died, and this was some evil temptation of the Nightmare, teasing him with a good woman that should have stayed safely beyond his reach.

"I can't stay here, Tempest." Even though there was nothing he wanted more than to lay beside her, he wasn't sure he could lay there and do nothing more. He wasn't a fool, he knew how this scenario would end, and it wouldn't be as he had promised downstairs.

"If you hadn't noticed, this place is rather deserted. There are plenty of sleeping rooms but very few beds." She seemed to grow surer by the second, taking charge and walking past him, her shoulder brushing his, leaving the tempting scent of her riding on the wind. She closed the door.

He swallowed hard.

"I have my bedroll and there is plenty of hay in the barn." He offered as he watched her toe off her boots and kick them under the foot of the bed. She came to a stop before him, still running the fabric between her fingers, but her trepidation was gone.

"Roryn, you idiot, I am asking you to stay with me."

"Tempest, you don't understand what you are asking of me." He could tell she was serious, but did she know exactly what she was proposing? "I can't sleep in that bed and not touch you."

"Well then," she let the slip of silk drift to the floor and trembled as her floral dress followed it, "I suppose you'll have to touch me."

Chapter Twenty-nine

"M ORTI, NO!" TEMPEST BATTED wearily at the thing disturbing her sleep. Couldn't Porta control her drool beast for just one night? "Ugh, how did you get in here?"

A hearty laugh against her mouth and the stone-hard press of a masculine chest on hers jolted Tempest from slumber. She'd been dreaming of her tower bedchamber back at the Pale Palace. It had been her favorite place to take a book, reading on a soft pile of pillows strewn about her balcony enclosure. One moment she'd been basking in the warm sun, the adventure in her latest novel strong on her mind, and the next, that damn dog-creature was licking every inch of her neck.

"Not Morti." Roryn cupped her breast and squeezed gently before brushing it with a kiss. "But if you are mistaking me for him, I'm worried that either I'm a really poor kisser, or he's a really good one."

Her embarrassment didn't stop her from arching against his palm, pleasure filling her as he responded by nudging his knee between her legs, enticing her to open for him. She did so readily, eager to please and be pleased in return. A glance out the window told her it had only been a few hours since he'd introduced her to the gratification to be found as their bodies united and she knew she would never be able to resist him.

She didn't want to and she wasn't going to pretend otherwise. Daring to be bold, she pulled his head down to hers, drowning herself in his kiss as she wrapped her legs around his back, moaning as he settled into the cradle her hips provided. His mouth dropped to the shallow indent where her pulse raced wildly, he sucked at tender skin there, and she shuddered at the ecstasy to be found in that simple sensation.

"I think I was perhaps wrong not to consider a career as a whore. It's quite fulfilling." Her teasing laugh turned into a gasp of lust as he bit her neck. He pushed aggressively against her, feeling her grow slick and hot for him.

"Someday you'll realize that you are mine, and you will never joke about such things again." His tongue laved at the red spot that his jealousy had left on her honeyed skin.

"Someday," she panted, "you will realize when to take a joke...and when to shut up and take your woman."

"That sounds like a challenge and I'm a competitive man." He rose to his knees, pulling her up until she sat astride him, supporting the curve of her back with one splayed hand as the other caressed the satiny skin of her behind.

How had he ever lived without her? In such a short time she had become as necessary to him as the air in his lungs, more vital to his survival than the beating of his own heart. She was perfection, fated to be the only woman that would ever settle the monster inside him. Even if she wasn't ready to acknowledge it, she was, and always would be, his.

He stared at her beautiful face above him, the amber glint of her half-lidded eyes seeming to reflect the glitter of magic heavy in the air between them. He stilled for a heartbeat before horror froze the blood racing through his veins.

"Son of a bitch!" He tossed her backward onto the bed, instinct had him covering her protectively with his body.

"What is happening?" She glanced over his shoulder, noticing the odd purple swirl of mist gathering on her vanity mirror. "Um, Roryn? Why is my mirror glowing?!"

He vaulted from the bed and his nakedness distracted her for a moment before his words settled in her mind. "Praxxys is summoning me."

He looked frantically around before gathering the scraps of her ruined red dress from the floor. Her gasp was pure surprised lust as his body covered hers once more, rubbing deliciously against all of her already inflamed skin. He groaned as he gathered her hands, stretching them above her head and raising her breasts high against his chest. "You are killing me, woman." He made quick work of tethering her wrists to the headboard, but he couldn't resist burying his face in the fragrant curve of her neck, sucking gently as she moaned.

"That's not too tight, is it?" He asked against her lips as he moved down her body, taking his weight upon his elbows.

"This isn't necessary!" She cried, sucking in a deep breath as his hips pushed, parting her legs wide as he pressed himself firmly against her most intimate place. She immediately knew it for what it was...a desperate promise.

"It is necessary." He laid his forehead briefly on hers. "And maybe a little bit fun." He placed a soft kiss on her nose and pulled back, leaving her empty with only the cooling air to calm her ache.

As an afterthought, Roryn tossed their tangled blanket over her torso and grabbed one of the tiny throw pillows to cover his manhood.

"You look ridiculous." Tempest said with a breathless petulance.

"You look delicious." He countered as he slit his palm with the tiny knife she kept on the top of her vanity. He drew a sigil the blood from his cut hand on the edge of the mirror's frame and muttered a few unintelligible words. The mist solidified into the darkly elegant form of the Warlock Emperor, dressed head-to-toe in a pristine black evening suit, the only touch of color the bone-white blade shoved into a golden sheath at his waist.

"You aren't wearing any clothes, my son. We have got to stop meeting like this."

"I thought you might want to see how a real warrior is built." Roryn's tone was hard, sure, with just enough irony to imply he had a sense of humor. It was the voice of the warrior she had met at the Evermore Inn, not that of the man who had held her so tenderly moments before.

Praxxys' laugh was deep, smoky, and Tempest couldn't help the catch in her breath. He, if it was possible, was an even more beautiful man than Roryn, if in an entirely different way. More polished, suave, seductive. His startling gray eyes were framed by the darkest and most luscious eyelashes she'd ever seen.

If she hadn't already hated him, that would be enough to make her decide to shun him with every fiber of her being.

"Ah," he said, and a shiver ran through Tempest as his eyes fell on her tied to the bed. She yanked her hands involuntarily, thankful

Roryn had managed to cover her important bits, no matter how scantily he'd done it.

"Is that my princess, Roryn? I would not have pegged you as a naughty boy."

"Of course not, Your Eminence. The heir had to be subdued, she proved to be a nasty piece, as you had predicted, Sire. This one was..." He gestured offhand, apologizing a thousand times in his head as he said it, "more pliable."

"Very good. Carry on then, Roryn. I won't make you kill her if you'd like to keep her around for a while. I quite like the idea of being a grandpapa." He winked and it was all Roryn could do to keep his expression steady. The idea that Tempest could be, even now, carrying his baby, sent a bolt of lust through him, followed immediately by the icy chill of fear.

What they were about to face was so dangerous. He didn't want to risk Tempest as it was but, if she were to be pregnant? He would tie her down for real and leave her behind to keep them safe.

"I'm enjoying this little gem of a town, currently." Praxxys was prattling. "Vyte, I think the locals call it. Such a viperous sounding, yet lame, appellation. I've been wanting to rename one of my holdings Noxmaria, what do you think, son?"

"Bright Curse you, fiend!" Tempest screamed, her trepidation at coming face-to-face, so to speak, with the infamous mage evaporating. Rage surged through her that he would so callously try to erase all the history of her people and stamp it with his personal mark of undeserving possession. "May your testicles find themselves too swollen to sit upon! I hope…"

"Tempest, be still!" Roryn roared at her, frightening her into silence, though she began to pull harder at the ties holding her. She redirected her fury at him, glaring daggers at his back.

Praxxys' steely gray eyes gleamed with joy as she struggled. He laughed heartily. "Tempest?" He repeated her name, rolling it around consideringly on his tongue. "How appropriate. That one is a spitfire, too? Perhaps when you tire of her, I'll seek out her company. She certainly is more than pleasant to gaze upon."

Roryn stepped aggressively in front of the mirror, causing the Warlock Emperor to laugh again, this time with a much darker undertone. His demeanor turned fierce, almost openly challenging, and his lascivious smile was a taunt in and of itself.

"Fine." He relented after a silent moment, holding his hands wide. "The healer is all yours. I expect you to bring me the heir in two days' time. There is a stone outcropping in the center of the Hlyn Plains, they call it Prophet's Pike," he shifted so he could see over Roryn's bare shoulder, arching a black eyebrow as he narrowed his silvery eyes at the girl on the bed, "but I think it reminds me more of, let's see...Praxxys' Point."

Tempest stared him down, fear that she dared to do so trying to make itself known, but the death magic inside her, the beast she must always deny, was surging so strongly in response to the Warlock Emperor's presence that it took everything she had to keep it contained. So, she stayed silent. Eventually, he grew tired of her insolence and focused his attention back on Roryn.

"Do you know it?" Dark hair spilled down the sides of Roryn's head as he nodded, hiding the heathenish tattoos that so displeased his emperor. "Excellent. The eclipse will begin at noon two days hence. I must have the girl there on time. With her, son, we will change this world forever."

Roryn bowed as the mirror began to swirl purple once more, Praxxys' stern face and off-puttingly intense eyes fading into the mist. He threw the pillow across the room forcefully, shattering the unlit oil lamp that had sat on her writing desk since before she was born.

"Roryn?" The Warlock Emperor's voice was an echo, strongly eerie in the dark, "That is a command."

A string of curses escaped under Roryn's breath as he stalked back and forth in the moon-lit room. He had known this was coming but, like the fool he swore he wasn't, he had not been prepared. How could he possibly disappoint Tempest by delivering her sister to her worst enemy? She would never choose him then.

"Roryn?" Tempest's voice wavered as she came to her own realizations. Tears began to streak down her cheeks. His glorious blue eyes met hers and he was across the room in a few steps, making quick work of untying her.

"Sweetest," he reached for her, folding her close to his chest, his wonderfully strong hands running comfortingly up and down her back, "don't cry, please. Let me hold you and we will figure this out."

"Dahlis aims to let Praxxys have her." She blurted, she didn't have to hear her sister's plan out loud to know the truth of it.

"I promise to protect her as well as I can, but if that is her choice, then we will stand by her as she makes it. It's not a death sentence," he added, bending to kiss her temple, "and not even a miserable existence. Praxxys needs her magic and for that, he'll keep her alive and treat her like a queen besides."

"No, Roryn, you don't understand. Dahlis doesn't have any magic. It's me he wants."

His eyes closed as agony shot through him. He held her tighter and began rocking her, as much to comfort himself as her. He had suspected, but it hadn't been a fear he'd allowed himself to truly consider.

"You cannot go to him, Tempest." He stopped moving, pulling away just enough to look into her eyes so that she could see how serious he was. "If you are thinking of doing so, I am telling you now to strike that notion from your mind."

"I will not let him destroy Dahlis when he finds out she doesn't have the power he desires." She insisted, the stubborn tilt of her chin leaving him with no doubt he had the battle of a lifetime on his hands.

"Did you forget you can no longer access your own magic?" He reminded her, squeezing her shoulders slightly. "What do you think he'll do to you when he discovers that?

"It's not my healing he wants." She turned her head away, staring out the window and refusing to look at him.

"You aren't making any sense, Sweetest." A soft finger on her chin shifted her gaze back to his.

"I...have another power." She admitted, a wobble of sorrow laced within the words.

"Another power?" A sinking feeling pulled the question from him in a whisper.

She closed her bright eyes and took a deep breath, as if to fortify herself. He held his own, afraid to make a sound lest it cause her to break. His heart beat double-time while he thumbed the tears from her cheeks.

"I have always had dual magics," she opened her eyes, determination and grief battling for supremacy in her soul. "One the lightest of light. The other...the darkest of dark. The Promise and The Nightmare. Now, without the ability to heal, I cause, I...am, death."

He sat back on his heels, facing her, his hands warm upon her knees. Even with the horror of her words reverberating inside him, he could not willingly go one moment without touching her. He had no words to comfort her for he had not expected to be faced with such an admission. Whatever he had thought her second power would be, this was not it. She was kindness and joy and empathy personified. He knew her soul like he knew his own and she wasn't a killer.

"That's not who you are, Tempest." He told her firmly.

"It is. I murdered Norc. That is why I carry his spirit. I am no different than the blade that bound you." Her jaw clenched, the delightful dimples he loved so much ticking with repressed emotion.

"Bullshit." He framed her face with his big hands, forcing her to look at him once again. "You wouldn't have killed Norc without a reason. The fact that he was a pompous ass from all accounts is more than enough call for it in my book. Defending yourself doesn't make you evil."

"I will understand if you no longer love me." His heart broke at how lost she appeared, delicate and gorgeous and immensely resilient. He didn't know much about her past and she knew almost nothing about his, but all that was meaningless, buried under the certainty that he would do whatever was necessary to build a future with her in it.

"That's not how love works, Tempest." He cupped the back of her head, leaning his forehead against hers.

"Show me how, then?" She pleaded, her lips reaching for his.

"Every day of my life." He promised.

A frantic edge suffused their touches, sending them burning out of control as the shadows haunting the night fled under the force of their desperation.

Chapter Thirty

Roryn took Tempest's empty bowl and stacked it in his own, leaving both sitting on the vanity to wash out later. Dawn was barely an hour away, but their growling stomachs had left him with no choice but to forage through the kitchen for a bite to eat. Luckily for them, remnants of Dahlis' broth and a loaf of bread had been left to warm on the hearth, so it had been a quick and fruitful jaunt away from the bed.

He was determined to spend every second she would allow him at her side. Preferably without clothes. "Now," his voice was gravely as he sidled back under the blanket beside her, "where were we?"

"You, sir, were going to let me use this on you." She twisted the much-abused silk strips from her red gown around her fists and pulled it taut, checking the strength of the fabric, smiling when she realized it would hold quite well. Pushing him back, she boldly straddled him, twisting the silk around his left arm and lifting it above his head.

"You continue to surprise me, Sweetest." His heart began to pound erratically, both in fear at being physically bound and in excitement to see how far she planned to take this. She threaded the fabric through the white-coated metal bars that made up her headboard, slowly leaning forward, her breasts temptingly close to his mouth as she secured his right hand.

"You'll stay right there," she pulled the knot tight, causing him to groan low and grit his teeth as her movement had him arching lustily under her, "and I," her mouth descended on his, her kiss gentle and apologetic as the taste of her tears coated her lips, "am going to save you."

His eyes widened for a second before they shut involuntarily, his body going lax under her. Tempest sat for a moment, memorizing his face, not ready to leave him when she just discovered how much he meant to her.

She loved him.

She knew it the moment he had first touched her hand. That first overwhelming zing of energy that bound two people in a promise of forever. She had ignored it, pushing back against Fate because, no matter who he was, she knew the beast that prowled within her was not capable of loving anyone. She had been afraid the goodness inside her wouldn't be enough to contain it. Now, without her light, she had to depend on her own sheer will to keep the dark at bay. She was starting to realize that it was a formidable thing, indeed, when she believed whole-heartedly in the cause she was fighting for.

If she wanted to keep him, she would have to prove herself worthy. She would free him from Praxxys, she would free everyone, and then she would gladly offer him the pieces of herself that remained. He was a strong man and, if there was any hope for her at all, it would come through his ability to heal what was left of her soul after the Warlock Emperor was done with her.

It was their fate to save one another.

She kissed his rough cheek and left the bed as the first pink and yellow glow of the sun appeared on the horizon. She stepped over the discarded floral gown and made quick work of slipping into the shirt and trousers that would make the long ride to Prophet's Pike much more bearable. Her hair was ratted and would take much more time than she currently had to tame so she shoved her brush into her small travel pack and whipped the curls up into a messy bun.

She looked at her reflection in the mirror. Her eyes were made brighter for the dark circles under them, but she couldn't regret her lack of sleep. A flush rose on her face and chest as memories of the night before flitted through her mind. She knew she'd be thinking about them, and him, her eyes touched regretfully on the unconscious form behind her, often as she traveled the path that would lead her to salvation.

Or to her death.

She shoved her feet into her boots and was standing in the hall before she had them fully laced. She didn't look back as she closed the door softly. She couldn't look back. The only option from this point was forward.

Dahlis was right where she knew she would be, catching the weak rays of the sun sitting on the boulder near the remains of the front door as she drank her morning tea. Tempest slid her travel bag to the floor inside before she stepped out.

"Good morning," Dahlis' smile was knowing as she took in Tempest's mussed hair and the love marks dotting her neck, "Or should I say, happy ending to a good night?"

Tempest blushed, horrified at the knowledge that her sister had known exactly what she'd been doing with her time, but she also felt weirdly compelled to start giggling and sharing all the glorious details. She settled for a smile and commented, "A *very* good night."

Dahlis' teeth shone brightly as she scooted over and patted the rock beside her. "I couldn't have imagined it would be otherwise. He seemed extremely interested in convincing you of his sincerity. That man wants you by his side so badly, he would absorb you if he could."

"That doesn't sound like a positive experience at all." Tempest sat and surreptitiously took Dahlis' free hand into both of hers, it was the way they would often sit together as children when the demands of being royalty became too much to bear alone.

"I don't know," Dahlis mused, "I think I would like such a relationship as that. He's a strong man. Staunch enough in his masculinity to let you be you while showing you the magic that you can be together."

"That is part of the reason I love him." Tempest felt her own strength fill her as she said the words out loud.

Dahlis leaned her head on Tempest's shoulder. "I'm happy for you, Tempe, but it's going to be hard. I suppose you have a plan for us to slip out while he's asleep and find a way to defeat Praxxys on our own?"

"Not exactly."

"You know he will be after your magic when he finds out I am next to useless in that department. Maybe our best option is for your gallant prince to escort me to his emperor as the curse demands. It's not his fault, after all, that the blowhard is operating under false information. If we can keep you out of his grasp until after the eclipse, then all his planning will be for naught.”

“I don’t think I can stay behind, Dahl.” Tempest felt the certainty growing in her by the second. Whatever was supposed to happen during the eclipse needed to occur and she needed to be there for it. “The darkness inside me wants me there. If I am willing, I think I can find a way to control it. The moment I think about not going, it begins to rage.”

“Then it’s going to have to be House Malorn against the known world,” she laughed without humor, “like it has always been. We can’t take Roryn with us. No matter how handy he would be to have in a battle, he is, regrettably, compromised by the curse.”

“I know.” Tempest closed her eyes, trying to absorb the feeling of having Dahlis near her, possibly for the very last time.

“Ah, thus the reason he is still abed. How long of a head start do we have?” She asked.

“I put him to sleep because I love him and I don’t want him to get hurt. Dahl,” she wrapped her arms around her in a tight hug and whispered in her ear, “I love you, too.”

The cup hit the ground with a solid crack as it left Dahlis’ limp fingers. Tempest held on one second longer then eased her sister onto the soft grass growing next to the destroyed wall of their childhood retreat. With luck, she would escape the worst of the sun's afternoon rays.

Tempest darted back inside for her bag and then loped the rest of the way to the barn. A symphony of neighs greeted her as she stopped along the row of crude stalls, one familiar face making her smile in particular. Her gelding bobbed his head up and down as she approached, hoping for an extra helping of grain, no doubt.

"Hello, my friend." She stroked Obertroess' regal nose and fluffed the hair away from his forelock. She opened the door and he trotted out as she grabbed his tack. He took the bit eagerly and stood remarkably still as she threw on his saddle and cinched it tight. He began to stomp in anticipation of a good run as she placed her foot in the stirrup.

"It wasn't nice of you to put Dahlis to sleep in the dirt. Her hair is going to be so nasty-full of ants when she wakes up." Tempest looked over Bert's back to see Porta staring at her from behind the door of Polli Nan's stall.

"I expect you to watch over her for me while I'm gone. I figure you can at least keep the bugs out of her ears until she wakes up." She finished mounting and gathered her reins.

"I'm going with you." Porta climbed the rickety wooden door, all elbows and knees, instead of letting herself out the proper way. "If anyone deserves to stab an emperor, I think it should be me."

"You can't stick a knife in anyone until you're thirteen. It's a Malorn Royal Dictate."

"Is not! Dahlis said she was slaying monsters when she was ten." Her tiny bottom balanced on the narrow wood as she crossed her arms over her chest, indignation clear on her face, but under it Tempest could sense fear.

"Monsters are different, and she was fifteen. You're welcome to wake her up and ask her yourself." She pressed her heels softly into Obertroess' sides and he walked forward, stopping of his own accord next to Porta.

The girl reached over and vigorously scratched the matted hair under his inky mane. She refused to look at Tempest, both at a loss for what to say. They'd butted heads more often than not but, especially these past few months, they'd become something more.

They'd become family.

"Is the Regent sleeping, too?" Porta asked finally, using her thumb to poke the kernels off a dried cob of corn. "I'm not picking any bugs off him." She let the loose kernels fall from her fist in front of Obertroess as the big idiot tried to lip the pieces out of the air. A growl in the rafters above their head let them know Lax the Destroyer was not pleased by their antics.

"Yeah," Tempest's hesitation brought Porta's eyes to her face, finally, "better let Dahlis be the one to wake him. He's kind of...not wearing clothes. And..." she blushed violently, "is a bit tied up."

Porta's jaw dropped before she started braying with laughter. "That is priceless, Tem! I think you are naughtier than Gussie the Hussy."

Tempest laughed, "Who knew, huh?". Lightning quick, she shifted in the saddle and kissed Porta on her grimy forehead.

"Tempest, you're coming back, right?" She snuffled loudly, dragging her nose across her bare arm, pretending it was snot she was wiping away and not the start of tears.

"You better believe I will, little sister." Tempest nudged the horse with her boot. With one last pleading snuffle at the corn cob, Obertroess sighed heavily and trotted off into the morning sun.

"Tempest!" The freckled girl hollered.

"What?"

"Comb your damn hair. You look like Morti's cousin." She didn't see Tempest's rude departing gesture through the wall of the barn, but she knew it was there all the same.

Porta jumped off the stall door and ran out into the sunshine, watching them as they disappeared into the tree line. Her little face appeared solemn as the sound of Bert's massive feet grew distant, but her mind was furiously concocting, discarding, and adjusting as she calculated how long it would take her to wake Dahlis and the naked regent.

Her thoughts jarred to a stop, and she had to chuckle. Sweet, unflappable Tempest had finally found something to twist her guts into knots and turn her mind into mush. Porta couldn't help but like her more. There was no way she was letting her face danger without help. She had lost her first family, she wasn't going to lose another. Not to mention, she wasn't about to let Tempest hog all the glory.

"Morti!" She called to the dog-thing that had begun to make a panting ruckus somewhere in the abandoned back corner of the barn, hoping beyond hope that he hadn't caught another rat. She'd leave his hairless butt here to rot if that was the case. That damp, always shadowed section of the building was too creepy for even her to explore.

She peered overhead, two glowing eyes stared steadily at her from the dusty loft. "What do you say, Lax, my cranky Destroyer of Souls, wanna go stab an emperor?" The kitten meowed, the first time he'd ever sounded happy. That was alright.

Porta was smiling, too.

Chapter Thirty-one

OBERTROESS WAS SPENT.

"I'm sorry, my brave boy." Standing on the edge of the path where the Dunshyre Forest gave way to the golden plumed wheat fields of the Hlyn Plains, Tempest unhooked the bridle and slipped it down her horse's noble face. She hugged him close and scratched his poll. Never before had she pushed him so hard. Never before had he met her request with such valiant effort.

She loosened his saddle and pulled it to the ground, leaving it behind as she faced the wide-open space before her. In the distance, she could see the gray and white stones that made up the outcropping of Prophet's Pike. She began to walk, unburdened by anything but her thoughts. She wouldn't need her weapons in this fight.

She was the weapon.

The fields were eerily silent, only the wind's whisper and the rasp of her pants against the stalks to keep her from insanity. To her left, rolling hills obscured all but the highest turrets of the Pale Palace. She didn't bother wondering if she would ever walk the streets of Vyte or read a book in her tower ever again. She didn't contemplate her chances of seeing Ben grow to manhood or Dahlis finally sitting upon the throne of Hlyn. She couldn't think of any of that. She kept her focus on the upcoming battle.

She couldn't think of him.

Overhead, two ravens danced in the breeze, the only other sign of life in an environment usually abounding with it. She didn't know if they were an omen but, if they were, she hoped it wasn't a bad one. She picked up her pace, keeping her eyes resolutely on the ground before her and concentrating on taking her next step.

The sun was edging higher in the sky, the twin moons creeping slowly closer and she knew she'd arrive at the place that was to decide her destiny just as they swallowed the light.

Hopefully, Praxxys would have no choice but to accept her bargain.

Before she was ready, the marbled rocks of the pike practically sprang out of the grass around her. It was a low ridge, not worthy to be called a mountain by any stretch, just one long, bare outcropping, flat and reaching far toward the distant Byyrin Sea.

She climbed up its ragged side, pulling her body easily up the ten feet to the top. She looked around, surrounded by the peace of a prosperous Hlyn. For miles in each direction, she saw no one traversing the plains or climbing the far mountains.

The Warlock Emperor wasn't here.

A hand touched her hair, stroking down the braid and tugging on binding, setting her curls free. She whirled around and came face-to-face with the man in her mirror. His hair was blacker than night, cut stylishly short with enough waves to brush his ears and neck. Skin pale as the white raven still circling above graced him with an added aura of agelessness that emphasized the flawlessness of his face.

"How...did you..?" There had been no one with her on the ridge, and, as a quick look around the empty fields proved, no horse to deliver him. With effort, she closed her gaping jaw. She needed him to see her as a canny foe, worthy of being molded into a competent tool. If she proved less, she feared he would take what he wanted and leave her body for those birds.

"I'm the Warlock Emperor, dear. I used a spell, have you heard of them?" He laughed, still staring at the long golden strands of hair tangled about his fingers. For the first time, she was truly scared. This was not a sane man standing before her. "It's not one I'm comfortable using often," he shook his hand, letting the curls fall back in place, "gives me watery bowels. But, I thought you would be worth the effort." His eyes, so gray as to appear a polished silver, moved to her face, "Wait. You are not the right princess."

"You are seeking a power only the Malorn bloodline can provide." It wasn't a question. "I will give it to you, for a price."

"I'm not interested in a healer whore." He stepped back, holding his pointed chin in his hand, as if he was examining a freakish oddity.

"The last man that called me a whore lived to regret it." Tempest's eyebrows met above her nose as anger ripped through her like a lightning bolt.

"I am not a man, dear, but, please, don't get your undergarments in a tizzle." He shrugged his broad shoulders, attractively encased in a plain black suit complete with a dazzling blue vest, his white shirt left open casually at the neck.

"I, myself, am not simply a woman." Tempest loosened the strongly leashed hold on her death magic, just the slightest bit.

A ripple of ecstasy charged through her veins and the Warlock Emperor's demeanor changed in an instant. A fire seemed to flicker behind his ungodly eyes and his lean, well-muscled body straightened perceptibly, practically oozing with focused attention. Twin dimples carved divots in his strong jaw as he smiled.

"No, not so simple at all." He walked around her, holding his arms behind his back, as if trying to appear harmless as he examined her from head to toe. "Rather perfect, in fact. Not one, but two unique magics and an ass fit for daydreams? No wonder my lonely boy found himself enthralled. Does Roryn know just how tantalizingly dark you are?"

"You, sir, are no gentleman."

"Shame upon my cursed ever-living soul! I'm sure my mother would be turning in her grave if she was anything more than a crusty pile of dirt with a face I'd forgotten a millennia ago."

"That is the saddest thing I have ever heard." A pang of empathy hit her by surprise. It could not be easy to watch everyone in your life die, lifetime after lifetime.

"Isn't it?" He spat off the side of the Pike, watching as it arched and fell into oblivion among the wheat field below. "I tire of this." He reached inside his simply cut, black jacket and pulled the wretched bone-white blade from its gaudy golden sheath. He waved it in a vague circle before her face. "Where is my Dragonbound?"

"He won't be coming. Roryn deserves better than what you have done to him, and I intend to see he suffers no longer." She set her jaw stubbornly, thankful for the anger that was keeping her from trembling. Being so close to his powerful, gods-blessed essence was wrecking her. The dark magic inside her was surging, wanting to join with his. Wanting to destroy him. Wanting to absorb him.

"I can smell him on you," he leaned into her personal space, a bare inch away from the skin of her neck, "so I know he isn't far away."

"That's more than a bit disturbing," she stiff-armed him, pushing him back a few feet until he was teetering on the edge of the cliff. "I'll thank you to keep your nose to yourself." She was no longer capable of cowering before him, the death magic was too strong, too cocksure, too much in control of her.

Laughing once again, Praxxys threw his arms out to his sides playfully, pretending to lose and catch his balance as he walked the precipice backwards. "Perfect, reluctantly obedient Roryn was told to bring the heir and he will have no choice but to do so."

"My healing power can cure more than maladies of the body." Pride filled Tempest. Although she could no longer heal, curing people, saving them, had always been her true strength. She had hated the power at times, feeling cursed to be so different from everyone else in Hlyn. It had made her who she was just as much as the dark urges filling her now had.

"If you had broken the curse, he'd be with you now, pushing you behind him and trying to stick me with his sword in a futile bid to free your puny self and your delicious sister from my evil clutches. Noble Roryn, most honorable Prince of those Salvadonian savages. I knew exactly what he was when I chose him. He is what I once was made to be."

Within a blink, he was in her face, his breath hot against her lips. "I told him he could keep you, but now I realize that isn't a good idea after all." His hand reached up as his intense eyes entrapped her, the dreaded blade sliding up the side of her face, cold on her soft skin.

Tempest stood silent. Fear was curdling her blood in her veins, but the knowledge that this would soon be over granted her a strange sort of peace. All she had to do was touch him. Then Roryn would be free.

"Ah," he said, severing a handful of golden curls and stepping back just out of her reach, "I see. You love him. What a moronic emotion on which to barter your life."

"What would a monster like you know about love?" The words were harsh and they hit with uncanny accuracy, even with a target as hardened as the emperor. His face turned to stone, the dimples gone along with the crazed streak of humor.

"I know it makes people vulnerable and easy to manipulate. Speaking of which, our corruptible hero has arrived." He unfolded her in a half-hug, his arm thrown around her shoulders. He turned them so they could watch the riders approach, pointing to the sky with a grim smile as the dual moons swallowed the sun.

"I won't be killing either your sister or your lover today, my Golden Dragoness." His promise was soft in her ear. "This is going to hurt you though." Darkness covered the Hlyn plains, one bright flash of light flickering over the far mountains.

He shoved the Dragonblade deep into her chest.

"Tempest!" Through a haze of slow motion, she watched Roryn, his beautiful face twisted in horror, draw his sword and launch himself from Trooper. Dahlis was right behind him, Canelope whickering with the fear pouring off her mistress. She looked up to see Praxxys smiling gently down at her, his eyes liquid reflections of regret and joy.

As she slipped from Praxxys' hold, her hands folded around the blade buried to the hilt inside her, burning with the fire of a hundred Nightmares through her flesh. Screams of terror and glee and blood and memories lost echoed from a thousand voices as the shadowed souls of the blade ached to make her one of them. They scrambled to claim her, to rip her apart, to absorb her until she was Tempest no more.

This wasn't the way it was supposed to go, she panicked. She hadn't expected to survive, but she'd hoped Praxxys would accept her bargain. It just went to prove she was still as naive as her mother thought.

Tempest felt a violent yank on her soul, pulling it from the slimy grasp of the Dragonblade's bloodshadows. A familiar spirit brushed against hers, pushing her further away from the hungry blade, surrounding her with a deep sense of regret and sorrow and...longing.

Norc? She questioned.

I didn't understand...many things. I do not ask for your forgiveness, girl. I can only hope for redemption.

She could almost see his face in her mind, solemn and resolved as he wrapped her dark death magic around him, entwining his wounded spirit in it before thrusting himself into the eager mouths of the soul-sucking bloodshadows. She felt him clinging onto her, desperate to not be lost, to end up as the nothing he'd always feared being.

I won't forget you, Norc of Thays. Her heart rejoiced, a reflection of his gratitude. He opened his hands, unleashing a bolt of power so blazingly white that it seared her soul, cleansing the dark and healing her broken edges.

Warmth exploded then into the depths of her being, racing along her veins, filling all her empty corners. Laughter bubbled against the frothing in her lungs as she felt the sweet embrace of her healing magic once again.

A light unfolds in the darkness, beginning what will have no end. Two sibilantly beautiful voices resonated with excitement, pleasure, and finality off the rocks of Prophet's Pike.

"Tempe?" Dahlis' crouched above her. Blood dripped from superficial wounds scattered about her body. Tempest reached out with her magic, healing them with barely a thought. She struggled to sit upright, strength returning in spades as her magic repaired her from the inside out.

"Roryn?" She asked, peering around Dahlis to see where he half-stood, half-stooped, favoring his left side, in front of Praxxys. Their weapons were scattered, broken, upon the hard rock.

"What now, my son?" Praxxys stood tall, no pleasure on his face but also no animosity. His eyes seemed by instinct to flicker to Tempest where she climbed shakily to her knees, pulling the

Dragonbone Blade slowly from her chest, healing herself as it slid out with a bloody gush. She stared at it for a second, entranced by the way it pulsed wildly, her death magic making it a weapon the likes of which had never been seen before.

"Roryn!" She yelled, sending it reeling across the rockface to stop against his boot.

She saw Praxxys' joy as Roryn picked up the blade. His silver eyes glinted gold as a sliver of the sun hit them. That gleam wasn't nature-born though, it was pure emotion, lighting up his countenance with an inner flame that out-shone any sun. It was all Praxxys. It was all ardent feeling.

It was hope.

Roryn shoved the blade into his master with the rage built of decades of servitude. Light blasted the Hlyn Plains, blinding everyone as the sun returned in all its brilliant glory.

"Thank you, Roryn." Praxxys' face was jubilant as he staggered back. The back of his knees hit a boulder, and he slid slowly down to sit against it. His hand lovingly caressed the blade as the death magic began to sing its song, turning his immortal body into something...more human.

"Thank you?" Roryn stumbled a half-step forward. Going down on one knee before the man he both hated and grudgingly admired. He knew Praxxys wasn't good, but he had never treated Roryn ill, past the binding ceremony that took away his freedom. "I don't understand."

"It had to be you. To be unmade, it had to be you...son of my heart, bound of the blood of the blade. We did it, Ryn." He panted, struggling for breath with a radiant smile upon his face. "So many years, I waited. I had almost lost hope when I saw you. I knew you would be the one, the only one." He choked on his words and his throat bobbed erratically for a few seconds, gulping past the pain and darkness consuming him. "You are my death. You were destined to be my salvation."

Roryn hung his head. So many things became obvious in that moment. How had he not seen? He couldn't forgive the evil done in the emperor's quest to end his pain, but...Roryn could understand it.

"Damnit!" Porta pulled herself onto the gray and white stones, scrambling to pull the satchel stretched across her stomach free of the cliff before she squashed its contents between her and the rocks. "I wanted to poke him with a knife, too! You guys never let me have any fun." She struggled to her knobby knees as Lax hissed his way out of the bag and directly back over the edge of the outcropping.

Porta peered over the side and shrugged. "He landed on his feet," she said reassuringly. A muffled wuffle from the bag preceded Morti's appearance. He turned three mangy circles before his eyes quit wobbling.

"What is that thing?" Praxxys was aghast, and enthralled. It could only be a very high minion of the Nightmare, he thought, come to escort him to the Neverafter! A tear ran down his cheek as the creature approached, crawling onto his lap and lifting his spidery club-toed paws onto his chest so that he could lick Praxxys' dying face.

"Fuck!" Using the last of his strength, the emperor-of-all, beloved-of-none, pushed the dog violently away. "That thing stinks worse than my corpse soon will!"

Tempest quietly kneeled beside Roryn. She touched his shoulder and his pains dissolved. Her arm dropped to his lower back, supporting him as she met the eyes of the most vile, most devious...saddest man she ever met. "I can heal him."

"You will do no such thing!" Praxxys coughed emphatically. "I worked hard for this death and I will take my due!"

She turned to Roryn, squeezing him gently in understanding as he shook his head. He would abide by the emperor's final wishes.

Praxxys smiled, reaching forward he offered Roryn his hand. They clasped forearms, not quite friends, but no longer enemies. The Warlock Emperor, Praxxys R'nevoran, Beloved of the Bright, fallen to the Nightmare, sighed in relief as he prepared to take the last step into forever.

"We've changed Telryuun for all time."

Epilogue

THE TWO RAVENS LANDED, abnormally large for their species, one white as the Promise, one dark as the Nightmare. They circled Praxxys as he lay prone upon Prophet's Pike. His blood painted the rock under him in a macabre circle of death. They cocked their heads eerily, but their eyes were unnaturally sentient.

Wake, our son. Their voices said in unison. *Rise, Most Beloved.*

Praxxys felt a jolt as his spirit returned to his body. He had no idea where it had been, but...it had been quiet. Peaceful. He was draped respectfully in a horse blanket and the fire glowing faint on the horizon told him Roryn hadn't abandoned him entirely.

Was he alive? Caught in a soft version of the Nightmare? He had worked very hard to be dead and if he wasn't, even now, melting into a gloopy mess of flesh and bones, he was going to be very upset.

Get up, son.

He sat up, the blanket falling away from his chest and revealing the tears in clothing where the blade had ended him. There was no wound. Son of all Bitches! He smacked the ground angrily and the Dragonbone Blade fell from the blanket where it had been wrapped. He reached for it, only to be confronted by two sets of glowing eyes.

"Who are you?" He asked, grumpy at being awakened. He had never been a morning person, and he was even less of a woken-after-death person.

You know us, son.

We are everything that grieves in sorrow. We made you the Brightest, knowing full well that Nothing is All. Bright is unbalanced if not tempered in Dark. It is our fault that you had to find your own balance in the temptations of the Nightmare.

This isn't real. He thought. He was dead and this was his comeuppance. Of course he deserved eternal confusion in the Nightmare instead of the peace of the Promise, or even the indifference and rebirth of the Nothing.

We give you life, one single human life, yours to use for dark or for light, for there is need for both in this world...but be wary, your choices will end it or save it. We grant you a companion.

The ravens stalked forward and clasped the Dragonbone Blade between them, their needle-tipped claws scratching the gold. A golden mist began to swirl about them, and they disappeared along with the blade. In their place a black and white bird began to caw aggressively. Tossing its head back and forth, as disoriented as Praxxys himself. It launched itself clumsily into the air.

The voices echoed in his head as he watched the mottled crow fly into the dark.

Find the Dragon Queen and unite her court.

The Nightmare comes.

About the Author

ASF DeWeese

Dreams can become reality, even when you drag your feet.

I call myself ASF DeWeese in the writing world because I used up all the good names in my fantasy ones. Like many other talented writers, I've always wanted to be a published author. It has taken me so, so, many years, but, despite myself, I can proudly say that my once seemingly unattainable dream is now reality.

As a life-long resident of enchanting Southern Indiana, my imagination has always been…excessive. Hey, when you are surrounded by cornfields and cranky squirrels, you need an occasional exciting escape!

In my books you'll find dragons and romance, adventure and abnormality, and quirky heroes and their fantastically ugly Chihuahua sidekicks.

I'd love to have you follow me into my fantasies.

Find me at https://www.linktr.ee/asfdeweese

Stain Upon the Soul

Book Two of the Dragonbone Blade series, coming 2026.

All he wanted was to end it all.

Once he burned the Brightest, favored by the gods of Telryuun. Now, Praxxys, the eternal Warlock Emperor, is consumed by the shadows of the Nightmare.

She will not forsake her people.

Born to be queen but destined to rebel, Dahlis fights against the tyranny of Praxxys' rule while hiding her own dark secret.

Sparks fly, but it isn't dragonfire creating the intense heat between them.

With souls stained by a past they can't forget, will they put aside their hate to build a better future or embrace the flames that threaten to destroy the world?

www.ingramcontent.com/pod-product-compliance
Lightning Source LLC
Chambersburg PA
CBHW070402310726

48977CB00003B/520